SHADOW
STORM
CHRISTINE
FEEHAN

PIATKUS

PIATKUS

First published in the US in 2021 by Jove
An imprint of Penguin Random House LLC
First published in Great Britain in 2021 by Piatkus

1 3 5 7 9 10 8 6 4 2

A CIP catalogue record for this book
is available from the British Library.

ISBN: 978-0-349-42840-6

Printed and bound in Great Britain by Clays Ltd, Elcograf S.p.A.

Papers used by Piatkus are from well-managed forests
and other responsible sources.

MIX
Paper from
responsible sources
FSC® C104740

Piatkus
An imprint of
Little, Brown Book Group
Carmelite House
50 Victoria Embankment
London EC4Y 0DZ

An Hachette UK Company
www.hachette.co.uk

www.littlebrown.co.uk

For Domini, who is the original Shadow Rider.
You keep on going against impossible odds when
few could—or would—ever continue.
Just know that you inspired this entire series.
You are Emmanuelle.
To others, you may be in the shadows,
but I will always see you.

FOR MY READERS

Be sure to go to christinefeehan.com/members/ to sign up for my PRIVATE book announcement list and download the FREE ebook of *Dark Desserts*—a book of yummy desserts to make when you're needing something sweet. Join my community and get firsthand news, enter the book discussions, ask your questions and chat with me. Please feel free to email me at Christine @christinefeehan.com. I would love to hear from you.

ACKNOWLEDGMENTS

As in any book, there are so many people to thank. First, Domini, who inspired the series, for always editing, no matter how many times I ask her to go over the same book before we send it for additional editing. Brian, who in spite of COVID-19 and having to use Skype to keep up power hours with me and keep me on track has been persistent. Thank you for always being there when I've gotten behind, insisting I could get back on track. You always have faith in me! Denise, you take the business on for me, leaving me free to write. Sheila and Renee, you know what you do for me, my amazing team!

SHADOW
STORM

CHAPTER ONE

Petrov's Pizzeria was owned and operated by Benito Petrov, a great bear of a man, and his son, Tito. Those who frequented the pizzeria and stood in line, sometimes for an hour just to get in, considered it the best pizza in Chicago—and that was saying a lot. It didn't seem to matter what night of the week it was, getting a table was always difficult, and on weekends, it was nearly impossible. Takeout was a brisk business, and that was always a wait as well.

The pizzeria was right in the heart of Ferraro territory, a large section of businesses and homes that were owned, rented, or leased and protected by the Ferraro family. There were whispers and rumors about the family and had been for years. It was said one could go to them with a problem and that problem would mysteriously go away.

Stefano Ferraro was head of the family, and he ruled with an iron fist. They owned banks and hotels, race cars and nightclubs, and they ran all sorts of other businesses, but they could be counted on to take care of the small problems in their territory. They knew the business owners by name and often were seen patronizing the local deli or pizzeria.

Benito kept a booth just for their family and a smaller table set aside for their bodyguards. It was always empty for them, even at his busiest times. They'd never asked him to do so, but then they'd helped him out of more than one problem, and he liked their business. They always insisted on paying, and they tipped his waitresses and waiters more than fairly. It was a win-win situation.

Tonight, only the youngest Ferraro had slipped into the pizzeria through the side door, her bodyguards and Elie Archambault with her. Everyone hoped there would be an announcement very soon of an engagement between Emmanuelle and Elie. Emme was a favorite of everyone in the Ferraro territory and she'd seemed far too sad lately. Elie seemed to make her laugh, and they wanted Emme happy.

Emmanuelle Ferraro laughed as she dipped a salty bread-stick into oil and took a bite. The booth in the shadows managed to hide her from most of the other patrons in the restaurant, which was why this particular table was always held in reserve for the Ferraro family. She was extremely grateful they had a place to go just to be "normal" when she never felt as if she could truly relax anywhere else. Eating pizza at Petrov's with Elie Archambault was the most relaxed she could ever get, and she was extremely happy that she could have this little time to pretend her life was ordinary.

"I can't believe the first thing you put on the plus side of this list was having babies." Elie glared at her.

Her laughter spilled out again at the feigned horror on his face. He was handsome. Shockingly so. All masculine and hard edges. That black hair that spilled across his forehead and made women want to tame it.

"I am not just a sperm donor," he stated with great dignity.

She waved the breadstick at him. "Don't be such a baby. This is very serious stuff. My mother expects little Archambaults running around. *Tons* of them. Like maybe a dozen. Think about that, Elie. We would make beautiful babies. And since my mother and the devil have some sort of pact between them, and she *loves* you and the thought of your babies, that tops the list for pros. I hope you're really good with kids and like the idea of staying home with them. I'm sure she'll be around a lot because she's not allowed in any of my brothers' homes. She's been banned from every single one of their houses."

Elie groaned. "That goes on the con list. The staying home with the kids *and* your mother."

"You already wrote my mother. She's at the very top of the con list." Emme pointed with her breadstick. "Number one."

"Your mother warrants putting down there twice. Add staying home with a dozen children to that con list. I'm a shadow rider. I don't stay home with children. That would be *your* job."

Emmanuelle made a face at him. "Why? Because I'm a woman?"

"No, because you're the one with the mother insisting on twelve children. Move on or we're never getting through the list," Elie commanded, helping himself to salami and olives. He glanced down at the list and sighed. "Your second pro is that I like the same pizza you do? Emme. Couldn't it be that I'm really damn good-looking?"

"No, because you already know you're good-looking and that makes you arrogant." She gestured toward the "con" list. "I think that's number like six or seven. Arrogance. I had a difficult time deciding whether or not to put it up at the top of the list. I think I should have."

He stared at her with his dark, gorgeous eyes. They looked almost velvet in the dim lighting. "Really? You put arrogance on the 'con' list?"

"You put 'moody.'"

"You are moody," he pointed out matter-of-factly and took the rest of the salami and olives without a qualm.

She made a face at him. "I suppose that could be true. But

I have reason to be. See your number one reason on the con list, Elie. My mother."

"I have reason to be arrogant. My hot good looks that you left off the pro list. That's an asset to you at any event we attend together. Think of all the women you can make jealous."

Emme rolled her eyes. "You just ate the last of the olives. That makes *me* jealous. You know I love olives. I've told you a million times to stop hogging all the olives." She wadded up a napkin and threw it at him.

He caught it one-handed without even looking up. "You shouldn't talk so much," Elie said, glancing down at the pro side of the list. "You're right, we do like all the same things. That's a big plus. And I can dance. That's a plus on my list, too. I like that you can."

"Pie's up, you two." Tito Petrov placed a large pizza on the tabletop. "Need a refill on your wine?"

"Olives," they both said simultaneously and then burst out laughing.

"The double order of olives on your pie isn't enough?" Tito asked, one eyebrow raised. When they shook their heads, he sighed. "There's something seriously wrong with the two of you—you know that, right?"

Elie waited until Tito walked away and then he nudged Emme with his knee. "He's right. We're sitting in here like two idiots going over a list of pros and cons to decide whether or not we should get married. Bottom line, we can't have sex with each other. Where does that leave us? I can't cheat on you, because I love and respect you too much to do that to you, and I'm not going the rest of my life without sex."

Emme sighed heavily. "I know. I feel the same. What's wrong with us, Elie? You *are* gorgeous. Totally attractive. Hot as hell. Why do I have to think of you as a sibling? It's just not fair."

"I guess we're going to have to marry strangers. That just sucks." Elie picked up a piece of very hot pizza and regarded her with his expressive dark eyes.

"And then what? We cheat on some poor innocent partner because we don't love them? How fair is that to them?" Emme asked. She broke off a piece of the pizza as well, picked up several loose pieces of olive and added them to the slice.

"When I go with an arranged marriage, I'm not cheating," Elie said.

Emmanuelle noticed he was already acting as if he'd made up his mind. Really, what was there left to them? She tried to make a joke out of it. Keep the night fun. "So, have you considered bringing in partners to live with us? It would be horrifying to my mother."

She danced her eyebrows up and down, a wide smile on her face at that mere thought. "As well as scandalous to the rider community. Can you imagine? It would solve all our problems. They could stay home and take care of the dozens of little shadow rider babies my mother will insist we have. *And*, we won't be the good couple. All my brothers have managed to be so deliciously bad that my mother wouldn't dare go unannounced to their homes. If we don't do something equally as bad, she would be turning up uninvited at all hours of the day or night. Bringing in lovers for us would be so perfect."

Elie threw his head back and laughed. "Emmanuelle Ferraro, you are a handful."

She took a bite of the pizza and nodded her head, feeling very pleased with herself. "I am. I had to be, growing up with all those brothers. Stefano especially. No one crosses Stefano, not even my mother. Not even when he was a kid. Now, of course, she doesn't dare 'drop in.' She's been banned for being so mean to Francesca, but even if she hadn't been, she wouldn't have dared just showed up. When Stefano wants sex, it doesn't matter where he is, what room he's in, he's all over that and he's very inventive and unapologetic. He's a crazy man, so Eloisa would never drop in on him."

Elie laughed again. "I have to admire your oldest brother. It feels like he's always been in charge of the Ferraro riders. Everyone defers to him."

Shadow riders meted out justice to criminals who fell through the cracks—those with too much money or power or who were just too dangerous to be convicted. Safeguards were in place to ensure no mistakes, and those they assassinated had committed horrendous crimes—at the end of the day, they were trained killers. They had begun their training as toddlers.

There were portals in the shadows. A very few people were born with the ability to be drawn into those portals and move from place to place. It wasn't a pleasant sensation; in fact it felt as if one's entire body was being pulled apart, skin, bones, every cell, as one was taken at high speed from one area to another. Those riders had to be trained physically from an early age and have a tremendous amount of stamina to be able to withstand the pressure of the shadow tubes.

"Stefano's been in charge of our family and our riders since I was born. He was the one taking care of me, not my parents," Emme said. "My mother wasn't in the least bit maternal. Stefano got up with me in the middle of the night. He was the one who set all the rules. Once, I remember, when I was about four, she was really angry with me and slapped me. He came roaring out of nowhere, and she backed right out of the room when he scooped me up. She actually left the house, he was so angry. I realized then the balance of power had shifted from her to him."

"How interesting. Stefano had to have been so young when he started taking care of all of you."

Emme inclined her head. She'd often wondered if her oldest sibling had ever had a childhood at all. Sometimes it made her sad to think of all the responsibilities Stefano had taken on at such a young age. Still, he had met Francesca, the love of his life and the heart of the Ferraro family. All of them loved her. Who could not? Well, maybe not Eloisa, Emmanuelle's mother. But then, Emmanuelle wasn't certain if Eloisa was capable of loving anyone. Now Stefano had Francesca, who doted on him, adored him and had provided him with Crispino, a beautiful son.

"What about Ricco?" Elie asked. "How does he keep your mother from showing up without an invitation? I can't imagine Eloisa not respecting Mariko. She's a shadow rider and a darn good one. I've seen your mother with her. She's curt, but at least respectful."

Emme had a mouthful of pizza, so she nodded while she chewed to indicate Elie was on the right track. Ricco was her second-to-the-oldest sibling, and he was a powerful, fast shadow rider married to a very respected rider who looked like a delicate, beautiful woman when in fact she was a warrior who could cut out the heart of a monster. When Emme managed to swallow the pizza, she flashed Elie a wide smile.

"Shibari. My brother practices the art of Shibari and loves to tie his beautiful wife up without a stitch on. It's a very erotic practice when they do it together, and apparently after warning Eloisa several times to stop dropping in on them, he didn't put any of the safety precautions in the shadows to stop her and she walked in on them. As you can imagine, it was embarrassing for her. Ricco was in the zone and acted as if he didn't even notice her there. She was livid and left, but she never went back." She took another bite of pizza and watched his face as she chewed.

"Sex seems to be a recurring theme here."

"You have no idea. Stop putting all the extra olives on your slice. I'm watching you."

"There are plenty of olives. Giovanni and Sasha? She's a sweet little country girl."

Emmanuelle nearly dropped her wineglass. "Really, Elie? You've been around our family for how long now? There is no way one of my brothers is going to be madly in love with a woman who doesn't have the kind of wicked sex drive he does. And if she doesn't start out that way, he's going to teach her."

Elie's expression shifted. It was subtle, but Emmanuelle had been trained from the time she was a child to notice every detail of anyone around her, and she had come to love Elie Archambault almost as much as she loved her brothers.

She hurt for him because, like her, she knew he was heartbroken and he believed whatever had happened couldn't be fixed. Elie had aligned himself with her almost from the time he had come to Chicago seeking to be trained by her cousin Enzo as a bodyguard. Why one of the best shadow riders in the world would want to be a bodyguard instead of a rider was a mystery, but eventually, when Stefano realized who he was, being Stefano, he had managed to get Elie to take rotations as a rider, pulling him back into their world.

Emmanuelle was grateful Stefano had done so. Elie had improved their speed and technique. He was amazing to train with, but more importantly, Stefano had brought him into the family. He'd needed them as much as she had needed Elie. Shadow riders had to provide children. It was as simple as that. There weren't enough of them left, and Emmanuelle was getting too close to the age where she would have to accept an arranged marriage.

She had fallen in love. The curse of every Ferraro—they fell in love once and never again. She had very bad taste in men, and her choice had turned out to be a liar and a cheat, and worse, he'd been playing her all along. The pain was still excruciating. Sometimes she could barely breathe, it hurt so bad, but she was a Ferraro and a rider, and she had purpose.

Elie never said what happened—why he had come to Chicago and said he would accept an arranged marriage. By turns there was anger, guilt and pain in him. Of all her brothers—and Emme had six—Elie reminded her most of Stefano. He could be very bossy. Very arrogant. He had charm, but beneath that charm was pure steel.

"I think Sasha and Giovanni are exhibitionists at heart. You don't dare go to their house, because they aren't going to be indoors. If you walk up to their car, they might be going at it in their back seat, or front seat. They're both crazy. Sasha has no inhibitions whatsoever. I called down the elevator once, and he had her pinned against the wall right there. Did he stop? No. He told me to shut the doors and go away."

Elie laughed. "Yeah, I actually had a little incident with

Gee and Sasha once, but I thought it was just me. Caught them going at it in the parking garage. It's private, but still." He smacked her hand as she scooped up olives faster than he could get at them. "Woman, that's going to cost you."

"You're lucky it was just once. They're very inventive."

"And Vittorio?" Elie lifted one eyebrow. "Grace is as sweet as they come. Well, other than Francesca. Although she's hell on wheels in that event planning business of hers."

"Vittorio is very dominant with Grace. He takes excellent care of her. Grace adores him and gives him anything he wants. It drives Eloisa right up the wall. She thinks Grace is a pushover because she doesn't oppose Vittorio on much. I think Grace brings him much-needed peace, and I love her for that."

"What you're really telling me is that Vittorio is a bond-age kind of man."

Emmanuelle rolled her eyes. "I'm not going to say that out loud in a public place *ever*. Sheesh. He's my brother. I'm going to pretend I never heard that word."

Elie flashed another grin. "No wonder I fit in so well with your family. Bondage. Exhibition. Shibari. Having my way whenever and however I want it. Yeah, I fit."

She glared at him. "Shibari? What do you know about Shibari? Don't tell me you actually knew what Ricco did all along?"

"Of course. He's a proven artist. One of the best. I've been interested in it for a long time and have gone to him and his mentor since I first came here. I was practicing when I was in Paris." He sent her a quick grin.

"I'm covering my delicate ears. I don't want to know any-thing else you do."

Elie laughed, but his eyes didn't light up. They stayed dark, almost lifeless. She hated that for him.

He changed the subject. "Taviano and Nicoletta? They just got married."

"I honestly have no idea, but I imagine he isn't any differ-ent from my other brothers, although he has to be gentler with Nicoletta." Her brothers were all very dominant men. Shadow riders had to be, and when one came out of the shadows, the hormones and adrenaline raged. The combination was a very powerful aphrodisiac. She experienced it all the time.

Riding the shadows was extremely dangerous. Moving from one place to another at breakneck speed. Choosing the right tube and ending up at the correct address, usually in a city far from one's own, in order to bring justice to a criminal who otherwise would get away with a major crime. There was no doubt that shadow riding was both exhilarating and dangerous.

They had lost Ettore, her youngest brother, in the shadows. Stefano had gone in after him, found his body and brought him out. He had warned Eloisa over and over that Ettore had no business in the shadows, that his lungs couldn't take it, but in their family, imperfections weren't tolerated. Ettore had been forced to work out longer and harder, to prove himself worthy of being a Ferraro. Had Stefano been aware of what their mother was doing, he would have put a stop to it, but Ettore had never told him. He had practiced and practiced and, in the end, his frail body hadn't held up under the terrible severity of the shadows.

Emmanuelle leaned toward Elie, taking a chance. Looking at him directly. "Are you going to tell me what you actually did, Elie?" she asked softly. "You don't have to, but I think you should tell someone, and you know I'll love you no matter what."

Elie hesitated. Looked away from her. It was the first time she'd ever seen shame in his eyes. She didn't like it and felt that particular expression didn't belong on him.

"I love you, Emme. If I tell you, it doesn't put me in a very good light. You're going to think less of me. A hell of a lot less of me, and I deserve it. It isn't like I have that many people in my life who do love me. I count on you."

"We all do things we're ashamed of, Elie," she assured him. "Everyone. There isn't a person on earth immune. We'd all like to think so, but we're not. You don't have to tell me, but I'm here. I just want you to know that. You've held it in a long time."

He sighed. "You get a lot of pressure being a Ferraro. You have to be the best of the best and train all the time. Can you imagine what it's like being an Archambault? We go from family member to family member even as toddlers. There's a hierarchy within the family, and depending on your abilities—and you're continually assessed—you're sent to various families to train. They're all extremely strict, very exacting."

He stopped when Berta the waitress approached to take the empty pizza pan from the table. "Dessert?" she asked brightly.

Both nodded. "The usual," Elie said.

"Same with drinks?" Berta asked.

"Yes," Emme confirmed.

Berta went away happy.

"I never had a chance to know my father. I was one of the really promising Archambaults. I picked up everything fast. Languages, art, anything I studied, including how to kill. First time out. It didn't matter what it was. That meant I was sent from one family to the next. I liked being in the shadows, and I liked learning. But it didn't give me a feeling of home. It didn't ground me."

Elie rubbed the bridge of his nose and looked at her. "I was taught languages and how to kill. I was taught to ride shadows and keep maps in my head. I didn't know the first thing about being in a family. Growing up as a teen, you can imagine how they encouraged me to be the best at what I did. Faster, stronger. Not one time did they ever mention family. Not even my own parents. My mother or father. I became arrogant and full of myself. You know how you get coming out of the shadows, coming off a job, so hot you just want to grab the nearest partner and fuck. Well, it was easy for me. I was good at that, too. Really good at it, and from a very young age. That made me more than arrogant in that department."

Emme nodded. It was the truth. And she couldn't see too many women turning Elie down. She rested her chin on the heel of her hand and looked at him across the table. His voice was low with self-loathing.

"I'm not exactly Mr. Nice in the sex department, either, Emme. Just so you know. All this was going on while my father had cancer. I didn't know. The powers that be decided I shouldn't be told. They asked my mother not to tell me, and she didn't. I wasn't even there when he died." There was bitterness in his voice for the first time. "I was eighteen. They were still deciding my life for me, and I was still letting them."

"Eighteen is a kid, Elie, and if you had been moved from family to family, of course you were letting them decide your life. You didn't know any other way to live."

"My mother needed me and I didn't go to her."

"You barely knew her." Emmanuelle didn't point out that his mother had allowed the Archambaults to take her baby from her and send him from family to family, never bringing him home. She guessed it was because his mother and father liked being alone together. If they visited their son occasionally, that was enough for them. Not all people were meant to have children, and riders were forced to. It didn't always turn out for the best—at least not for the child. His mother hadn't insisted her son come home to her after her husband had died, either—and she could have. Emmanuelle didn't point that out, either.

"I spent another five years working and learning, riding the shadows and building my reputation," Elie continued. "I built my reputation with women as well. I preferred models. Tall. Elegant. Long legs. Hot as hell."

She'd seen the photographs. He'd been all over the magazines, escorting the top runway models in Paris. He'd broken hearts—a lot of hearts.

"I was called into Jean-Claude Archambault's private home for a formal meeting. He was a member of the council. I was told it was time I settled down. There was a girl. A *girl*,

Emme, eighteen fucking years old. A rider who couldn't cut it. He actually said that. Too soft. But good genes. The best genes for producing riders. Good family. A virgin. He said that, too. He named her. Brielle Couture." His voice softened when he said her name.

Elie raked both hands through his hair, shaking his head as if he could somehow stop his thoughts. Take back his history. "I was so damn sick of Jean-Claude and all the rest of the Archambaults running my life. Dictating to me what I could and couldn't do. They'd been making noises for some time that I'd better stop running through so many models so fast. They'd heard of the nights that I spent in the sex clubs, and they didn't approve. They wanted it stopped."

Emmanuelle could believe it. The paparazzi were relentless when it came to wealthy bachelors and scandal. Anyone with Elie's looks, his money, his penchant for famous models and sex clubs would definitely attract attention.

"They knew my tastes ran pretty dark when it came to sex, but they were going to throw some little girl at me that didn't know what the hell she was getting into just to prove to me that they were the ones in control of my life. They didn't like what I was doing, but it didn't stop them from giving me more rotations than any other rider in Paris, or having me train with younger riders to try to bring them up to skill levels they couldn't possibly achieve. For Jean-Claude to dictate to me, tell me I had to marry this *child* who couldn't possibly handle my brand of sex, was the last straw. I wasn't having it. I told him off. The problem was, when I told him off, I told him off in entirely the wrong way."

Berta was back with two Italian sodas and the ice cream they both loved. She put it on the table between them and hurried away to serve the next customers.

Emmanuelle found herself tense, only because Elie was. Whatever had transpired in that house had been bad. It was there on Elie's face, pressed into the lines that rarely showed.

He picked up a fork and dug at the very outer edge of the ice cream treat, keeping his eyes on the plate in front of them. "I told Jean-Claude that he was out of his fucking mind if he thought he was going to saddle me with a little child that didn't know the first thing about sex and would faint at the things I'd demand of her. I told him her breasts and hips were too big and once she had a kid, she'd be a cow for certain, that she was well on her way in that department already. I pointed out that I wasn't in the least attracted to her and what did he want me to do, close my eyes the entire time I fucked her? I ended rather triumphantly, telling him to go fuck himself, that I was done with him telling me what to do, and I stalked out—right out into his sitting room. Where little miss eighteen-year-old virgin Brielle Couture sat with her hands folded in her lap and her face so white it looked like I'd slapped her. She'd heard every single word."

"Elie," Emmanuelle whispered.

"I accidentally stepped into a shadow tube that connected with hers. The jolt was unlike anything I'd ever experienced. I knew then what a mistake I'd made, not just in hurting her, because I felt that right down to my bones, but because I knew she was the one meant for me. I tried to backtrack, but there was no way to do that."

"Eighteen is so young, Elie. She wouldn't have any confidence in herself, especially if she couldn't make it as a rider, either. And to hear your evaluation of her as a woman, that would humiliate her beyond all comprehension. No, there would be no way to back out of that one." Emmanuelle felt terrible for him and for the unknown Brielle. "What did you do?"

"I apologized to her. I told her I was talking out of my ass because I was so angry at Jean-Claude, which was the truth and I hoped she heard that, but I could tell she didn't. She didn't even look at me. She just nodded her head, said it was all right, that she understood, and she left. She didn't run. She walked. Head up. She was actually quite magnificent. I wrote to her several times. My letters came back unopened. I went to her apartment, but she refused to answer the door. I thought about just going in, but that would be wrong, so in the end, I followed my mother to the United States. She was just as tired of the Archambaults telling her what to do as I was."

There was something in Elie's voice that alerted her. "What happened with your mother, Elie?"

"Turns out, she wasn't all that thrilled to see me, either, Emme. She said I looked too much like my father. She didn't really know me. It was nice to have dinner occasionally, but seeing me every day was just a little too much. It was easier for everyone to think my mother and I have this great relationship and that I came here to be with her after my father died, so I let all of you think that."

"I can understand, and actually, in a way it's the truth. The timeline is a little off. Your mother didn't come here right after your father died, did she?"

He shook his head. "When I realized she didn't need me hanging around, and I needed action, I joined the military. You know the rest. While I was in the military, I continued to ride shadows because I couldn't resist them and to stay in practice. I was careful never to get caught. When I came to Chicago, I was going to end my riding career and be a bodyguard, but I guess once it's in your blood, you can't just let it go."

"And you're needed, Elie," Emme reminded gently.

He nodded. There was no denying that fact. There weren't enough riders. There never would be. "We're back to needing those babies, aren't we, Emme? The ones we can't really have together. Are you going to tell me how you managed to fuck up your life? I can't imagine that you called your man a cow. And how I ever even came up with such a demeaning term for a woman who looks as beautiful as Brielle, I'll never know. She isn't a tall, elegant model, and she actually has breasts and hips, but *fuck*, Emme, what I did to that woman. I hurt her beyond any imagination." He scrubbed his hand over his face as if he could wipe away the memory.

Emmanuelle studied his expression for a long time, and then she sighed. She had to give him something. "I just chose the wrong man. You saw him dozens of times, Elie."

He lifted his head and looked at her. "Valentino Saldi is not a rider, Emme. Ferraros fall in love once, same as Archambaults. Saldi couldn't compromise your shadow."

She took a sip of her Italian soda, her gaze darting around to the tables closest to them, landing specifically on the one where their bodyguards ate pizza and drank coffee. "I tried to talk to my brothers about this more than once when I was a kid, but they wouldn't listen to me, Elie."

She lowered her voice to the point that he would have to hitch forward. If he really wanted to hear what she had to say, she wasn't taking any chances. Elie, to his credit, leaned toward her, even though he did take a rather large forkful of ice cream.

"You were around the council a lot. Did you ever hear of anything other than pure shadows weaving two people so tightly together they can't get away?"

Elie sat up straight, his dark velvet-brown eyes moving over her face inch by slow inch as if he was examining her carefully. "What the hell does that even mean, Emme?"

She sighed. "Apparently, you haven't."

Elie leaned toward her again. "Is there any evidence? When we look at shadows, we can see the knots tangled. Can you see something in the shadows binding you when they're reflected on a wall?"

She nodded slowly, her teeth biting down on her lower lip. Once again, she glanced toward the table where their bodyguards sat enjoying food. "From the very first time I was ever around him at a party. I snuck out and went with a friend of mine. I wanted to see if I could do it because my brothers were always going places but I wasn't supposed to." She flashed him a little grin. "Naturally, I slipped right past them all."

"They weren't expecting it, were they?"

"Nope, not from the good girl, little Emme." Her breath caught in her throat. "Val was so good-looking, and I was so young and impressionable. I stayed across the room. He was a Saldi, and I was a Ferraro. I knew I shouldn't be there. I knew Stefano would lose his mind. I didn't dance. I stayed in a dark corner. I didn't want him to see me. I don't know why I was so afraid of him, but I was, and I've never been afraid of anyone."

Elie shook his head. "That should have told you something right there, Emme. You should have acted on your instincts and gotten the hell out of there."

She nodded because it was the truth. "I know. I knew then. I felt trapped. I was afraid if I moved, I'd call attention to myself." She swallowed hard, wondering what to tell him. Elie had been so honest, it was only fair she be just as honest. But he was an Archambault and a rider. She didn't want Val dead, and if she wasn't very, very careful, if she didn't walk a fine line, that could be the result of the conversation.

"I could barely breathe when Valentino Saldi looked across the room and his eyes met mine for the very first time—they were extremely intense, Elie, and so damn green. The pit of my stomach dropped away. I couldn't have moved if my life depended on it. He stood, a casual, almost flowing move, very controlled, and my heart accelerated. I was a trained shadow rider, and I couldn't stop my reaction. I knew he was going to walk right through that crowd straight to me. His shoulders were broad, his hair thick and glossy black. He was the most handsome man I'd ever seen. I remember every single detail so vividly."

Emmanuelle pressed the heels of her hands to her eyes. Even now, after all this time, after all the things she knew about Val, her memories of him still had the power to move her.

"I had to fight for air when my lungs were burning. The dim lighting threw shadows on the wall. I'd deliberately sat in the corner near a shadow so I could step into a tube to escape if there was an emergency. I remember thinking maybe it wasn't such a good idea. Something very peculiar was happening as Valentino approached. He stopped, frowning, when his shadow hit mine. I felt an overwhelming jolt, and I could see it hit him, too. It was a physical, sexual fireball rushing through my entire body straight to my sex."

"How could that happen when he isn't a rider?" Elie asked

in a low voice, frowning. He looked every inch an Archambault in that moment. A member of the famed French family with many branches—the only family that could bring justice to riders when they went rogue.

"I have no idea. I really don't." Emmanuelle couldn't look at him. "I was sixteen, Elie. I'd never experienced anything like that in my life, and I was embarrassed. I looked at the wall, expecting to see our shadows knotting. I'd been told what could happen, of course, but the actual experience was so mind-blowing and frightening for someone so inexperienced, I was stunned."

She pressed a hand to her hair and found it was trembling, just as it had been that night. "I glanced at our shadows on the wall, expecting to see them tangling together the way it was described to me, but that wasn't happening."

Elie frowned, forgetting he had a forkful of ice cream halfway to his mouth. "It wasn't?"

She shook her head. "There were these ropes, like a million cords rushing toward my shadow. It was terrifying. I could see them coming out from his shadow. Each time one of those ropes touched my shadow, it wrapped around it really fast, almost like a chain. I knew immediately if I didn't get out of there, and more managed to attach, I was going to be in trouble."

Her heart had gone crazy. She'd been so scared. "I felt as if I was being taken prisoner. The only thing I could think to do to save myself was get rid of the light throwing the shadow. That meant I didn't have a way to escape fast, but whatever was happening to trap me would be stopped. Honestly, the phenomenon was so frightening, I nearly had a panic attack."

"Emme." He breathed her name and reached over to take her hand. "You didn't go directly to Stefano?"

She shook her head. "It wasn't Valentino's fault any more than it was mine. I could tell he was just as shocked. The awareness between us was very sexual. He was older, and he didn't like it. We talked for a little while, and I found him to be very sweet and gentle. He was a gentleman the entire time and ended up escorting me home. I thought that would be the end of it, but found myself obsessing over him. Evidently, he found himself obsessing over me."

"Why didn't you tell Stefano?"

"I actually tried to. He found out I'd snuck out, and he was furious. I kept trying to talk to him about what happened, but every time Valentino's name came up, all of my brothers lost their collective minds. I was afraid they might actually hurt Val if I did manage to describe to them what happened to our shadows and how it made me feel. In the end, I kept it to myself."

"But you continued to see Val after that?" Elie prompted.

She nodded. "It was difficult to stay away. I tried. I was afraid of him, of the way I was so drawn to him, and I didn't want my shadow anywhere near his. I was careful to stay in the dark or absolute light, where our shadows couldn't touch. I learned to be very aware all the time."

"Was he? Did he seem aware of the phenomenon?" Elie asked.

Emmanuelle knew it wasn't just her friend and almost sibling questioning her now. This was definitely an Archambault. She pulled back, sitting up straight and drinking her Italian soda to give herself time to think before answering. Was she still protecting Val? Why would she be? That made no sense. Still, she was reluctant to talk about this.

"Yes, he was definitely aware of it as well. We both found it disturbing. I couldn't talk about shadow riding, of course, so I pleaded ignorance as to what it all could mean. Eventually, we couldn't—or didn't—ignore the physical pull between us. He waited until I was old enough—eighteen." That was putting it mildly. The need to be with Val had been raging. Brutal. Irresistible. She had thought he had felt the same way. Most days, she still couldn't get from one breath to the next without needing him. "I was still as careful as I could be, watching over my shadow." That was true, although she hadn't been careful enough.

"Did he, at any time, allude to shadow riding?"

"No. Had he done that, I would have gone to Stefano immediately." She would have. There was no doubt in her mind. She would never have risked her family. Never. She knew the truth was in her voice for Elie to hear.

"Did he really betray you, Emme? The way you said he did?"

She nodded slowly, the hurt ripping through her every bit as physical as it was emotional. She had stood in the shadows, in his bedroom. She hadn't been able to hold out any longer, and she'd gone to him, ready to commit to their relationship.

"I was going to tell him I loved him. I would have given up shadow riding for him. Being a Ferraro. Everything I am, to be with him. I went to him, and he was with another woman. In his bedroom. She asked about me, told him she'd heard he was with me. He kind of snickered and said I was just business. He'd been ordered to make me fall in love with him and was fucking me to get me to spill the Ferraro secrets. Did he really want to be with a spoiled baby who didn't know jack about sex? That's why Vittorio beat the shit out of him at the hotel that day. I inadvertently said something. I had before, but no one was really listening to what I said, I guess."

Elie groaned. "For fuck's sake, Emme. I practically said the same thing about Brielle. How can you even look at me?"

"Clearly, you aren't Valentino Saldi," Emme said. "You hate what you did to Brielle and tried to apologize. She just didn't give you the chance."

Elie was silent for a long time. He swirled his straw and then looked up at her, his dark eyes pure velvet. "Has Val ever tried to explain to you what he said and did?"

She felt the color drain from her face. Her body went stiff with shock. "Yes. Many times. I can't listen to him. I don't dare let myself." She whispered the confession like a terrified child.

"Why, Emme? You're a Ferraro. A shadow rider. Why are you so afraid of Valentino Saldi? It shouldn't matter how sexually attracted you are to him or how emotionally attached. You can hear lies. You can *hear* them. You know if he speaks the truth. Brielle could have heard the truth if she wanted to hear it. She didn't. She chose to live with that hurt, and she condemned me and someone else to an arranged marriage because she didn't have the courage to at least let me explain. Yeah, what I did was wrong. It was so fucked up it wasn't funny, but she's not without blame, either, because she didn't even once let me try to explain in all the times I reached out to her."

Emmanuelle wanted to put her hands over her ears and drown him out. "Sometimes the cut is so deep, Elie, you can't bear to ever go there again."

"Maybe you're right, Emme. But think about the poor bastard you're condemning to living with you who will never have real love from you. Your loyalty, yes, but never your love, and he'll know it. He'll feel it every damn day of his life."

"That's not fair and you know it. You can hardly compare Valentino Saldi, a *criminal*, with your situation. That's what you're doing."

"Technically, Emme," Elie said, complacent as always, "we're criminals. We're assassins. We kill people, any way we look at it. You don't know what Val does or doesn't do. Even Stefano isn't certain of Val. I know because I asked him."

Emmanuelle's phone vibrated, and she pulled it out of her pocket with a little sigh, grateful for the respite. She didn't want to talk about Valentino Saldi anymore. She didn't want to think about him. She hadn't slept in months. She'd cried so many tears she was pretty certain she could have filled a lake. Still, there was an emptiness in her, a pain that just wouldn't go away. There was no way to explain that to Elie. He'd said hurtful things to a woman, but he didn't know her. She'd spent time with Valentino for years. He'd made love to her. He'd taken her rough, gentle, slow, fast, looking into her eyes.

She was *not* going to cry right there in the pizzeria. She

clutched her phone like a lifeline and looked down at the message. For a moment she didn't actually comprehend what she was seeing. Not who it was from or what it meant. Dario. Val's bodyguard and lieutenant. She thought she'd purged every number. Blocked them all. Why would he reach out to her of all people, even if there was an emergency? This made no sense. Her heart began to pound in alarm.

911. Tell no 1 or he's dead. Hurry. Place you met last.

CHAPTER TWO

"Stupid, stupid, stupid, Emmanuelle," Emme whispered to herself as she stood just inside the mouth of the shadow she'd ridden to the North Shore home on Lake Michigan that Valentino Saldi's birth mother had had in her family for generations. The land had never been taken out of that name and transferred to his adopted name. "You should have told someone you were coming here," she whispered and pulled out her phone with the idea of texting one of her sisters-in-law.

Closing her eyes tight, she knew she couldn't do it. If Val was really in trouble, then she wasn't going to make things worse by giving him up. Taking a deep breath, she sent a text. She was laying herself bare. Making herself vulnerable all over again. Maybe even getting herself killed.

I'm here, Dario, where are you?

Thank G. In main bedroom. Hurry.

She had really studied the layout. There didn't seem to be any guards. No snipers on the roof of the building. Still, she caught another shadow and rode it toward the house. The tube was dizzying, the walls curved, the views going by at such a speed that if anyone was waiting to take her prisoner, they were nothing but a blur. Still, it was necessary to try to look around her as she passed through the gates and down the drive, at the lawns and, in the distance, at the lake.

Twice she had to hastily step from one shadow to another, but she moved fast. She was adept and very skilled at her work. The last portal took her up the long steps and under the door right into the house. She was familiar with the interior. She'd met Valentino there many times. It had been the one place they felt confident they could go without either family finding them.

Emme's mouth went dry and her heart beat faster. She tried not to allow any memories to get to her. She was only there to make certain he was alive and well. Dario Bosco was Valentino's bodyguard as well as his lieutenant, but more importantly, he was his cousin. Dario, in her mind, had always been a question mark. She didn't quite understand his loyalties, but then she didn't understand any of the workings of the Saldi family.

"Damn it, Emme." She heard the whisper of Dario's voice, coming from the main bedroom. "Hurry. Hurry." He sounded like he was talking to himself.

Looking quickly around for cameras—there hadn't been security cameras activated before, and she didn't find any now—she stepped into another, smaller shadow that shot her straight to the main master bedroom. To her horror, there were smears of blood on the door frame. She could smell blood. The door was partially open, and she pushed it, staying to one side in case it was all a sham and she was being set up.

"Thank fuck you're here, Emme. Hurry up. I didn't know what else to do. He said not to call you, but he's going to die if you don't help him."

She was already at the bed, staring down at Valentino Saldi, the love of her life, the man she would have died for, killed for, given up her entire life for. There was too much blood on his clothes, soaking into the sheets.

"He needs to be in a hospital."

"If I could take him to a hospital, I would have," Dario snapped. "Tell me what to do."

There was only one thing she could do if she was going to save Val's life. "You'll have to trust me, Dario. You won't like this, but he's going to die if I don't get us help now."

She yanked out her phone and texted the emergency code to the one person she trusted the most in the world. She knew he would come through, no questions asked. He might flay her alive later, but right now, right when she needed him, he would come fast and bring help and get every single item on the list she sent to him to her as quickly as humanly possible without asking why. Even when she said who it was for and that he'd been shot and that he was dying.

"Dario, is anyone else in this house? I need to know now." Emmanuelle began removing Val's shirt as fast as she could. He'd been shot multiple times. She needed to see the entry and exit wounds.

"Giuseppi, his father," Dario added unnecessarily. "He insisted on holding off Miceli's army when they came at us while I got Giuseppi out to the SUV. It's armor plated. By the time I got back, they'd nearly overrun the entire house. Valentino had been shot so many times I thought he was dead, but he'd crawled to the door, and I dragged him out and then carried him to the car. I don't know if any of our boys made it out alive. We knew Miceli was going to make his move, but we thought he'd wait another couple of weeks. We'd heard he had an auction for young girls coming up. This seemed like a stupid time for him to chance fucking that up, so we weren't really ready for him."

That was almost more than Emmanuelle could take in. Miceli was Giuseppi's brother and Valentino's uncle. And an auction for young girls? Did he mean Miceli was *selling* young girls? What the hell was going on? She had to concentrate on saving Valentino. He'd lost too much blood. The wounds didn't look like they were in bad places, only that he'd lost so much blood he could be bleeding out.

"Is Giuseppi armed?" She stuffed the shirt into the worst of the wounds and pressed down as hard as she could.

"Yes. And I am as well." He lifted the gun in his hand.

"Does Giuseppi need medical care?" Not once had she taken her gaze from Val's body, trying to assess exactly how bad he was.

Stefano strode into the room, ignoring Dario who spun around, gripping his Glock and nearly landing on his ass. Her brother went straight to the other side of the bed, his gaze moving over Val, and then ripped back the sheet to begin stripping off his bloody trousers.

"Dario? Is Giuseppi wounded? Are you?" Emmanuelle persisted.

"The old man is fine. I took a couple of hits. Nothing major."

Stefano glanced over his shoulder. "That's why you look a little gray and nearly fell on your ass when I walked in. Sit down."

Few people disobeyed Stefano when he used that tone, but just in case, Emmanuelle wanted to reassure Dario. He was set on guarding Giuseppi and Val.

"My entire family will be showing up, and they'll be armed to the teeth. They'll make certain no one gets to them, Dario. Just sit down." Inside she was chanting *Hurry, hurry, hurry*, much like Dario had been doing.

Vittorio was next, striding in, and with him were Enzo and Enrica, two of their cousins and bodyguards. They were carrying trays of items. Vittorio had a home on the lake and lived close. He had a small medical unit there and thankfully had many of the things they needed to start the lifesaving process for Valentino.

It was Vittorio who put the IV into Val's vein, not Emme. Her hands were shaking too badly. Fortunately, their surgeon lived on the lake as well. Stefano had sent a car for him and his team. He was on retainer, paid enough that he came, no questions asked.

While they set up for surgery in the master bedroom,

Enzo and Enrica began to unload weapons from the trunk of the car and bring them into the house. They found the main security room and turned on the cameras. Ricco and Mariko arrived next, and Mariko immediately went into the bedroom to help the nurses with Dario. Emmanuelle was sent out under protest.

"Baby, what's going on?" Giovanni turned up, circling her waist with his arm.

"I'm not certain. Dario sent me an SOS, so I came here. Valentino's been shot several times. Giuseppi's in the other room. I'm going to go check on him now. He's probably very concerned about Val. It looks as if Miceli tried a takeover."

"Can we expect that his men will show up here to try to finish the job?" Giovanni asked.

"I don't know." She didn't. She didn't want to be away from Val, but she wasn't of any use in the surgery room. She wasn't the nurse or doctor type. She was more the assassin type. "But we should be prepared, just in case."

She walked quickly down the hall to the closest guest room and knocked on the door before calling out, "Giuseppi? It's Emmanuelle. Dario called me. May I come in? My brother Giovanni is with me."

She listened for movement. Giuseppi was older. He and Greta, his wife, had adopted their nephew, Valentino, when his parents had been killed. They'd never had children of their own, and they clearly loved Val. She knew they did. Greta had adored him, and Val had reciprocated that feeling, but then Greta had been easy to love. Both Giuseppi and Valentino were mourning her death from cancer.

"Come in, Emme," Giuseppi called out. His voice sounded stressed, but he also sounded like the Giuseppi that had ruled an empire for decades. He might have been down, but he wasn't out. His brother had tried to kill him, but worse, Miceli had tried to kill his son.

Emme made certain to keep her body in front of Giovanni's. As she came through the door, she could see Giuseppi sitting in a leather chair in front of a gas fireplace, the chair turned toward the door. He had a blanket over his lap, but the gun was on top of the blanket and pointed directly at her.

She ignored the gun and went straight to him, her relief at seeing him alive shocking her. Tears burned behind her eyes. "He's still alive, Giuseppi," she whispered, as she hugged him. "Stefano and Vittorio are with him. They brought a surgical team. Dario's wounded. They'll work on him, too. I didn't see how bad Dario was. He refused to even sit down until we had Val prepped for surgery."

"Dario always looks after Val," Giuseppi assured her, patting her shoulder. "Let me look at you." He held her at arm's length, his eyes running over her. "You look scared for him, Emme. Valentino is strong. He'll pull through."

She nodded, but Giuseppi hadn't seen him. There was so much blood. Too much. She wanted to bury her face in her brother's chest and sob, but they needed to secure the house. "How many men do you have that you can count on to be loyal?"

Giuseppi sighed. "Valentino and Dario shot four that were traitors in our own house. That saddened me greatly. These men were ones I had known most of their lives. I have no idea how Miceli managed to get to them, but I will find out. I would never have believed they would turn on me."

Looking at him, Emmanuelle felt a small shiver go through her. Giuseppi always seemed to be a sweet old man. He told her stories and laughed with Greta, bringing his wife flowers, sneaking her the occasional doughnut that she wasn't supposed to have. Right then, looking into his eyes, Emmanuelle saw the killer in him, the head of the Saldi crime family, which he'd ruled with an iron fist for so many years.

"We need to know if Miceli knows about this house, Giuseppi," Giovanni pushed. "And if we can count on any of your men to aid us if he sends an army after you and Val."

Giuseppi smiled at her brother—a shark's smile. "Who would have thought that the Ferraros and Saldis would have to fight together to survive?"

"Why is Miceli so determined to take over?" Emmanuelle asked.

"Human trafficking makes a tremendous amount of money, Emme," Giuseppi said. "Val tried to tell me some time ago that Miceli was selling women. I thought, at first, he meant the strip clubs. We have plenty of strip clubs. I visited all of them. We have high-class clubs and very raunchy clubs, but the ladies know the score, and no one makes them do anything they don't want to do. I visited every single one of them with Valentino and Dario. We made surprise visits and talked to the staff and girls. I saw no hint of human trafficking."

"I thought Miceli had his own territory," Giovanni said.

Giuseppi steepled his fingers but did so directly over his weapon. "True, but he must answer to me. I checked every one of his clubs. His girls were not treated with the same respect as mine, but they made no complaints, and I made certain to speak to them privately. If they were trafficked women, they certainly did not seem to be, and Valentino didn't think so, either."

"Val didn't drop it," Emmanuelle guessed. She knew how stubborn Valentino could be when he was certain he was right.

"No, I tried to get him to focus on who was pushing drugs and weapons in Ferraro territory, who was killing and leaving bodies to take us to the very brink of war with Stefano, but he said he was certain Miceli was throwing out red herrings to get us to look at anything but trafficking. I argued with Valentino so many times. Terrible arguments."

For a moment, Emmanuelle felt sorry for the older man. He looked tired and sad. His wife had been dying, and his son had been angry and accusing his uncle of horrific, vile and treacherous deeds. How many times had Val tried to call her? To text her? She'd blocked him, and he'd found other ways to get around it and had communicated with her until she couldn't stand it and shut that down as well. He'd needed to reach out to someone he trusted and talk over his worries about what Miceli was up to. She'd been too hurt to listen to him.

Giovanni wrapped his palm around the nape of her neck. "I take it Val found Miceli's trafficking ring?"

"Someone was abducting beautiful, very young girls, taking them off the streets all over the country. Very young. Under-age. Virgins. So, fourteen or fifteen. They would bring them in from other states and hold them in a warehouse. Five to eight at a time. Little, terrified girls, in these tiny, dirty cells for however long it took to bring in five of them, and then they'd clean them up and put them up for auction. Miceli would hold an exclusive event and auction these children to the highest bidder. They'd bring in millions for him."

Emmanuelle's stomach turned. "How did Val know?"

Giuseppi frowned. "He knows things. He always has, even as a child. I should have remembered that, but Miceli is my brother, and I didn't want to think he would do what Valentino said he did."

Emmanuelle had the feeling the older man wasn't talking about human trafficking, but she didn't ask.

"To answer your question, Giovanni, as far as I know, Miceli has no idea about this house, but one can never be certain. As far as my men, I would guess I could gather about twenty-five if needed, but I couldn't guarantee that they would all be loyal to me."

"Let's put that on hold," Giovanni suggested. "Since we're just not certain if Miceli got to anyone else. Val would skin us alive if anything happened to you."

"I need to get an update on his condition," Emmanuelle said. If she didn't, she was going to lose her mind. She forced a smile. "If Dario's good, I'll send him this way."

Giuseppi nodded. "You do that, Emme."

Emmanuelle needed to get out of the room and just take a deep breath. Valentino had been investigating Miceli for human trafficking. More, he'd been risking his life. Miceli was a vicious little weasel and he wanted complete control over the Saldi empire. Valentino had talked about his worries in this very house with her, how he was afraid that Miceli might try to kill Giuseppi and that he was certain it was

Miceli who was behind the car bombing that killed his parents, making him an orphan.

He told her Miceli's legitimate sons, Angelo and Tommaso, had once intimated that it might have been Giuseppi who had disposed of his youngest brother, Valentino's father, but Val had violently disagreed and wouldn't even entertain that idea.

Emmanuelle noted that Taviano and Nicoletta, her youngest brother and his wife, were there, talking with Enzo and Ricco about securing the house and grounds. She gave them a wave and a smile of thanks. Her family. They came when called. All of them. There was Elie. He sent her a grin and shook his head, striding toward the back of the house.

Sasha, Giovanni's wife, strode in, Enrica, Emme's cousin and a trained bodyguard, at her side. Both women were cool under fire. Sasha was hell on wheels with a rifle. Enrica was the sister of Enzo and Emilio, the top bodyguards of the Ferraro family, and she'd trained with her brothers.

Demetrio, Drago and Leone, all three bodyguards and fierce protectors of shadow riders, split up and walked outside, taking up the assignments given them by Enzo and Emilio. Emmanuelle was fairly certain one or more would be on the roof. She knew they were good with rifles.

Tomas and Cosimo Abatangelo talked quietly with Enzo for a few moments and then went outside as well. Their youngest brother, Raimondo, was sent down the hall toward the security room. He looked a little sulky, but he went without argument; a good thing, or she knew Enzo would have ordered him to leave. They were setting up for possible war, and there was no room for insubordination.

Emme first went into the hallway bathroom and scrubbed her arms and hands, and then used a paper towel to open the master bedroom door. She didn't want to carry in any more germs than she already was. The smell of blood hit her hard. Dario sat in the leather chair near the door, his gaze fixed on the men and women surrounding the bed and the patient there. Clearly, someone had already seen to his wounds. He had his shirt off and there was a wide bandage around his ribs and another around his left bicep.

"Have they said anything?" Emmanuelle found herself whispering.

"That it isn't nearly as bad as it looks. Mostly, that he lost tons of blood. They've started getting it back into him, and if they can keep that coming, he'll be fine," Dario said. "Where did they get all the blood? I mean, it's clear that your brother is giving him that blood, but . . ."

Dario took a deep breath. He pulled his gaze from the bed, the blood and the gore with an effort and met her eyes. "Thanks, Emme. I don't know what I would have done if you hadn't come."

"It's Val. I had to come. You knew I'd come the moment you typed nine-one-one." She saw on his face that he'd *hoped*, but he hadn't known. She'd held out a long, long time. Maybe she'd even made Val believe she was over him, as if that could ever happen.

"How can they know that Vittorio's blood will match up with Val's?" There was worry in Dario's voice. On his face.

She hesitated. He kept looking at her. "Vittorio's blood matches up with everyone's. That's our little secret."

"That's impossible."

"He has a rare blood type, only a couple of people in the world have it. We don't talk about it, Dario. Just like there're things you don't talk about, we don't talk about that." She changed the subject. "Giuseppi thinks he has at least another twenty-five loyal men, but I'm hesitant to let him call them. I'm hoping Miceli doesn't know about this house." She'd always wondered why Dario was so loyal to Valentino when he was actually Miceli's son. He was illegitimate, and Miceli hadn't acknowledged him for years, but he was his oldest son. No one had known about Dario for years.

"Yeah, at this point, I'd be careful. Valentino and I have a few men we know for certain we can count on, but Miceli was really splashing some big money around. Times get hard, and there are bills to pay. I don't know, Emme, loyalties can get tested. And the younger ones, it seems they're so easily bribed with money and pussy." He winced. "Sorry. I shouldn't talk like that in front of you. Val would beat the crap out of me." He grinned at her. "Well. He'd try. We're pretty damned even most of the time." He leaned his head back against the leather, looking exhausted.

"I have brothers, Dario," she reminded. "Why don't you go in with Giuseppi? He could use an update on Val. He's acting tough, but he's really afraid for his son."

"I don't know, Emme."

"If you were going to have to shoot someone for trying to hurt him, you would have had to do it already," she pointed out. "Give yourself a break. I'll watch over him."

"I doubt if you're going to shoot one of your brothers," he said, his voice a mixture of amused and dry.

"Don't bet on it. I think about it often." She sent him a little smirk. "Do you need help getting up?"

"Don't be a smart-ass, Emme."

Dario didn't look as if he could make it out of the chair on his own, so she hadn't exactly been being a smart-ass, but he was Valentino's right-hand man, his lieutenant, the enforcer. She didn't want to think too much about what that meant in the Saldi world. She couldn't exactly judge him. He protected Giuseppi and Valentino, and he did it in a permanent way. Dario was as tough as they came. She could never tell whether he liked her or not. He didn't give much away.

He'd briefly shown interest in Nicoletta, but when Taviano had announced she was his fiancée, Dario had seemed to respect that boundary and backed off. That made Emme wonder if his interest had been genuine. She couldn't imagine anything stopping Dario from going after a woman if he truly wanted her. Dario was a mystery, but right now, he needed to rest as much as possible, because they would need his ability with his guns if they were attacked.

"Don't shoot Val, either," Dario cautioned as he pushed himself out of the chair.

Emme stepped back and got the door for him. "Giuseppi

is armed. It might be best to let him know you're coming in. He looks a little trigger-happy."

"Will do. And I want updates on Val every fifteen minutes. Who's running the show here? I'll need him to coordinate with me. Introduce us before you lock yourself away here. I want you to make it clear I'm looped in at all times." Dario's voice had turned hard. Scary. He'd gone back to that man she was never certain of.

"Stefano is always in charge, Dario—you know that. But Enzo and Emilio run the control room and will send all orders to every guard, sniper and soldier. They have eyes and ears everywhere."

She was already texting Enzo to meet them in the wide hallway outside the guest room where Giuseppi was. She also cautioned the bodyguard to treat Dario with the utmost respect. As a rule, the two families were uneasy around each other if not straight-out enemies. The feud went back over a hundred years, which was just plain silly in Emmanuelle's mind.

She followed Dario out of the master bedroom, and immediately found she could breathe easier. She hadn't realized she was holding her breath, trying not to take in the scent of blood that hung so heavily in the air. Valentino had lost so much. She couldn't think about whether or not she'd gotten her family and surgical team there in time. Right now, the most important thing was to set up to protect him and his father from his murderous uncle and nephews.

Enzo came around the corner right as they made it to the alcove just opposite Giuseppi's door. Dario sank into a chair, his face gray, sweat beading on his forehead. He ignored it as Enzo came straight to them. Emme performed the introductions, although the two men had met multiple times over the years, just not as allies.

"We chose these rooms for a purpose," Dario stated. "This guest room has a panic room. It's virtually a vault and has enough supplies for a couple of weeks. I can stash Giuseppi if need be, and no one will be the wiser. If something happens to me, he'll be there. There's also a similar setup in the master bedroom, although trying to stash Val anywhere, wounded or not, won't be easy."

He indicated his phone and Enzo drew close, so Emme did as well. There was a layout of the inside of the sprawling house, all the rooms, but it looked more like a child's drawing than an actual professional blueprint. Dario pointed to several places where there were colored scribblings, as if a child had attempted to color but couldn't stay in the lines and then, becoming frustrated, had just slashed with crayons all over.

"Everywhere you see these, we have armories. Some are in the floor, the walls, the attics. We stashed them everywhere. This place was our last stand. We knew Miceli was going to come at us and we couldn't trust anyone. Val and I renovated this lake house as fast as we could over the last year."

Emme hated the way Dario's voice was so thin. He clearly was hurt. She risked a quick glance at Enzo. Would Dario be telling the Ferraro family details like this if he expected to survive?

Enzo put his hand on the small of her back, a comforting gesture, but he kept his eyes on Dario's phone. "And these squiggles?"

"Those are doors to get into the walls. Inside, the walls are narrow. All of you are big, much like Val and I are, but the women wouldn't have any problem moving through the house in the walls. It's another way to escape. One exit leads to the garage, one to the boats, and one to the vault in the guest room. I can make it through there, but my shoulders hit either side. A bigger man might have trouble if he's not careful, especially in the pitch dark. They didn't put any lights in there. You have to have a flashlight or some kind of light."

"Send this to my phone. I can share with the Ferraros," Enzo said.

"Give me your fuckin' word that Valentino and Giuseppi come out of this alive." Dario sent the information to Enzo's phone.

"How the hell can I guarantee that? I wouldn't be here if I wasn't trying to save them," Enzo snapped. "I think you lost a little too much blood yourself."

Emme swallowed down her fear for Valentino. "Dario? You believe Miceli knows about the lake house, don't you? You really think he's going to come for Giuseppi, Valentino and you, with an army."

Dario looked up at her, his dark eyes moving over her face. "Yeah, Emme. Miceli's going to come. When he does, it won't be pretty. He hates all three of us. You have no idea the kind of hatred someone like that can have. What he's capable of and what he's taught his sons to be. I don't want them to get their hands on you. Valentino has gone to great lengths to ensure they don't."

She frowned. "What does that mean? When did Miceli ever try to get me?"

Dario shook his head. "I'm tired, Emme. I'm fucking tired. Go find out how Val is and send me an update. I'm going to lie down for a few minutes. Enzo, keep me in the loop."

"You got it."

"When he comes, Enzo, he'll try to overrun the place. Boats, ground, maybe even air. He'll strike hard."

"We'll be ready."

What had she gotten her family into? This was Saldi family business, and now her entire family was involved, other than Francesca, Stefano's wife, and his son, Crispino, who were safe in their penthouse at the prestigious Ferraro Hotel with Vittorio's wife, Grace. Emme knew that Stefano would never have left without first securing his wife and child, as well as Grace, surrounding them with protection.

Her phone vibrated, and she yanked it out of her jeans pocket. Stefano. Her heart jumped. Clenched. If something had gone wrong with Val, he would have just said so, right?

Without a word, she turned and hurried back to the master bedroom, anxiety making it difficult to breathe.

"Is he alive?" The question tumbled out of her mouth before she could stop it, revealing too much, but then what did it matter? She'd already asked Stefano to come, to put their lives on the line for the man who had betrayed her.

Emmanuelle hurried over to the bed. The doctors and nurses had cleaned up the surgical site. Valentino lay on fresh sheets, thanks, she was certain, to Mariko. Vittorio sat in a chair, legs sprawled out in front of him, an IV in his arm, fluids going into him, just as fluids were going into Val. Val looked pale, his dark hair emphasizing the unusual color, but thankfully, most of the blood had been washed off.

"Bullets didn't hit anything vital," Stefano reported. "I never saw anyone so lucky. He was mostly in danger from blood loss."

"He was hit several times," Emme whispered. Tears burned behind her eyes. She didn't want anyone to know. Crying was weakness. *He* was her weakness. Valentino Saldi. Her failing.

Stefano curled his palm around the nape of her neck. "Vittorio gave him so much blood, he's more Ferraro than Saldi now."

"Dario says Miceli has an army and that they'll come here, Stefano. I didn't mean to involve our entire family in their war. He was dying, and I just called you. I always call you when things go to hell." She turned her face up to his. "I'm sorry." She loved Stefano with all her heart, but she loved Valentino with every breath in her body. "I couldn't let him die."

"I know, baby. I would have been very upset if you hadn't called me. When things go wrong, that's what you're supposed to do. We rely on each other. We're *famiglia*. That means something, Emmanuelle."

He dropped a kiss on top of her head. "Valentino is a good man. I told you that before. I know things went south between you, and I don't in any way approve a relationship just because of what kind of family he comes from, but I know he's a good man. I have no problem helping Val, especially when he's been working to take down a human trafficking ring and a high-priced auction." He touched his phone, the mass text she'd sent when she'd gotten updates of any kind of news on why Miceli had attacked Giuseppi, Valentino and Dario.

She put her arms around her brother and laid her face against his chest, right over his heart. She needed comfort, and Stefano gave it to her without hesitation. He wrapped his arms around her immediately.

"Do you think that's what Grace was almost caught up in?" She glanced over at Vittorio. He was clearly paying attention.

Vittorio frowned. "I've been thinking it. They were very specific that someone wanted Grace. Not just anyone, but Grace. Dario said that these auctions are young girls, and although Grace was a virgin, she wasn't a teenager, and they had no way of knowing she was a virgin."

"I thought you knew who wanted her, that Miceli owed him a debt," Emme said.

Vittorio shook his head. "Stefano and I talked it over many times. That scenario didn't make sense. No, someone else wanted her, and Miceli wasn't going to own up that he was involved in any way."

Alarms began to go off in Emmanuelle's head. She pressed her lips together as if to hold back secrets. How many secrets could she hold back? And for what? She pulled herself out of Stefano's arms and leaned over the bed to stare down into Valentino's face. His eyes were closed. His lashes were as black as night and long, too long for a man to have. She'd always been envious of his lashes. Now they stood out starkly against his pale skin. He normally had the most beautiful dark complexion, as if he had a permanent tan. She loved his coloring.

"You're awake." She made it an accusation.

The lashes fluttered but didn't lift. "Floating. Doc gave me something, but it's wearing off." His voice was tinny, faraway.

Good. Maybe he'd tell the truth for a change. "There was a reason you noticed me all those years ago, Val, the same reason Dario noticed Nicoletta and Miceli wanted Grace."

Stefano stepped closer to her, one hand on her back for support, as if he knew she was guessing and whatever answer Valentino gave her was going to rip her apart even more. Vittorio sat up straighter in his chair.

Val's lips, the ones that looked chapped and dry but had always been velvet soft and perfect and could kiss like heaven, pulled into a little half smile. "My girl. So smart. Love you so much, Emme."

"Valentino. Why did you single me out?" She made it a demand. "Why was Dario looking at Nicoletta? What did Miceli want with Grace?"

His hand moved on the bed. Sliding. Seeking. She looked at it, trying not to respond. Hating that she wanted to touch him. That she needed to. She closed her eyes and then let herself feel his skin next to hers. The moment she did, she knew it was a mistake. There was no blood. No trauma to keep her head occupied. There was only Val and Emme. Before she could pull her fingers away, he turned his hand and captured hers with surprising strength. Never once did he lift his lashes.

"Val, I need an answer."

"You already know the answer, Princess."

It was another blow, a hard punch in the gut, even though she was expecting it. Now she knew what her sisters-in-law had to have felt like when they first learned they met certain "criteria" to be with Ferraros.

She tried again to pull her hand away, but he refused to relinquish his hold on her. "I saw the bindings tying our shadows together, but I don't know how, or what it means, Val." Deliberately, she spoke aloud, even if it came out a whisper, because if she didn't she would never be able to tell Stefano and Vittorio why there were tears streaming down her face.

She felt her brothers' shock. Stefano dug his fingers into

the side of her waist. She didn't look at him, or at Vittorio. She could only look at Val. Was there some way to undo it? If so, was it like the riders? Would she forget him? Did she want to forget him?

"Not going to talk about anything that would give you an excuse to run away from me again. Too tired right now, Emme. Give me a couple of hours, babe." His voice trailed off.

Stefano tightened his hold on her for a moment and then jerked his head toward the door. Vittorio got up, starting to remove the IV from his arm. Mariko came out of the shadows and did it for him, using a much gentler technique than he would have. She remained behind, watching over Val while Stefano led Emme out of the room.

Emmanuelle felt a little like she might be going to her doom. She kept her chin up while she explained to both brothers about how each time she was near Val, and their shadows touched, those little ropes insisted on tying themselves around her shadow, binding her to him, almost as if she was a prisoner. She'd learned to be careful, but the pull between them was so strong that often she didn't pay as much attention as she should.

"Why didn't you tell us?" Stefano demanded.

"I tried to tell you," Emme said. "Often, especially when it first happened. I was terrified. Every time I brought up Val, you were furious, Stefano. You yelled at me before I could find the right words to describe what was happening. I tried over and over to tell all of you that I couldn't stay away from him, but you acted like I was some helpless female caught up in him because he was hot. No one would take the time to listen to me. Eventually, I'll admit, I gave up. More, I didn't want to say anything because I knew I was in love with him and I was afraid of what you'd do. It only just occurred to me that maybe Dario saw something in Nicoletta like Taviano did. Is that possible, Stefano? Can the Saldis bind a rider to them differently, but still bind them?"

Stefano and Vittorio exchanged a long look. Stefano put his arm around her shoulders. "I don't know, honey. I've never heard of such a thing. I'd have to ask a council member. I can ask Alfieri without going into details. I'm sorry I didn't listen to you, but you know you should have told us."

Alfieri Ferraro was a distant cousin from Sicily who sat on the International Council of Shadow Riders. He would know, or have access to those who would know, the answer to the question if anyone would. The feud between the Saldis and the Ferraros had started because the Saldis had taken offense when the Ferraros refused to align themselves when asked. They had openly opposed the Saldis and had helped others against them. In the end, the Saldis had made a concentrated effort to wipe them out, every man, woman and child, to stamp out the very existence of the Ferraros. Few other than the shadow riders had escaped, dispersing across the world, vowing to come back stronger to find a way to prevent a massacre from ever happening again.

Emme nodded. Stefano was right, especially if it proved that the Saldis could bind female riders to them for some purpose and Nicoletta and Grace had been unknowingly in danger. Her phone vibrated, and she yanked it out quickly, saw the text and groaned.

"Eloisa just drove up with Henry. Great. That's all I need. I'm going back in the room with Val. I can't face her right now, Stefano."

"She came to help defend him and Giuseppi," Stefano reminded. "No matter what she says or does, she is *famiglia*, and when push comes to shove, she will fight at our side."

That was true, but Emmanuelle didn't want her there.

CHAPTER THREE

Eloisa walked through the door, Henry right behind her. Emmanuelle tried not to stare at her normally elegant mother. Tonight, Eloisa wore dark trousers with slashes of gray through them. A wide belt held multiple loops. Hanging from those loops were so many kinds of weapons, but each was encased in something that prevented them from knocking against one another, so they remained silent.

She had on a black-and-gray top with long sleeves that clung to her body like a glove. Across her front diagonally was a strap holding multiple weapons. Around her neck was a black scarf that looked as if it might actually be a hood. Behind her, Henry was dressed and armed similarly.

"Eloisa, Henry," Stefano said. "It's good that you came. "Giuseppi is unharmed, but Dario and Valentino are both in bad shape. They've been investigating a human trafficking ring these last couple of years, certain Miceli was behind it, and unfortunately, they were right. He's been bringing in teenage girls and auctioning them off to the highest bidders. Giuseppi tried to shut it down, and Miceli turned on him.

Valentino fought off an army so Dario could get the old man out alive. That's it in a nutshell, but we expect Miceli to try to finish them."

Eloisa nodded briskly. "Does Giuseppi have anyone he can count on?"

"From what I understand," Emmanuelle answered before Stefano could, "he thinks he does, but Dario isn't as certain. Dario said that Miceli has been bribing even men Giuseppi has had in his organization for years. The younger ones like the money and access to girls that Miceli promises. He said there are a very few that are loyal to Val, but not many they trust with Giuseppi's life."

Emmanuelle braced herself for her mother's biting, sharp tongue. Anything to do with Valentino Saldi had always been ugly between them. Eloisa glanced at Henry and then to Stefano and Vittorio.

"At least they had the good sense to call on us. Where is Giuseppi?"

"He and Dario are in the guest bedroom down the hall," Stefano said, indicating it with his cell phone. "I can send you all the particulars. We're all keeping in touch that way."

Henry's phone chimed first and then Eloisa's.

"You gave blood, Vittorio," Eloisa observed.

"He would have died otherwise. He was shot multiple times," Vittorio clarified.

"Say what you want about that boy," Eloisa said. "He does love his father. He would do anything at all for that man."

She said it as if Val couldn't love anyone else. And maybe he couldn't. Emmanuelle already knew Giuseppi had ordered Val to get her to fall in love with him so he could learn the Ferraro family secrets. There had been another woman in his bedroom, and he'd actually said that to her. He'd compromised a young girl, made her fall in love and continued duping her. And then there was the binding of her shadow. He had known all along, and he had deliberately sought her out for that as well. Was that something Giuseppi had ordered?

If Miceli knew and went after Grace because of it, and Dario had looked at Nicoletta because of her abilities, then Giuseppi had known. Someone had to have clued in Dario and Valentino. She couldn't look at her mother or Stefano another minute. She needed to be alone.

"I'll go outside and look around, Stefano. I know we've got people out there, but it might be good to have one of us looking out as well." She sent him an imploring look. She just needed to breathe fresh air. Be alone. Just for a few minutes.

"Good idea, Emme. Stay in the shadows. Let Enzo know."

"Of course." She nodded at Eloisa and Henry without really looking at them and stepped into a shadow, letting it carry her right out the door.

The minutes she was in the shadow she felt it tearing her apart, skin, bones, every part of her, just the way Val had. She knew if she got close to him again, if she looked at him, touched him, the terrible cravings would start all over again. They had something to do with the way the ropes coming off his shadow had bound hers to his.

The shadow took her to the lake itself. The moon was no more than a sliver, but it was bright enough to cast a ribbon of silver to stream a shadow trail for her. Dark purple clouds shimmered over the lake, an ominous portent of the storm advancing on them. She thought that very fitting. There was a storm brewing between Val and her. Between the two Saldi factions. Between the Saldis and the Ferraros. It was all coming together quite soon in a terrible clash of violence. She was used to violence. She had been raised on it.

She crouched low in the mouth of the shadow tube and stared out over the water, trying not to remember all the times she met Val at this very spot and watched the sun set over the lake, his arms around her. More than once, she had glanced over to see her shadow on the ground and those ropes swirling around it, tying it tight, only now they looked as if they were knots upon knots, impossible to pull loose.

Emmanuelle forced herself to remember looking up at Valentino's face, catching him looking at their shadows with a look of intense satisfaction. Her heart had suddenly gone crazy with trepidation, an ominous warning rushing through her bloodstream. She'd wanted to pull back and reassess, think things through, but then his mouth was on hers and she wasn't thinking anymore.

That was the way it always seemed to go. Once Valentino was kissing her or touching her, all her worries disappeared. The lessons she'd learned had been harsh. She couldn't get near him, because the moment she did, something in his voice, in his eyes, always drew her back, always made her believe, no matter what the evidence showed.

She looked around before she stepped out of the mouth of the tube and then walked to the deck she was so familiar with. She'd spent time with Val here often—their secret hideaway. She'd fantasized more than once that this was her home with Valentino, and they were safe here. No one would ever get to them, tell them they couldn't be together.

She curled up in one of the beach chairs, pulling her legs up and wrapping her arms around her knees, staring out over the choppy water. She just needed a few minutes to gather herself together, and then she'd be able to handle whatever Miceli Saldi threw at them. The moment she allowed herself to sink into sorrow for everything she had lost, she felt it—that melody playing along her nerves, sending it throughout her body.

Emmanuelle gasped and sat up straight. Damn him. She'd managed to stop that sensation over the last year. Block it out completely. Somehow, those ties imprisoning her shadow so completely had connected her nerve endings to his so that along with sexual awareness, a terrible, brutal, merciless need for him, there was this . . . beautiful music that soothed when she was upset. At night, when she was alone and unable to sleep, he would send this music to her. The melody sang along her nerve endings, overcoming her sorrow, and easily, because it moved along her nerves, comforted her body, she would fall asleep.

She didn't want Valentino to touch her in any way. He didn't have that right. She wanted to find a way to undo their connection. So far, that hadn't happened. If shadow riders were divorced, their shadows untangled. There had to be a way for her shadow to be freed from the chains he'd bound hers with. It wasn't just his melody, it was extremely sensual, bringing her body alive, making her aware of herself as utterly feminine, and his—and him as totally masculine, and hers. That they belonged together.

The ties wrapping her shadow so tightly had prevented any other eligible shadow rider from connecting with her. She had traveled extensively to other countries, and there were many riders looking for a female. Not a single male's shadow had managed to form one knot with hers. She knew it was because Val had tied her shadow up so tight, she was his prisoner.

Emmanuelle rubbed her chin on the top of her knees. She should have told Stefano. Made him listen. She hadn't because she was afraid Stefano might kill Val, and she was still protecting him. She told herself she didn't love Valentino Saldi, she couldn't love him after all the lies and betrayal, but she knew she did. That humiliated her.

She wasn't a weak woman. She had self-esteem. Or she used to. Until Val. She had confidence in herself as a woman, until Val. Now she was a rider—a damn good one. One of the best. No one could take that from her, not even Val.

"Babe, you're crying." Elie leaned down and swiped a tear out from under her eye with the pad of his finger.

"I'm not *crying*," she denied. "The wind is wreaking havoc with my tear ducts."

He grinned at her and sank down without invitation into the chair beside hers. "I get that, even if you're the worst liar on the face of the earth." He picked up her hand. "He's going to be all right."

"Yeah, he is. I don't know if that's good or bad." But she knew it was good. Just bad for her. "Miceli is coming for him. I can feel it."

"Why?"

"I don't really know that much about the politics in their

family," Emme confessed. "I tried not to hear too much. I didn't want to know. I wasn't ever going to tell Val anything about my family, so I didn't think it was right to get too much on his. Still, it wasn't that difficult to realize, when I heard Miceli talking, that he lied quite often. He acted like he had Giuseppi's best interests at heart, but he didn't. He hated that Valentino was next in line to run things. Miceli had his own territory, but he had to answer to Giuseppi. If Giuseppi stepped down or died, Miceli would have to answer to Val."

"Ouch," Elie said. "I can see how that might smart. Having to answer to his own nephew, one much, much younger."

"Val was adopted by Giuseppi and Greta. He's a Saldi, but the youngest son's child. Val's parents were killed in a car bombing. Giuseppi and Greta had no children, and they took him in and eventually adopted him. Miceli had Dario with a woman he was never married to. He didn't claim him for a long time. Then he married and had two sons, Angelo and Tommaso, both of whom would have been in line to be head of the family had Val not been legally adopted."

"So they probably hate Val as well."

"For certain they do."

"Why is Dario with Val and not Miceli?" Elie asked. He rubbed Emmanuelle's fingers over his forehead, back and forth.

She took comfort in that physical touch. Val had been able to stop her from connecting with other men on a romantic level, but she had managed an emotional attachment to Elie she desperately needed. She was eternally grateful.

"I don't know the answer to that. Dario certainly isn't going to tell me, and Val never has. I think Giuseppi stopped doing a lot of the things Miceli wanted to keep doing that made a great amount of money and that made Miceli angry. I'm only speculating. This split seems to have been brought on by Valentino discovering a warehouse used for auctioning young girls to wealthy men and women. He shut it down. Apparently, that wasn't well received by his uncle."

A shadow fell across them. Taviano stood close. "Emme,

it seems Val is extremely agitated. So much so that Stefano and Vittorio can barely keep him down. Stefano says to get in there and find out what's wrong so he doesn't undo all the good the surgeon's done. Vittorio can't spare more blood."

She frowned, getting to her feet immediately. "Did anyone check on Giuseppi? Reassure him his father and Dario are okay?"

"Of course."

Emmanuelle stepped into the shadow tube, the pull on her body vicious, wrenching at her until she felt completely pulled apart and disoriented. She stepped from one shadow to the next, letting this one carry her inside the house. Taking a deep breath, she let herself have a moment for her body to catch up with the reality of her mind, and then she straightened her shoulders and strode into the master bedroom.

The moment she pushed open the door, Valentino's vivid green eyes were on her, hot with anger. He was sitting up, bandages covering his arm, shoulder and chest, stark white against his olive skin. He had more muscles than most men had, and even sitting in bed covered in bandages, he appeared threatening. Those eyes of his were on her face, a gathering, threatening storm, just as fierce as the one outside.

"I take it you can handle this, Emme," Stefano said. "We'll leave you to it."

Emme stepped away from the door, her gaze on Val. He was clearly spoiling for a fight. That was good. Better than him trying to pretend he was sweet. Stefano and Vittorio went out of the room without a backward glance. Emmanuelle was very grateful her older brothers didn't treat her as if she were a little child they had to protect. Instead, they made it seem as if Val was the one throwing the tantrum and she had been brought in to calm him down.

They stared at each other for a long time. For what seemed forever. Emmanuelle struggled not to fall into those brilliant green eyes. She kept her features composed, her back to the door, her eyes on the man who had trapped her into something she knew was very explosive but equally as wrong.

Before, she would have been the first to speak. She was so much younger than Val, always seeking his approval, so afraid of losing him. Now she waited. She'd learned patience over these last two years. She'd learned humility. She'd learned many other useful things. She kept her gaze on his.

"I don't like his fucking hands on you, Princess."

That was the last thing she expected Val to say. For a moment she couldn't process it, or the raw jealousy in his voice. She blinked rapidly, turning his statement over and over in her mind as if she could change it. Frowning.

"For the last two years, all I've seen is that man with you, sitting with you, eating with you, arm around you. Making you laugh. Taking you to the club. Dancing with you. Your fucking mother loves him, and she hates everyone. He's always pushing your hair out of your eyes. Thought about killing the son of a bitch so many times, Emme. You have no idea. You fucking have no idea how many ways I thought about killing him. I can be inventive."

"Maybe that wouldn't be such a good idea to try, Val. Not everyone is so easy to kill." She kept her voice very mild, but a part of her was in a state of near panic. What if Valentino had really tried to kill Elie? Elie Archambault was one of the fastest shadow riders she'd ever met. Few could best Elie, and Val was not a shadow rider, trained from birth as an assassin.

"The point is not whether or not I would kill an innocent, Emme, and the answer is, I would *not*, but that I'm damn sick of you letting him put his hands on you. Even now, when you know I can feel him doing it."

She let herself breathe. Valentino wouldn't kill an innocent. She kept her eyes on his. "What does it mean when your shadow throws all those ties around mine until you tie my shadow so tight, I can't get loose?"

"What do you think it means, Emmanuelle? You feel it every time we're together."

"It's more than that. Tell me what more there is, Val. When I was sixteen years old and we were at that party, you

saw our shadows on the wall and the way your shadow reacted to mine. You saw it then. It wasn't just about sexual
attraction. What happens when we're tied together like this?"

"Come over here and sit on the bed."

She shook her head. She didn't dare get that close to him.
"I'm fine right here."

"You want to talk about this, then you come over and sit
on the bed right next to me."

"Why?" She narrowed her eyes suspiciously. "It shouldn't
make any difference where I am, Val. This doesn't change
anything between us. My family is still going to protect your
father, Dario and you from Miceli and his army. It's what
we do."

"You want to know these answers, Princess, you get over
here and sit next to me, otherwise we can talk about your
friend Elie."

Valentino was as stubborn as hell. She knew when he
made up his mind to do something there was no stopping
him. She needed answers. The fact that Dario had looked at
Nicoletta and Grace had been in danger of being kidnapped
by Miceli worried her. She knew it was rumored that ancestors in the past had married into the Saldi family. If that was
so, had the shadow rider genetics been passed on, or at least
something similar? Did the Saldi family have something of
their own that meshed with Ferraro genetics?

Reluctantly, Emmanuelle crossed the room and slid onto
the bed beside Val. She kept as much of a distance as possible. Fortunately, the bed was king-sized, so there was plenty
of space, and she stayed right on the edge. She didn't like getting close to Val for self-preservation's sake. He probably
knew that.

"So, talk, Val."

"Thanks for coming. I told Dario not to send for you, but
he doesn't listen to me. Your family coming, that's huge.
Knowing Giuseppi's safe. Thanks for that."

That voice. Up close, his voice was like an actual caress

smoothing over her skin. He brought every nerve ending alive with his voice. She tried not to shiver, tried not to let one single response to him slip where he could see, but already, she knew those nerve endings connecting them like sins would tell him everything he needed to know.

She lifted her chin. She refused to hide away like a child. There was nowhere to run. He had tied them together in a way she didn't understand. Only he did. In order to get free, she had to know what he had done to her, why and how it worked. Pretending he didn't affect her was just plain silly. So shivering or getting goose bumps, well, that was just part of what happened when she was close to him.

"No problem, Val. I'm sitting here, close. You recognized something in me when I was a teen and you saw my shadow. I saw it on your face quite a few times. You always managed to distract me with kisses when I was getting worried. I'm asking for answers. What did you see, Val?" She forced herself to look into those brilliant green eyes, even though they made her heart beat too fast and her stomach melt.

"I want you to actually listen to me all the way for a change, Emme. You never let me finish anything. You get hurt and then you rush off and I don't have a chance at explaining. You're going to be hurt."

She nodded. "I'm kind of used to that now. Breathing your name equates with being hurt. I've asked for this explanation, and I do want it, so I'll listen all the way through." She just didn't want to look at him while he told her about another betrayal.

The silence was so long she almost lifted her gaze to his again, but she couldn't make herself do it. She sat with her back to the headboard and took long, deep breaths, contemplating the toes of her boots.

"Giuseppi told me there was a story of a way the Saldis could go from one place to another gathering information and even, if circumstances were dire enough, sending a spy to watch a rival family prepare for war. Of course, no one believed such a myth. This was handed down from father to son, but always, in spite of the feud between the families, the rumors revolved around the Ferraros and the Saldis."

"I don't understand. You'll have to make yourself clearer." She knew Val. He was hedging. There was a story. He didn't want to give her the details. He knew she wouldn't like them.

Valentino sighed. "I don't suppose you'd consider sliding over here on my good side and letting me put my arm around you. I haven't touched you in a very long time, Emme."

"And you aren't going to, Val. The last time I saw you, I stood in the doorway of your bedroom and you had a very naked blonde in your room. You might not remember, but I do. She was kneeling right in front of you. You told her that your father had ordered you to get together with me, but I didn't know jack about sex."

"Does that really sound like something my father would order me to do, Emme?" Val asked quietly.

Her heart jumped. She couldn't do this with him. She dropped one hand to the comforter on the other side of her body, out of his sight, and fisted the material as tightly as she could. "It doesn't matter right now anyway. We need to stick to one subject at a time. Please explain what you meant about the story Giuseppi told you."

Valentino cursed under his breath. He'd always had a foul mouth, much like Stefano. "It was like a stupid myth handed down from father to son, only the way he told it, I knew it was real. He said the story came from the old country. That our ancestors said it was sacred and if we ever found a woman with shadows that our shadows ran to and tried to tie, that we needed to pursue her and hold her to us."

Emmanuelle lowered her lashes and tried to force her heavy heart not to ache so much that he would feel it. "At the party, you saw my shadow, and your shadow threw out all those ropes. I could tell you were shocked."

"So were you. You broke the light on purpose."

She nodded, conceded that she had. "The sexual jolt scared me. I'd never felt anything like that before, and then seeing the strange patterns on the wall was a little over the top. I just wanted to go home." Until he started talking to her in that voice of his and making her feel safe when she wasn't. "Don't stop, Val—explain how it works."

"Supposedly, each time our shadows came together, my shadow would tie yours closer to me, imprison yours, so to speak, but in some way, connect us on a molecular level. The more we were bound together, the closer that level became, until it was difficult for us to be apart."

She tried not to view what he was telling her as more of a betrayal. Certainly, it was the truth. She could barely breathe without him. She had no idea if he felt the same. He certainly had no problem inviting another woman to his bedroom. Letting her touch his body. She shifted, thinking to slide from the bed, needing to pace, but his hand snaked out, shackling her wrist.

"You promised me this time you'd listen, Emme. All the way through the entire explanation. I told you some of it would be difficult to hear, that it would hurt, but you asked, and I'm giving you the truth. I need you to hear me all the way through. I didn't play you."

She pressed her lips together to force back any words of condemnation. She *had* agreed to hear him, and she needed to hear everything he said. She had to know how Saldis could tie Ferraros' shadows to them so she could undo whatever had been done between them with the least amount of damage to both parties.

"Yes, you're right. Go on. It was a silly reaction. Explain how your shadow ties mine. I don't understand that part."

"I'm not altogether certain I do, either," Valentino admitted.

He didn't loosen his fingers, keeping that cuff around her wrist. Emmanuelle knew it was absolute lunacy to allow his skin to remain against hers. She was aware of each of his fingers pressed tightly to her wrist, her bare skin, and now his thumb slid back and forth in a mesmerizing caress that threatened to tear her heart right out of her chest.

"Those early years, when I would see you, you would

purposely distract me so I would forget to protect my shadow, didn't you?"

"Yes. It gave me the opportunity to bind your shadow tighter to me."

"Why? What happens if you do that?" Emmanuelle asked, turning to look at him. Needing to see his eyes. "Tell me what you do know, Val, because you must know something or you wouldn't have done that."

"I know that each wrap binds you closer to me, and I can feel that. The more the binding, the more I want. The more I need. I find I send for you, call you to me, just to secure more ties to your shadow so I know you're mine and no one else can ever claim you." Stark possession was in his voice. Raw need. "Do I know that's wrong? Hell yes, Emmanuelle. It's like some terrible, brutal obsession I can't control, and it gets worse every time I'm near you. That need to own you. To put my ring on you so everyone knows you're mine. So no one dares to hurt you. Or tries to take you away from me."

Valentino shook his head, his breathing labored enough that Emmanuelle had to look at him, suddenly alarmed. She reached out, running her fingers down his neck to find his pulse.

"Breathe, Val. Everything's all right. I'm here with you."

He was really upset, going somewhere she didn't want him to go, not when it agitated him so much and he'd been wounded. He didn't just sound possessive, he sounded protective, and that broke her open when she needed to be completely closed off to him. She couldn't have sympathy for him. He was her greatest love and her greatest enemy.

"You don't understand, Emme. If I can see your shadow, and what it means, others can as well. You're tied to me. I made certain. So tight no one dares to try to take you. Dario saw Nicoletta, and he worried for her. Grace was in such danger. Miceli saw her. Angelo. Tommaso. Three women who could be tied and used for these purposes, and all at once. Not only does Miceli have to kill me, but if he doesn't succeed in killing me, he has to kill you because you're tied to me."

"How do we get untied? There has to be a way."

Most of the time, Valentino looked at her with gentleness. So much so that she forgot he was the son of a crime king and capable of the very things she had trained in from the time she was a toddler. His features hardened. Her heart nearly stopped. He looked entirely different. Scary different. Not at all like *her* Val. His hand was still around her wrist, and now his thumb slid back and forth on her skin as if soothing her, as he knew he was scaring her.

"I should have asked more about the story Giuseppi told you," she said, lowering her lashes so he couldn't see her expression. "How would you be able to spy on an enemy? How would that work?"

Some of the tension eased from Val's body. His thumb continued that slow glide back and forth over her inner wrist. "According to the story, you can move from one place to another using the shadows." He fell silent.

Emmanuelle's heart jumped. Began to pound. She realized his fingers had settled over her pulse.

"Emme? That's how you got past the guards and into my house. Into my bedroom." He made the statement quietly.

She didn't confirm or deny it, but she did try to pull her hand away from him. He settled his fingers firmly around her wrist again.

"Don't, Princess. We're talking this out, just like we said we would. You asked me. If the story is correct, you move in the shadows, but you're tethered to me. If I have a very small hold on you, I can only use that hold for small things like having you listen in on meetings in the enemy's home, but I have to be close enough that the ropes will extend through the shadows to where I want you to listen and see the enemy."

"So I would spy for you and bring that information back to you."

"That's the way the story goes."

"In essence, what I heard in your bedroom that night was really true. Giuseppi really did tell you to find me, hold on to me to ferret out the Ferraro secrets, just not in quite the way you told her. And I didn't know anything about sex. You had to teach me everything. You didn't lie, Val; I can't fault you there."

His grip tightened on her wrist, although he was gentle. His thumb moved along her skin, and this time she felt the strange melody running along her nerve endings that always sent that peculiar awareness of Valentino charging through her like electricity, bringing her alive in a sensual way that devastated her after the things he'd said about her to another woman.

Emmanuelle thought about the young girl—Brielle Couture—whose self-esteem had most likely been destroyed by the things she'd overheard Elie say about her, just as hers had been when she heard Valentino say terrible things to another woman. She knew she would never forget a single word Val had said to that woman in his bedroom for as long as she lived. Men didn't realize the long-reaching effects the things they said or did could have, especially on a young woman in love.

"Baby, you have to know it was never like that for me. Yes, my father told me the story. *Both* fathers told me that story. It's handed down generation after generation, but I don't know if Giuseppi believed it or not. I didn't tell him about you. I felt guilty not telling him, but something stopped me. I didn't want anyone to know. Not my parents, not Dario, whom I regard as a brother—no one. What was happening between us, I didn't understand, but it was intimate, and belonged just to us. Eventually, Dario knew, but no one else."

He turned her hand over. "You were a kid, Emme. A teenager. I was a grown man. I was already very experienced, but I'd never been hit so hard like that in my life, the way I was attracted to you. And it was wrong. I knew it was wrong, but I couldn't stay away from you. I did try. I told myself you were too young and that what happened between our shadows wasn't real, but none of that mattered, only seeing you again."

She heard the raw need in his voice. The truth. She'd always been able to distinguish lies from truth. That was a gift of being a rider, an essential one. She'd begun to doubt her abilities after being with Val. So many times, she thought he was telling her the truth, that he loved her the way she loved him, and then she would catch him in some terrible deceit. After so many times, she had to believe her eyes, not her heart.

"I found myself compromising my code, my honor—nothing mattered but seeing you."

"You were careful with me," she conceded. He had been in those early days. She couldn't say he hadn't seduced her—he had.

She had never looked at another man after Val, but he hadn't done more than kiss her. A lot. There was a lot of kissing. Eventually, there was a lot of touching. He brought her to orgasm with his fingers. He taught her how to bring him to pleasure with her hand. Then her mouth. He did the same with his mouth. He had waited until she was eighteen before he took her virginity.

At first, she barely remembered what was happening with their shadows. She was so wrapped up in the wild, almost feral way they came together. She could hardly stand being away from him. She was obsessed with him. He seemed to be the same way about her. Both of them knew their families would object, and they were careful. Valentino didn't like that she had to hide from her brothers, but she insisted, knowing Stefano would forbid any kind of relationship between them.

Emmanuelle noticed the expression on Val's face when they were sitting together out by the lake after they'd made love. He was looking at their shadows, and he looked very satisfied, almost smug. She had turned her head and was shocked at the amount of cords wrapped so tightly around her shadow, as if it were imprisoned by his. She had sat up straighter, turning to him, her heart pounding, for the first time in three years with him afraid. Val had tackled her, laughing, kissing her, distracting her.

That night, she'd stayed awake all night in her bed thinking, realizing she had to tell her brothers. That alone was terrifying. Her confession hadn't gone over very well. She hadn't even gotten to the part with her shadow when they all began yelling and threatening Valentino. They forbade her from ever seeing him again. Eloisa began to accuse her of being disloyal to the family. She'd tried to stay away from Val, but in the end, it was impossible. The pull to be with him was too strong, and no matter how hard she tried, she always ended up going back to him.

"Keep going on with your story, Val. I think I understand what you're saying. I would be able to go into the shadow, spy on a rival with you sitting in a car outside if our tether, for lack of a better word, were short."

"Something like that, I guess. If it were stronger, you could be at a greater distance from me. You could, say, be across town. I wouldn't have to be close to you for you to get the information for me."

"And if we were really tied tight together?"

"The bonds have to be wrapped and knotted so close and so permanently that there is no way to undo them. You already know our neuropathways are connected via those ties and shadows. Supposedly, the more bonds I put on you, the more permanent they become, and the more we're bound together."

"Then what would happen?" she asked. She found she was holding her breath. She already knew the answer.

"You would take me with you. I would travel from place to place with you. In the shadows. Those ties have to be that strong between us."

"That's what you were doing every time we were together. You were wrapping as many ties around my shadow as you could, as fast as you could. If I noticed, you deliberately distracted me." She kept accusation out of her voice, just stated it as fact, because it was.

Valentino didn't deny it. "Yes. I didn't know what it would take to make us a permanent couple, but your family and mine objected to us, and I wasn't going to lose you. I knew if Miceli or his sons found out your capabilities, it was possible they would make a try for you, and that would put you in danger. If you were permanently tied to me, there would be no reason for anyone to try to kidnap you or to tear us apart."

She flicked him a look. "And you could benefit greatly from the uses you could get from having a spy, or being able to move through shadows, if that is all true, right?"

Val pressed his fingers into her wrist. "Don't hold on to anger and hurt when we have a chance to work this out, Emme. Yes, I knew things you didn't, but you knew things I didn't. You still do. We have families to protect. I never asked you questions. I accepted that you would protect your family, just as you accepted that I would protect mine."

"How do we work out the other women, Val? Do we work out that I get to sleep with other men? Is that the way our relationship is supposed to go forward? I guess we should have talked about what we both expected. The idea that another man could touch me after you was abhorrent. I thought it would be the same for you, but clearly I was wrong."

"You weren't wrong, Emme." Valentino let go of her wrist for the first time, bringing his hands to his lap. He stared down at his empty palms. "Touching anyone but you or allowing any other woman to touch me feels disgusting."

"And yet you did."

"If you think I stuck my dick in her, I didn't."

"She was naked, Val. In your bedroom." Her lungs nearly seized all over again. She couldn't breathe.

She was back in that room, looking at the man she loved more than life itself. She'd gone to him prepared to tell him she'd give up everything for him. She would live her life with him. She knew if she chose Val, she would never ride the shadows again. Her mother would disown her. She would be considered the wife of a criminal. It didn't matter. She loved him that much.

She had ridden the shadows right into his home, bypassing his guards, straight into his bedroom. He hadn't been alone. There had been a tall, busty blonde, completely naked, facing Val, on her knees, looking up at him and inquiring about Emmanuelle.

"I thought you were all about that little Ferraro girl."

"Really, babe?" Val had said, his fist in the woman's hair. "I had orders to make her fall in love with me, which was damn easy to do." He sounded like he was snickering. "Do you really think I want a spoiled baby who doesn't know jack about sex?"

Her world had shattered, not just her heart. Val had looked up then, his eyes meeting hers. For one terrible moment, she thought he looked as devastated as she did. She'd stepped back into the shadow tube and let it take her. She hadn't ever allowed him to talk to her about that night since. Really, what could he say?

CHAPTER FOUR

E mmanuelle, breathe," Valentino said. "Princess, you're not breathing."

She wasn't. She couldn't get air. It was silly, really. She was over this. She had been for the last two years. Okay, maybe the last year. She'd taken a year to grieve. To put up barriers between them. She'd had to find a way to block out that sensual melody he could play on her nerve endings when she felt so sorrowful. It had taken time—and distance. She'd taken rotations for work in foreign countries. So many of them, exhausting herself so she couldn't think.

Emme forced air into her starving lungs. "I just want to know how to undo the ties between us, Val. You don't need to explain things. I didn't ask about other women because I was too naïve."

"I know it looked bad. It sounded bad. It hurt you, Emmanuelle, and I'm so sorry for that, but that woman had been sent by Miceli. I wasn't about to let her take back information to him that you meant something to me. By that time, I knew he was part of a human trafficking ring. He knew I was trying to find a way to prove it to Giuseppi. I didn't have a clue about the auctions, only that he had a hand in young girls being kidnapped in other states."

Emmanuelle wanted that information more than she wanted to dwell on her own hurt. She'd heard rumors about far too many young girls disappearing. They were taken from malls. On their way home from school. From after-school classes. From jobs. Just about anywhere, never to be seen again unless a dead body turned up.

"The woman you saw—her name is Marge Marino—is deeply entrenched in Miceli's organization. She runs one of his strip clubs for him. She'll do anything he wants her to do, including kill someone. She's one of his most trusted enforcers. I was pretty shocked when she started coming on to me. Nothing big at first, just kind of smiling at me and then rubbing up against me. Eventually, she called and asked me to have lunch with her. She kept coming on to me and once in a while slipped in a question about you. Miceli and I were dancing around each other. He knew I was investigating his activities."

Emme didn't say anything. This was the woman who had laughed with Val over Emmanuelle's lack of knowledge when it came to sex. Running a strip club where anything went in the back rooms, Emme could imagine that Marge had a vast experience that she didn't.

Valentino groaned and reached for her wrist again. He settled his fingers on her skin gently but firmly. She knew she shouldn't let him. She should even feel repulsed, but she ached. Hurt. Needed comfort, even if it was from the enemy. She stayed very still and didn't look at him.

"There were all kinds of rumors about the two of us. Miceli wanted a way to get to me. All he had to do was confirm that I was crazy about you, Emme. We were careful, so no one ever managed to see us together, but I had to deny to everyone that you mattered to me. I knew the moment Marge started coming on to me and slipping in sly little questions about you that he'd sent her."

Emmanuelle tried to push away the images of the woman, naked, laughing with Val at her expense. Unfortunately, they were burned into her memory for all time. Subtly, she tried to pull her wrist free of his hold.

Val clamped his fingers tighter. "Will you just listen?"

"Why? Are you going to tell me how good she was at sucking your cock for you?"

"She was never going to suck my cock. For fuck's sake, Emme. Every time Elie put his hands on you, I knew it. We're tied together. If another woman touched me or put her mouth on me, don't you think you would have known it? I had to convince her you didn't mean anything to me and that Giuseppi was trying to get dirt on your family. More, I had done a little bit of establishing some groundwork of my own, acting like I was more open to some things my father wasn't in terms of trafficking."

Emmanuelle was silent, trying to process what she'd seen, the sound of his voice now, both stark truth and even annoyance at her for not believing him when he'd tried to explain over and over and she hadn't let him. She forced herself to remember what Elie had said to her when they'd been in the pizzeria together. Sometimes things weren't what they appeared and people needed to be heard out.

It was difficult to get past the sight of the naked blonde or the sound of the shared laughter. Maybe that was the worst of it. The humiliation. Did Brielle feel that same humiliation every time she looked in the mirror the way Emmanuelle did? Emme wanted to go find Elie and kick him just the way she wanted to kick Val.

"How were you going to avoid her sucking your cock when she was so very intent on doing just that and still have her go back to Miceli and report you were one hundred percent on board with whatever she wanted?" Emmanuelle didn't even care that there was sarcasm in her voice. She couldn't wait to hear his explanation.

"Dario. He knew the setup. He knew what Marge was there for. The moment she stripped down, got on her knees and crawled to me, I sent him the signal to interrupt us. Fortunately, she asked the question I was waiting for. Or unfortunately, due to your timing. In any case, Dario arrived, walked right in with an emergency, ignoring Marge and telling me we had to go now."

"I see." Emmanuelle wasn't certain she could believe him. She didn't know what to believe. She'd had two years of reliving that scene.

"No, Princess, you obviously don't see. Did you see my fucking cock hard as a rock like it is for you? No, you did not. I had to stroke myself to pretend I was the least bit interested, and even that wasn't working. I tried thinking of you, and putting you in the room with her didn't work. Suffice to say if you'd paid attention to me and not her, you would have noticed something was a little different from when I'm with you. I've got a monster when you're around, babe—hard to miss. Where the hell was it?"

Emmanuelle's heart clenched hard in her chest. She had looked at Valentino. Right into his eyes. His gorgeous green eyes. He'd looked as devastated as she felt. As shattered.

There were so many things wrong with their relationship. Too many things. Even if they straightened out what had happened with the blonde in the bedroom, she knew the ties binding their shadows together were far too dangerous to her family. She could never allow that to stand. If she told Stefano, he'd walk right into the room and shoot Valentino without even discussing the subject. She knew he would. He would never allow the shadow riders to be in danger.

She had to find a way to disentangle herself from Val, and then she could warn the riders of the dangers the Saldi family presented. Someone had to have known. That story had to have been told at some point in the past. It needed to be told to children in *every* family, in every country, to protect the riders.

"Did I want that woman's mouth on me, Emme? Did I show one single sign a man would have with a naked woman crawling all around the floor, willing and eager, that I wanted her? You know damn well I didn't. I wanted to find out about the trafficking ring. I wanted to protect you. And I wanted to make your family as safe as I could."

Emmanuelle forced herself to look past the woman to Valentino's body. His body was superb. Muscles on muscles. Tattoos drifting over his chest, back and arms, each one as beautiful as he was. He didn't do colored ink; it was black and white. He had a little memorial wall tattooed on his body for his mother and father. Now Greta was there as well.

Emmanuelle's name was inked on his chest in a nest of knotted ropes. Tied to his name. Bound to him. A captive in those ropes. Couldn't Marge see Emme's name tattooed there? It was intricate, letters swirling in the ropes; maybe Marge hadn't cared enough to look or Val had given her an explanation she'd bought.

She rubbed her temples with her free hand. He still hadn't let her wrist go, and she hadn't fought too hard to break free. The pad of his thumb felt soothing on her inner wrist, and she needed it. She felt the burn of the tears she refused to shed.

He did have his cock in his hand. Caging it. Almost as if he were protecting it. And no, it wasn't the beast it normally was. He had a wide girth as a rule. She knew because it was difficult to take him in her mouth. He was long as well, adding to the difficulty, but he'd been patient when he was first with her. He always bottomed out, and sometimes that hurt, making her sore. That had made his accusations of her knowing nothing about sex all the worse, because damn it all, she hadn't known anything. He'd taught her everything she did know. She'd practiced, worked hard to learn to do the things that brought him the most pleasure.

"Maybe, Val, you're not the best instructor when it comes to sex," she muttered, scowling down at the blank screen of her phone, not wanting to think she had misjudged him for two years. Could she have gotten it so wrong?

Val pulled her hand to his chest. Over the bandages. "Finally, you're starting to believe the truth. I didn't let her touch me. I didn't mean those things. My father doesn't know about our shadows being tied together. No one does but Dario. Only the three of us."

He brought her knuckles to his mouth. "You didn't talk to me for so long. I couldn't find a way to make things right between us, and Miceli was getting bolder. He was recruiting the younger members in our territory, promising them more money, and I kept hearing rumors of young girls being taken off the streets, but I couldn't track them down. Then in your club, and in some of your businesses, things started to go wrong, and I knew it was Miceli, but again, there was no way to prove it. After the kidnapping attempt on Grace, I was worried that Miceli, Angelo or Tommaso had seen her shadow. The people murdered in Ferraro territory definitely were a very big message to me to back off. Miceli wanted to take the territories in one direction and Giuseppi in another. There was war brewing between them. I knew that. And your family was right in the middle."

She snapped her head up and looked directly at him, eyes wide. Her family had thought the Saldis wanted to go to war with them. Not with each other. Valentino was saying that Giuseppi and Val had tried to protect the Ferraros. At least, to her, it sounded that way.

"Why didn't you go to Stefano and talk to him, Val?"

Val shook his head. "Your brother made it very clear he would like to see me dead, not that I blame him. You were so young, Emme. I had no right to you, but once I met you, I couldn't stay away. I did try. I want you to know that. I did try."

"You never told me how we can undo the bindings on the shadows," Emmanuelle persisted. It was important, and she had to keep to that if she was going to save his life.

His features hardened again, just like they had before. His hand reached out and caught her chin, pulling her closer to him, so that she tipped sideways in the bed. He framed her face with both hands and stared directly into her eyes, forcing her to look at him when she wanted to look away.

"Do you honestly think I'd let you go? That's not going to

happen, Emmanuelle. The only way you're ever going to be free of me is to put a fucking gun to my head and pull the trigger. If you want out of our relationship, you may as well do it now. Don't hide behind your brothers like a coward, just do it yourself, because I'm not letting you go. You're lying to yourself if you say you don't love me, because you fucking do."

"I never once said I didn't love you, Val. I'm trying to keep you alive." One of them had to be calm, and she was no liar. "Let go of me now. We have to figure out a way to undo the way our shadows are tied together, and you know it." She forced her voice to be even. "Neither one of us will be able to get on with our lives if we don't. All this nonsense of spying and moving from one place to another . . ."

"Don't start trying to lie to me, Emmanuelle. I've been around you now for years. I've watched you. Everything you do. Everything you say. I watched you when you didn't know I was around. When you didn't want me around."

"That's stalking behavior, Val." She tugged at her hand, wishing her stupid heart weren't reacting to his declaration. It never seemed to matter what Valentino said or did. When she was too close to him, all she wanted was to be closer. Her brain turned off, and her body turned on.

"You think I don't know that? You think I don't know that everything I've ever done when it comes to you is against every code of honor I have?"

Was there a kernel of bitterness in his voice? She met his blazing-green gaze again, and the pit of her stomach bottomed out. There was a storm brewing there, and storms with Valentino were bad. "That's not love, Val. It's obsession. You saw the way our shadows reacted and felt that jolt. It's a rush."

"It's not just a rush, Princess. I have a hell of a lot more experience than you do when it comes to sex. What we have together is off the charts."

"It's still not love, Val. This is still about our shadows, not about us. It isn't real and it's wrong." What woman would go into a relationship with a man knowing she was only worth something to him because of his shadow's reaction to hers?

"It doesn't matter whether it's wrong or not, Emme. I don't care if you want to call it obsession. Not when it comes to you. We aren't going to try to break the ties between us, not that I think it's actually possible. If anything, we're going to keep strengthening them."

She twisted her wrist and yanked it away from him, rolling off the bed and coming to her feet. "That is the last thing we'll be doing, Val. I mean it. We aren't going to have a relationship even if we can't break the ties. Once this is all over, and hopefully we defeat Miceli and his army, I'll have no choice but to tell my brothers about this."

He raised an eyebrow. "Why? This is between us, Emmanuelle. It's always been between us. We work it out, no one else."

"Because your family is a threat to ours. Grace was threatened. Nicoletta could have been. Obviously, I was."

"Baby."

His voice went soft, that voice that always played along her nerve endings like his melodies, running through her body and spreading like electrical charges. He waited until she looked into his eyes. Until she was drowning there.

"I have never, at any time, been a threat to your family. I've only tried to protect them. You know that. In your heart, no matter how angry or hurt you are, you know that to be true. I've protected you and what's between us, and I've kept it between us."

He was making it so difficult to do the right thing. She had no choice. He had to see that she had no choice. She hadn't admitted she was a shadow rider. That she could move from one place to another, but he knew. She saw the knowledge in his eyes. He'd told her that he'd watched her. Just knowing the truth of her family would put him under a death sentence. If he knew about her family—and he would someday head one of the most notorious crime families in Chicago—the Ferraro family would be compromised in all of their vast businesses.

She backed away from the bed. This was far worse than she had ever imagined. She had seen the bindings on her shadow. The ropes were so heavy and so many, the loops intricate and the knots numerous and so complicated, she doubted if an expert would be able to get them undone.

Expert. The word slid through her mind. Ricco was more than an expert with rope and knots. Was it possible she had the solution right in front of her? If she was patient, after this was over, she could go to her brother, swear him to secrecy and then have him unravel the rope and knots for her. He wouldn't like her tricking him into silence, but she would promise to tell Stefano and the others the story the Saldis passed from father to son, explaining it was all too real and the riders needed to be on guard.

The moment the solution was within her grasp, she breathed a sigh of relief. Val would be safe, whether he liked it or not. He might think he knew they could slide into the shadows, but he had no way of proving it. If he talked about it to anyone, they would think he was crazy.

"What are you planning, Emme?" Val demanded. "I can see you're working on something I'm not going to like. My wounds weren't that bad. Mostly, I lost a lot of blood. I'll be up fast and will be able to help in a few hours. That means whatever fucked-up plan you're devising to get rid of me isn't going to work."

It would work. It *had* to work if she was going to save his life. She lifted her chin at him. "Fortunately, Val, you never did get to dictate to me what I could and couldn't do."

He swore under his breath and planted one palm on the mattress, acting as if he might swing his legs out of the bed. The door opened and Dario strode in. Val settled and Emmanuelle let out the breath she'd been holding.

"I can see you two are getting along," Dario said and dropped into the chair that allowed him to see both the bed and the door.

"What are you doing here?" Val demanded. "I thought you were looking after the old man? He's all right, isn't he?"

"Would I be here if he wasn't?" Dario snapped.

"You didn't take any pain meds, did you?" Emme asked.

She couldn't help herself, she moved closer to Dario even though his dark eyes warned her to stay back. Although his expression showed irritation, that was all on his features; there was near agony in his eyes. Vittorio had said his wounds were worse than Val's, although Val had suffered severe blood loss. "Dario, you need to take pain meds."

"You know as well as I do that Miceli will find this place soon if he doesn't already know about it, Emme. I can't take a chance on being impaired."

"How bad were you hit?" Val asked.

Dario shot him a glare but didn't reply.

"Take something mild. You aren't going to be of much help if you can't move around very well," Emme pointed out, trying not to sound concerned.

Dario had pulled out his phone and was frowning down at the screen, but he glanced up, eyes shooting daggers at her. "Don't worry about me, Emmanuelle. Worry about Miceli. He sent his fucking men after Giuseppi and Valentino. I told him if he ever did that, I'd kill him myself. I guess he didn't believe me."

There was truth in every word he uttered. Truth and venom. He really detested his father. Miceli had done things to him, or he knew things about the man that had made him this way. She glanced over at Valentino, wondering if he was aware of just how much Dario despised Miceli. She could see Val had full knowledge. For some reason, he had always trusted his cousin and treated him right when no one else had. She imagined it must have taken even Giuseppi a good amount of time before he trusted Dario to guard his precious son, yet he had come to do just that.

Emmanuelle wished she'd been nicer to Dario. He was a hard man. Closed off. She thought of him as a killer. But then, what was she? Did she think she was so much better because she told herself she meted out justice to criminals? She was still an assassin. She wasn't sanctioned by the government. No law enforcement agency was behind her. In fact, they often tried to find out who was behind the killings of those who had, for a short time, seemed to escape justice.

Dario was a man whom the world saw as a killer. Valentino was the son of a crime boss. She was the princess of a billionaire mogul family. They were a dynasty. They had an empire all over the world. Hotels. Banks. Casinos. Clubs. They lived out in the open, a glitzy life among celebrities and stars. The paparazzi surrounded them whether they were on a racetrack or jetting off to some secluded island for a weekend. It mattered little what they were doing; it was always noteworthy. Reporters followed Giuseppi and Valentino occasionally, but not because they wanted to get great pictures; they were looking for news stories to tie them to crime.

"Stop looking at me like I'm going to fall apart any second, Emme," Dario said. "I don't kill so easily."

"She didn't look at me that way," Val complained. "I think she thought about shooting me."

"I'm still thinking about shooting you. You can thank Dario for saving your life," Emmanuelle said, with a little sniff, not looking at him.

Dario sent her a ghost of a smile. "Don't reconsider on my behalf. He's been a pain in the ass for the last couple of years, pining away for you. If you aren't taking him back, put him the fuck out of his misery. It would be a mercy to everyone who knows him."

The door opened again, and Eloisa stepped inside the dimly lit room and closed the door behind her. She glared at her daughter, and Emmanuelle knew she had deliberately waited before spilling any of the usual venom she reserved for her daughter in front of Henry or her sons.

"I knew I would find you in here with *him*. Valentino Saldi." Eloisa didn't look at the man on the bed, keeping her judgmental gaze fixed on her daughter. "You just can't leave the man alone, can you?"

"Are you looking for me, Eloisa?"

"Yes, Emmanuelle. I'm certain you were in here groveling,

begging him, as usual, to take you back while the rest of us are here planning out how to keep everyone safe," Eloisa said, her voice cutting. "For once, try to make yourself useful and ask Enzo what you can actually do instead of fawning all over a man to try to get noticed."

Emme straightened her shoulders, placed her hands on her hips and looked her mother up and down. Never once had she answered her mother back, not in all the years her mother had cut her down and degraded her. Humiliated her. Accused her of being a spy for the Saldis. She was just plain tired of everyone, especially Eloisa. She'd had it with everyone.

"I'm too tired to put up with your nasty insults tonight. If you want to stay and give Valentino your usual dose of ugly snark, be my guest, I'm sure he can more than hold his own against you and will be quite willing to tell you to go to hell. I just don't want to listen to your crap, and I'm not going to. Stay away from me tonight or leave. We don't need your help. Your experience with weapons isn't worth putting up with your vicious tongue."

She switched her gaze from her mother's shocked expression to Dario. "Who's on Giuseppi?"

"Enzo assigned Henry and Eloisa to him full time." He looked pointedly at Eloisa.

Emme swung around to confront her mother a second time. "Did you abandon your post just so you could harangue me? Giuseppi is a main target."

Eloisa turned bright red as she first looked at Val and then Dario. She glared at her daughter. "You *dare* to speak to your mother that way? In front of . . . of . . . *them*?"

"Right now, you're not my mother. We're about to go to war with Miceli Saldi. If you're not capable of staying in your position and protecting an extremely important target, then we'll assign someone else who can better protect him." Emmanuelle was unrelenting.

Eloisa opened her mouth twice and then turned on her heel, head high, and marched out of the room, closing the door with a very hard thud behind her. There was silence. Emmanuelle counted to twenty in the hopes that her mother would have made it down the hall.

"Dario, I'm certain you can protect Valentino should any of Miceli's men make it this far. You can lock his ass in the safe room."

"You aren't going to stay?" Val asked.

"No. If Dario needs extra help, he can reach out. Someone will come. I'm sure you'll be armed. There are a thousand weapons in this house." She started toward the door.

"Princess, come here before you leave." His voice had dropped low again.

She stopped with her back to him. Her nerve endings were singing. Electrified. On fire. His to hers. She forced her hand to the doorknob, grasping it like a talisman with her fingers.

"It's going to get intense, Emme. Anything can happen. Are you really going to leave us like this? Come here, baby. If you don't, I'll have to come to you. You know I will. I can't leave things this way."

She closed her eyes. That voice played along her nerve endings in a rush of heat. The melody was building fast into something hot and fiery she couldn't handle, especially since they weren't alone. The notes became flames, spreading like a wildfire, using the nerves throughout her body as the pathways, so fast, claiming every inch of her and then settling low and sinfully wicked in her sex.

She knew Valentino would leave the bed and come after her. She had known him long enough to know if he said something, he always followed through. That was what was so scary about his declaration of keeping her. He meant it. She heard the bed frame creak. Whirling toward Val, she saw that his hands were planted in the mattress as he swung himself around.

"Don't be a jerk," she hissed.

"Then you get your sweet little ass over here," Val said. "I'm not playing games, Emme. I'm not doing this with you anymore. I explained about Marge. You know I didn't want her there. I don't have other women. You can interrogate Dario. He's always with me."

"He'd lie his ass off for you, wouldn't you, Dario?"

"Yes." Dario didn't look up from his phone. "Not that he ever looks at other women. Don't involve me in your idiotic Romeo and Juliet fights. Emmanuelle, go over and do whatever he wants you to do so he'll shut the fuck up. You're going to do it eventually anyway. I can't tell you how truly sickening this is."

Emme stomped over to Val, glaring at him the entire way, but her heart was pounding and her stomach did somersaults. He looked so brutally handsome, even with his bandages. Maybe more so because of them. She ached inside when she looked at him. Her body burned for his. He burned equally as bad for her. She saw it in the heat of his eyes. At least she wasn't suffering alone.

Val had turned in the bed, so one bare leg hung over the side. The other lay atop the sheet, bare but bandaged. The moment she was close enough, he reached for her. Curling his palm around the nape of her neck, he drew her in between his thighs. It was too intimate to stand there, close to the heat of him. The sheet might have been gathered around his lap, but it provided little modesty—but then Valentino had never been a modest man. His erection was brutal, thick and unashamed, pressing tight against his abdomen. His sac was heavy on the mattress, outlined under the sheet.

Emmanuelle tried to keep her gaze fixed on his and her hands on his thighs. She shouldn't have wanted—no, needed—to touch him anywhere else.

"What is it you want from me, Val?" She wanted to make a demand; instead, it came out a whisper.

"Everything, Emmanuelle. I want everything from you." His palm was warm on her neck, almost too warm. His thumb slid back and forth in a mesmerizing glide over the artery in her neck. "Right now, I want you to kiss me. If anything happens to either one of us, I want that to be the last thing we have."

"Nothing will happen to you. I swear it, Val. My family is protecting you and your father. They'll protect Dario. Miceli isn't going to win this one."

"Kiss me, Emmanuelle."

Kissing Valentino was surrendering to him. Giving herself to him, heart and soul. There was no going back from kissing him. Staring into his green eyes, standing between his thighs, feeling the heat of his body so close to hers and the electric charge of their shared firestorm burning out of control, running up and down her nerve endings, she knew it was already too late to save herself.

Emmanuelle touched her tongue to her lips, already tasting him. Val had always been so masculine. Cedar and rain. A blend of leather and woods. Just his scent had set her body on fire when she would get near him. Now he smelled of those scents, along with gunpowder, blood and alcohol from all the cleanup they'd done on him. It didn't matter; he was still as sexy to her as ever.

His palm tightened around the nape of her neck, pulling her closer. The pressure was slow but steady. She just let him. Surrendering. Because that's what she did when she was with Valentino. Heart pounding. Stomach doing mad loops. Breasts aching. Nipples hard. Sex clenching.

His lips were gentle on hers. Nibbling. Teeth tugged with exquisite gentleness at her lower lip. He kissed the corner of her mouth. His lips were velvet soft on her upper lip, then his teeth bit down harder on her lower lip and tugged until she gasped. His tongue slid over the tiny sting, soothing it.

His lips shaped hers. Coaxed. She opened for him, and his tongue swept in. Ruthless. Merciless. Took her over. Fire reigned. Poured into her. Bright, hot sparks lit up her world. Lit his. They came together in a firestorm of such intensity they could have lit the world up. The flames ran up and down every neural path in their bodies, spreading out to connect between them, running back and forth, feeding their hunger for each other, keeping it raging between them.

Val slid one hand into her hair, closing a possessive fist in the thick, silken strands, to position her head to take fuller advantage. At the same time, he urged her closer to him, bringing her almost right onto his lap. She slid her arms up his chest, careful of his bandages, needing to feel him solid and real under her palms. Skin to skin. The kisses went on and on. The fire roared hotter.

Dario cleared his throat loudly. "For fuck's sake, you two."

His voice was like a bucket of cold water dousing Emmanuelle. She stepped back, or tried to. It was impossible with Val's fingers fisting in her hair so tight. He refused to let her go, his green eyes moving over her face, noting her heightened color and the guilt in her eyes, no doubt. She didn't try to hide it from him. What was the use?

With shaky fingers, she touched her burning lips. "We can't do that."

"We *have* to do that. I'll go out of my mind if we don't do that, Emme. What do you think it's been like for me these last two years, thinking about you going out of the country, so far from me, where I can't protect you? I tried to keep men on you, but you disappear so easily. My only consolation was, if I couldn't find you, then Miceli probably couldn't, either. I did my best to mislead him into thinking you didn't matter to me, but then I couldn't stay away from you. Vittorio had to beat the crap out of me at the meeting between our families. I knew why. I knew you told him about finding Marge and overhearing what was said. I let him hit me. I deserved whatever he wanted to dish out, but Miceli noticed I didn't really defend myself and I didn't let Dario interfere."

She lifted her palm to frame his jaw, her heart turning over. She didn't want to love him the way she did. She wanted to keep telling herself that she reacted to him physically because somehow their shadows were tangled together and once she got them apart, she wouldn't feel the same and neither would he. She knew it wasn't the truth. Valentino Saldi was forever her choice. In spite of knowing he was heir to the Saldi throne, she knew he was a good man.

"Who the hell is Elie Archambault to you, Emme? Why is he always with you? Touching you? He's constantly got his hands on you. He even kisses you." There was heat in his voice. Heat in his very direct gaze.

She rolled her eyes. "He doesn't kiss me."

"He kisses you. I told you, I can feel it every time a man touches you, and he's always with you and he's always touching you. You go clubbing with him. Tonight, you were with him while I was getting my ass shot off."

That was a distinct accusation. Emmanuelle dropped her hand from his jaw. He still had his fist threaded through her hair, so there was no going anywhere unless she put up a fight, and the bandages on his body kept her from doing that—at least she told herself that was the reason.

Dario's head went up, his gaze leaving the screen of his phone. He scowled at them. "That's probably why you got your ass shot off, you dick. You were paying more attention to your woman than the bastards trying to kill you. Maybe if you actually kept your mind in the game, and quit thinking with your dick, I wouldn't have had to drag you out of a war zone with you shot all to hell." His tone, as always, was mild.

Emme pressed her lips together to keep from smirking. No one talked to Val like that but Dario. She used to think Dario was just being mean; now she knew it was just the way they showed affection to each other.

"Shut the fuck up, Dario. I'm interrogating her."

"Is that what you call it? If it is, you're going soft." Dario went back to looking at his screen.

Emmanuelle would have given anything to see what Dario was looking at. She knew he didn't play games on his phone. What was he scrolling through with that never-ending black scowl on his face?

"Eyes on me, Emme," Val said. "I want to know who Elie Archambault is. Why is he always with you?"

She made a face. Honesty was always the best policy. "In

my family, arranged marriages are normal. Elie's as well. Elie and I are good friends. We both knew our families were considering putting us together, but we're more like siblings. It wouldn't work for us. We were trying to hash things out last night. How we were going to face arranged marriage with strangers when we couldn't face it with someone we cared about. Time was running out for both of us, so we were just trying to think things through." She tried to give a casual shrug.

There was a long silence while the room filled with sheer black anger. The tension stretched out until she wanted to scream. She'd known Valentino wouldn't like the truth, but she wasn't going to lie to him. She glanced at Dario. Even he was looking at her in pure shock.

"What do you mean, time was running out?" Valentino's voice was pitched very low. Never a good sign with him. His fingers tightened in her hair.

"I told you, Val. We marry by a certain age in our family. We have certain expectations placed on us. The men and women. If we don't find the person we want to marry, one is found for us. Arranged marriages are very common. I was very clear."

"Actually, Princess, you never said one word on this subject. Had you, we would have already been married and your entire family could go to hell. You're not marrying some stranger. Or Elie Archambault. You need to get married, you can damn well marry me."

"Such a lovely proposal. You're so romantic."

Her phone vibrated alarmingly, and she immediately pulled it from her back pocket and glanced down at the screen. "They're here. Your uncle's men. An entire army and then some." She looked over her shoulder as Val's fingers eased in her hair. "Dario, you've got this?"

He nodded.

She leaned forward and brushed a kiss on Val's forehead. "Be safe." She turned and hurried out of the room.

CHAPTER FIVE

How many?" Taviano asked as he peered at the screen over Raimondo Abatangelo's shoulder. The screen was lit up with what looked like green dots everywhere.

Raimondo grinned at him. "I'd say just about everyone. This guy must be a billionaire. He's got them coming in by boat and air as well as land."

Enzo spun around in his chair. "Stefano, Miceli isn't kidding around. He's determined to kill his brother and Valentino. This strike is to take them out permanently. Rigina just sent in a report on Miceli's personal financials, the ones Giuseppi has no knowledge of, and he is definitely a billionaire. Human trafficking has made him a fortune. He isn't about to give it up. Giuseppi, Valentino and Dario are really the only three standing in his way."

"That's not really true," Stefano said. "Miceli forgot the Ferraro *famiglia*. We stand with Valentino this time. Ricco, you and Mariko take those dropping onto the rooftops. You'll have to be very fast and efficient. We can't spare other riders. Nicoletta, Taviano and Giovanni, I'll need you to stop the ones coming in off the boats. Again, don't use finesse. Just get the job done. Be fast. Take them down any way you can. Enzo, get your best snipers to pick off as many as possible. Set them up to protect us as we're moving in and out of the shadows. Remind them to keep their line of fire off the shadows."

"Will do."

"Vittorio, you gave a lot of blood. Are you feeling up to working, or do you need more time?"

"I'm good."

Stefano took him at his word. "You and I will be the outside floaters, filling in wherever needed. Emmanuelle, you and Elie are going to be our land defense. You'll have Vittorio and me to back you up as well as our snipers. Henry and Eloisa are with Giuseppi, and Dario is with Valentino. If, for any reason, you have to go into their rooms, give a shout-out first or they will shoot to kill.

"Above all, be safe. Let's not lose anyone." That was a command.

Emmanuelle managed to keep a smile off her face. Stefano could always sound so gruff, even when he was so amazingly caring. She blew him a kiss and stepped into a shadow, letting it take her, letting the familiar feeling of being torn apart bring a kind of solace to her. Did she need to seek the physical pain as penance for putting her family in danger? She didn't know.

She stepped out of one shadow and into another that would take her to the driveway, right at the very curve where the tall, heavy gates were. They were locked, and she knew the trucks coming would have to stop in order to get those gates open. It wouldn't take them long, but they wouldn't want to make too much noise, so she doubted they would blow them. She could wreak a lot of havoc in a short period of time. No doubt Elie would be doing the exact same thing, and he was extremely fast.

As she was hurtling through the second shadow tube, it occurred to her that she'd rarely killed anyone other than as a justice seeker. She was sent out for one purpose—to administer justice to someone who had managed to escape it. She did so completely impartially. To kill to protect others was unusual in her family. It had been done to protect the ones they loved when called for, but it was extremely rare.

She was at the very mouth of the shadow, and she waited, allowing her body to catch up with itself, letting the feeling of being disoriented fade until she was once more wholly confident in her own skin. Across from her, looking out of another shadow, was Elie, a handsome devil, a heartbreaker, his dark eyes flashing a wicked promise of sheer fun, as if they were going into a fun house, not an actual war where people, including them, might die. He pretended to crack his knuckles. Emmanuelle couldn't help an answering smile. He was outrageous.

It was impossible to be too nervous when Elie was around, not that she was all that nervous. Emmanuelle was sure of her abilities, and she was pragmatic about death. One had to be, living the kind of life she did. She trained hard and was prepared for any possibility, so she didn't think about losing fights. She was a silent killer. She didn't engage enemies in battle. She simply killed.

The ground shivered beneath her feet, alerting her to the fact that several vehicles were approaching the gates fast. Valentino's property was gorgeous. The heavy stone fence was overgrown, with years of beautiful weeping wisteria climbing the walls. The plants attached to the stone had become a thick, impenetrable forest of masses of leaves, vines and, depending on the time of year, blossoms resembling purple waterfalls all along the fence. Only the gates were unfettered, and that was a constant battle between the plants and the gardener.

The line of cars stopped. Emmanuelle counted five SUVs and one truck. The truck looked like it carried an arsenal in the bed. She wasn't positive, because they had it covered, but she thought they might have brought a mortar. When she glanced up, Elie was already gone. She followed suit, stepping out of the mouth of the shadow for a split second to catch one that would take her to the lead car. Even if the man at the gates managed to unlock them, if everyone in the lead car was dead and it blocked the entrance, that would slow the other vehicles down.

Elie had already killed them. She shook her head and slipped into the next shadow to slide up to the second vehicle. The back passenger door was open as the men inside waited for the lead car to get the gates open.

"What's taking so fucking long, Don?" the driver demanded into his radio.

"There's like ten locks on this thing. I could blow it, but Angelo said we didn't want neighbors to get nosy and call the cops too soon."

"He doesn't even know if they're here," another one grumbled. "Tommaso said Valentino was hit hard. He saw Dario pull him out of the house. If he was really hit that bad, Dario wouldn't have risked moving him this far. He would have taken him to the theater."

Emmanuelle swung her head around. She recognized that voice. That man had been employed by Giuseppi. No one called the little building on the edge of Ferraro territory "the theater" but Valentino and Giuseppi. It was a running joke with them. The carpet inside was a gaudy red. The wallpaper on the walls was faded and peeling. The Ferraro family was going to clean it up and rent it out to a business, but they never got around to it. Val and Giuseppi sometimes went there and played cards when they wanted to escape their world for just a little while. They had a small refrigerator, an old couch and a table and chairs. Dario was always their bodyguard.

Emmanuelle thought it was funny that they didn't go to a restaurant like any normal crime family boss might have done. Giuseppi and Valentino had done something different and, to Emme, heartbreakingly beautiful and fun. This man, and she remembered his name—Val had called him Giorgio—had been trusted by Giuseppi. He'd obviously given a lot of information to Miceli and his sons regarding Val and Giuseppi and most likely even Emmanuelle.

"You'd better hope Dario was hit if Val was," another recognizable voice from the back said. "Dario will never stop hunting you. Doesn't know about me." There was smugness in his tone.

"Yeah, but if he catches up with Giorgio, he'll torture him and get the names of everyone who took Miceli's money, Brando."

The others burst out laughing. "You'd better make sure you kill Dario this time."

"He's not so easy to kill," the driver said. "Neither is that prick Valentino."

There were five men in the SUV. The driver and a passenger in the front seat. The passenger had remained silent. He hadn't turned around to join in with the banter in the back. She hadn't gotten a good look at his face, but had the feeling he was the man in charge. One shadow lined up with the back of the SUV, but just barely. It would get her inside, and allow her to kill at least two of those in the back, perhaps the third one, without alerting those in the front seat. She went over the moves in her mind until she knew exactly what she was going to do.

Seconds had passed when it felt as if minutes had. She stepped from one shadow to the next and was inside with the five men, aware of the close quarters, the smell of cologne, leather and guns. She snapped the first neck almost without thinking and was on the second, the middle passenger, as she emerged fully.

The signature move of the Ferraro kill was taught to them at a very young age, almost from infancy. Crispino was already learning, just in play, the technique of placing his baby hands on the head just so. Emmanuelle snapped the second neck, her touch so light, her movement so stealthy and quiet, so fast, that she'd dropped the first two bodies in a brief second and the third man, the treacherous Giorgio, had no idea she was behind him until he glanced over at Brando and saw him slumped down, head at an odd angle.

Her hands were already on him, fingers light, so he was unaware. His mouth opened to issue the alarm when she tightened her grip and wrenched hard, preventing sound. The moment she did, she was over the seat, pushing aside his body, her hands on the head of the man, the leader, in the passenger seat. This was her greatest risk. She was totally exposed to the driver. The windows of the SUV were tinted, but that didn't mean those in the car behind her might not see what was taking place.

The leader, at the sound of the crack of Giorgio's neck, had begun to turn his head. He was too slow. Emmanuelle was on him, whipping his head back and wrenching it in a smooth, practiced move. The driver let loose a string of curses, trying to drag his gun out of his shoulder holster, lurching toward her at the same time. The movement only drove his head straight at her, giving Emmanuelle the advantage. She took it.

She let go of the dead leader and gripped the driver face-first, ignoring his look of utter terror. Something smashed into the windshield, fragmenting the glass into a spider's web, but it held. She glanced up, even as she took a firmer hold and wrenched hard. The man from the first vehicle who had been trying to unlock the gates was running toward them, his weapon out. He had to have heard the driver swearing. He hadn't taken two more steps before he went down. One of the Ferraro snipers had taken him out.

Emmanuelle glanced around her, looking at the ground, hunting for a shadow that would take her close to the next vehicle in line. She'd used up only a couple of seconds, but shots had been fired. Those in the other cars would be antsy and looking for instructions from those in the air. No doubt there would be a flyover soon to assess the situation. All the bodies, other than the one who had been working on the gates, were in the cars.

Elie had taken care of the third SUV so she took the shadow to the fourth one, only to find that one filled with dead men, too. Elie had been working quickly. That meant he'd left the fifth one for her and he was already at the truck. There was one shadow that went behind the SUV, and she took that one. The vehicle was directly in front of the truck, so the driver was facing her. If she stepped out of the shadow, he would see her without question.

The truck held two men in the front seat and three in the back of the extended cab. There were another six in the long truck bed. She didn't see Elie anywhere, which meant he was in the shadows somewhere, just the same as she was, studying the problem. It never paid to hurry when they had a job to do. Others would take care of those coming in from the lake or dropping down onto the roof.

Emmanuelle heard the sound of a helicopter, and then the glaring shine of a spotlight quartered the ground all around the SUV and truck. It ran up the line until it got to the front near the gates, or at least she presumed that was where it was hovering. There was suddenly a flurry of activity in the truck and the SUV. Doors popped open. Men cautiously emerged, crouching close to the sides of the last two in line, but the others remained dark and silent.

The men looked at one another. One of the men by the front passenger truck door spoke into his radio, clearly trying to call out to others in the SUVs. When no one answered, the helicopter began to move slowly down the line again, spot lighting each vehicle, shining the glaring light directly into the windshield.

"They look dead. All of them, sir," someone in the helicopter reported.

"That's impossible." That sounded like Angelo.

Emmanuelle heard the voice clearly coming over the radio of one of the three men who had been sitting in the back seat of the SUV. The three had slipped out and were now outside, crouched down, weapons drawn. Two were on the left side, one on the right. The two on the left side had lined up directly, one in front of the back tire and one behind it.

"Have the pilot bring the helicopter around again so I can get a better look."

"Wait—" Immediately, sound was cut off.

Emmanuelle's heart jumped, and she nearly smiled. That first command to bring the helicopter around had been issued in a commanding voice that sounded just like Angelo, but she knew wasn't. One of the younger bodyguards in training, Leone, had an extraordinary talent. His voice could replicate almost anyone else's. Evidently, Emilio had ordered him to copy Angelo's voice and give the command to bring the helicopter around. The real Angelo had tried to tell his men he hadn't given that order, but he'd been jammed.

The helicopter pilot did exactly what he'd been told. Emmanuelle waited, adrenaline running through her veins. Heat coiling. The moment the pilot positioned the craft, several shots rang out, just as she'd known they would. She didn't wait to see if the snipers had done their job. She sprang into action, leaving the safety of the shadow, taking the first of her prey.

Emmanuelle was on the exposed man in the gathering darkness. He tilted his head toward the sky as the helicopter slipped sideways. She broke his neck before he could utter a single swear word, and then she was moving forward. It took only two steps before she was on the second of the three men she had marked. He had half risen to see the craft begin to spin. She caught him on either side of his face and wrenched, breaking his neck, dropped him and moved up behind the third man, who was wholly upright and had stepped out from behind the safety of the open door for one moment. He suddenly threw himself on the ground, yelling into his radio for his men to get down.

Emmanuelle realized he hadn't seen her and wasn't reacting to the dead men; he was reacting to the fact that snipers had taken out the helicopter. It was bucking and jerking in the sky, spinning out of control, tossing two men out the open doors as if they were rag dolls. Emme hit the ground and rolled toward her prey. She dug the toes of her favorite boots into the grass and pushed herself closer to him.

He had his head up, eyes watching the helicopter as it came down in a stunning display of wrecked, twisted metal.

"Shit, Angelo, what the hell was that? Dario or Valentino just took out the helicopter. I thought we had someone on the roof. Take that prick out." He shouted the order into the radio.

This had to be someone fairly high up in Miceli's organization to talk to Angelo that way. She couldn't imagine the man she'd known to be so arrogant putting up with anyone, even during a firefight, talking like that, unless they were one of Miceli's most trusted advisors, and even then, it was risky.

"If I knew where the prick was, I would have done that already," Angelo snapped, his voice shaking with fury.

The exchange, along with the crash, was the diversion needed to allow Emmanuelle to slide up on her prey and grip his head in her hands, jerking hard as she did so. He was big and strong, his neck thick. He rolled almost before she'd settled on him, going in the direction of her technique. He smashed her leg under him, pinning her to the ground with his superior weight, but she didn't lose her grip.

Emme's breathing never changed. Slow and even. The man had turned now, and was punching at her, shoving up with his hands, yelling into his radio for aid. She had seconds before the men from the truck would come around to help him. Nothing else mattered in the moment but her job. She focused completely on breaking his neck.

The man bucked like a stallion, using his weight, realizing for the first time that his opponent was a woman. He reached one hand up and caught at the front of her jacket, feeling the swell of her breasts. Then he punched hard, over and over. She ignored the pain and counted, knowing his entire concentration was on hitting her. She breathed in and out. On the sixth punch, she wrenched hard, heard the familiar crack and reached for the gun that he'd dropped in the grass when he'd rolled over her leg.

As the first man rounded the hood of the SUV, calling out to ask "Mo" what was wrong, she shot him three times, twice between the eyes and once in the heart. She immediately lay flat. She didn't struggle to get her leg out from under the heavy body. The ground was soft from the rain, so she wiggled gently to see if she could create a little space, but the entire time she searched for another man she'd glimpsed coming toward her from the truck. He would have heard the gunshots very clearly.

"Mo? Talk to me, Mo. What the hell's happening out there? Get moving. Just drive through the gates. Blow them if you have to," Angelo commanded.

There was no answer. No vehicle moved. Emme scanned under the SUV, looking for the last man. There was no sound to give him away. The blast had been loud, and now a fire was roaring in the distance, but she kept her entire attention on the one hunting her. She stayed on her belly, ignoring the pain pounding through her body where Mo had repeatedly punched her. Something moved behind the SUV, but she didn't see legs or feet. He had to be on the bumper. She hadn't seen the vehicle move, which it would have when his weight had been added to it. He'd used the distraction of the helicopter and Mo's fight to plan out his attack.

She kept wiggling her leg, inching it out from under Mo's heavy body. It took patience to keep slowly working the leg as if she had all the time in the world and any minute someone wasn't going to be shooting at her, possibly with an automatic weapon. She kept her breathing slow and even. Breathing in and out. Letting her body, her training, take over the way it had done for years. She relied on that discipline, that training, had confidence in it.

A boot slowly dropped down to the ground right next to the end of the SUV. The leg came into view as the man wholly committed to climbing off the vehicle. He took one step forward to allow his other leg to drop down. She could see the partial end of a gun as he planted the second boot on the ground. Two-handed, Emmanuelle fired three shots into the exposed calf and knee, going right up the leg with each bullet. The man screamed.

She yanked her leg free and rolled under the SUV to the other side and was up, crouching low, searching for any shadow she might slide into, even as she checked the truck to see the status of the enemies there. Both the back passenger and driver's-side doors were open. A body hung out of the back passenger door.

"Pull back," Miceli's voice ordered. "Now. All of you. Pull back immediately."

"We can still do this," Angelo countered.

"Be quiet," Miceli snapped. "Pull back now, everyone. This is that girl, Angelo. Emmanuelle. I know you're here, sweetheart. You're defending him. Valentino. He isn't worth it. He's been playing you since day one. I thought you knew that. I thought you found his true character out."

His voice had gone from a whip of menace, of complete command, to that of a sweet older man talking gently to a young, mixed-up girl. Emmanuelle could clearly hear him over the several radios on the men lying dead on the ground.

"It must have been so difficult for you to grow up like you did. A mother who doesn't love you, never wanted you and is so ugly to you, abusing you every chance she gets. How humiliating for you. It's no wonder you were ripe at such a young age for a grown man like Val, who was experienced in seducing women, to take advantage of you."

There were no shadows for her to disappear into. Nowhere she could go to escape the voice that was telling not only every one of his men her story, but her family and cousins as well. Miceli was doing so deliberately to provide a distraction so his men could safely pull out. He knew the Ferraro family was helping Val, Dario and Giuseppi. He knew their reputation. He didn't know how they did what they did, but like everyone else, he both respected and feared them. He wasn't willing to lose more men to them.

"I always have a place for you, Emmanuelle. You're a beautiful woman. Angelo and Tommaso both have long wanted to ask you out, but Val had made it plain that he had a claim on you. They would treat you with the respect you are due. They wouldn't cheat with other women the way he does. They wouldn't lie to you. You wouldn't have to put up with your own family calling you names and disrespecting you. We would protect you from all that. Come to us, Emmanuelle. Val is pure poison. He will turn on Giuseppi. He is out only for himself. I tried to tell my brother, but he looks at Val through the eyes of a loving father. I can't save him, no matter how hard I try."

The man she shot in the leg crawled to the truck and hauled himself into the driver's seat. He closed the door and wrenched the steering wheel, turning so the truck lurched forward awkwardly. The body hanging out the door of the back cab slid farther so the head, the torso and even the hips were out. The tips of the fingers dragged macabrely on the ground. The dead man's boots seemed to be hung up on something inside the truck, or he would have been ripped out.

Two other men in the back raised their heads for a moment, semiautomatics at the ready, eyes scanning around them as the driver quickly made a U-turn to make a run for it. Emmanuelle had a good shot at the driver, but didn't take it. They were running, and it didn't seem right to kill men who were retreating. In any case, she couldn't get a clear shot at them without exposing herself, and there were too many of them not to take a hit from return fire.

"Think about it, Emmanuelle," Miceli kept on. "Come to us."

"Cut the bullshit, Miceli," Valentino snapped. "You tried to kill my father. Your own brother. What kind of man are you? There is no place on this earth that you can go that I won't find you. There will be no truce. No peace. You wanted war. You thought Giuseppi weak because he loved Greta and he stayed close to her while she was dying. You thought I wasn't paying attention. That was a mistake on your part, Miceli. A very big mistake."

There was no reply. Dead silence followed Valentino's declaration. His voice had been low. Deadly. She knew that voice. He meant every single word. He would never stop until Miceli was dead.

She just sat in the grass watching the truck disappear down the long drive, heading away from the lake. It wouldn't be long before emergency vehicles began to show up. It wasn't as if one could hide a helicopter crash, or the fact that a bullet had taken out the pilot. A war had been fought here at the lake house. Stefano, Giuseppi and Valentino could decide what they wanted to tell the police. She didn't want to see or talk to anyone.

She wanted to feel a sense of peace. She'd had that for just a little while when she'd been with Valentino here at the lake house before she'd gone to his room and seen him with the blonde he'd identified as Marge. She pulled her knees up and tucked her chin down to rub along the tops of her legs. They'd been happy together—at least, she'd been happy. She thought Valentino had been happy as well. Who knew about others? How did one know? Her brothers were happy with their choices. They seemed to adore their wives.

Lights crisscrossed the yard and then ran along the grass, throwing shadows in all directions. She knew Emilio had set those lights up in order to ensure the riders could go anywhere and escape quickly if need be. They would be checking rooftops, basements, every nook and cranny, just to make certain no one had been left behind to try to assassinate Giuseppi. She should help, but she knew they didn't really need her.

Already, several of their people were leaving. Stefano didn't want the police to associate them with the Saldis. It would be interesting to see how this was explained.

"Emme?"

She closed her eyes as a hand came down on her shoulder. She hadn't even realized her eyes had been burning. The wind was blowing. The clouds looked so purple in the dark sky, spinning and churning rapidly. She'd put her blurry sight down to that.

"Stefano. I was just about to check in with you." She still had the gun, and she placed it very carefully in front of her. "I'm wearing gloves." She had no idea why she pointed out what he could so easily see.

"I wasn't worried, honey." Stefano sank down beside her.

"The cops will be here soon. I'm sending away as many as we can spare."

She nodded. "I figured you would have to."

"Do you want to leave?"

"Yes. But I can't. Not until I know he's safe." She leaned into her older brother, needing his comfort.

Stefano wrapped his arm around her immediately. "It's clear that you really are in love with him, Emmanuelle. I didn't want to believe it. I don't even know how it can be true. A Ferraro can only really love once. That one person. An all-consuming love. That means your shadow has to be involved."

Emmanuelle closed her eyes and remained silent. Breathing. Hoping Stefano let it go, knowing he wouldn't. He was the head of the family. He was responsible for all of them.

"Emme? Is your shadow in some way compromised by Valentino Saldi?"

It was a direct question. One didn't lie to Stefano. Hot tears leaked out, spilled down her cheeks. At once she felt that stirring along her nerve endings. The music, the symphony. Him. Valentino. Reaching for her. Trying to comfort her. Trying to draw her back to him.

"Emme?" Stefano repeated, his inquiry infinitely gentle.

She nodded, unable to speak. It felt as if a terrible weight had been lifted off her chest. But now she had to worry that her brother might actually kill the man she loved.

Stefano let her cry. Holding her. Rocking her. Only for a minute or two. They didn't have time. Cars were making an exodus, skirting around wreckage and dead bodies.

"Okay, honey, you're going to have to tell me what happened."

"There is no quick version, Stefano, and I don't want Eloisa to know." She looked at him. "I don't. I don't care if you think I'm being childish. I've had it with her opinions. This has been so terrible for me. It's been difficult for Val as well."

"Why didn't you come to me?"

"I tried to, several times. You got so angry every time

Valentino's name came up, and then . . . I don't know. I didn't want to end it. I knew I would have to." She hung her head, ashamed. It was the truth. When she'd been with him, their world had been on fire, a brilliant white-hot flame of sheer beauty. Somewhere inside, she'd known it would have to end, but she'd clung to it as long as she could—until that night she'd dared to go to his house. To his room. Prepared to give up everything for him.

"All right, honey. Let's do this. The story is very simple. Valentino, Dario and Giuseppi were hit by someone, we don't know who, that's not our business. Vittorio was called as one of the nearest neighbors, and we were with him, so we all came. I've already sent word to the doc, so he can document the surgery and not get in trouble. He has to report gunshot wounds to the cops. Vittorio gave blood. It's known he has medical supplies in his unit at his home. It will sound plausible. While we were here, we were ambushed, and our bodyguards fought off the attackers along with some of Giuseppi's men."

Emmanuelle sent her older brother a small smile. "It looks a little like a war zone."

"That's true, but it isn't my problem. Fortunately, some of Giuseppi's men, the ones defecting, were here, so it does look as if he lost a few of them. Giuseppi will do most of the talking, so whatever tale he wants to spin will be fine with me. After, I'll take them to the hotel."

Emmanuelle shook her head. "Stefano. Francesca and Crispino." She couldn't imagine her brother risking his beloved wife and child, no matter how safe the penthouse was.

"There are more suites than just mine, Emme. I've already ordered one prepared. Drago and Demetrio have gone ahead to make certain the suite is entirely secure. I've already informed Dario of my intentions, and he's agreed it's the safest thing for now until Val can gather his men. I can provide a safe place for him to do that."

"You would do that?"

"I can't let Miceli get away with human trafficking and

auctions, Emme. If Valentino has a way of shutting it down, I've got to help him. Once we get them settled in the suite, we can talk about how Valentino managed to compromise your shadow."

Emmanuelle hoped he still felt the same way about helping the Saldis after she talked to him. She stood up with her brother a little reluctantly. The sirens were getting close. They stepped into the shadows and were taken fast to the house. Emme's choice of shadows took her straight to the front door. She had no idea where Stefano's shadow tube had taken him.

On the massive verandah, one hand on the wide column, she turned to look out over the lake. Once again, the night seemed peaceful, as if nothing had happened. There were no sounds of fighting, only the wind tugging at the water playfully, so that the dark blue surface had white caps rocking and splashing like wild surf.

The orange flames from the fire had died down, although the wind gusts would occasionally cause a sudden updraft so a fiery blaze would shoot into the sky and then go back down as the wind faded again. Her stomach was in knots. Tight, ugly knots. Was it because Miceli had spilled her private business to everyone? She pressed her fingers to her throbbing temples. She was used to her mother's ugly, cutting, derogatory comments. Pretty much everyone knew her mother's opinion of her. But still, it was rather humiliating to have Miceli talk to her like some actor in a theater play.

The front door opened and Dario walked out. He wasn't walking with his usual swagger. If anything, he was a little hunched, one hand pressed against his side, hidden under a jacket. He raised an eyebrow when he saw her. Instead of sweeping on by and ignoring her as he normally did, he dropped into a chair and looked up at her.

"That was a smooth operation your family ran, Emme." There was genuine admiration in Dario's voice. He didn't give respect or admiration easily. Most of the time he was expressionless. He reminded her a lot of her brothers.

"Yeah, they're good at all kinds of things." She was non-committal. She had always been careful never to talk about her family around Valentino, Dario, Giuseppi or even Greta. Thankfully, they didn't ask her many questions, but even when asked the nicest, most basic question, such as how was everyone, she had trained herself to think carefully before answering cautiously.

"Just so you know, Val never touched another woman, Emme. I don't interfere in relationships. It's all bullshit to me, but what Miceli said about him and the way he feels about you, that's not true in any way. You have enough to deal with without listening to that bastard."

She gave him the briefest of smiles. "What are you really doing out here, Dario?" It didn't make sense that he'd come looking for her when he was wounded. He was hurting. He refused to take painkillers. He didn't want anything impairing him when he was defending Val and Giuseppi.

"Came looking for you."

"Val send you?"

"Says you're upset. He needs to see for himself you're not hurt. Physically, that is. He wants to help with the rest of it. Doesn't like anyone else comforting you when he can do it."

Those dark eyes bored into her. Saw too much. He was like Stefano. Ruthless. Merciless. No give in him. Loyal to a fault, but willing to do things unimaginable to her. Unfortunately, she knew Val was the same way. In the early days, she hadn't thought so. She'd believed him to be sweet and kind because he always was to her.

Valentino might have been Giuseppi's son, but he'd been adopted. She had thought he wasn't of the same bloodline. He didn't have those violent tendencies. She was so positive. She'd been nineteen when Greta had told her that Val's father had been Giuseppi's youngest brother. That was when she realized he *did* have the same bloodline. More, he might have been even more ruthless than Giuseppi. He just hid it better.

Dario came from that same line of ruthless blood. She had no idea who his mother was; Valentino had never said, only that Miceli had refused to marry her or even claim Dario as his child for many years. There was quite a bit of mystery surrounding Dario. She should have had Rigina and Rosina Greco, her cousins, both investigators and hell on wheels with computers, find out everything they could on him. It was very hard to hide from either one of the women once they decided to hunt you with their keyboards.

"He'll have to get used to it, won't he?" Emmanuelle dug her fingers into the column and turned her gaze out over the lake. "The cops will be swarming all over this place. He'll hate that. *I* hate it. This was our place." She knew Dario would hear the sorrow in her voice, but she didn't care. He knew she loved Val. What was the point in trying to hide it?

"Why are you giving him up? Are you back to being the good little girl? Your family telling you what to do, Emme?" Dario taunted.

"I wish I were the good little girl, Dario. I wish they had ordered me to give Val up. They did when I was a kid." She had to be honest. "But then they left it up to me, until he hurt me. Until he shattered me. Don't ever love anyone that much, Dario." She whispered the last to him, turning to look at him. "I have to let him go and there won't be anything left of me. I know that, but there's his world and there's mine. Just don't love like this."

"I'm not capable, Emme." Dario studied her face. "That night. When you came to his room, how did you get into the house?"

She shrugged and turned away from him. "I'm a Ferraro, Dario. I can do a lot of things."

"You were going to leave your family for him then, weren't you?" He stood up, stepping back to allow her through the door. Too many vehicles were hurtling up the drive toward them, sirens blaring.

"Does it matter?" She stepped into the entryway.

"I think so."

"Yes. I would have given up everything for him."

"What's the difference now that you know for certain he wasn't cheating on you?"

He deliberately trapped me. She knew he had. He knew things she didn't. She couldn't say that aloud, although she was certain Dario had that same knowledge.

"I'm a little more mature now. I understand his world a little better, and maybe him. He's far more ruthless than I realized, and more caught up in a world of crime than I could probably live with."

"And the Ferraro family isn't?"

Emmanuelle didn't answer. She avoided the master bedroom. Instead, she headed to the control room, where Enzo and Emilio were casually wiping clean every camera as if none of them had been recording.

CHAPTER SIX

Emmanuelle loved Stefano's home. One wouldn't ordinarily think of a hotel penthouse as an actual home. The suite took up the entire upper floor. Before Francesca, the rooms had been cold, without personality, more like a place to do business than a place to live. Once Francesca had moved in, every room had undergone a transformation, just as Emmanuelle's oldest brother had. The transformation might have been subtle in Stefano, especially to an outsider, but all of them could see the happiness in him. That was the way Emmanuelle thought of the penthouse—a place of absolute happiness.

The kitchen was often the gathering place. Taviano and Francesca both loved to cook and were excellent at it. The table was large, and they would surround it, talking and laughing and filling Emmanuelle with hope and love of family, something she needed when she knew she had lost the love of her life—the only man she would ever love. Over the last two years, Stefano's kitchen had saved her sanity more than once.

Sometime over the last year, Elie had been accepted as a family member, coming and going just as her brothers did, in and out of Stefano's home and sitting with them at the kitchen table, laughing and talking, sharing that same love. Emmanuelle knew he needed it the same way she did. He'd lost his one chance at the real thing as well. She could see the knowledge in his eyes, even if the others couldn't.

She'd asked Stefano not to invite anyone but her brothers to the meeting. He'd raised an eyebrow, but he'd complied. She hadn't even wanted sweet Mariko or Nicoletta there. She didn't know if she was ashamed of the things Miceli had said over his radio, knowing his men as well as every single one of her people could hear. She only knew she felt as if she were being crushed under a terrible weight. No matter which path she chose, she would lose.

Valentino, Dario and Giuseppi were just two floors beneath them. They had a suite half the size of Stefano's home. It was enormous, one they could easily live in, with multiple bedrooms and bathrooms. They could have guards with them as well. Stefano had assigned only his most trusted staff to clean and stock their suite. Drago and Demetrio would check them before they entered the room to clean. There would be no substitutes.

Emmanuelle had deliberately avoided going to see Valentino, afraid she would lose her resolve. She *had* to tell Stefano the truth, now that she knew other riders could be in jeopardy. She hadn't known before, but she had no excuse now. She couldn't settle, pacing back and forth, the buildup of nervous energy overcoming the pain that had begun to come through from the pounding she'd taken from Mo's fists.

"Emme, you need to just come out with it. Get it over with."

Stefano's voice always grounded her. He spoke low. A velvet growl of command. No one would ever mistake him for anything but the leader. When he said to do something, you just did it.

She couldn't look at her brothers, feeling as if she'd

betrayed them. Vittorio loved Grace so much. Grace had almost been kidnapped. Everyone thought it had been over a gambling debt her foster brother owed, but now she knew it was because Grace's shadow was like her shadow. And Nicoletta . . .

"I love Val the way you love Francesca, Stefano. The way all of you love the one person you're married to. I've loved him for so long, and I don't want anything to happen to him. I don't think I could ever forgive any of you if you hurt him." She had to get that out there. "I don't even know if I'd be able to stop myself from retaliating." That was the truth as well.

Her eyes were burning. Was she crying? Had she turned into a baby? That was the last thing she needed to be right now. She had to make her brothers understand. She might know she couldn't be with Val, but she wouldn't tolerate them killing him for what he'd done. There wasn't anything different from what any of them had done when they found their women. She knew Stefano had deliberately tied Francesca to him using their shadows. She was fairly certain the others had done so as well.

"Emmanuelle." Stefano handed her a crystal glass with an inch of amber liquid in it. "No one is going to hurt Val."

She took a deep breath. She had to just say it. Tell them. "The Saldis have a story they hand down from father to son. They apparently have done so for generations. It's some kind of requirement. I only found out this information today or I would have told you immediately. I had no idea. None."

She paced across the room to stare out the long row of windows that overlooked the city. There were so many lights one couldn't see stars. Below her, the lights of the city itself were dazzling. She pressed the crystal glass to her throbbing head.

"The story has to do with finding someone whose shadow throws out tubes. Like mine does. Like Grace's. Like Nicoletta's."

She felt the stillness behind her. The sudden tension in the room. Her brothers were extremely intelligent, and it wasn't that difficult to connect the dots. In fact, she'd just laid it out for them.

"I came home the night of the party when I was sixteen and I tried to tell you what happened, Stefano, but you were so angry that I'd snuck out, you couldn't hear anything I said. I didn't even know what I was saying. It sounded so stupid. Ropes tying up my shadow? Chains surrounding it? I felt ridiculous. After you yelled at me, I was more rebellious than ever. I just decided I'd had too much to drink and I imagined it."

"Ropes binding your shadow?" Ricco asked.

He would be the one to make the inquiry. It was easier to face him than Stefano. Or Vittorio. She forced herself to look at Ricco. He was a genius with rope. With knots. He might be her savior. She nodded.

"I noticed my shadow on the wall, and as Valentino approached me, I felt this jolt of physical awareness. It was very hard. I'd never felt anything like that in my life. When I looked at my shadow, there were what looked like ropes swarming around it, binding it really fast from his shadow to mine. It terrified me. I broke the light."

She took a sip of the amber liquid and felt the fiery smoothness slide down her throat. Scotch. "I didn't know it at the time, and neither did he, but just the small number of ties bound us together and forged a connection. It was difficult to stay away from each other."

"Are you certain he didn't know the significance?" Giovanni asked.

"At the time he didn't, at least that's what he says, and I couldn't detect a lie," Emme said. "He was older than me and didn't want to go near a teenager. I didn't want to start a war between our families. He became an obsession. I couldn't think of anything else. We met again accidentally, at least I think it was that way. I was so careful to keep my shadow out of reach of his. He was careful to keep a physical distance between us."

She took another sip of the Scotch. "I wish I could say I

continued to be as careful, but I didn't. He never touched me, other than kissing me, until after I turned eighteen, but I didn't guard my shadow the way I should have. We would be talking and laughing. I would be having such fun. Then that physical jolt would hit so hard. He would be kissing me, and I just wasn't thinking the way I should have been."

Ricco held up his hand, a small frown on his face. "I'm not clearly understanding, honey. Tell me exactly what happened to your shadow."

"The more times mine was open to his, the more of the ropes his shadow was able to tie around mine until mine was held captive. Completely. Our shadows are merged together so tightly now, bound by these ropes. And they connect us on some kind of neurological level. I can feel him running along my nerve endings. He can feel me. If I'm sad. Happy. He knows if I'm with another man. That kind of thing. We can close off from each other. I did that, but it took me almost the entire two years I was away from him. I was still bound to him."

"What do the ropes look like on your shadow?" Ricco asked.

"Very intricate knots. I know I can't undo them. I don't think they can be cut, not without killing both of us. I didn't have enough time to ask him a lot of questions. He admitted to me he thought the story was a myth until it happened to us. He didn't ask Giuseppi any questions because he didn't want him to know about us. He was worried about the ramifications."

"You might want to tell us what that means," Stefano said.

His voice wasn't as gentle as it had been earlier, and Emmanuelle shivered.

"Miceli was trying to give his men time to retreat, but he really did want to entice you to come to him. He knows you believe Val cheated on you. He knows Eloisa disrespects you. He gave it his best shot to bring you into his fold. He is well aware of this phenomenon with your shadow. He tried to have Grace kidnapped. And Dario was interested in

Nicoletta, although to his credit, he backed off when Taviano told him he was engaged to her." Stefano pinned her with his dark blue gaze. "It's clear Miceli knows and wanted Grace, at least, because of her shadow. Why?"

"If a few ties are on the shadow, the shadow can be used as a spy, if her lover is close. If more, he can be farther away. If there are many and they are irrevocably tied together, then he can travel with her wherever she takes him."

There was once again silence in the room. Tension. Her stomach knotted, fingers tightening on the glass until she was afraid the thick crystal might actually shatter.

"Emmanuelle, when did you find this out?" Stefano asked.

"Just before Miceli's crew showed up. I was questioning Val. I knew I couldn't be free of him, but didn't know why. I know I love him, and it's the real thing. A Ferraro thing. I wasn't certain how it could be."

"How imprisoned is your shadow?" Stefano asked.

She pressed the glass to her temple again. "It's so weighted down I feel like I can't breathe without him. In terms of what it takes to make that last part of the Saldi story fit, I don't know how close I am to it, or if we're already there. I suspect we're very close, Stefano."

"He had to have known," Stefano condemned Val.

Emmanuelle nodded slowly. "Valentino did his research once he realized what was happening. He knew. Just like all of you, he decided he wanted me and he was going to keep me. He deliberately tied me to him, and I was so silly I just let him do it." She wasn't going to pretend she didn't have blame in the situation—she did. She'd gone to Valentino of her own accord.

"What a fucking bastard," Giovanni snapped.

Vittorio swirled the liquid in his glass. "Isn't it funny how we can totally look at Valentino Saldi and call him out for doing exactly the same thing each of us did with the women in our lives, binding them to us without their consent? Hell, we seduced them, we played every card we had to make sure they belonged to us. We were masters at it, and we didn't care that they didn't have a chance, yet he does it and we want to call him the lowest worm on the face of the earth. I think that makes every one of us a hypocrite or worse."

Emmanuelle wanted to kiss him. Vittorio. Of course he would stick up for her. She could always count on him. He hadn't even looked at her. He hadn't acted in any way as if he was standing with her. He'd simply stated a truth.

"Damn it," Taviano exploded. "Vittorio's right. You can't look at Val without seeing the way he looks at Emme and you just know . . ." He trailed off. "But there's the cheating. We don't cheat."

Color crept up Emmanuelle's face. "I might have gotten that wrong. I should have listened to his explanation. Elie told me to, but I just couldn't bear to, and then there was the shadow thing that terrified me."

"There was an explanation for a naked woman being in his bedroom?" Vittorio asked. He'd been the one to beat the crap out of Valentino, and Val hadn't lifted much of a hand to defend himself.

She nodded. "Miceli had sent her to get information from Val. Val didn't want them to know I was important to him. Dario was already on his way to interrupt them when I showed up. He'd been signaled when she took off her clothes. Apparently, she runs one of Miceli's strip clubs and has something to do with the trafficking ring. Val can tell you about her and all of that when you talk to him about Miceli's operations."

"And you're satisfied that he really didn't cheat on you?" Taviano pushed.

"I can hear lies as well as any of you," Emme said. "But question him all you want." She had the feeling they would no matter what she said. She was their baby sister, and they were determined to protect her no matter what.

"Can you see the ties binding your shadow when he's not with you?" Ricco asked.

She shook her head. She'd spent hours staring at her shadow, trying to figure out how to undo what had happened.

"When he told me the story Giuseppi had told him over and over, I realized that was the real reason Grace had been targeted, not to pay a gambling debt. And I'm certain Dario looked at Nicoletta for the same reason. Suddenly, after centuries of this story being nothing but that, these men see three women with shadows that their shadows react to. If that gets out, all of our unclaimed riders could be in trouble. I had no idea. I had no way of protecting myself."

She put the glass down on a coffee table and wrapped her arms around her middle to try to stop shivering. "Now I'm in love with a man I can't have. I have to go into an arranged marriage so I can produce babies with someone I'll never love. I'll wreck his life. He'll always know I don't love him. It won't matter that I won't cheat on him. He'll know. And what about the woman he should be with? Our marriage will wreck her life as well."

She knew there was despair in her voice because there was in her heart. She'd thought about the scenario so many times. If she didn't do her duty to the shadow rider world and produce children, she was just compounding her sins.

"You're getting ahead of yourself, Emmanuelle," Stefano said. "Way ahead of yourself. We take one step at a time. The very first step is with you and Val. It's easy enough to call his family criminals and say we're not, yet we kill as often, if not more. We tell ourselves we're the good guys, but every now and then, I have to look at myself in the mirror when I put my son to bed, knowing I've been teaching him how to kill, and he's just a baby."

There was another long silence. Giovanni sighed, the first to break the mutual stillness. "It is all in the perspective, isn't it?"

Vittorio nodded and finished off the Scotch in his glass. "I agree with Stefano on first things first. We have to find out how far this thing has gone between the two of your shadows, Emme. Let's get you together and take a look. Does Dario know?"

"Yes. Dario knows everything, but for some reason, Valentino doesn't want Giuseppi to know. He's been careful, and even tonight, when he was telling me the story, he said he hadn't told his father. I was still upset because when he was talking with Marge—the blonde in his bedroom that night— he said his father ordered him to seduce me. I told him in a way it was the truth. The story was all about finding someone with my kind of shadow and seducing her. Right? I met the right criteria, and he did exactly what his father wanted him to do."

There was bitterness in her voice. She felt that same silly burning behind her eyes and fought against it. "His choosing me had nothing to do with *me*. After I was legally of age, I would meet him at the lake house. I was so happy. He was this amazing, wonderful, caring man. Later, looking back, I realized every time I started to question the weird phenomenon of his shadow binding mine, he would kiss me until I couldn't think. He knew what he was doing by then, and he controlled the situation."

"Emme." Stefano said her name very gently.

"Don't. I know you're going to defend him. I can tell. You're going to try to make me feel better, but it won't work. I *was* stupid. I was all the things Eloisa said I was, with the exception of betraying our family. I never once talked about us or riding shadows. I didn't know about his family's myths. I had no idea they had any way of binding a rider to them and using them to spy or go into the shadows or if they can tie a rider permanently to them. Still, for all that, I saw our shadows. I saw the ties. I *felt* them. I felt our connection growing. Sometimes I even saw the look on his face of pure satisfaction when he looked at our shadows. It made me uneasy, and I still didn't stop seeing him. I went to his house that night to tell him I'd give up everything for him. And I would have. I would have given up being a rider for him."

"You love him that much?" Vittorio asked, his voice soft.

"Absolutely, I do." Her voice rang with conviction.

"Is he aware you're a shadow rider? That all of us are shadow riders? Does he know what that is?" Stefano persisted.

Emmanuelle was very careful. She was on shaky ground now. To know the secret of the Ferraro family could get someone killed. That was one of the reasons she had asked Stefano not to include Elie in their meeting. He was an Archambault. She'd revealed a little too much to him already, passing it off as being a young girl who'd had too much to drink, but still, it might have gotten him thinking, especially when she was so connected to Valentino. Elie Archambault could make one call and get the authority to take out a rider, let alone a civilian who threatened an entire community of riders. She hadn't wanted Eloisa there because her mother would have taken malicious joy in making the call to the council.

"He doesn't know. He may suspect. There is the story of the woman, the spy moving in shadows, the tether binding her to her man so she can't escape him. I'm not even certain how it works because we didn't have much time for him to explain it in detail. I said nothing to him. Dario asked me how I entered Valentino's home without his guards catching me, but I didn't answer him. Val never asked me a question about my family, and I never asked questions about his. It was one of the things that made me believe he really cared about me."

Emmanuelle lifted her chin. She wasn't going to hide from her brothers. She knew they loved her. Eloisa might not. She knew her father never had. Valentino wanted her physically. He couldn't hide that fact from her, and he wanted her for whatever her shadow could provide for the Saldi family.

"Would you take him into the shadows if he asked you to?" Giovanni asked.

"No. That's what I don't really understand about this story. Something had to have been left out. For instance, if Grace had been taken by Miceli and he tied her shadow to his, why would she go into any shadow to spy for him, if he knew she could? What could he do to force her? Cause her pain? First, Grace isn't a rider. She doesn't know how to get into the shadows. It wouldn't work, and he'd just be angry. If he got his hands on me, I'd cut his throat the first chance I got. Unless they have some way of stopping us from doing that."

Emmanuelle was back to pacing across the floor. "I think Valentino told me part of the story, not all of it. And when I asked him how to undo the ties, he refused to answer. He just said he would never let me go." God help her, there was a part of her that was thrilled with his declaration, and she was too ashamed to admit that to anyone. She barely could admit it to herself.

"Clearly, the only way we're going to get answers is to talk to Valentino," Stefano said. "Although I doubt he's going to be forthcoming if he thinks we're trying to take you from him."

"If he already suspects we can move around in the shadows, but Emme isn't admitting our family secrets to him," Vittorio said, "why would he want to give up his family secrets to us? He has no incentive to do so."

"Maybe a gun to his head?" Giovanni muttered.

Emmanuelle pressed a hand to her already knotted stomach. Her breasts hurt, the bruises now making themselves known. Mo must have landed a blow just under her breasts as well. She was beginning to feel a little beat-up. The adrenaline of being in the shadows had worn off, and exhaustion was setting in.

"Gee, I love you, but now isn't the time for your dark humor." She knew he wasn't really joking, but she was going to pretend he was. "I'm looking for positive help for both of us, Val and me, not just me. He's trying to shut down a human trafficking ring. He's been trying to do so for well over two years, pretty much alone. I wish he'd come to us, but like I said, we didn't talk about our families. He doesn't know what we do. He didn't know we could help him. He has to have tons of information by this time."

Stefano watched her pace for a few minutes, his eyes narrowed and watchful. "Miceli has to have cops on the take, otherwise Val would have managed to give them whatever information he had to shut this ring down if he couldn't do it with Giuseppi's men."

"From what Dario indicated, they might not know who they can trust in Giuseppi's organization anymore," Emmanuelle said.

"Are you injured, Emme?" Stefano asked.

One didn't lie to Stefano. "I took a couple of punches, but fortunately I'm only bruised, nothing major. There's not much that can be done for bruises."

"Mariko can take a look," Ricco offered. "She's good with healing."

"Thanks, Ricco." Emmanuelle smiled at her brother. "It really is nothing. Just aches a little. I'd like to get this over with so I can rest. Stefano?"

"I've texted Val. Told him it's urgent I have a meeting with him tonight. That I'd like to bring Ricco and you with me, Emme. That it is best if Giuseppi isn't present, and it is up to his discretion if he wants Dario there, but we will be discussing his association with you."

"His reply?" Vittorio asked.

"He corrected me. He said he would be more than happy to discuss his relationship with his woman. Giuseppi has eaten, showered and retired for the night at the opposite end of the suite with two of their trusted bodyguards on him. He said come when we're ready."

Emmanuelle could feel the tension in the room rising the minute Stefano relayed Valentino's reply. He had thrown down the gauntlet, declaring she belonged to him. Val could be just as arrogant and annoying as her brothers. He'd been raised the way they had, training to take over an empire, learning to fight, even to kill.

She knew Val's life hadn't been easy. She knew he'd seen things that had been traumatizing. He'd done things he wasn't proud of and didn't want her to know about. That was the life he'd been born into, just as she'd been born into hers. She'd told herself she would ask him what his family was into before she committed to him, but then she'd gone to him, prepared to accept him on any terms. Now, she knew, she couldn't do that. Now, she knew, everything was very, very different.

Before, Emmanuelle had been absolutely certain Val loved her. When they came together physically, the chemistry was explosive. Sex was certainly not love. Even if that lasted their entire life together because of the connection of their shadows, she still wanted to be loved for who she was. Everything they had together had been built on deception.

She gingerly hugged her brothers before going to the elevator with Stefano and Ricco. Stefano caught her chin as they rode to the correct floor. "You want out at any time, you just give an indication and we'll take you out."

She nodded, blinking rapidly. She loved her family so much. "Thank you, Stefano. This is difficult for him as well. We're just kind of in this place where we don't know what to do."

He cupped her chin, looking into her eyes even as the doors slid open and Drago and Demetrio appeared, looking for a moment as if they might shoot first and ask questions later. Stefano refused to look away from her.

"I made absolutely certain that Francesca couldn't escape me, Emmanuelle. I knew she was mine. She belonged to me. I wasn't about to let her get away. I've never regretted that decision, and I've worked every day to see that she doesn't regret being with me. I'm not a nice man. I'll never be one. You and I both know Valentino isn't a nice man, either. I don't want him for you, and I'm not standing up for him, but I am saying, just because he used every method he had available to him to tie you to him doesn't mean he did it for all the wrong reasons." His thumb slid along her jaw. "Keep that in mind when you listen to him." Stefano dropped his hand and stepped back, indicating for her to precede him into the suite.

Emmanuelle pressed her hand over her thudding heart. She just wanted this over. Seeing Val after all this time, two years of avoiding him, of learning to live without him, of not feeling him running along her nerve endings like a song, was just too much. She needed downtime. Somewhere she could go to be alone and just stare off into space and not think. Not feel. Not hurt anymore.

Dario stood in the foyer. "I assume you gentlemen are armed."

"You assume correctly," Stefano said. "Not that it matters. I'm quite capable of killing someone without a weapon."

Dario didn't smile—in fact, when his dark eyes slid over Emmanuelle, he frowned. "Emme. Are you injured?"

She wasn't even walking, and he asked the same question Stefano had. So much for being stoic. She shook her head. "Nope. Just fine."

He stood there, blocking the door, staring at her with his dark, piercing, *accusing* eyes. She rolled hers. "*Fine.* Not that it's any of your business, but I took a couple of punches. Hurts like hell but only bruises."

Dario had his phone and was texting fast, one-handed.

"Great. Sending that little bit of info straight to your boss? Is that really necessary? He doesn't need to know."

Dario just looked at her and then opened the door. Emmanuelle could see that Valentino had cleaned up. He'd taken a shower and changed his bandages. His color was far better. He looked fresh, and she looked . . . wilted. The moment she walked into the master bedroom, his dark eyes moved over her, assessing her for the damage Dario had reported.

"Come here, Princess." His voice was low, a soft melody that immediately sent a wave of comfort along her nerve endings, spreading through her body and finding the bruises.

She heard his swift intake of breath and knew he shared the pain, that he'd found just where she was injured. Their connection was so strong it was frightening. He held out his hand to her, his gaze on her face, eyes meeting hers.

She didn't want to go to him. She almost couldn't bear his touch, but then starting out first thing with him in any kind of altercation while her brothers were in the room was a losing situation all the way around. What did it matter if they were skin to skin? He was already inside, twisted and knotted in every nerve ending she had, wrapped around her heart and maybe even her soul.

She made certain she went to the side of the bed where the

light would highlight her shadow, and if he moved, his. Her brothers had come to see what their combined shadows looked like, and she was determined to allow them to see, even if that meant Valentino's shadow would be able to over-power hers even more. She hadn't mentioned her fear of that to Stefano. Maybe she should have.

She'd been so careful to keep her shadow safe from Val ever since she realized he knew what was happening and was deliberately imprisoning her. Sometimes, like now, she was afraid, feeling as if it were too late for her, and she was al-ready his prisoner and she couldn't escape. When that hap-pened, she wanted to fight her way out.

Emmanuelle wasn't a quitter. She wasn't a fleer. She was programmed to be a fighter. A survivor, and she would fight to the death.

"Baby, stop." Val's thumb slid over the back of her hand. "What's wrong? Just breathe. You did this earlier, as if you're having an anxiety attack."

His voice was pitched low, and he had leaned forward, his lips against her ear. When he spoke, the movement against her skin was sensual, as it could only be with Val. She felt each stroke slide deep, an arrow of pure fire shooting to her sex. She didn't want to feel the way she did about him. She didn't want him to be the one to make her feel so alive, but he always managed to when no one else could.

"I told them as much as I could about us, Val. I had to." She made her confession, feeling as if she'd betrayed him.

"It's all right, Emme. I expected you to. We just have to be very careful who finds out about this. There are men who would try to take you and some of the others."

Stefano approached the bed, but stayed at the foot of it. Ricco did as well. Both were very aware of Dario closely watching their every move without seeming to.

"We'd like to see your shadows," Stefano said. "If you could shift positions so you're to the left of that light fixture, your shadow will hit the wall next to Emme's."

Emmanuelle's heart began to pound. Adrenaline poured

into her body as Valentino once again turned his head to meet her gaze. This time, his eyes held hers. Dark green. Incredibly sensual. He obeyed Stefano slowly, shifting his body those few inches until his shadow moved, a dark phantom on the wall. The moment that velvety apparition appeared close to hers, thick ropes reached for her shadow, quickly looping around it.

The moment the first rope touched her shadow, Emmanuelle felt the brutal sexual jolt hit her like a freight train. It was vicious, a firestorm, rushing through every nerve ending, lighting her up with a million white-hot flames. Val's hand tightened around hers, nearly crushing hers, and his eyes went hungry, the lines in his face carved deep with a mixture of something she couldn't name and pure carnal lust.

The ropes swarmed so fast to her shadow, it was a takeover. The shadows were too close. Her shadow was already weighed down, unable to move quickly out of the way, even when she tried to pull away from Val. His hand clamped down tighter over hers, and he pulled her closer to him, edging their shadows inches closer, giving his shadow more of an advantage.

Emmanuelle noticed each time the ropes themselves were different, as were the knots and loops binding her. These ropes seemed to sink into her shadow, merging with it. They were thicker and the knots so intricate she could barely process them before they were sinking into her shadow among all the other ropes with their loops and knots.

"Turn off the light," Stefano ordered.

Valentino didn't react to the command. He pulled Emmanuelle to him and took her mouth. She heard thunder in her ears. Lightning struck a million places in her body all at once. There was chaos reigning in her mind. She felt pure fire rushing through her veins like a firestorm out of control. She nearly crawled onto the bed with Val to get closer to him, to feed that wicked craving that wouldn't let up, wouldn't let go, just fed and fed, growing stronger and stronger until she needed to straddle Valentino and take everything her body demanded. She pulled back abruptly before she lost herself completely.

The ropes were too heavy. Her shadow was completely lost. *She* was lost. She knew she was. There was no saving her, no matter what Ricco tried to do. She looked up at Valentino, meeting his eyes, seeing the knowledge there. Forcing herself to see that not only did he trap her deliberately, but he did so without remorse.

"The light." This time Stefano snarled the word, a low, harsh command, and he was already striding around the bed toward the offending and very expensive sconce on the wall. It was clear he had every intention of smashing it.

Dario snapped off the light. "Sorry. Was a little slow."

Emmanuelle knew he was giving Val more time to trap her in those heavier ropes, the ones that sank through her shadow into her skin. She felt every one of them penetrate deep, binding Valentino to her even tighter until there didn't seem a way to separate.

She turned her head to look at Ricco, her only hope. Her one real hope. Ricco, the rope master. He knew every knot known to man. If there was one person on the face of the earth who might have been able to free her, it was her brother. She had been unaware of anything or anyone but Val when he was kissing her, when their shadows were touching, but Ricco had stepped close to study the knots.

Ricco remembered everything. He would be able to draw an exact duplicate of what he had seen on the wall, even though it was gone. There were so many ropes, so many knots. All different, all various sizes and shapes. All tangled together. And now, so many sinking into her shadow, and how could she tell them, into her body?

Ricco's eyes met hers. He gave a small shake of his head to indicate to her to stay silent. He didn't want to speak yet in front of Valentino and Dario.

"You trapped Emmanuelle's shadow, Val," Stefano said, moving back across the room to take one of the very comfortable chairs facing the bed. "Why?"

Val frowned when Emme tried to pull away from him. "Sit up here with me while we talk this out, Princess."

She wanted to go to one of the guest rooms and inspect the damage done to her body, and then just lie down on a bed and go to sleep. On the other hand, Stefano wasn't going to take half answers from Val, the way she had. He would want to know the entire story.

"You'll have to let go of my hand so I can go around the bed."

He studied her face for a full thirty seconds, clearly weighing whether or not he could trust her. Finally, after rubbing the back of her hand one more time with his thumb, sending a little dart of fire down her spine, he let her go.

Emmanuelle reached up and took out her tightly woven braid to help relieve the headache pounding at her temples as she made her way around the four-poster bed to the opposite side so she could get on the comforter. The Ferraro Hotel had spared no expense. Every blanket, every sheet and certainly the comforter and mattress were luxury at its best. The moment her body sank down onto the bed, it felt like heaven.

She thought about staying as far from Valentino as possible, but it seemed childish, and she knew he would never stand for it. She scooted close to him without touching him. Val simply reached over, wrapped his arm around her waist and dragged her up against him. As always, his skin was hot and warmed her instantly. She didn't fight him. She leaned into him, absorbing his heat and resting her head on his chest.

"Emmanuelle told us the short version of the fairy-tale story Giuseppi gave to you about shadows and what to look for. I want the *entire* story. The version you gave Emme makes little sense. Tell me everything," Stefano demanded. His voice was back to his usual low-key tone, the one that said no one ever crossed him, so just give him what he wanted.

Val sent him a little half smile, wrapping a thick strand of Emme's hair around his fist. "Give me a very good reason why I should do that."

Stefano nodded. "Because Miceli got a small taste of

what it is like to be enemies with my *famiglia*. You have placed my sister in an untenable position. We are either your allies or your enemies. If we are your enemies, what Miceli saw is nothing in comparison to what will rain down on you and your organization, Valentino." Again, Stefano's tone was extremely mild. He could have been talking about the weather. "So you choose. Are we allies or enemies?"

CHAPTER SEVEN

think he's making me an offer I can't refuse, Dario," Valentino said, a faint smile on his face. It didn't reach his eyes. He studied Emmanuelle's brother through half-closed eyes. He'd always known this day would come.

He wasn't giving Emme up. He knew he'd lost her trust and he had to earn that back. He'd loved her almost since the day he'd laid eyes on her, when it was forbidden and made him feel like scum. He'd done his best to protect her back then, at least until she was old enough, and then he'd just stopped pretending he was a good man. He wasn't. He never would be. He'd do his best to try, but in the end, he was heir to the Saldi territory, and if he didn't take it and hold on to it, Miceli or one of his sons would take it and the underbelly of Chicago would get far uglier than it already was.

Giuseppi had always provided a balance in that world. He ran things with an iron fist. No one ever fucked with him because if they did, he hit them hard and fast. He demanded loyalty, but in return, he gave it back. He was fair. He didn't ask for more than anyone could give. If someone was injured in his employ, even low-level soldiers, he paid for their care and their funerals, and he saw to their families. On the other hand, no one lied to him. No one cheated him. No one ever betrayed him.

Then Greta had gotten sick and Giuseppi hadn't been paying attention. Valentino should have been. He'd been upset about losing his mother as well. He knew Emmanuelle didn't want to be part of his world, and truthfully, she didn't belong in it. Then he'd gotten wind of the sex trafficking ring Miceli was running. When he began investigating, he'd had no idea how far-reaching it actually was.

Miceli and his sons had begun to show interest in Emme. He knew they had somehow discovered her shadow, just as he had. Then Grace had nearly been kidnapped. Dario had tried to watch over Nicoletta. Things had gotten out of hand fast when Val and Dario began to suspect that some of Giuseppi's trusted capos had defected to Miceli. That meant they had traitors in their organization. Anyone could try to assassinate Giuseppi.

"You're offering an alliance between the Ferraro family and my family." Val wanted Stefano to confirm it. To say that shit out loud in front of Emmanuelle. If he went back on his word—and Val couldn't imagine that Stefano would; his word was considered gold—Emme would never forgive her brother.

"Giuseppi Saldi has the largest territory covering Chicago. Every other crime boss answers to him. You are his heir, and at this time, with Greta's death, and Miceli making his move against his brother, I would have to say he's turned the reins over to you. So yes, I know what you do and who you are. And I'm offering to align my family with yours in an effort to defeat your uncle and protect you, your father and your organization. But you have a price to pay."

"That price will never include giving up Emmanuelle."

"Is that even possible at this point?" Stefano asked.

Val felt Emme turn her head to look up at him. He knew when he answered, he would feel condemnation. He would see it in her eyes. He stroked a gentle caress down her long, silky hair, giving her brother the truth. Trying to tell her he would always take care of her. Be there for her. Stand with her. He knew she didn't want his world. He'd tried to get out of it. Hell, he didn't want it, at least not at first. But he couldn't let Miceli have it. Or Angelo. Or Tommaso. He was born into the life, and he was responsible for those under him as well as those needing his protection on the streets.

"No. It's impossible to break us up without doing permanent damage to both of us. In the early stages, I believe it could have been done by someone such as Ricco. Perhaps even in the secondary stage, although it would have taken time and tremendous patience. Both parties would have had to agree. But at this stage, it would be impossible. We're tied together on a molecular level. I can't explain it because I have no understanding of how it could happen, only that once so many of the ropes wrap around her shadow and they begin to thicken like the ones you saw, they sink into her shadow and our shadows merge. When that happens, a pathway seems to forge between our bodies until they merge as well."

Emmanuelle felt as if she might leap off the bed and run from him at any moment, but she wasn't the running type. More likely, she was going to launch herself into an attack when the full import of his statement hit her. She was truly his prisoner. There was no way out for either of them, other than death or perhaps a vegetative state. Her body vibrated with coiled tension, and all along her nerve endings, he felt inflamed sparks charging with fierce fire. Her breathing was slow and even, but that didn't mean anything, not when it came to Emme.

In all honesty, he hadn't believed any of the bullshit story Giuseppi had repeatedly told him, and eventually Dario as well. Even after he'd met Emme and seen and felt what happened when their shadows came together, he couldn't comprehend how they could merge their nervous systems. It was science fiction. So was spying through shadows. Dario and he had discussed the story countless times, especially after meeting Emmanuelle and seeing her shadow. They still couldn't figure out how it would work.

"You freely admit you deliberately compromised Emme, knowing if your shadow merged too deeply with hers there would be no chance of going back?" Ricco asked.

"Absolutely. I did so every chance I got and would again," Val said. He wasn't about to lie to them over that. They could all go to hell as far as he was concerned, but they better understand, they couldn't keep Emmanuelle from him. He loved her. It was impossible not to love her. Maybe if they'd taken better care of her over the years, he would have backed off, but he didn't see that they had anything to be superior about.

Emmanuelle rolled over, heedless of his injuries, going right over the top of him, her smaller body all muscle, shockingly fast and strong, hands going for his head as if she might break his neck. There were tears in her eyes, determination on her face. Val didn't protect himself from her. She deserved to take her shot. It was Dario who got there, anticipating her reaction, just as Valentino had. He knocked her one hand away from Val's face with a solid punch to her forearm.

She made no sound at all as Stefano, arms around her waist, dragged her off Valentino, toward the other side of the bed. "I've got you, honey."

Val caught her with equally strong arms. "Don't, Stefano. She wasn't going to kill me." He pulled her back to him, bringing her right to his chest, one hand pushing her face against his shoulder. "This is hard to hear. I know that, Princess. I should have told you first. I was so in love with you, I would have sold my soul to the devil to have you. I did sell my soul to him."

She lifted her head to look up at him, her brilliant blue gaze meeting his. Searching his as if looking for something. What the hell? Hadn't he ever told her he loved her? Didn't she know? He'd told Marge he didn't. They hadn't really talked since. When they had, it had all been about possession. The shadow.

He brushed his lips gently across hers. "I love you so much, Emmanuelle, sometimes I can't think straight."

"I was going to break your neck. You should have protected yourself."

He smiled at her, because she was the most beautiful woman in the world to him. "No, babe, you wouldn't have. You love me too much. Dario should have known that."

"She would have broken your damn neck, you idiot. She's lethal as hell. You fall in love with a woman like that, you'd better not piss her off." Dario sounded exasperated. "Ask her brothers. They know."

Valentino studied her face. Yeah. She really would have. "You know that would have taken both of us out. Not too happy you would have contemplated ending your own life just to get back at me. Let's not go there again. If you're royally pissed at me, take your shot, but don't make it so fucking permanent."

"I'm not happy with you." She rolled off of him and sat tailor fashion, pulling her hair up to put it in a knot on top of her head.

"I'd like to continue the conversation," Stefano said. "It's late and I'm certain everyone's tired. We need to get this done. How do you get your woman to spy for you? That seems a little vague."

Val studied Stefano's face for a long time, allowing the silence to stretch out between them. Stefano was in one of the darkest parts of the room, his pinstriped suit making it even harder to see him. All the Ferraros wore those suits, including Emmanuelle. He knew Emme didn't wear much under her suit. He'd had years to watch the Ferraros. He'd had Dario watch them. They were careful. Very careful. Emme was careful. But he noticed how they could disappear at will into those shadows. He didn't know how. It didn't make sense, but they could do it. Suddenly, all the stories, all the old history, the feuds between the families, weren't so much bullshit anymore.

"It appears that the woman we can tie to us can move about undetected in the shadows." Val kept his eyes on Stefano. The man was stone. He didn't so much as blink, but he was fully aware that Val and Dario both knew that the Ferraro family could move freely through the shadows, and that information hadn't come from Emmanuelle.

Valentino could tell Dario was ready for an attack on them. He was as well. Stefano was weighing the danger to his family.

"I've known for certain for a year, Stefano," Val said. "I suspected long before that. Had I wanted to use the information to harm your family, I would have done so." He leaned his head back against the headboard. "The last thing I wanted to do was alienate Emme further."

"If the woman is taken against her will, how is she forced to work for you?" Stefano persisted. "Had Miceli succeeded in kidnapping Grace, if she could have entered the shadows, which she couldn't, how could he force her to work for him?"

Valentino and Dario exchanged a long, puzzled look. Eventually, Val shook his head. "I have no idea. None. Threats? Torture? I wouldn't put anything past Miceli or his sons."

"Is there anything in the myth that would indicate a way to coerce the woman?"

Seduction. According to the story, the merging shadows provided heightened chemistry. Val had experienced that firsthand. The sexual chemistry was explosive. He wasn't going to mention that again. He simply shook his head.

"Unfortunately, I don't have the luxury of asking Giuseppi too many questions. That might be the only way to get the answers you're looking for, and I'm not willing to risk it," Val said. "I'm not certain he has the answers anyway."

"Why?" Stefano asked, steepling his fingers and regarding Val over the top of them.

Val shrugged. He loved his father. *But.* He'd grown up with him. He'd been with him, learned from him, seen and done things he didn't want Emme to ever know about.

"He's very old-school. I don't altogether trust him when it comes to certain things regarding the business. Protecting Emmanuelle has to be my first priority where it wouldn't be his. If he thought she could move through the shadows, he would be ruthless using her against his enemies. He might also think he could get away with blackmailing her by threatening her family. He doesn't quite get that some women are capable of being just as ruthless when protecting their own as he is."

Stefano's expression didn't change. Val hadn't expected to be able to read him. He ruled his family with an iron fist, but he loved them fiercely—and he guarded Emmanuelle. All of her brothers did. Val knew he never would have gotten away with stealing her if she hadn't allowed him to do so. That had been her youth. He'd taken full advantage.

When that first jolt of sexual awareness had hit him, he'd thought a firestorm had struck him. He'd known what those ropes tying her shadows to his meant, he just hadn't believed it. He'd talked to her for a long time, calming her, forming a plan, deciding then on what he would do. He'd discarded his plan dozens of times, but the pull to her had been too strong to ignore.

Looking at Stefano, he could believe what he'd long suspected—her family was made up of lethal assassins. They did move through the shadows. That was another reason he didn't want to let Giuseppi know about Emmanuelle. If his father was ever so irrational as to make a mistake and threaten her, her family could wipe them out and no one would be the wiser.

"How did you plan to get Emme to spy for you?"

"I never planned on using Emmanuelle to spy for me." Valentino's voice rang with truth because it was the truth.

For the first time, Stefano looked away from him to Ricco. The two brothers exchanged a long look Val couldn't interpret.

"Why did you bind her to you so irrevocably if you had no intention of using her as an advantage for your business?" Stefano asked.

Val's gut tightened. He kept his gaze from straying toward Dario. He should have sent him out of the room, not that he would have gone. Dario might have been considered his enforcer, his bodyguard, but Dario didn't take any shit from him and never left his side if he thought he was in danger. Both of them were well aware the Ferraros were extremely dangerous. Dario hadn't been happy allowing both brothers in the room along with Emmanuelle.

"Every chance you got, you placed more ropes on her shadow, until you knew it would be impossible to separate the two of you," Stefano persisted. "You did so deliberately. Tell me why."

They were either going to believe him or they weren't. Valentino Saldi wasn't a man with feelings. He was considered ruthless, merciless and brutal. In a way, binding Emme to him only served to show he was all of those things. He saw her. Wanted her. And he took her. He might have started out seducing her, unsure what their connected shadows meant and wanting to find out, but after spending a small amount of time in her company, he was like a drowning man needing oxygen. Emmanuelle was air to him. Sunshine. Everything good. He'd never laughed more. Never felt better than when he was with her.

"I fell in love with her, and I didn't want to lose her. She was the only good thing I had in my life."

How could he explain himself to a man like Stefano Ferraro, who didn't appear to have a chink in his armor? He had to do things that required him to shut off his soul. To step out of his humanity. His own father required those things of him and then to go shower, change and join his mother for dinner as if nothing had taken place. He had been dead inside for so long until that party. Until Emmanuelle.

Emme managed to bring him back to life. To make him feel a spark of humanity. Each time he was with her, she brought out something better in him. He couldn't give her up or he was lost. He knew it was selfish. He even knew he was risking both of them. He also knew he was that ruthless, merciless, cruel man who would kill for her without a qualm if anyone threatened her. And he had Dario. Dario would protect her the way he did Val.

There was a long silence again. His phone vibrated. He

glanced down at the screen. Emme looked over his shoulder. He should have covered the message.

You're such a pussy, Val.

Val flipped Dario off, but at least the room didn't feel the tension, which was stretched so taut it could have been cut with a knife.

"What do you need, Val?" Stefano said.

Val let out his breath slowly. The Ferraros were going to help him. They weren't going to try to take Emmanuelle from him. He knew he still had a few hurdles to get through with his woman, but if her brothers believed he loved her, then she had to start believing it.

"I can't look weak, and that means calling a meeting immediately. My people will know that Miceli hit us hard. They may have heard rumors we were killed. I'm certain Miceli will have fueled those rumors to disrupt business. That can't happen. We don't want chaos on the streets. I have to know who my enemies are. I'll need a place to meet with my capos. That will be the most difficult part. Finding a place we can protect. The moment word goes out, Miceli's spies will let him know, and he'll have another chance to hit us."

"I have conference rooms hidden here in the hotel that can be used, ones even more protected from civilians than what we used before," Stefano offered. "You wouldn't have to travel far. Your soldiers would have no idea what connections you have, and I can guarantee protection from every direction from inside the hotel as well as underground and the entrances and exits. I can have my cousins here by tomorrow afternoon to help with your protection. No one will see them or us, for that matter, unless anything goes wrong."

It was an offer Val couldn't afford to refuse, even if it came with strings—as long as those strings didn't include giving up Emme.

"In return?"

"You keep the existing truce with my family. All drugs and other crimes out of our territory. No human trafficking in your territories. You stay silent about our family. If a whisper gets out, all bets are off and we come after you, Emme or no Emme." Stefano's tone meant business.

Beside him, Emmanuelle moved, as if she might decide to slide away. He always felt as if she were on the verge of flight. He caught her wrist, just as he had done on so many other occasions, holding her to him.

"Those terms are more than generous, Stefano, when you're risking your lives."

"I'm not unaware that someone has to do the job you do, Val. You set up what you need, let me know and I'll work my end. I'm heading home to my wife. Emme?"

"Emmanuelle and I have things to work out," Val said, tightening his hold on Emme's wrist. He didn't look at her, willing her to go along with him. To stay with him. Willing her to want to work it out.

She remained as taut as a piano wire, but she didn't move off the bed. "I'll stay here for a little while longer, Stefano."

"If you're certain."

"I am."

"I don't want you heading off alone tonight. Miceli knows you're important to Valentino," Stefano said as he stood. "You can use any of the guest rooms in our home, or one of the hotel rooms if you choose."

"Or she can stay with me," Val pointed out, trying not to swear. The man had offered him protection, to be an ally when he needed it most, hadn't tried to take Emmanuelle back and yet was still acting like Emme belonged with the Ferraros, not with Valentino.

Emmanuelle heaved a huge sigh. "Good night, Stefano. Ricco. Thank you for all your help tonight. I appreciate you so much."

"Yes, thank you," Val echoed.

He was grateful the two men walked out, closing the door behind them. Dario stood up and crossed to the far side of the bed, where he could study Emmanuelle's face.

"Now that they're gone, tell us how hurt you really are."

"I told you. I was punched a couple of times. I was counting, breathing, but maybe he got in a few more punches than I thought, because I'm pretty sore."

"Show us."

Emmanuelle sat up straight. "I will not. I'm not wearing anything under my jacket."

Val turned to her, putting her at arm's length. She was very pale, and she was breathing shallowly, something she didn't ordinarily do.

"Take off the jacket, Princess. We have to see what's going on so we can help."

"Dario's here."

Dario made a sound of total exasperation. "Don't be ridiculous, Emme. Do you think I haven't seen women's bodies before? Take the damn jacket off and let me see the damage. I'm fucking tired and I want to go to bed."

Val's hands were already at the buttons. He'd always been intrigued by the fabric and the strange makeup of the buttons down the front. He'd never encountered the feel of the material before. As her seams widened, he saw the dark purple-and-black bruising spread across her generous breasts and down lower, just between and under them.

He swore. "What the fuck, Emme? Why didn't you say something right away?" His fingers brushed lightly over the damage.

Dario went to a pack and removed a first aid kit. "You can't let damage like this go. You know better."

"Are you both going to give me lectures every time I screw up?" she asked, closing her eyes, pretending she wasn't sitting on a bed with her jacket open and two men looking at her black-and-blue naked body. At least she was spared having her brothers in the room.

"Yes," Val and Dario said in stereo.

"That goes on the 'con' side of the list," she murmured as Val spread some kind of cream over the bruising on her breasts.

"I want to go to bed, Emmanuelle," Dario said. "But you have to give me your word of honor, no matter how mad he makes you, or how scared you get, you won't kill him. Or even wound him. If you have to, take a little break and sleep in one of the chairs in here. But I need your word you won't kill him yourself and you'll stay with him and protect him while I get some sleep."

Sometimes Val wanted to strangle Dario with his bare hands. He was the one protecting Emmanuelle, not the other way around. "Get the fuck out. I'm taking care of her. She doesn't need to sleep in a chair and look after me. I can take care of myself."

His phone vibrated and he looked at the screen. Keeping her in the room with you, idiot.

He looked up at Dario. Dario's expression gave nothing away. He and Emme were in a staring match while Val smeared the cream on the bruising just below her breasts.

"Word of honor, Emme," Dario insisted.

"You know I have a temper, Dario. It might be hard to keep. He makes me so angry sometimes."

"I'm well aware."

"He's absolutely stubborn and wants everything his way."

"Yeah. I've known him a long time. But I can't let you kill him."

"Not even a little wound? The gunshots didn't do much to him. Stabbing him might straighten him up."

Val tried not to laugh, but he couldn't help the smile. She sounded so sincere.

"Not a scratch. Word of honor, Emme. And you have to stay in the room with him."

She heaved a sigh. "Fine, Dario, but you owe me."

Dario shoved his phone into his pocket and had been turning away from the bed, but he turned back with a shocked expression. "What?"

"Yeah, if I have to behave, no matter how outrageous he gets, then you owe me. I'll think about your repayment."

Dario glared at Val. "I don't know if you're worth the crap I have to put up with sometimes." He stalked out and shut the door just a little too firmly.

Emmanuelle burst out laughing. "I've never managed to rile him."

Val tugged at the sleeves of her jacket. "Take this off. You can wear one of my tees. Dario grabbed a few we had at the lake house. You'll be more comfortable. There's some Tylenol on the nightstand. And just so you know, you've managed to rile Dario plenty of times."

"I have?"

She slid off the bed, away from him, and the moment she was where he couldn't reach her, he had that same feeling he always got—that he might lose her. He immediately threw back the covers and put his feet on the floor. He was far stronger than anyone thought. He had three wounds that were of any significance, one of which hurt like hell and two others that he certainly felt but were nothing in comparison to the one throbbing so painfully.

"Yeah, babe, you infuriate him."

"I do? That's great. Someone needs to infuriate Dario. I thought he was pretty much unflappable."

"That's what they said about me until you came along."

He watched her as she sank into the chair her brother had occupied. She was beautiful. His Emme. He could breathe again, now that she was in the same room with him. Two long years where she wouldn't even speak to him. Interestingly enough, she hadn't blocked Dario's number, but she'd blocked his. She'd kept that line open, his only faint hope.

Emmanuelle looked up from where she was bent over, unzipping her boot, a look of amusement on her face. She hadn't yet covered up, and her full breasts tumbled forward, the bruising dark spreading out over her otherwise flawless skin. She could never be called thin, and he liked that. He had never wanted thin. He liked that she had breasts and hips. He liked her curves. He liked everything about her.

"Two fucking years, Emmanuelle." He said it quietly.

"I know how long it's been, Valentino." She pulled off the boot and set it aside. Keeping her head down, she unzipped the second boot.

"You wouldn't give me a chance to explain. To talk to you. That gutted me."

Her boot dropped to the floor, and she sat up slowly, her blue eyes finally meeting his. She saw pain there.

"Too many things between us, Val. You know that. The ropes. The blonde. Your family. Mine." She shook her head. "I know you told Stefano you loved me, but that wasn't the entire reason for binding me to you. Not in the beginning. I saw your face. You were so smug about it. You knew exactly what you were doing. I would lie awake at night thinking about how you looked and how you distracted me by kissing me. I let you do that. I let you take me over. I was ashamed of myself for not fighting, for putting my family in danger."

"We're going to take this one step at a time. I did tell your brother the truth. I do love you. I felt very smug and satisfied every single time I managed to get more ropes around your shadow. In the beginning, you were good at hiding from me. But eventually you let your guard down. I was happy about that. Elated, in fact. I did know what I was doing. I started researching our weird Saldi myth. If I could find a way to tie you to me permanently, you better believe I was going to do it."

She stood up and pulled the tee over her head, allowing the material to drop around her curves. He was taller than her by almost a foot, and the shirt hung on her. She reached under the hem and opened her trousers.

"Your family was never in danger. If anything, my family is in danger from yours. Baby, I don't want you to ever feel shame because you want to be with me. Is it because of who I am? A Saldi?"

Emmanuelle shook her head. "You know what we do, or you can guess. Your family is out in the open where mine is literally hidden in the shadows. It would be a little hypocritical of me pointing fingers at you."

He still wasn't exactly certain what her family did, but they had taken care of Miceli's men efficiently. More than efficiently. Thinking like a leader, he had to admit, forming

an alliance with Emme's family would be more than benefi-
cial to him.

Val didn't like the fact that she carefully folded her trousers, then unfolded them and arranged them over the back of
the chair.

"Come here."

Emmanuelle sighed and turned her head to look at him
over her shoulder. She looked so damn heartbreakingly young.
His woman was fierce, and yet right then, she looked vulnerable and afraid. He hated that he was the one who'd put that
look on her face when she should always feel safe and protected with him.

"You do know it doesn't really matter what we feel for
each other, don't you? It isn't like we can sneak around like
we used to." She ignored his directive and walked around the
room, one hand moving along the wall, staying as far from
him as possible. "You have a life already mapped out for you,
Val. You said yourself you can't change it. My brother even
implied you couldn't. You're taking over as head of the Saldi
family, aren't you?"

She turned her head to look at him. Once again, her blue
eyes met his. He felt the impact of those twin brilliant gems
piercing him all the way to his heart.

"Yes, I am." He made the statement quietly, watching her
closely.

She nodded. "I have a life as well, Val. I have responsibilities. I have a job I don't want to give up."

"And what is your job?"

She hesitated. "One I trained for and I'm good at it. I work
with my family."

"Why would that mean you can't be with me, Emme?
Many women are married and still have jobs. Did you think
I would be so controlling that I would insist you wait at home
chained to my bed?" He would dictate that if he could, but
she might cut his throat. Emmanuelle was not the kind of
woman to take kindly to dictators, no matter how much she
loved him.

"Yes." She frowned at him. "You're very controlling. You order, you don't ask. I don't think you've ever asked."

"I haven't?" She made him want to smile.

"No."

"Then I'm asking now. Please come here to me." He widened his legs and pointed to the spot between his thighs. He wanted her close. He needed to touch her. To feel her skin. Her heat. To know that after two years of silence, she was really there with him, even if she was still struggling with the idea of being with him.

"I walked into that one, didn't I?" A hint of laughter mixed with resignation in her voice. She left the safety of the opposite side of the enormous room and came toward him slowly.

Val's breath caught in his lungs. His woman. She smelled like heaven should smell. She looked like redemption. He waited for her to come all the way to him. She took her damn sweet time, but he didn't hurry her, knowing she was struggling. The one thing Emmanuelle had for certain was courage. She faced every threat head-on, and he was a threat to her freedom. To her way of life. To so many things. Still, she came to him.

"We don't make sense, Val."

"We make perfect sense, Emme. We make our own sense. You're just afraid. You've always been afraid of what we'd be together."

She shook her head. "Your way of life is brutal, Valentino. I can see the toll it takes on you. On Dario. You're both good men, and yet you have to do things, terrible things neither of you like, but that you do anyway."

She pressed her hands to his thighs, careful to keep her palm from coming too close to the bandage on the left one. He could feel the imprint of her hand, her fingers, on the hard muscles there and was grateful he was skin to skin with her.

"What of you, baby? You do things you don't always want to do." His hand came up to trace one of the worst bruises that spread over the curve of her right breast. He mapped it out over the material of the T-shirt from memory alone. It was easy enough since he never forgot anything to do with Emmanuelle.

"What I do happens fast most of the time, and no one sees it coming. You." She stopped and shook her head. "I can see things in your eyes, Val. You turn off. You go cold. You just stop being human. A person doesn't do that unless they have to. I heard stories about the things Giuseppi did in retaliation if someone betrayed him. I didn't want to believe it because when I met him, he seemed so sweet, but then I heard Stefano talk to him a few times, and I knew the stories were true. The fact that I tried to talk to Stefano about us and he wouldn't listen was also a good indicator that the stories were true. They are, aren't they?"

Val had always known this moment with her would come. He wanted to wrap his arms around her and hold her tight. Already, there was so much keeping them apart. He had to give her the truth. She was giving him the truth. If they could just find a way to get beyond the two violent storms colliding, they might have a chance of making it. He just needed Emmanuelle to want to fight with him, not against him.

"The stories are true, Emme. I imagine you heard the milder versions. I lived them. I was forced to participate in them. More than once, it was a family I knew, a kid I went to school with. One I liked. Growing up like that, you grow up fast, you learn you can't trust anyone. I had Greta telling me one thing and Giuseppi another. I didn't trust Miceli, Angelo or Tommaso, but Dario and I became inseparable. At first Giuseppi tried to change that, but I wouldn't let him. It was the smartest thing I ever did."

"Giuseppi really tortured men? Killed entire families?"

"Giuseppi often had me do those things for him once I was in my teens, Emme. Dario and me. That was my life. The minute I entered his household, Giuseppi began training me to take over. I had to be the best at everything. That meant killing and torture as well. And let's not forget about taking me to the strip clubs to learn my skills there."

Val expected to see horror and rejection on her face. She stood in front of him, her eyes soft, her expression filled with compassion, with love, as only Emme could look at him. She leaned into him and put her head on his shoulder.

"I don't know what we're going to do, Val. I really don't. I love you more than anything, at least I can give you that. Just don't say *wife*, or *marriage*, or anything remotely like that. I'm not having a child of mine raised like you were. You probably would never want a child of yours raised like I was."

"Not by your mother, anyway." He made a poor attempt at humor as he closed his arms around her. It felt right to hold her. She belonged in his arms. "Wash your face and do whatever it is you like to do before you go to bed, but Princess, sleep here tonight. Dario will be happy. You can slip home tomorrow and get a few things. I imagine you'll want to help out with security."

She nodded. "I imagine so. Stefano always heads up the operations. He is the ultimate law, and everyone answers to him. The cousins will come in from New York and LA. Maybe San Francisco, but most likely LA. Elie's here, and that's good. He's fast. And we've got a good ground crew. Dario can set up someone he trusts to liaise with them."

"Dario will most likely do that himself. Stop talking and get ready for bed."

She flashed him a smile. "There you go again."

He raised an eyebrow.

She just shook her head.

He knew exactly what she was talking about. He hadn't asked anyone to do anything in years. He had been groomed to be head of the family. Everyone obeyed his orders—with the exception of Dario. And now, most likely, Emmanuelle.

CHAPTER EIGHT

Valentino had to put Emmanuelle completely out of his mind in order to become who he had to be. The moment Dario had returned to the room, she had disappeared into the bathroom with her clothing, dressed and then was gone. She hadn't even kissed him good-bye. He would be talking to her about that, but much later. Right now, the Saldi *famiglia* needed to know they had a strong leader, that Giuseppi had stepped down and Valentino had risen to lead them.

"Custanzu Parisi has been in my life since the day I was born, Dario," Val said as he dressed carefully, putting on his suit jacket. "He's been my father's advisor and friend for nearly his entire life. He was best man at his wedding and sat at our dinner table for years."

Dario holstered his favorite weapon and then added a second to the harness on the other side of his chest. He said nothing.

"No one knew the layout of our house with the safe room or the hidden escape route to take Giuseppi out other than you, me and Parisi. No one else. There are no blueprints. No workers to be asked. No staff in the house ever knew. Miceli didn't know. If you didn't betray Giuseppi, and I didn't, that leaves only Parisi. That leaves a man my father loved like a true brother. Did you have Bernado look into his financials?"

Valentino had found Bernado Macaluso when the kid's mother had been working as a barista in one of the coffee shops he frequented. The boy had been a little strange and had always been on an old iPad. One day Val had noticed the kid and his mother both were upset. She'd had a black eye and bruises. The kid had been beat up all to hell and the iPad was gone. Val had told himself to stay out of it, but he'd never been able to stand looking at women with bruises. He'd followed the two home, had found out her landlord had demanded more than his rent and that she had nowhere else to go.

Valentino had taken care of the landlord, found a nicer place for them to stay, bought the kid a new iPad and a computer and a friendship had been born. Not just friendship. Loyalty. When Bernado's mother had gotten cancer, Bernado had gone to Val, and Val had made certain she received the best of care until she passed. Bernado worked for him exclusively as his tech whiz. Right now, he was the bookkeeper as well. Dario and Val were still looking for someone to help take that load off.

Dario nodded slowly. "I sent the reports on his financials to you, along with everything else Bernado found. Parisi liked the strip clubs. We all know that. Apparently, Marge is fond of taking video of her more wealthy clients and especially any of your father's men."

"We have strip clubs, Dario. Why use Miceli's?"

"Miceli started running dungeons beneath the strip clubs; an edgier addition, he called it. You were briefed."

Val nodded. There were so many things he had been briefed on during Greta's illness. Too many things his father had let slide and that he was trying to catch up on. He hadn't visited the newer additions to Miceli's strip clubs. They paid their dues on a regular basis and brought in a shit ton of money. He had so many other fires to put out that he had put that on a waiting list.

He didn't give a damn what others wanted to do with their sex lives as long as it was consensual.

He narrowed his gaze at Dario. "It is consensual, isn't it? Parisi didn't screw up and rape someone, did he?"

Dario sighed. "You have all the videos, but does it matter whether they're fake or real? He didn't come to your father to fix things. He has a wife and grown children. Grandchildren. He took what Miceli offered and sold out not only Giuseppi, but you."

There wasn't so much as a whisper of venom in Dario's voice. His voice matched Val's. They could have been talking about the weather, not about a man they knew they were going to make an example of. He wouldn't be killed clean. He couldn't be. Every single member of their family as well as those in neighboring territories had to know what would happen if you betrayed a Saldi. If you double-crossed one. If you lied to one or cheated one.

"All the capos on the list you trust, Dario?"

Dario gave him a faint smile. "I trust you, Val. And maybe Severu Catalano. The others on the list I believe are with us. They have good crews and are in control of them. They earn good money for the family. The ones on the second list are suspect. The ones on the third have their hands in our pockets, which means they are stealing from us. Bernado sent you reports on how deep. The second list, he's running their financials and looking at surveillance, but we aren't going to know if all of them are caught in Miceli's net."

Valentino shrugged. "I'll know when I see them today. Have you checked out the conference and interrogation rooms where Stefano is allowing us to take Parisi and anyone else we need to talk to?"

Dario nodded. "Very good accommodations, although, Val, it's risky to get too far in bed with Stefano Ferraro. The hotel is fine, and the conference rooms, that's smart. Forming an alliance, I get that. Using his interrogation room, that could get us in real trouble. I searched for hidden cameras and will again, but how far can we really trust them?"

Valentino understood Dario's worry. He had the same one himself. On the other hand, where could they safely take prisoners? To their own warehouses? They owned cops, but at the moment, they didn't know who they could trust. That had to be sorted. They had to come out on top. Feared. They had to take back the streets and shut Miceli down. He either trusted Stefano or he didn't. At this point, he didn't have enough men he could trust to take back the streets. He had no choice but to trust Stefano.

"It's a calculated risk, Dario, but Stefano loves Emme. Emmanuelle is bound to me. She can't get away. He doesn't want to risk her. He also despises Miceli and what he stands for. He'll want to help me stop the trafficking ring and shut down the auctions. He's not going to betray me. That would be the same as betraying Emme."

"He could hold on to a video and use it later."

"The risk isn't Stefano seeing us. I have the feeling what we do won't be anything new to him." For Valentino, the risk was Emme seeing what he did. That ruthless, merciless man who would torture Parisi, cut him to pieces and leave him on his doorstep while Val's clever computer whiz kid took apart every business and bank account, stripping the family of their money, leaving them with nothing. Instead of having the care that Giuseppi had always shown the family of even a fallen soldier of the lowest rank, Parisi's family would have nothing. That would be the fate of a traitor. Giuseppi would have killed the entire family. He would have done so in front of Parisi if he could have, or he would have told him what he was going to do while he was watching him being hacked to pieces. That was the old way to send a message, and it was one that never failed to be understood.

Dario sighed. "I get what you're saying, Val. Emmanuelle is going to have to accept who you are. You're head of the Saldi family. If she's going to be your wife . . ."

Val lifted his head, hands on his tie, eyes staring straight into Dario's. "There is no *if*. She is going to be my wife. She will be the mother of my children."

Dario shook his head. "You never make anything easy. The Ferraro family can move through the shadows, Val. I've watched them carefully for the last few years. Once you told me about Emmanuelle's shadow and I observed it for myself, I watched her closely first, and then her brothers. They're clever. They wear those suits for a reason. They entertain for a reason. They always have an alibi."

Again, their eyes met. Valentino nodded. "They can be anywhere and no one would know. They can hear their enemies speak. If they want to come into a home and kill someone undetected, they can do so and leave without ever being seen."

"I researched until I found the original Saldi myth as well," Dario said. "Over the years, fathers told sons watered-down versions, or perhaps portions were lost in translation. Who knows? Perhaps because no one ever saw a woman with a shadow ours rushed to imprison, they did come to believe it was a myth, just as we did."

"After the massacre of the Ferraro family, there must have been so few of them and they scattered over various countries in order to remain safe," Val said. "It would have taken years to build their families back up. It's no wonder no Saldi ever ran across one of them. Why didn't you pursue Nicoletta harder, Dario, once you saw her shadow?"

Dario shrugged. "I wanted her safe from Miceli, but she wasn't mine. I'm not nice. She needed nice. I'll never be that. But Miceli wasn't getting her."

Val nodded. He moved his arms to make certain he had a range of motion and he could do so without pain. It was the wound in his leg that worried him the most. "When I stand, you're going to have to cover for me. That's the one time I'm awkward and someone might notice. It just takes a few seconds for my body to adjust and then I'm fine."

"I know we needed to get on this immediately, Val, but I don't like it. We're really having to rely on Stefano and his family for your protection. I did see the security room. Emilio and Enzo showed me everything. Very high-tech, better than anything we have. Bernado was drooling over their equipment, and they had no problem letting him in the room with them. He's in seventh heaven. I will say Stefano's cousins are very forthcoming anytime I ask for information. I was given full access to the underground levels as well as blueprints. Emilio sent those to my phone after giving me a personal tour."

"Cameras?"

"Everywhere, but out of sight. He will have them off in the conference room unless I signal I want them on and Bernado will tell him. Normally, I wouldn't allow phones anywhere you're speaking, but in this case, Bernado, with the equipment Emilio has, can tell if anyone is recording and it will give us one more tool to find traitors," Dario said.

Valentino nodded. "I will bring my father in myself with you escorting us."

"When he leaves, who do we trust enough to bring him back? Because I'm not leaving you alone with known traitors," Dario stated.

Val shook his head. "Have you considered, even once, that I give the orders?"

"Not really."

Val refrained from smiling, but was grateful he had Dario. He might have been appointing Severu Catalano as his official advisor, but it was always going to be Dario he listened to first. "Stefano's bodyguards will take him back up. You have to admit, they're every bit as good as anything we've got and we can trust them."

Dario nodded. "Bernado will have eyes on them all the way back to this suite. No one will be able to get to him here. I presume they'll stay to guard him."

"That's the plan."

Valentino glanced at his watch. "Let's get this done. We'll need to talk to Giuseppi about Custanzu Parisi. If he hasn't figured it out yet, it's only because he doesn't want to know the truth. He can't go into the meeting without knowing.

That will make him look weak. I don't want that for him. Not ever."

His chest felt heavy as he walked with Dario through the large suite to his father's room. They'd given him the bedroom with the best view of the city. Val gave a perfunctory knock and opened the door. His father sat in the leather armchair facing the gas fireplace that wasn't on. He looked tired and sad.

"Should you be up, Val?" Giuseppi didn't look as Valentino crossed the room and greeted him with a kiss to the top of his head. "We should put this off for a few days."

That told Val his father knew his best friend had betrayed him and he was more than ready to hand over the reins of his empire to his son.

"You know we can't do that without losing everything. The meeting has been called, and capos are waiting. You have only to make a short appearance and announce you are stepping down and I am taking over. I will handle everything from there. Demetrio and Drago will escort you back to this room. It is safer here until I know who to trust and who Miceli has corrupted with his flesh trafficking."

Giuseppi heaved a sigh and then pushed up with both hands off the arms of the chair. "He always said there was so much money to be made in those markets. Young children. When I say *young*, I mean he talked of selling little boys and girls. And then there was his idea of taking teens and selling them. Using them in moving brothels. Women to be sold or used the same way. He kept coming to me over and over, and I kept turning him down. He showed me the numbers to be made, more than weapons, more than drugs, but I wouldn't hear of it. I kept my word to the Ferraro family, but more, the idea sickened me. Everyone has a line they won't cross. That was mine."

"I feel the same way," Valentino assured him. "Why do you feel guilty?"

"I tried to talk to him. To convince him, but I didn't try

hard enough. Women came easy to him, and he never respected them. He treated them cruelly and discarded them as fast as he acquired them. He raised Angelo and Tommaso to be like him. The way he treated Dario's mother. The things that happened to his own son. He wanted to raise Dario the same way, but it was too late." He looked across the room at Dario, his faded eyes filled with sorrow. "Your mother was beautiful and so sweet. She was cursed the day she caught his eye."

As always when his mother was mentioned, Dario shut down, his features completely expressionless, his dark eyes looking like the pits of hell.

"You know who betrayed us," Val said. "You have to know."

Giuseppi sighed again. "There was only one other. He tore out my heart."

"I will take care of it," Val said. "You have only to pass on the reins to me. I will identify the traitors in our family. I may miss one or two at this meeting, but in the end, I will find them all. The message will go out today that we are strong, that we will not tolerate betrayal and it is business as usual even if it is war with Miceli. And it is war."

Giuseppi took Val's arm and leaned heavily on him for a moment before straightening. "You're certain your injuries will allow you to do this? You can't show any weakness, Val."

Valentino raised an eyebrow. "I am your son. I never forgot one single lesson. Not one single word. You know that about me." It was the truth. Valentino retained everything, even when he wished he couldn't. "There is no need to remind me." Even to his father, he couldn't show weakness. He was taking over whether Giuseppi liked it or not. There had been too many mistakes, and there couldn't be any more. Already, the war had spilled onto the streets. He didn't want innocent blood spilled.

The reporters were all over the story at the lake house, with helicopter crashes and bodies found on rooftops and in boats and vehicles. It looked like a war zone, all men known to the police as soldiers for the mafia, yet the explanations

Stefano and Vittorio as well as the doctor had given about the attack left the Ferraro family, Giuseppi and Valentino in the clear. Lawyers for both families had stepped in and fielded questions after they had briefly spoken with law enforcement, but that didn't stop the frenzy of reporters from trying to find answers.

Fortunately, the Ferraro Hotel was a luxury hotel, and it was business as usual. Famous clientele came and went. No one thought anything of the expensive cars driving into the exclusive parking garage. Once there, those cars were directed to a private elevator and taken to a garage on an underground floor to be first vetted by guards before the occupants were allowed out to be escorted to the conference room.

Demetrio and Drago pushed open the double doors to the conference room and entered first. Instantly, all talk stopped. No one knew them, and this was a private meeting. The two stepped to either side of the door, and Dario strode in. He scanned the room with dark, piercing eyes. Nothing escaped him. Nothing. He noted each man, whether they looked nervous, excited, passive or like they were just waiting to see what was going to happen. His gaze touched on Custanzu Parisi. He was seated at the right hand of the table. The advisor to the Don. The shark. He was smiling. Looking relaxed. Serene.

Giuseppi entered, walking in with a straight back and straight shoulders. Head up. His gaze sharp and a smile of greeting on his face for his capos. Valentino strode in behind him, tall, his frame muscular, looking fit, eyes scanning the room just as Dario's had. Giuseppi went straight to the head of the table, nodding to those calling out greetings. Valentino took the seat to his left. Demetrio and Drago stepped out of the room and closed the double doors. Dario stood back against the wall, facing the capos, in between Giuseppi and Valentino.

Valentino knew the lighting in the conference room created shadows, and somewhere inside those shadows were guardians to help Dario should they be attacked. Bernado,

Emilio and Enzo were watching each of the capos in the room, sweeping them for electronic equipment as well as hacking into their phones for personal information.

"As you can see, the rumors of my demise are premature," Giuseppi said with a quick laugh. "My brother has declared war on us. He attacked me and my son and nephew at my family home and then again at the lake house." He smiled the smile of a wolf and picked up the espresso that Val had poured for him from one of the small carafes the Ferraros' select staff had set out in front of each chair. Taking a sip, he placed the cup precisely on the table and looked around. "He lost a small army, but no doubt he will try to regroup and come at us again. I believe it is a young man's game to wage war such as this, and given the success he has achieved, I have decided it is time to turn the reins of the Saldi empire over to Valentino, my son."

Giuseppi rose and turned to Val, who also stood. He took Val's hand, where the ring sat heavy on his finger. "You will do the things our family needs for you to do."

Valentino inclined his head. Giuseppi turned to the man at his right, the one who had been there since he'd been a boy. Giuseppi took the man's face between his hands and kissed each cheek and then slowly turned and walked from the room without a backward glance.

There was a long, heavy silence. Valentino allowed the silence to stretch out after the double doors had swung shut with a thud. He surveyed the faces looking up at him from around the very large oval table. The Saldi territory was extremely large. He had deliberately, long before he took over, cultivated men he was certain he could count on. Those Dario had placed in strategic positions in case the ones they suspect of being traitors had already conspired to assassinate him.

Twice he saw Parisi glance toward one of the capos to his left, an older man by the name of Pius Banetti. He didn't make the mistake of looking at the man, but he also had been a friend of Giuseppi for years. Bernado had flagged him as suspicious simply because unexplained money had begun to show up in his account two years earlier. Small sums that had begun to increase monthly. Crews made their own money, but it was always accounted for. That money was not explained, nor could Bernado find a source from any of the businesses Banetti and his soldiers ran or were responsible for.

"First, before we get onto anything else, I want you to know what I expect of you. It will be business as usual. There will be no slowing down. I will expect reports from each of you, and regular payments. Anyone already behind has one week to catch up or you will present yourself to me when called on. Hopefully, you will bring the missing cash at that time with an explanation." He let the threat hang for a moment. He already had a vicious reputation. He didn't need to lay details out for anyone.

"Know that my people have been paying attention to the books and scrutinizing each business. There have been too many shortfalls lately. My mother was ill, and my father wasn't paying as much attention as he could have been. His friends, ones he took care of for years, took advantage. I see this and it angers me. Any who have cheated him during this time of his mourning, when they should have been supporting him, had better bring to me what is owed."

He kept his tone soft. There was no need to raise his voice. His word was law. He had cultivated his reputation over the last few years, working at Giuseppi's side, doing the dirty work, showing no mercy, his features blank, eyes dead. That reputation stood him in good stead now. The capos, old and young, exchanged nervous looks or stared into their espresso cups.

"The Saldi family does not sell children. We have made that very clear to everyone in our territories. We do not tolerate the selling of children in our streets. We don't take them from their parents and sell them. Any who have profited from this business is a traitor to us and will be considered so. You will be hunted, dealt with, and so will your families. Every single one of you swore an oath to my father. To the Saldi name. To me. You knew the rules of our business and understood them clearly."

A ripple of unease went through the room at the reminder of not only what the betrayer would suffer but also the families of the betrayer. Out of the corner of his eye, Valentino caught the blur of movement as Alceu Regio, a longtime capo with Giuseppi, went for his gun. He was seated to the left, where they had placed the capos they were the most suspicious of. These were the ones who had frequented Miceli's strip bars. They had been friends with both Giuseppi and Miceli, and friends with Parisi. The men had either gone to school together or lived in the neighborhood growing up.

Dario had deliberately seated those capos in between the men he trusted the most. He had done so carefully, just as a precaution, an added insurance, if in the event that he couldn't get to anyone making an attempt on Valentino's life, or one of the Ferraros couldn't, those capos they trusted could.

Before Regio could pull his weapon, he was dragged from his chair by the two capos seated on either side of him, two of the men Val and Dario had cultivated over the last two years and had recommended to Giuseppi to be brought into the family as young capos. They had Regio stripped of all weapons and his hands bound with zip ties. He was escorted to the far side of the room.

Valentino barely gave him a glance and continued speaking as if nothing had happened. "Miceli could not have carried out his attack without help. There are those within our family, men like Regio, who betrayed us." He turned to look at Parisi. "A trusted brother."

Custanzu Parisi widened his eyes in shock. "Valentino. What are you saying? Surely, you aren't accusing me of betraying your *famiglia*? I have known you since you were a boy. I've known your father since he was a boy. I have been at his side for longer than you've been alive."

"And you betrayed him. You led Miceli's assassins right to him." Val kept his voice low and even. He was surprised at the sudden surge of rage erupting in his belly and shooting through his body, the need to hurt this man like he'd hurt Giuseppi. "We found the evidence. The videos. The money. You betrayed him. You betrayed your family."

For a long moment, Parisi stared at him, as if making up his mind whether to continue to deny the truth or just admit it. Finally, he sighed. "I told your father countless times it was a mistake to love a woman. He wouldn't listen to me. One marries for many reasons, Valentino. You marry to gain territory. You marry to form alliances."

"It is *Don* Saldi. Do not forget who you are speaking to."

Parisi inclined his head and then looked around him at the lush conference room. "You chose wisely when you pursued the young Ferraro girl. She is impressionable. I told Giuseppi this. To make an alliance with her family is the ultimate coup. That is an acceptable goal with a woman. One marries to have children. But you don't love, Val. Don't make that mistake. If you take this oath to lead, you give your life in service and you can't be divided the way Giuseppi was. I was his advisor, his underboss, but he refused to listen. He put Greta before our *famiglia*."

Val hit him hard. First one cheek, then the other, snapping his head left then right, nearly breaking his neck. He did it casually, when he didn't feel casual at all.

"My father always put the business first. Always. You wanted to sell children. He didn't. That had nothing to do with him loving his wife. Some men can love their women; others merely are cheaters and have no integrity. Had my father been paying attention, he would have realized that if you could break your vows to the woman giving you children, you would break your vow to him, to our brotherhood."

There was utter contempt in his voice because he felt utter contempt. He jerked his head toward Parisi, and the same two young capos, Luca Amato and Quintu Noto, who had taken control of Alceu Regio, pulled Custanzu Parisi none too gently from his chair and bound him as well.

"Pius Banetti, you have been frequenting my uncle's strip

clubs and accepting money from him in large amounts. Perhaps you would care to explain to all of us why Miceli has been paying you so much cash," Val continued, leveling his gaze at the capo, who also had been a longtime friend of Giuseppi's. To Valentino, these three men were the worst of the betrayers.

Banetti tried to bluster, beads of sweat visible on his forehead. "Val, you must have it wrong." He looked behind him to see if either of the two capos who had put Parisi in restraints were close to him. When they weren't, out of sheer desperation, he went for his gun.

The two capos on either side of him instantly were on him, one driving his wrist to the table, pinning it there, the other hitting him hard across his cheek with the barrel of a gun. Blood spurted, and Banetti slumped sideways. The two dragged him backward away from the table.

Romeo and Tore Vitale were also newer recruits Dario and Valentino had been instrumental in bringing in as made men and then up through the ranks to captain their own crews. Like Quintu Noto, Caj Lastra and Luca Amato, Valentino and Dario had kept the closer ties secret even from Giuseppi, other than to drop a word now and then to advance the five capos in the eyes of the Don.

"Gentlemen, if you would escort the prisoners to the interrogation room, the rest of us have a small amount of business to conduct," Valentino said. He knew that would put the others at ease. There were two more capos suspected. He hoped they were just lax in their business, and not traitors. He would give them the chance to prove themselves one way or another.

Dario moved for the first time, walking ahead of the four capos with their prisoners to the double doors. When the doors opened there were two men waiting to lead the capos with their prisoners, Tomas and Cosimo Abatangelo, bodyguards for the Ferraro family and unknown to the majority of the Saldi capos. The doors swung closed again, and once more there was silence. Dario turned back to the room, his dark eyes sweeping over the rest of the men there, no expression on his face.

Valentino had deliberately allowed the others to catch a glimpse of the strangers leading his trusted younger capos to an unknown location. That would just enhance the mystery surrounding him. He had defeated Miceli's army at the lake house and turned the police investigation back on Miceli. He didn't appear to be at death's door. He had ferreted out three of the worst traitors in the organization. He had use of a luxury hotel and knew his way around in it. He had seemingly made allies of a family long sought after by not only the Saldis but many of the other families throughout Chicago and other states, and in other countries. For Valentino to have pulled it off signaled a major feat.

Valentino knew Emmanuelle and her family were somewhere hidden in the shadows. They'd heard every word of Parisi's speech. The worst of it was, in some ways it was the truth. It was a coup to have Emme tied to him and an alliance formed with the Ferraro family. Every one of her brothers would hear that and be upset on her behalf. Elie Archambault would be angry as well. And what of Emme? She was looking for reasons why they shouldn't be together. She also had her doubts about Val's sincerity when it came to why he'd tied her to him. He pushed all that out of his mind. He had to conduct business. Go forward.

"We are at war, gentlemen, but I expect business as usual. Your soldiers will carry on just as they normally would. They will learn to be on alert at all times and watch each other's backs. As for Miceli and his attempt to kill my father and me, we will retaliate and take over his businesses. Everything. We will be raiding each of Miceli's businesses and taking them down. Already, we've stripped his bank accounts, including his offshore ones. He'll need his capos to pay him from those businesses, and we're taking those away from him."

Dario suddenly moved up behind one of the capos sitting on the left side. He had been a man they were on the fence about. Dario reached around him and took a cell phone from his hands and tossed it onto the table in front of Val. When the man tried to reach for a weapon, Dario stopped him, a knife to his throat. He leaned in close.

"I'll be visiting your family, Arturo, you treacherous fuck. Kill them all? Kill everyone in the room? Does that mean you, too? Or are you wearing this red tie so they'll know who you are?" Dario didn't wait for an answer. He slit the man's throat and then, as he let go, slammed the blade into the back of his skull.

Valentino reached for the cell. The message to Angelo Saldi, Miceli's son, was clear, although even though Arturo had hit send, the message hadn't gone out. It had been blocked by those keeping watch in the control room. Arturo's body slowly slumped forward. The capo beside him shoved him down and onto the floor.

Val still faced over forty capos, most of whom his father had "made," which meant he was still in quite a bit of danger. The territory was large, and they needed men for legitimate and illegitimate businesses. Most of the captains ran their own crews separately and rarely interacted with one another. Meetings such as this one, bringing them all together, were rare for a reason. One traitor knowing of such a meeting and giving the location could have a team of assassins suddenly showing up. If any of the others were in on the conspiracy to wipe out the rest of the Saldi men, they weren't wearing red, or any distinguishing clothing that Val could see.

"Severu Catalano." He beckoned the man to whom Dario and he had been the closest as they had grown up. Severu was a couple of years older than them, and had been in the organization longer, but he had proven his loyalty to both many times. He was calm, intelligent and not afraid to oppose Valentino's point of view if he honestly thought he was wrong. He was good at strategy, at not missing details. Like Valentino, he had served in the military, and he was utterly cold and ruthless when need be.

Severu stood up slowly and walked around the table to

come to Valentino's side. He looked puzzled and had a shade of wariness in his brown eyes, but otherwise moved right up to face Val. He didn't look to see where Dario was, nor did he have a hand near his weapons.

"It appears, Severu Catalano, that I am in need of an underboss. I didn't have the time to discuss it with you ahead of time. The position is for life and carries tremendous responsibilities." Valentino stared intently into Severu's eyes. They'd known each other a long time. This was a dangerous role he was asking of his friend. The man, like Val, like Dario, would always have a target on his back.

Val detested putting Severu on the spot, but there was no one else. If he didn't take the position, there was only Dario whom Valentino trusted to that extent, and he had plans for Dario. Dario wouldn't like those plans and would fight him all the way on them, but would eventually see it was the only solution to the problem that would be cropping up hopefully very soon if all went the way Valentino planned.

"I would be honored to serve you and our family," Severu said without hesitation. He kissed Val's ring, and they embraced. He took the chair at Val's right that Parisi had been forced to vacate.

Val knew many of the capos would consider Severu too young to be underboss, as many of them had been in the outfit years longer and had more experience, but they were his father's men, not his. That meant that over the years they had also been around Miceli. Miceli had charm when he wanted and he could be persuasive. Every chance he got, he brought up his belief that trafficking was the new way to make the most money. Others were doing it, and the Saldi *famiglia* should as well, otherwise they would fall behind.

The dead body was removed and all signs of his demise with him before the servers were called in to bring the food. All talk ceased until they were gone.

The rest of the meeting was spent with capos mainly reintroducing themselves to Valentino, swearing their fidelity and letting Severu know their businesses and when they turned their profits over to the bookkeeper. What they owed, and if they were behind. Three were behind, one seriously.

Valentino sat at the head of the table as each capo came to him and laid out their information in a succinct way. Caj Lastra was in his thirties, with dark hair and even darker eyes. He was a good-looking man but for the strain in the lines showing on his face. He swore his fidelity, renewing his oath, and seemed sincere, but again, Val caught the tension in his jaw and around his mouth. He was one of the men Val and Dario had brought to Giuseppi's attention and had helped guide to his current position. They had counted on him to be loyal to them.

"There is a problem with your bookkeeping," Val stated, not giving the man a chance to make any mistakes by trying to lie his way out.

"Yes, Mr. Saldi, there is a problem, and it is becoming more of a problem. I haven't been able to find the leak. It's been going on for the last seven months. It started small and has continued every week, someone siphoning the profits. If it came from one business, I would be able to pinpoint the thief, but it doesn't."

Bernado confirmed that Caj was telling the truth. He had been going over his books thoroughly and said the thief was hacking in from outside and transferring money out of the accounts. Each transfer was for different amounts, and each was taken at different times, seemingly random. Caj had paid what was due to Giuseppi in full up until three months ago, all the while paying his men without taking his own cut. But the money disappearing was becoming substantial to the point he couldn't pay both Giuseppi and his men. His soldiers needed the money to live on, so he paid his men, giving Giuseppi less and less.

"Why didn't you come to my father and tell him this was a problem?"

"I went to Parisi after the fourth month, when I could see it was an outside source. I told him the problem, and he assured me he would talk to your father and they would help me. I didn't hear from anyone after that."

Valentino was afraid he would hear that often from the men owing money. The capos would have gone to the underboss and laid out their troubles after first trying to fix them. Parisi had been betraying Giuseppi as far back as two years earlier, nearly three. Maybe longer. Most likely, Parisi was setting up the capos for Miceli, making them ripe for his money.

"We will give you help with this problem, Caj," Valentino said. "We have someone who will speak to you alone and ask you questions. Severu will introduce you to him over an encrypted line. You will give him full access to your books and answer any question freely, as if you were speaking to me."

Caj nodded his head. "I appreciate any help you can give me."

"Until it is fixed, we will suspend the profit sharing as there are no profits. Come to Severu if you need help with your soldiers. You can't look weak to them, and you want to take care of them. Has Miceli contacted you directly? Or his sons?"

Caj nodded. "Tommaso phoned me once and then came to see me, asking for a sit-down. I heard him out. We have the East Side corner buildings for rent or lease. They're used mainly for large commercial ventures such as garages, or the larger butcher operations for beef or pork where they are cut up, packaged and frozen before being shipped out. The East Side is mainly our legit operation. We have some smaller businesses in there as well, but for the most part the warehouses are quite large and anyone who leases there needs the space. We vet very closely. Those businesses are all ours, of course—at least, we own the majority of stock in them."

"What did Tommaso want on the East Side?"

"The buildings at first. He offered a large amount for them. When I said absolutely not, he wanted to meet in person. I took the meeting because I was interested in what he had to say. There's one corner warehouse three stories high, extremely large, with a deep basement that runs nearly the length of the entire building. He wanted to convince me that could be turned into a lucrative strip club with another, even more lucrative club below the first one, a more exclusive club catering to kinky tastes for men and women willing to pay huge fees to play."

Valentino drew in a deep breath. He had a lot to talk to Parisi about down in that interrogation room. He hoped Stefano had given him the tools he would need. If not, he had his hands. It would take longer, but he had broken men with his fists before. He needed to find out what each of the other capos behind in their payments had that Parisi wanted before he confronted the monster to see what deal he had made with the devil.

CHAPTER NINE

Emmanuelle stood just inside the alcove of the door where the Ferraro family entered and exited the hotel in private. Leaning against the wall, she pressed a hand to her churning stomach. She'd never felt so violently ill in her life. It wasn't as though she'd never seen anyone beaten or tortured before. Her brothers were guilty of such behavior when they were extracting information from someone. Emilio and Enzo were as well. It was just that . . . this was Valentino. *Her* Valentino.

She had never seen him look so hard. She'd known he could be, but not like that. So cold and distant. So completely emotionally turned off. He'd never raised his voice. He hadn't raged. He'd smashed a man to pieces with a hammer, one part at a time, asking him questions in that same low, very calm voice. So soft. Almost gentle.

She shuddered. She knew that voice. So patient, as if there were all the time in the world. Ask a question. Listen to the sound of sobbing. Of pleading. Val hadn't repeated himself. He'd waited the exact time he'd said he would wait and then

CHRISTINE FEEHAN

swung that heavy hammer and broke another kneecap. Or an elbow. Or a hand. He hadn't hesitated. He hadn't flinched. He'd simply done as he'd said he would, following through as if Parisi were a child and his lies wouldn't be tolerated. *Just tell the truth.*

The screams had been inhuman. Then the words had come tumbling out. Children as young as three, as five, taken from their parents. So much more lucrative to sell. Easier to handle. To keep. Miceli had started with women, but had gone to snatching young teens, preferably very young. Miceli knew someone who'd suggested young children were worth so much more. Did Parisi know anyone willing to pay very high prices for young girls and boys? He wasn't a pedophile. He liked women, but he knew several men who liked them very young.

The more body parts Val had smashed, the more Parisi had spouted information. He'd given up names of others in territories bringing teens to sell. It had taken longer to get the names of the ones bringing in the children. He hadn't known where Miceli and his sons held them. Angelo was in charge of the children. Tommaso was in charge of the teens. Miceli's underboss, Dino Lombarto, oversaw the entire operation, along with Marge, particularly the women. There was someone in one of the other *famiglias* overseeing the entire network, but Parisi had no idea who.

Emmanuelle knew the information was needed. She knew it was absolutely important to rescue the children, the teens and the women, and to put a stop to the network. It didn't matter that closing one didn't stop others from springing up. It meant saving those already out there. It meant stopping the insanity from continuing.

It was just that . . . this was Valentino. He was utterly cold. Utterly inhumane. So capable of turning off all emotion. She pulled out her phone and texted Henry, keeper of their large fleet of cars. She was tired and didn't want to ride shadows. She wanted—no, needed—to feel human.

Need favorite Porsche ASAP. Can you deliver? If not, I'll take cab to garage. Hotel Ferraro. Private entrance.

Stefano had cars in the private parking garage he'd let her borrow, but that meant saying something to him. Technically, the cars belonged to all of them, but she needed space from everyone.

On my way now.

She could always count on Henry. He was like the sun rising every morning. It didn't matter if it was raining, you knew the sun was there somewhere, even if you couldn't see it. She wished Henry could have been her father. Why couldn't Eloisa have fallen in love with Henry? Maybe she had, but Henry wasn't a rider. He had no way to wrap his shadow around Eloisa's, and being a rider was all that was important to Eloisa.

Emmanuelle would have given up being a rider for Valentino. Val would never have given up his world for her. She could see that. Watching him in that conference room with those men, most far older than him, but all respecting him, some even fearing him, she knew she had been so naïve when it came to her childish fantasy of the two of them running off together and making a life away from their families. That had been her hope. She thought it had been his hope as well.

"Emme? Are you crying? I don't think I've seen you cry since you were a little girl." Henry reached a hand out to her to help her up.

She dashed at the tears on her face. She was turning into a regular faucet. That was what Valentino had reduced her to. Taking his hand, she scrambled to her feet, allowing him to pull her into an awkward hug. Henry wasn't the hugging type. Even when she was little, he would pick her up if she fell, dust her off and pat her shoulder, telling her she was fine. She was somewhat shocked to feel that embracing him was like hugging an oak tree. His body was pure steel under his clothing. He kept himself fit. That was what working for the Ferraros did to you.

"I'm good. Just having a little pity party. You know how it is." She pulled back just as he let go of her. The bruises on her chest were sore enough that coming up against anything hard was painful.

He dropped the fob for the Porsche into her palm as his gaze moved over her face. "If you say so."

"Do you need me to give you a ride home?" It was the last thing she wanted to do, but she made the offer.

"Eloisa is picking me up."

That shocked her. It was late. More than late. Eloisa didn't put herself out for anyone, although Henry might have been the exception. The two recently had been together constantly. Emmanuelle had even wondered a couple of times if they were living together but had dismissed the idea as ludicrous.

"Thanks for rescuing me, Henry. As always, I knew I could count on you."

"I was surprised you didn't just take the shadows."

"Stefano wants all of us to be more cautious until we understand more of what happens to the brain when we're inside the shadows," she said. That much was true. Eloisa had brain bleeds, significant enough damage that Stefano had insisted all of them have brain scans before they were cleared to take jobs again, especially if they had headaches. She had one now, and it was a significant one, although it had nothing to do with riding shadows.

Because she didn't want to engage in any more conversation and she definitely didn't want to see Eloisa, she slid behind the wheel of the Porsche, blew a kiss to Henry and entered the street. She was trained to watch for anyone tailing her, and she was extraordinary at getting rid of them as well. She could outrun just about anyone, including the cops. She kept a map of the city in her head at all times, including alleyways and entrances and exits of parking garages.

As it turned it out, she didn't need any of those skills as she made her way home, far from the actual city. She loved her house. It was closest to Taviano's home, but still miles away, with a heavily wooded area separating them, although there was a long winding path to take on foot, if one knew it, which she did. She'd only made that trek once to ensure she could use it in an emergency.

The property had come up for sale, and Taviano had put

a hold on it instantly, knowing she would love it. The unbelievable house came with three precious acres of land, difficult to get, and she wanted privacy. The grounds were gated, giving her even more privacy. The land close to the house was landscaped with mature trees and plants with explosions of colors.

The side drive wrapped around to another house, a smaller version of the main one, which she called her couch house. There was a heated pool she did laps in at night to tire herself out so she could sleep. At least she tried to tire herself out. It didn't matter if it worked or not. The pool was awesome, and the landscaping surrounding the pool and house was lush. She loved it.

The house itself was stunning. She loved the way it was clearly designed as an Italian Renaissance Revival country home. She felt the architects had succeeded. Two stories, it had a sweeping bridal staircase, which was one of her favorite features. The rooms were grand sizes. There were four suites on the second floor for guests. Each suite had a wonderful view of the lake, the pool, the forest or the lush landscaping. The suites were complete with their own enormous bathrooms and sitting rooms.

Technically, there was a third story. Emmanuelle called it an attic, but the spaces had been renovated at one time into offices. She had the cleaners keep them up, but she never used them. The attic ran the length of the house, so each of the four rooms was gigantic, too big for her to contemplate what one would do in such a large space other than turn it into a workout area. Her gym was in the basement, where it was cooler, and no one had access to it but her.

Her kitchen was fabulous. She actually really enjoyed cooking, although she never told anyone because Francesca and Taviano were the two chefs in the family and she wasn't up to their capabilities. She dabbled in cooking. She learned by watching the cooking channels. It was fun and relaxing, and no one was around to see her mistakes.

The impressive foyer had mahogany wainscoting. There

was a formal living room and a sunroom that overlooked the beautiful landscaping. The dining room led into her kitchen, and even the sunroom had an archway that gave a peek into the large, sunny room. Perhaps because she was Italian, she felt like the kitchen was the heart of her home. Certainly, when she was visiting Stefano and Francesca, dining was one of the happiest times she spent with her entire family.

There was an expansive island and gleaming mahogany cabinets, with limestone and marble countertops. The Sub-Zero and Wolf appliances didn't mean that much to her, but seemed a huge selling point to her real estate agent, so she was happy to have them. She did appreciate the walk-in pantry and the eat-in area along with a butler's pantry. She spent a lot of time in her kitchen and, from there, used the French doors leading to a sun porch facing the lake.

The luxury master bedroom was a little over the top, but she couldn't resist the gas fireplace, walk-in closets, dressing room and private balcony facing the forest. The suite cornered so that part of it faced the lake as well. The master bath was nothing short of spa-like. That had been a selling point. When she came out of the shadows, her body hurting like hell, she enjoyed soaking in that deep, hot Jacuzzi with the powerful jets coming at her from every angle.

The shower was just as luxurious, a large, glassed-in two-person room-like stall with a complex overhead rack of hundreds of small fountains that could rain down in various colors, if one desired, while other jets sprayed from all sides. She allowed the patterns of colors to run through as she washed her hair and conditioned it and then let the hot water pour over her skin, hoping to ease the pain of the physical punches she'd taken to her body.

She loved Valentino Saldi. Nothing was going to change that, but he hadn't exactly told Stefano the entire truth. He hadn't told her the entire truth. She had seen firsthand what lies did to shadow riders. Eloisa was a prime example, and she was not going to be turned into her mother, a bitter woman who'd turned on her own children because she wasn't loved.

Did Val love her? The answer was yes. He loved to fuck her. The physical attraction between them was so hot and wild she couldn't imagine it ever fading. She'd seen older riders and knew it hadn't faded for them. Their shadows saw to that. She also knew that wouldn't be enough for her. She wanted to be loved for herself.

She'd thought Valentino had fallen in love with her, just as she'd fallen in love with him. She had been naïve, not realizing it was all about loving her body. Her family. Her shadow. Whatever it was that he knew—and she didn't. He kept secrets from her, vital ones. Not just family secrets. She could forgive that. She kept family secrets. They both had a silent pact not to ask. This was different. He was hiding something he should have disclosed to her.

Her towels were in a warmer and felt nice against her abused body. She needed nice. The bruising looked worse. Her body still ached. Hurt. Her heart hurt. Her soul. She thought about the way Valentino had looked facing the capos in that room. He belonged there. He had always intended to be there. The things Parisi had said about loving a woman hadn't changed the expression on Val's face at all.

She knew once in the organization, once a made man, you didn't get out unless you died. Blood in, blood out. That was the way of life Valentino had been born into. He was now the reigning king. He looked every inch that king, and those around that table had treated him with that respect—and fear. Watching him in the interrogation room, barely working up a sweat, completely dispassionate as he took apart human beings who had betrayed his family, she could understand that fear. She felt it herself.

It wasn't as if her brothers couldn't be the same. She'd seen them be that way, but Valentino was utterly removed from her. So far away. She knew if she had sparked a nerve ending, looking for him, letting that fire travel to him, the flames wouldn't have found him. The Val she knew was gone. The man in that room was someone else. Someone terrifying. Someone who had trapped her, bound her to him and refused to let her go, but he had left her.

Her top drawer held her night attire. She normally slept in the nude. She didn't like anything to twist around her, not even the sheets, especially after the shadow tubes, but she planned on filling out the complicated arranged marriage questionnaire. She had printed it out, although it was strictly an online program no one else was ever supposed to see—not even members of the council. Supposedly. She had her doubts about that. The questionnaire was very personal and exacting. Some of the questions made her blush. She didn't want anyone to see her answers—not even the computer.

Emmanuelle pulled on a nearly nonexistent crimson thong that matched the nearly sheer crimson silk top that slipped over her head and draped in a deep vee in both front and back, held up by only spaghetti straps. The material barely covered her breasts. She didn't mind; she felt hot and unsettled as she reached for the thick sheaf of papers and for the hundredth time began to reread them, this time with a pencil, determined to fill them out.

Emmanuelle's eyes opened wide, awareness rushing in, her hand sliding under her pillow, fingers searching for the knife she kept there. It was gone. She inhaled, dragging the masculine scent into her lungs. She should have known. The only person who could enter her home without her knowledge was Valentino. He was too much a part of her, already connected to her—a shadow sliding into her house without tripping a single alarm.

She sat up slowly, pulling the sheet with her, aware she'd fallen asleep wearing only the crimson top and thong set, which left little to the imagination. He still wore his suit, the one that cost the earth and had been tailored to fit his wide shoulders and perfectly sculpted body. He looked what he was, invincible, the reigning king of the underworld, a man not to cross. His eyes were dark green, his gaze fixed on her like she was prey, not the woman he loved.

"What are you doing here?"

Valentino sat in the chair beside the bed, facing her. He held a thick mass of papers in his hand, up high, along with a lighter, the flame flickering. "Do you want to tell me what the fuck these are, Emme?" His voice was low, that same voice he'd used in the conference room when he was identifying the traitors to his organization. Almost a caress. Almost velvet.

She gasped and crawled toward the edge of the bed, at the last moment making a lunge for the papers as he lit the corners of them with his lighter, the greedy orange flame rushing up the paper. She'd spent forever trying to fill out those papers, agonizing over every answer. "You have no right to be in here. It took me forever to fill those out. And they were *private.*"

He shouldn't have read them. No one was supposed to read them. Some of those answers were extremely private. No one was supposed to see them. She had printed out the papers and would eventually transfer those answers back to the computer program that would supposedly match her with the correct mate and then destroy her answers so no one would ever see anything she or her chosen partner wrote other than the two of them. It was a newer program, and one the riders hoped would make the arranged marriages more workable.

Valentino easily held the burning papers out of reach as he leisurely carried them to the wastebasket, allowed them to drop inside and burn to ash. "An arranged marriage? You decided to enter into a marriage with someone you don't know? Why would you even consider such a thing, Emmanuelle? I noticed you made a point that your husband has to be from Europe and you two must live, work and stay there."

He turned back to face her. His eyes were fierce. So dark green they were fathomless. Merciless. He was beyond angry. "I'm so damn sick of you deciding you're going to leave me. You're not. Do you really think you'd be safe there from me? I would find you in Europe. You say no cheating. You want someone who would respect the marriage vows. You say in those papers that you would do the same."

He took a step toward her. Stalking her. Her heart began to pound and her mouth went dry. She sank back onto her heels suddenly afraid of what he might do. She'd never seen Valentino like this. The tension in the room coiled as tight as the tension in her stomach.

"But you aren't so certain you can keep those vows if you're around me. That's why you're insisting on finding someone in Europe, isn't that right, Emme?"

She pressed her lips together and curled her fingers around the sheet. Of course, he was right. The physical pull between them was far too strong. She would never be able to resist him. She wasn't going to chance cheating on her husband. She wouldn't be like Phillip, her father, using the shadows to sneak around for sex. She would stay in Europe and do her best to make her husband happy. When she made up her mind to do something, she was very good at it.

Val halted just at the end of the bed. "I've had enough of this bullshit, Emme. I really have. I'm not even going to pretend to understand why you would want to enter into an arranged marriage, but it wouldn't stop me from going after what's mine, and you'd better be very clear on that. You're mine. We made that agreement a long time ago."

Fury ripped through her. "No, Val, *we* didn't. *You* made the decision for both of us. I had no idea what was happening. You didn't give me the courtesy of letting me know. I was a teenager. You were an adult. You had knowledge of what your shadow was doing to mine. You could have told me, but you chose not to."

"You wanted to be with me. I asked you multiple times, Emmanuelle. We talked about our relationship, how difficult it would be, but how it would be worth it. You agreed. We both agreed. I wasn't alone in that decision."

She sat back on the bed, shaking her head, wanting to

throw something at him, hating the way he reverted to calm when she was a mess. He always did that, becoming the adult while she was a child. He was older than her, and he led their relationship. He always had. She had been caught in the sensuous web he created, and he surrounded her with heat, with fire. She never seemed to be able to break free long enough to take a breath and think clearly.

She couldn't let him get away with it this time. She was fighting for her life, and she knew it. In a way, she was fighting for his life as well. She was no pushover. She wasn't her mother. She loved Valentino, and the moment he treated her the way Phillip had treated Eloisa, she would kill him, or force him to kill her.

"I was too young to know better, Val. I was so caught up in the sex that I didn't realize what was happening to my shadow until it was too late. You counted on that, didn't you?" She didn't take her eyes from his. Holding that steady gaze. She had to know the truth.

He didn't so much as flinch. He'd settled easily in the chair again, facing her, looking every inch the man in charge, just as he had in the conference room. It was unsettling to think she was facing the crime lord and not the man she loved, but she refused to back down. She wasn't living with half truths.

He nodded. "Yes."

One leg was out from under the sheets, her normal way of sitting or sleeping. He reached for her ankle and wrapped his long fingers around her bare skin. The moment they were skin to skin, she felt that connection deep, the sizzling flames flashing along her nerve endings, spreading fast through her body like a wildfire out of control. She tried to pull her leg away, but he tightened his grip.

"Do you think you're the only one affected by the heat between us, Emme? I can't think about you without wanting you. I can barely take a breath without needing you. I may have been older than you, but I was in uncharted territory as well. So yes, I counted on the sexual attraction distracting you long enough for me to bind you to me. I had no intention of letting you get away from me. Not then. Not now. Not ever."

Part of her wanted to pry his fingers from her ankle and then kick him right in the head and hope she knocked some sense into him. He sounded like the worst kind of stalker. Another part of her wanted to yank him down on the bed and make love to him. That was what was so terrifying about being close to Val. It was impossible to think straight.

Emmanuelle took a deep breath and let it out, forcing air through her lungs, needing to be clearheaded. Valentino couldn't distract her. Her body was hot. Her breasts heavy. She was grateful for the bruises because the aching let her feel the soreness even more. She didn't want hands on her. Especially Val's. He could be rough at times, and right now, her body couldn't accept rough.

"You implied you wanted out of your father's world, but you were never going to leave it, were you?" She kept her eyes on his. Steady. Forcing him to give her the truth. "You had no intention of ever leaving, did you?"

He didn't so much as blink, those dark green eyes looking so much like a predator's she quaked inside, but she didn't let her fear show on the outside. She was a Ferraro. She could protect herself if she had to.

Val shook his head slowly. He gave her the truth even though it shredded her. "I tried to lie to myself a couple of times, but I always knew I would be taking over for my father. Once I knew Miceli was up to no good, I didn't hesitate. And I knew it very early on. Years earlier."

"You wanted to take over," she persisted.

He nodded. "That's true. I was raised to stand in my father's shoes. I don't know another life. Even before he officially adopted me, we talked of it."

She hated him almost as much as she loved him. Betrayal ran deep and hurt like hell. "You didn't trap me because you loved me, Val. I heard what you said to Stefano about loving me, and it rang with truth. At the same time, it was a lie. The lie was as big as the truth. You had another reason. Trapping me even back then, when I was so young, it was never about me as a person, or even about the sex—all of that came with it, but there's another reason, one much more compelling. The real reason you're forcing me to be with you. It has nothing whatsoever to do with loving me. Tell me what that is."

She glanced around her bedroom because now she couldn't look at him, this man she loved more than life. More than her own life. For the first time, she realized that her soft night-light was glowing, throwing shadows on the wall. Her shadow. His shadow. She thought he'd moved the chair to face her, but he'd deliberately positioned himself so their shadows would merge. The ropes swarmed over her, weighing her down, thicker and tighter than ever. There was no hope of ever getting free, yet he was still adding to the bindings.

Emmanuelle gestured toward their shadows. "You're still doing it. There's no doubt in my mind there's something else, Val. You can't force me to stay. You know I can find a way to escape. Tell me what that reason is."

He continued to look at her, his eyes heavy. Hooded. A chill went down her spine. Was there a way he could force her to stay with him? Force her to go into the shadows for him? She had all kinds of confidence in herself, knew she was lethal and yet just for a moment, she was afraid of him.

"You're already afraid of me, Emme. You're my heart. My soul. The one good thing in my life. Why would you be afraid of me? Why would you think I would ever hurt you? And don't tell me I did anything your brothers haven't done, because you'd be lying to yourself and to me. I've seen it in them. Killers know killers. I recognized them early on as well. Why do you think I made the decision to take you?"

She reached for her pillow and pressed it to her churning stomach. "I don't know, Val. That's what I'm asking you, and you keep avoiding the answer. What's the real reason? Dario knows. You know. I think you're the only two people in the world who do."

His thumb moved over the bare skin of her ankle. "There

are some things that are ours, Emme. Yours. Mine. The Saldis'. Not the Ferraros'. You have a tendency to think of yourself as a Ferraro and you go straight to Stefano. I don't blame you for that. In fact, Stefano saved us. I'm grateful for the alliance."

"You were counting on an alliance. As much as Dario said you told him not to contact me, that was bullshit. You both wanted me there, knew I would come, and you counted on me calling Stefano."

He didn't deny it. How could he? Valentino always had a plan. She should have known, but even had she figured it out ahead of time, she still wouldn't have allowed him to be killed.

He gave her a faint smile. "The most difficult time for me was early on. You protected your shadow, Princess. I had to be patient, and I was really afraid one of the others might notice the phenomenon. Dario helped me watch over you, but it was very nerve-wracking. I was afraid you'd go to Stefano and he'd put a stop to you coming to see me when I called you. I counted on your protecting me."

"I did go to him."

His eyebrow shot up. "Why didn't he stop you from coming to me?"

"He didn't listen to me that first time. After that, I did protect you."

He looked so satisfied she wanted to throw something at him again. Instead, she clutched the pillow. "Valentino, I'm not going to be sidetracked. I want to know what you're hiding."

"Marry me. Right away. I'll tell you everything. But only when you're my wife."

She scowled at him. "Are you crazy? Do you even listen to anything I say? Absolutely not." She pressed the heel of her hand to her forehead. "Can't you see why this won't work? You can't hear me when I talk to you. You don't understand what I'm saying to you. I'm not another woman, Val. I'm a Ferraro. I'm every bit as lethal as you are in my own way. You think because I love you that I wouldn't ever harm you. Given the right circumstances, you would be wrong. I'm not willing to risk it."

She heard the absolute, utter despair in her voice. There was no resolving a situation when Val was so certain he was right. He was stubborn in the same way Stefano was. As head of the house, everyone else bent to his will. As head of an entire organization, a huge territory, Val would expect everyone to do exactly as he ordered—including her. That wasn't Emmanuelle. She'd often defied her brother. That was what had gotten her in this mess in the first place.

Val shrugged carefully out of his jacket and reached for his tie, loosening it, his eyes never leaving hers. "I always listen to every word you say, Emmanuelle. You're important to me. I've had these last two years to go over every word you said. Every word I said. I know every breath you took and when you took it."

Emmanuelle didn't know how to save herself when he was like this. His voice a velvet caress, smoothing over her skin, raising goose bumps. His words shooting arrows straight to her heart, to her soul. He knew what to say to get to her. His eyes never leaving hers so she was held captive, drowning in him. That's what he did to her. That's how he mesmerized her every single time. She turned weak.

"Do you really think I would ever cheat on you, Emme? That I could stand another woman touching my body? That I would want another woman's mouth on my cock? That I could put my cock in her body after being inside of you? Is that what you really think of me, Princess?" His tie was dropped to the chair, and he sank down and removed his shoes, not once looking away from her.

Her stomach did a slow somersault. The very large room was suddenly too small. He filled it with his masculine scent. Just with him.

"You expect me to believe a man like you, a man with your sex drive, has gone two years without a woman?" She flung it at him like an accusation, trying to save herself in desperation. Already, she was aching for him. Felt empty, her blood pounding with excitement. Racing. Hot with need. With craving. With obsession. This was Valentino.

One by one the buttons of his shirt opened to reveal his chest. That chest of his. Rock solid. All muscle. Even the scars, old and new, fresh wounds, couldn't deter from the perfection that was Valentino Saldi.

He smiled at her. A predator's smile. He knew exactly what he was doing to her. Her heart was racing. He saw the rise and fall of her breasts beneath the thin, nearly nonexistent top she wore as she struggled to keep her breathing under control. Her fingers fisted in the sheets.

He glided and was suddenly looming over her, his palm wrapped around her throat, fingers on one side of her neck, thumb on the other. His strength was enormous. She'd forgotten how truly strong he was. He tipped her head back so she was staring into his dark green eyes. Eyes that held no mercy whatsoever.

"Do you expect me to believe that a beautiful woman with a voracious sex drive such as yours has gone without a man for two long years, Emmanuelle?" His voice was very soft, but it carried a warning. "I wonder if you ever considered how often I might be lying in my bed awake going a little insane thinking of another man touching you."

His free hand stroked her right breast gently under the little silken top she wore. His thumb brushed her tight nipple back and forth. Each light brush sent darts of fire straight to her core, scores of fiery arrows that were like lightning strikes, every single one of them.

"Go ahead, Val, I can't resist you. That's why we're here, at this point, but I won't marry you and I won't stay. I'll let you seduce me and distract me because that's what you always do to get your way and I'm so damn easy." There were tears in her voice, but there wasn't a single one in her eyes. She wasn't going to shed one for him. Or for herself.

"Is that what you think I'm doing, Princess? Seducing you? Distracting you so I don't have to give you answers?"

He reached out and caught the hem of the silk top she wore, pulling it over her head and dropping it on the chair behind him.

There had been a note of dark humor in Val's voice, but she couldn't detect any on his face. His gaze was riveted to the bruises on the swell of both breasts and just below, in the valley in between.

"Isn't it?" She could barely breathe. The look on his face distracted her too much. Rage was back. His eyes were alive with a swirling promise of absolute death, but a long, slow one to any man who would do such a thing to her.

"Give me a name, Emmanuelle. Who the fuck did this to you?"

"He's dead. I killed him," she reiterated. She had told him after the doctor had worked on his injuries. "It happened when Miceli's men attacked the lake house. I was taking out the men in the vehicles coming up the drive."

The pads of his fingers moved to the valley between her breasts to lightly trace the dark, angry black-and-blue splotch there. He was making it so hard to think. His other hand was still around her throat, but so gentle. His head remained bent and so close she could see the spill of his thick dark hair and his long lashes as he examined the colors running down the lighter olive of her natural skin tone.

"There were quite a few men in each of the SUVs and trucks. By the time I got toward the end of the line, they knew someone was attacking them and they were waiting, set up for that. Those in the truck behind the SUV were also watching. There was a helicopter in the sky with a spotlight as well. It was a tricky situation."

"I told Dario to order you inside."

His fingers stroked lower, to the very top of that tiny scrap of crimson material she called panties. Her thong was already damp. More than damp. His long fingers slipped inside and caressed her bare mound. She kept herself shaved because the sensation inside the tubes of being pulled apart was easier without hair. She normally braided the hair on her head very tightly before going into the shadows to keep from feeling as if she were being scalped.

"I wouldn't have come inside even if Dario had gotten a message to me. My family was running the operation, Val. I go where I'm assigned, just like everyone else. I'm good at my job."

"All communication went through Emilio, and he made that very clear to Dario. To me. Stefano was giving the orders. He had given out all the assignments. Lie back, baby."

"Val, this isn't a good idea. You were shot. You're not healed yet. I was beat up. We haven't worked anything out."

"This is the only idea. Two long fucking years, Emmanuelle. Do you honestly think I'm going to wait any longer for you? We can talk after. I'll be gentle with you. You can be gentle with me."

He never stopped moving the pads of his fingers along her mound. Now they dipped even lower, skimming along her bare lips, feeling the dampness, her slick heat. He slid one finger through her wetness. Her feminine channel clenched hard. Every individual muscle. It was disturbing to need him so much. He'd barely touched her, and yet every nerve ending in her body was totally alive and aware of him.

Emmanuelle's breath caught in her lungs, leaving her raw and burning for air. It was always like this if she got too close to him. Inside her body, flames licked through her veins, the fire burned bright and hot. Tension just coiled tighter and tighter.

She would have believed him, but he didn't sound gentle. There was a distinct growl to his voice. An edge. The hand wrapping around her throat tightened just a fraction. Miniscule, but she felt it. The hand sliding through her wetness brushed her clit, and she jerked as if he'd touched her with a white-hot flame.

"Lie back now, Princess. I'm not waiting another minute to taste you. I've been craving the taste of you since the moment you got on the bed with me and I could smell your unique fragrance. Nobody smells like you do." He pulled his hand from her thong and lifted his fingers to his mouth and licked, his eyes watching her, tongue curling around his fingers as if savoring the cream.

"I'm not sure that's a compliment."

His hand slid from her neck, so gently, over her breasts to her belly. He spread the heat of his palm on her, nearly taking up her entire stomach, his fingers splayed wide. "It's a compliment, Emme."

Very slowly, but relentlessly, he applied pressure until she complied with his order, letting herself fall to her back.

Her heart accelerated until she thought it might burst from her chest. "Valentino." She whispered his name. She didn't know if she thought to stop him. She didn't want him to stop. Not when his face was carved somewhere between carnal lust and love. Not when desire was stark and raw and dark in his eyes.

"You don't need these, baby." He caught the crimson thong and pulled it over her hips and down her legs to toss it onto the chair, leaving her body bare and completely open and vulnerable to him.

CHAPTER TEN

Valentino stood for a moment at the end of the bed, looking at the woman who was his. Two long fucking years he'd waited for her to come to him. She lay sprawled out, naked, her gorgeous body his for the taking. He wanted to devour her. Spend endless hours with her, hearing her scream his name when she came for him over and over. Hell, tie her to the bed and keep her there until she realized they belonged together. She was so skittish, so damn certain he didn't love her. How could he not? How could anyone not love Emmanuelle Ferraro? She was so convinced they didn't belong together, when really, she knew damn well they did.

He ran both hands from the tops of her thighs all the way to her ankles, a slow assault, just to feel the shape of her. To feel her in the palms of his hands. He'd always loved knowing he could do that—just touch her anywhere. He loved holding his woman. Pulling her onto his lap. Kissing her. Sliding his hand under her shirt just to feel her silky skin. He wasn't the kind of man who needed to show ownership of a woman by grabbing her breasts or ass publicly, but he loved to stroke the pad of his finger along her ribs or belly. She had such soft skin over amazingly firm muscles. Emme was soft silk over a framework of steel, and that, to him, was sexy as all get-out.

He caught her thighs and pulled them apart. Widened them even farther as he stepped closer. "You're so damn beautiful, Emme. I wonder how many times you can come for me? How many times you can scream my name before it sinks into your head that there's no going back?" He murmured the question against her inner thigh softly. Musing. As if it weren't a warning. As if his intention wasn't to show her she was his. He was hers. They belonged. They were meant.

Startled, her head lifted and those intense blue eyes met his. She couldn't fail to see his intentions. He'd had enough of her running. He was putting a stop to it one way or another. He didn't give a damn if Stefano Ferraro came out of the shadows and tried to break his neck, or one of her other brothers decided to end his life with a gun. Hell, he faced death every damn day of his life, and had since he was born. At least for Emmanuelle, he had a good reason.

"Valentino." She whispered his name.

"Yes. Valentino. You should have come to me, Emme. You knew I didn't cheat on you. You fucking knew it. You should have come to me. You clung to that because you didn't want to face the real truth. Your real fears. You know I do love you and you do belong to me and that scares the holy hell out of you."

He bent his head and pressed his lips to the inside of her left thigh and sucked. Gently at first. Harder. Longer. Leaving his mark. She reacted the way she always had. A little moan. Moving her leg as if she might try to take herself away from him, but when he clamped down on her, she didn't fight him. She pressed into him, sighing. Wanting him. Needing him the way he needed her. He moved his mouth up one-half of an inch. So close to that hot junction between her legs, the one crying out for him.

Right now, his cock felt like a monster, caged only by the

cloth of his perfectly tailored suit. That suit wasn't fitting so well, applying far too much pressure to his already aching shaft and balls. He tore his zipper down to give himself a little respite. The relief wasn't nearly what he needed, but it was enough to allow him to hear past the roaring in his head.

She moaned softly as he spread little kisses up her thigh from her knee to her bare lips, first one side and then the other. He took his time. Making her wait. He blew gently. Steadily. Licked at the liquid heat and then suddenly sucked her clit. She nearly jumped out of the bed. A small cry broke from her. He stopped immediately.

"Babe. I'm just getting started. Didn't I say I wanted to devour you? You can't be trying to run away like that."

"I can't help it, Val. It feels so good. I haven't . . ." She broke off. "You always make me feel things I've never felt."

At least she gave him that. She might not have wanted to, but she'd always been starry-eyed and a little shocked as if every single time he'd fucked her, or made love to her, it was her first time and he was the most amazing, incredible lover ever.

He spread her thighs wider, placing her legs over his forearms, and then leaned down, one hand on her belly to hold her in place. He went back to those slow, delicious licks and flicks with his tongue. Teasing. Building the burn. Never quite giving her what she needed where she needed it. He used his free hand to brush her clit or circle it when his tongue wasn't there. He curled his finger inside her, stroking that very sensitive spot that made her go a little wild. He pulled back and used his tongue like a weapon, plunging in and out and then withdrawing just as she was close.

He'd missed her taste. He'd missed her response. He'd missed every single thing about having his woman under him. The sight of her in such need. Her fragrance surrounding him. That soft skin and tight channel with scorching, silken walls waiting for his aching cock. He nuzzled her thighs, breathing her in, taking her deep into his lungs, keeping her there.

"Val! What are you doing?" she wailed. "I'm so close."

"You need to come, baby?" He could feel her. Coiled so tight. Her body hot. Flames licked at both of them. Every nerve ending on fire. His. Hers. Nothing separated them.

"Yes. Hurry."

"You need to know who makes you feel like this, Emmanuelle." He put his mouth on her. Let his tongue work her hard. Bring her right there. He lifted his head. "Who would that be, Princess? Who gives this to you?"

"You are being a *dick*." Her head popped up again and her blue eyes darkened as she glared at him with demand. With a threat. "Do you have even an *inkling* of an idea what I do for a living?"

He laughed. He had forgotten he could laugh. Only Emmanuelle made him laugh. He lived in fucking hell, and she brought the sun with her. She knew how to brighten his world.

He went back to work: Fingers. Mouth. Tongue. Teeth. Bringing her close. Losing himself in her taste. In her scent. The softness of her thighs. In the fact that he loved her. That he could feel that overwhelming emotion the way he did for her. That she was right there with him again. He had her back, and he would be damned if she slipped away again.

She was thrashing now, her body close. He felt the tightness in her belly, her thighs, the small silken muscles clamping down viciously on his fingers. He withdrew again, kissing her thighs, wiping his face on either side of those creamy legs while she wailed and threatened.

"Better talk to me, Princess. Say what I want to hear. Who gives you what you want? Because my woman is marrying me, not some fucking stranger in another country. No other man is *ever* going to make you come. Promise me, baby."

Her head was up suddenly, her blue eyes looking straight into his eyes, and he knew he'd given her too much. Revealed how much it hurt. In his voice. Now it showed in his eyes. The knife she'd driven into him deep. Twisted. Kept twisting.

She'd left him for two long years, believing he'd betrayed her, when all she'd had to do was listen to her own body, hear his voice, to know the truth.

She was going to give herself to another man. Those fucking papers. He'd read every single question and every single one of her answers. Damn her to hell for thinking she would give herself to another man. That hurt more than any bullet, any knife ever could.

He looked at what was his. His woman spread open for him. So beautiful. All liquid and hot. Waiting and wanton. Pulsing and needy.

"I promise, Val. No arranged marriage. I promise that much."

Her voice was very soft, a mere thread of sound. She was telling him she wouldn't ever marry someone else even if she didn't commit to him. That was something, at least. He bent his head and pressed a kiss to her stiff little clit. She jumped.

He went back to one of his most favorite things, bringing his woman as much pleasure as possible. This time, he didn't stop, encouraging one orgasm to roll into a second, much longer one. She was sobbing his name by the third. Yeah, she knew who gave her intense pleasure.

He eased her down gently with his fingers and then rid himself of clothes. "I missed you, Emme. I missed you so much." He wanted to make love to her slowly, hold her in his arms, but he hadn't been with his woman in so long, and he wasn't going to last this first time. "You on birth control, Emmanuelle?"

"Yes."

"I swear to you I'm clean. I really haven't been with another woman. I want to feel you, take you bare." He'd always preferred to be in her bare, although he'd never, not once, before Emme, been with another woman without a condom.

"Tell me it's okay, Princess." He was right there, the thick, wide head of his cock fitting in her snug, hot entrance, his heart beating too hard, while blood pounded through his body, a firestorm raging that might never be fully sated.

"Yes, hurry, honey." There was urgency in her voice.

His hand tightened on her hip. He couldn't help the possessive streak he had. He felt possessive of her. He hoped she felt the same for him. His fingers dug into her flesh to hold her still, and he surged forward, a hard thrust, driving the thick, long length of him right through those tight, hot silken muscles that didn't want to give an inch.

Fire raced up his spine. Flames licked over his entire body. She was so tight. He'd forgotten what it was like being inside her, trying to force his way into that silken canal. She didn't want to open for him, but he forced the invasion, a thick, wide drill, penetrating every inch, burying himself as deep as possible. Making them one so they were sharing the same skin. Nothing felt so good. Nothing was like Emme. She was pure fucking fire.

"You're too big, Val. It's burning. Stretching." Her voice came in ragged little pants.

She hadn't been with anyone else for two years. A long time for her body to wait for his. He took a deliberate breath, threw his head back and let himself just feel to give her time for her body to adjust to the size of his invasion.

"It was always like this at first, baby. Remember? Then so good. Relax for me. Just relax. Give yourself to me."

She always did. Emmanuelle had trusted him in the past with her body. He'd worshiped her over and over. Taught her so many things. He felt her relaxing. Felt her silken muscles, so scorching hot, adjusting to his size. She was a snug fit, and in their time together, that fit was always that same tight glove that stretched around him so perfectly.

Emmanuelle took a deep breath, and Val felt the muscles contract and then relax just enough to allow him to move without fear of hurting her. He started as slow as he could to give her a chance to get used to his cock dragging over her sensitive bundle of nerves. She jolted every time he hit them so perfectly. She'd forgotten and reacted, her body shivering, shuddering, coiling with tension, winding with pressure fast.

He caught her hips and surged into her over and over,

letting himself go, needing this first time with her to stake his claim. The flames ran up his legs, his spine, danced over his skin, colors flickered behind his eyes. Yeah, this was what he remembered. What he needed. Only Emme could give him absolute ecstasy. Nothing, no one else came close. She was the real addiction. Once you had her, there was no going back.

"Put your legs around my hips, Emme."

She did so immediately, wrapping him up, locking her ankles around him, opening herself up even more to him so he could be in her that little bit deeper. He wanted to be closer. Inside her. As deep as he could possibly be. He used the strength in his legs, in his hips, driving into her, roaring, claiming his woman, taking her back.

The streaks of fire became jagged strikes of lightning, a white-hot sensation that refused to let up, nor did he want it to. He drove into her, feeling her contract all around him, biting down hard, that silken fist that was the most beautiful, perfect storm of fire and thunder, pounding through his veins, hot as hell. Val rolled his hips, grinding into her with each ferocious surge.

Emme gasped, her head thrashing. "Too much, too much." But she moved with him, her body rhythm countering his, hips pulling away and hammering down over his cock in a twisting, spiraling motion that nearly had his eyes rolling up in his head.

They came together in a fury. Then she was locking up on him. A blazing firestorm. Hotter than anything he could remember. "Fuck," he shouted. The word ripped from him as her silken fist clamped down on his cock like a vise, like a python squeezing him, strangling him.

She clung to him, crying out his name while he kept yelling, "Fuck," his head thrown back as pleasure ripped through him, threatening to destroy him through sheer force. Her orgasm seemed endless, biting at his cock, milking him, determined to get every drop from him. He soaked her inner walls, long ropes of his seed triggering more orgasms in her.

"That's it, baby, take it all—been too long without you.

Plenty where that came from." There was. So much more. All for her. He was jerking inside her, his cock in that hot haven where he belonged. Where he wanted to stay forever.

Val wasn't so certain his legs were going to support him. She'd milked him dry, but his cock wasn't going to stay satisfied for long. He knew that. She wanted to talk, to get things straight between them, and it had to be done. He was there for that reason, but there was no way he could be with Emmanuelle and not claim her body again and again.

He kicked aside his clothing and slipped up onto the bed beside her, wrapping his arm around her waist to lock her to him before she could escape to the bathroom and build up her defenses. Kissing his way up her belly to her breasts, he was careful when he brushed gentle, soothing kisses over the bruises.

"You have no idea how much I want to follow this bastard to hell and make him pay for hurting you."

Her fingers slid through the thickness of his hair. She'd always done that. Massaged his scalp. Idly played with his hair. He'd never objected because it always felt like such a connection between them. She almost always did it after they had sex. When she didn't, it bothered him. He'd find himself wondering why.

"Don't you think being dead is payment enough?" There was a hint of laughter in her voice.

"No, absolutely not." He levered his body to one side when he really wanted to blanket her, to press his weight over hers and hold her under him so she couldn't leave him again. "He should have died slow, in agony, thinking about each punch." Before she could move, he laid his head on her belly. "Some things are just not forgivable, Princess. Punching you is one of them."

"I don't know why," she said softly, her fingers working through his hair, "but when I'm with you, I always feel at peace. I shouldn't. We're so different, and we're so totally wrong for each other, but for the first time in two years, I feel like I can breathe."

He closed his eyes and let himself bask in her honesty. That was the other thing about Emme he'd always admired. Even when it cost her, she gave him such truth. Little pieces of her soul. He wrapped them up, just like the ropes did her shadow, trapping them, so he could take them out when he desperately needed them. When he was drowning in filth and blood. There was his Emmanuelle to let him know he would have something to go home to—until she left him alone for two long fucking years.

His palm tightened against her hip, fingers digging into her flesh. "We're not wrong for each other, Emme. We never were. Our families are more alike than you want to believe." He felt her stiffen beneath him, and he refused to move, tightening his hold on her. "Settle down. Just for a few more minutes. Give us a few more minutes just to be us."

The tension receded from her body. Clearly, Emmanuelle wanted the same thing he did—time. A little time. Just to be left alone in their own world, even if it was a fantasy and would end the moment the sun began to rise.

Miceli had to kill him. He had no choice. He'd declared war, and there was no going back now. He'd made his attempt, thinking, with Parisi's help, he would trap them as Valentino and Dario hustled the old man into Giuseppi's safe room, or catch them like rats in the walls as Miceli positioned shooters at either end. Emme had said he brought her peace. She did the same for him, even when he knew there was no peace and there wouldn't be until his uncle and cousins were dead.

He pressed kisses into her belly, wishing his child already lived there. Grew there. If he didn't survive, he knew she would always keep their children safe. Emmanuelle, as gentle and as compassionate as she could be, was also a skilled warrior and would fight to the death. She'd come for him, just as he'd known she would.

He'd gone to the lake house because he knew it was loaded with weapons and had a safe room he could stash Giuseppi in and when Dario sent for Emme "against his will" she would come. He also was banking on the fact that she would call her family. That was the biggest risk. Val couldn't fight Miceli alone.

His uncle had gathered too big of an army against Giuseppi during Greta's illness with cancer. Val didn't know how deep the rot in their organization ran. He only knew that some of the captains weren't taking care of business and some had taken money from Miceli. Either way, that was a breakdown, indicating Giuseppi had lost control, that he'd lost strength. Valentino had to send a message fast that he'd taken that control back and that he was stronger than ever. He'd utilized Emmanuelle's family at the lake house and then sent messages to the five families that one didn't fuck with Valentino Saldi and get away with it.

Yeah, Emme gave him peace, and he needed it. He knew she would look at his strategy and feel used—feel he'd used her family. He had. He couldn't deny that. He would use any means necessary to keep Giuseppi safe and take back their position as one of the strongest, if not the strongest *famiglia* in Chicago. In the end, he'd do the same to keep her safe and their children. He'd learned to be ruthless at a young age. He wondered if Stefano had done the same. Why were some children allowed to be children and others placed on a path that took them somewhere dark and twisted?

He reached up and took one of Emmanuelle's hands. He'd always loved her hands. They felt small and delicate next to his large ones. His were callused. His knuckles had been broken and hardened from being in fights. He had scars. So many. He liked to run his thumb over the back of her hand to feel her soft skin and then the pads of his fingers over her palm, memorizing the lines there, that map, some said, of her life.

"I love you so much, Emmanuelle. Never forget that. Did you forget that while you were away from me? Did you let yourself forget that you were my world?" He rolled over the top of her again, fitting his hips between her legs.

He had to use his knees to spread her thighs far enough

apart for him to fit and then prop himself up so he wouldn't mash her sore body where some asshole who needed to be dragged from the very depths of hell just so Val could torture him and send him there all over again had bruised her. He scooted down her body again so he could dip his head to brush kisses on her belly and then swirl his tongue around her belly button. "Need to know, baby. How could you push me out of your head so easily? I talked to you every single night. Told you about my shitty day. All the things I was worried about. How I was so certain Miceli was behind kids disappearing, but I couldn't find the pipeline. How I felt knowing those kids were scared. Hurt. Trapped. No protection. My fault for not finding them. Needed you, Emme. I fucking needed you."

He rubbed his face over her stomach, the stubble along his jaw causing abrasions on her soft skin. She'd always had delicate skin, and the sight of his marks on her always aroused him, not that it ever took much.

"I'm sorry, Val. Yes, I heard you whispering. I couldn't always understand you. I tried to drown you out with music. With anything I could to get your voice out of my head."

Her honesty was painful even to her; it was there in her voice. Her hands were back in his hair, trying to soothe him with gentle strokes, gentle caresses. He wasn't certain a lifetime of soothing would ever take away those nights of wondering how many children had been taken from their homes, or off the streets, out of shelters, snatched from a park. How many had been left to a lifetime of sex trafficking because his leads had always ended up in dead ends?

"You cut the ties between us after that first year." It was an accusation.

"Not entirely. I tried," she admitted. "It was so painful to love you so much and know I couldn't have you. I needed to be free if I was going to move on."

He sank his teeth into her hip, that sweet curve that had always driven him insane. It spoke of pure femininity to him. Emmanuelle was all about curves. He loved her breasts, hips and ass. She had gorgeous legs, but those curves drove him up the wall. Right now, just the fact that she could contemplate needing to be free of him and moving on deserved a little punishment. He bit down hard enough to cause her to gasp before he lapped at the spot and then kissed and sucked it gently.

He looked up at her. "I guess I can't get too upset with you." That was a fucking lie. He was furious, but he'd learned a long time ago to lock that shit up tight. "I got to such a low point when I couldn't get a line on where they were holding the kids, or who was grabbing them, that I considered having sex with Marge or one of her girls at Miceli's Dungeon in his strip joint."

Val said it deliberately, knowing it would hurt her. Knowing she would hate it and that she was responsible. Knowing it was the truth. He held her responsible for him even thinking about it. He'd lain awake night after night, detesting himself for not being enough, not being able to prove Miceli or his crew were involved in the trafficking of children. It was bad enough when he knew it was adults, but children? That got to him as nothing else could have and made him feel an absolute failure.

Emmanuelle had deserted him and wouldn't answer him no matter how he'd tried to reach her. She'd blocked him. He'd tried seducing her body from a distance. He'd tried pleading. He'd tried ordering. Mostly he talked to her, shared with her. Talked out loud to bounce ideas off of her, hoping she would hear and respond, want to help him. She never did. She cut him off. Cut out his heart. Left him in the dark with screaming children and accusing eyes filled with horror.

"I didn't have any way to get the information I needed. Becoming a man-whore was my last resort. You weren't coming back to me. You made that clear. It felt like you ripped my heart out, Emme. My soul. There was nothing left and after I found a place where I didn't feel, I thought I could do it."

He nuzzled her belly again, let the dark shadow on his jaw slide over her soft skin and leave faint red marks behind. "I thought I didn't feel anything. I thought there was a black void. I can take a man apart and go somewhere inside me where there is nothing at all, Emmanuelle. Nothing. Just a blank space. I face another woman putting her hands on my body, or her mouth on my cock, and there's no blank space. I can assure you of that. There's pure rage. It comes up so fast and so ugly it scares me. I don't know how it is for you, but there is no chance that I will be cheating on you. If that happened, you can believe the woman wouldn't survive it."

He felt a shiver go through her body at the dark edge to his voice. At the honesty. She knew he was telling her the truth because he was. She hadn't been with another man.

"I'm so sorry, Valentino. Your world feels so frightening. I don't know why."

Now her hands moved in his hair to comfort her, not him. Sometimes she curled her palm along his shoulder, feeling the muscles running beneath his skin.

"I had no idea or I never would have put you in that position. I hate that you even thought about going to another woman just to get information. I would have tried to get it for you. Maybe I am a coward, so out of my element, but just the thought of a man like Miceli being able to do what I do, which could eventually happen, is terrifying. Once you have someone like me in your family, what's to stop another crime family from taking our daughter by force? Or you deciding that family is a good, decent family and telling them about the ropes binding shadows? Worse, we're at war, and the price to stop it is giving our daughter as a bride to another family? Or another family is looking to merge territories and wants peace with you and again, that price is our daughter?"

She clearly had studied the ways of the families. What she was asking was entirely possible; the last two were huge possibilities. Daughters were raised to know that they could marry within the families for business purposes. Sons often did the same. Arranged marriages weren't unheard of at all. The families were much more careful now. They conducted business out of the spotlight and had many legitimate businesses. But yes, their daughter easily could be the bride in an arranged marriage.

"I can't tell another crime family about the myth and you and me. That story is handed down father to son. If they don't hear of it, if their father stops telling it, as many have, that's on them. If our daughter is in an arranged marriage, we, together, will make certain it is one she will want. Whoever she is with doesn't need to know she has the ability to go into the shadows, and you said yourself, it is possible she won't be able to."

"She will have the genetics to pass on, Val," Emme said. "And if the marriage is arranged, how can she want it?"

"I meant we would never arrange a marriage with someone she didn't want."

Emmanuelle's hand moved to the nape of his neck, fingers massaging the tight muscles there. She had strong fingers for being so delicate. She'd always had such a strong will. He'd loved it and detested it. Emme went his way until she didn't, and then there was no convincing her. He had to be more careful with this second chance, yet he knew himself. He was a man who took charge and expected those around him to follow his lead—especially his woman.

"I'll love you until the end of time, Emmanuelle, and beyond. No matter how crazy or angry you make me. Just don't do this again. Don't throw other men in my face. It was all I could do to give you time. I can't do this again. We can work all this out. Just don't do this again."

He had wanted her to come back to him on her own. He'd hoped she would see that they were meant to be together. He had taken her choices from her at a very young age, and he'd told himself she needed time to grow in confidence, to learn who she was. Between her brothers and him, and that mother of hers, Emme had to fight just to stand on her own. He wanted to give her that chance. But there was Elie Archambault. He'd never wanted to kill a man more.

Valentino had kept eyes on Emmanuelle at all times, even when she disappeared out of the country—and that hadn't always been easy. She would take her family's private jet and go, supposedly to see relatives to have a vacation, to have fun shopping, or skiing, or whatever the hell she was pretending to do. He knew it was none of those things. When she came home, she was always with Elie again, and it seemed the only time she smiled anymore was when she was with him.

If Emme had fucked Elie, Val knew he couldn't have stopped himself from killing the man. Nothing would have stopped him. Nothing. She hadn't. The two had the strangest relationship. They were close. Very close. Almost inseparable. That hurt. She gave Elie her friendship. Her laughter. When they went clubbing and the man danced with her, Val watched the videos of the two of them endlessly, and it was pure torture.

"You thought you were giving me time?"

"I know I was. I know you thought it was something else, but for me, it was giving you time you needed on your own. I watched over you in case Miceli or my cousins went after you. I know they thought about it a time or two. Had they done so, the war would have started a lot sooner."

He pressed kisses up the right side of her rib cage, along each rib, careful of any bruising. He wanted to make love to her, a slow, burning assault on both of their senses, not the fast, dominant fuck he'd taken that had sent both of them into such a sexual frenzy. He'd been away from her for so long he'd needed to get that out of the way. Now they both needed something else, something that defined the way they felt toward each other.

"Dario said you told him not to call me."

He lapped at the little indentations between her ribs that took him underneath the swell of her right breast. He kissed and sucked gently, nibbling his way around her full mound, wishing she wasn't so bruised. There was little space to leave anything of himself, or anywhere he could pleasure her. She liked breast play, and the son of a bitch who had punched her had taken that from her.

Val transferred his attention to the left side of her rib cage and took his time before answering her, pressing kisses and flicks and licks along those little indentations. "I did say that to him," he confirmed.

"You knew he would ignore you." Her breath hitched as he reached under her left breast and gently repeated his actions, kissing his way up and over the purple-black mound to her nipple. He used his tongue first and then oh-so-tenderly drew her into the warmth of his mouth. He took care not to constrict around her sore nipple, just let his heat surround her for a moment before he let her go.

"I did. Dario always ignores every order I give him."

Her arms came up to cradle his head to her as he switched to her right breast, soothing it with the warmth of his mouth. He loved her. His mouth said it for him. His hands, too, as they gently shaped her, stroking caresses over those dark bruises. His cock was a monster again, thick, his girth pulsing and throbbing with need, her heat calling to him. He felt her slickness with the broad crown, so ready for him, in the way she always was.

She never turned him away, no matter how many times he turned to her. It would be easier this time, with the combination of her heat and his seed helping to make her even slicker. He would need that to ease his way inside.

He kissed his way over the curves of her breasts to her throat and then over her stubborn, sometimes very defiant chin. His teeth scraped back and forth against it. He was overly fond of her chin. He knew he always would be. He kissed his way up to her bottom lip and brushed his lips gently back and forth over hers.

She had the softest lips anyone could imagine. Like velvet, only softer. Her lips were generous and plump and curved upward to give him a smile even when she mostly wanted to try to frown at him. He tugged at her bottom lip with his teeth just because he liked to bite at it. She knew he did. That was one of those things that sometimes earned him the fake scowl. This time it earned him her hips squirming closer to his—her hot little gasp right into his mouth.

Valentino had always loved the way Emmanuelle was so responsive. He kept the first kisses gentle. Tender. So loving, Emme had tears in her eyes when she looked at him. He removed them from her cheeks with the pads of his thumb.

"Don't, baby. We're here now. Don't think about anything else. We're together now."

He pushed deeper into that silken vise that was home to him. His breath left his lungs in a long, raw rush, and he wasn't even more than an inch in. She was just that tight. That hot. He wanted slow, and it was both paradise and hell. Entering her slow meant he never was certain he was going to make his way in. He'd forgotten that.

He couldn't trap her wrists and hold her hands above her head like he preferred because he didn't dare let her chest take his weight. He had to hold himself off her just enough while he forced his body to inch his way deeper into that tight inferno. "Baby, you feel so good I think the end of the world could come and I wouldn't know it."

He leaned down, licked her neck and then bit down. She gasped, and he was able to manage another inch.

"It's just that you always feel like it's impossible for you to actually fit."

She whispered the confession to him, her blue eyes staring up at him. Wide. Worshiping. Loving. Making his damn heart stutter. Bleed. There was so much feeling he *didn't* remember, even though it was there in his mind. Like this moment. His cock stretching her body so that it felt as if she was resisting him, trying to fight him, to keep him out.

He circled her clit gently with a finger, whispered to her that he loved her, that she was beautiful. To relax for him. He didn't want to drive through her folds hard and fast and just take her the way he could, burying himself deep, forcing her body to accept his. He did that often. Too often. He'd done that already. This was not that. This was a slow burn. A smoldering, inch-by-inch claiming of her body. Sharing her skin. Her mind. Her heart and soul. She not only surrounded him with that scorching sheath so tight he felt her every heartbeat, but she surrounded him with love every bit as tight. Wrapping him completely in everything Emmanuelle.

"It's too much." Her voice was ragged. Now she was moving, her hips bucking, fighting, either pushing to get him inside, or trying to throw him off of her.

"It's not enough," he denied. "It's never enough for either of us. Your body was made for mine. It remembers me. The way we are together."

"Val."

A little sob in her voice. She always got that little hitch when she was climbing high. No way was he stopping, not with her body strangling his, pulsing around his cock like the tightest, hottest mouth trying to milk him of everything he had in him. He was no more than halfway in her, and already he could feel her body coiling tight. That tension winding in her. Preparing. Needing. His Emme responding to him.

She tried to dig her heels into the mattress and push her way up toward the headboard as if she might be able to slide out from under him. At the same time, she raked her nails up his back, and then anchored her hands on his shoulders, trying to avoid the bandages. She tried to press her fingernails deep to hold him to her.

That bite of pain added to the climbing waves of ecstasy her body always sent through him as he buried himself in her, inch by slow inch. Inevitably, he managed to sink all the way to his balls, and hold himself deep. It felt like paradise to be able to feel every beat of her heart. To know every inch of her sweet pussy so intimately. She contracted around him until it was as if his cock felt her every breath. Hot and silky. Anticipating.

He caught her hips in his hands and slowly dragged his cock back until his crown was once more right at her entrance. Her breath hitched. His did as well. He pushed into her slowly, letting the flames lick over him, lick over her.

"I love you, Emmanuelle. So damn much." He whispered his truth as he repeated that slow, easy action, a smoldering burn that threatened to consume them both. He didn't take his gaze from hers. Looking into her eyes. Letting himself drown there. Wanting her to drown in him.

For a man like him, who swam with sharks, who put his trust in very few, and for whom one misstep could not only doom him but other entire families, a woman like Emme was the most perfect treasure in the universe.

"Valentino." His name came out in that whisper she had. That way that made the earth stand still for him no matter what was going on around him. She could make him lose himself completely in her.

She didn't look away as he moved in her. He wasn't a gentle man, or a poetic one, but he knew when he moved in her like this, looking into her eyes, this wasn't about heart to heart, it was about soul to soul. He may have been the one to wrap the ropes around her shadow and capture her, prevent her from leaving him, but she'd taken his soul long before he'd secured her to him. She'd been the one to make him her prisoner.

Val made love to her slowly, taking his time, building the pleasure between them to an intensity that shook both of them, and then continued to build it. Emmanuelle held him tighter, the tension in her growing, the alarm on her face spreading.

"Babe, it feels like we're going to go up in flames. That you're destroying me. I'll never be the same."

"Let go for me."

"No, not this time. If I do, it won't just be me anymore. You know that." There was real panic in her voice, in her eyes.

He did know. He'd already gone there. He was nothing without Emmanuelle. She had to give herself completely to him. "Let go, Emme."

"I can't. I don't know yet. I have to know. This will destroy me."

She was right. "We'll never be the same. There's no Valentino without you, Emmanuelle—no Emmanuelle without Valentino. Give yourself to me." He made it an edict. A law. The truth. He leaned down and sank his teeth into that sweet, sweet spot between her shoulder and neck.

She cried out and her scorching-hot sheath clamped down on his cock. He gave a strangled roar of pleasure as a thousand fists pulled and squeezed, mouths sucked and tongues lapped, all molten hot, swirling around him in a frenzied fury.

Emmanuelle's orgasm went on and on endlessly, or one ran right into another until the two of them were so drained they couldn't move and lay still, fighting to just breathe. In spite of feeling every wound in his body, Valentino had never been happier, especially when Emme curled into him and let him just pull up a sheet so they could rest together.

CHAPTER ELEVEN

Valentino lay with his head in Emmanuelle's lap. How many times had he done so at the lake house when they had hidden away from everyone? He had known even then that their time was limited. Maybe he should have tried to tell her that things were going south with the family business. She'd been trying to get him to commit to leaving. She wanted them to both leave Chicago, to strike out on their own together, to make a life without their families. She was ready to give up everything for him, but he knew he would not leave the *famiglia*.

Blood in. Blood out. That was his life. That would be her life as well. She humbled him with the way she loved. She gave him everything, and he was still holding back. He didn't want to, but he knew if he told her his plans, he would lose her. Back then, he'd tried to find something to give her, something for her to hold on to when she realized he was going to keep them in Chicago, that he was going to take over his father's business.

Now he needed to talk to her. Tell her what she needed to

know. They'd slept for a short hour, showered briefly and returned to bed. He'd snapped the night-light back on, telling her he wanted to see her face. He did, but he had other motives. He always had other motives, but he needed to see her face. Her expressions. She wanted him to talk to her about the Saldi myth, and he needed to be able to read her. This was going to be difficult all the way around.

Her fingers stroked through his hair, soothing him. He had all but forgotten how that made him feel. Loved. Cared for. She had a way of soothing him and allowing his brain to quiet. He always thought at such a fast speed; it was nice to be able to slow things down and just enjoy a little peace with his woman.

"When I first felt our shadows connect at that party, that jolt of physical awareness, it was sexual, so fucking hot, I couldn't breathe. I couldn't talk." He glanced up at her face. "When I realized it was for you, and you were a kid, I was ashamed of myself for feeling the most physical attraction I had ever felt for a woman in my life."

Emmanuelle didn't say anything; she just sat there, eyes half-closed, those long lashes of hers veiling her expression so he couldn't see what she was feeling. He went on. She wanted to know, and he was going to tell her.

"I knew my birth parents loved each other. It was evident in everything they said and did. They were inseparable. Sometimes I wasn't always sure they had room for me." He gave her a faint grin. "I'm kidding. They both spent plenty of time with me. I might have been an only, but I was never lonely."

He reached up and traced her lips. "I wanted a family. I always knew I wanted a family and that I would love my wife and children the way my birth parents loved each other. The way Giuseppi loved Greta and she loved him. The way Giuseppi and Greta loved me."

He fell silent. His adopted father was such a dichotomy. He loved his family wholeheartedly. Was gentle with Greta, although very strict with her about separating business from his home life. She could never inquire into his business affairs without severe reprimands. He'd expected Val to follow in his footsteps, and he'd showed him every aspect of the business, especially the harshest, most vile tortures, ones that included keeping a man alive for days using drugs and IVs so he would suffer endlessly if Giuseppi deemed he deserved it. Killing families of traitors while the traitor watched before torturing him so they would be made an example of was also something he would do without a qualm if he thought it was deserved—even families he knew.

Val had learned early what was expected of him, and he accepted his fate, that mantle of authority. He recognized that the organization was, in some ways, a protection for the rest of the civilian population. There were always going to be criminals. Always. How bad those criminals got, and how out of control, depended on how strong leadership was within the organization. Giuseppi was a strong leader, and he refused to allow certain types of crimes to take place in his territories. Anyone trying to bring in human trafficking or selling drugs to children, things Giuseppi was opposed to, would earn a death sentence, but not just a death sentence; he made an example out of you—and that wasn't something anyone wanted.

"Why didn't you ever consider leaving?"

Valentino stared up at the ceiling. He told himself he would be honest with her. The simple and very real answer she would accept—blood in, blood out—but he knew the truth was much more complex and she would always know there was more. He slid his palm along her bare hip and down her thigh. Drew circles there.

"One can't walk away from this business, Emmanuelle. Especially someone like me. Once in, you're in for life, and I was born into it. Had I tried to leave, I would have been hunted down and killed."

He wanted to leave it there, but her silence told him she knew there was more. That was his woman. Too damned intelligent. A Ferraro. Lethal as hell in more ways than one. He found her hip again, traced her hip bone, and then moved his exploring fingers up to her rib cage.

"I like control. Power. I was born into that as well. It's stamped into my DNA. When I was with Giuseppi in meetings with the other bosses and I was a kid, I couldn't help looking for each of their weaknesses. Ways to use those things against them. Ways to make our family stronger. I was always thinking that way."

"Like you do with me."

He turned on his side to face her, one arm wrapping around her narrow waist. Again, she was right. "Yes. I would do anything to keep you. I'm not going to lie to you, Emme. Not ever. You're not easy, baby. You're hard to read. You don't give anything about your family away, and I respect that. I always have. I treat you carefully."

"You use sex."

Val let the smile show in his eyes as his gaze drifted over her body. Already, his cock was stirring again. It didn't surprise him. He'd been without her far too long, and he'd never been able to be around her long without wanting her. Just thinking of her could make him as hard as a fucking diamond. He'd had to learn to discipline his mind when he went into meetings to keep her out.

"I do." He admitted it readily. He saw no reason not to. "I use anything I can to keep you wanting me. You're the most maddening woman in the world." He bent his head and nuzzled her breast very gently, inwardly cursing that anyone could hit her so hard they would put such dark bruises on her body. "Sometimes I feel like trying to hold on to you is like trying to hold water in my hands."

"I don't mean to make you feel that way, Valentino."

Her voice was soft, and he could hear her love surrounding him. Enfolding him. That's what she did, and it only made him feel all the more desperate to hold on to her. That feeling of being blanketed in her. Wrapped in her love. He was so fucking obsessed with her. Consumed by his dark need of her.

"I don't want to be with you because your shadow reacts to mine or somehow we have good sex because of it."

Her blue eyes met his, and he could see her insecurity. As

if he wouldn't want her for herself. She was priceless. He couldn't blame her. He was her only experience, and damn him to hell, it had better stay that way. He resisted the urge to bite her, although if she kept saying things like that, he wasn't going to be able to stop himself for long.

"We don't have good sex, Emme. Our sex is off the charts. Fucking insane. That's what it is. I can feel that you love me. You wrap me up in your love. How is it you can't feel mine for you? Because, believe me, Emmanuelle, I feel love for you. You bring me to my fucking knees every time."

It pissed him off that she could make him so weak. So vulnerable. She had the strength to leave him. To walk away. To fill out papers arranging a marriage—a *marriage*—to another man while he was a robot barely able to sleep or eat. Anger pulsed through him, hot and vibrant.

He caught her hips, flipped her body over so she was on her belly and jerked her up onto her knees. She gave a little breathy moan, somewhere between his name and a sound of desire. He smacked her ass cheeks hard with the flat of his hand, over and over, spreading fire through her while she pushed back, wanting more. Her pussy was hot and glowing with her welcoming liquid. Slick with her need of him.

Her nerve endings, so connected to his, had reacted the moment his had flamed to life, burning with desire, with that hot, out-of-control storm of heightened anger, of his wrath that was raging lust, love and anger. His cock was a fucking steel rod, his girth stretching the skin to the very limits, pulsing with his fury at her for thinking she could be with another man.

He didn't wait, he slammed home, and streaks of lightning shot up his spine. Fiery flames licked over his skin, threatening to burn him alive. He didn't care. He caught her hair in his fist, forcing her head back, forcing her to arch her back, pushing her bottom higher in the air as he took her roughly. His thigh hurt like a mother, but then it went numb as the fire consumed him from the inside out.

Her pussy was an inferno, burning him alive. His cock felt

like a monster, too big for that tight little tunnel. She was silk and flames surrounding him as he pistoned into her, hammering deep, the friction threatening to send them both to hell—or nirvana. Who the hell knew or cared? He only knew that he couldn't stop. She used her strength, pushing back into him, almost as hostile or as lustful as he was, adding to the frenzied grasping over his cock—building the coiling need in her body.

"Don't you dare, Emme. Not without me." He gripped her hair tighter, snarling the command. He was hoarse he was so caught up in the inferno. Sinking into the flames. Refusing to give into the building pressure rising in him. It was too good. Too insane. Pain or pleasure? He didn't know anymore, only that he couldn't stop.

Her breath was so ragged, a musical symphony matching his own. That scorching-hot sheath clamped down like a vise. Surrounded his cock with a million sucking mouths. With a million flaming tongues lashing him as the mouths sucked greedily. He roared again as she sobbed his name.

Colors danced behind his eyes as blue and orange flames raced through his bloodstream and burned through his legs and belly. He'd never had such a hard, jerking release, over and over, the hot seed coating the walls of her sheath, triggering multiple hard orgasms in her, one rolling right into another so that she collapsed forward.

Valentino barely was cognizant enough to catch her before she could fall on her sore breasts. He had to roll both of them to one side so they could lie together on top of the bed, his cock still in her, feeling the aftershocks as they squeezed and gripped at him rhythmically.

It took a long time to get his breath back. "Are you okay, baby? I went a little crazy."

"I think we had angry sex," she ventured, her voice breathy.

"I think we did." He wrapped his arm around her waist. "Did I hurt you?" He'd been rough. He'd always been rough, but they hadn't had sex in a very long time—well, if you didn't count the first two times—and she was still as tight as hell. He should have been more careful.

"Val, I was just as rough. Couldn't you tell I loved it?"

"I think I was too busy being selfish."

She laughed. That laugh of hers got to him every time. She was so damn perfect for him. She closed her eyes and rubbed the back of her head on his chest.

"Val, you were talking to me about sitting in on meetings with your father when you were young. Learning weaknesses and growing up wanting control and power. I need to know these things about you and what all that has to do with me and the shadows. It's important for us as a couple."

Confessing his greatest sins to her, his character flaws—would she look at them that way? The Saldi myth that wasn't all just a myth, and part of it could be a nightmare—was torture.

"I didn't want Miceli, or any one of those sitting in the meetings, to ever have the chance to wipe out my entire family in order to take over my businesses, my territories or anything else I had because they coveted it or perceived me as weak," he said. "I'm not weak. I wasn't raised that way. I can do what's necessary to protect my men and their families, and I can protect my own. But my woman . . . my children . . ."

He stopped and rolled away from her to look back up at the ceiling. He couldn't face her when he felt so vulnerable. He was a grown man spilling his guts to her. Letting her see his darkest fears. Now he wished he hadn't insisted on the night-light being on, even so dim. He'd just had his cock in her, hard as a fucking rock, and now he was talking about what scared him the most.

"I wasn't going to take a chance that a car bomb was going to wipe out my wife. Or my kids. I knew firsthand what that felt like."

He would never forget the moment when Giuseppi and Miceli had come to him to tell him his parents were dead. The sorrow on Giuseppi's face, the compassion for him. The sly cunning in his uncle Miceli that only a child would see that would forever make Val leery of him. There had been a kind of triumph, almost a glee in his eyes that Miceli hadn't been able to hide. Val had suspected him of having the car bomb planted, but at his age, there was no way of proving it. When Dario had come to live with him, the two of them had worked to uncover evidence, but it had never been enough to take to Giuseppi, just enough to convince both of them that Miceli had devised a plot to murder his own brother and sister-in-law.

"I watched Giuseppi worry every day about my safety and Greta's. And then there was Dario—what he went through. But there was that absolutely ridiculous fairy tale of a story I'd heard, first from my birth father and then from Giuseppi."

Unerringly, he found her hand and threaded his fingers through hers. Her hand always seemed so small and delicate in comparison, but she was strong and she was lethal. He knew she could kill with those hands. If anyone could help him keep his family safe, it was Emme.

"I even talked to Dario about the stupid myth. We laughed about it. Then I went to that party and there was the most beautiful girl I'd ever laid eyes on, sitting across the room in a corner, watching me. Women came on to me. I never had to go to them. I waited, but you didn't come. Then I realized who you were. A Ferraro. The enemy. What the hell was a Ferraro doing at what was essentially a Saldi party? Worse, you clearly were underage. You were there surrounded by a pack of wolves. And believe me, honey, they were wolves. The thought of you with them scared the hell out of me, and I didn't even know why."

"You were definitely the hottest man I'd ever seen."

"I'm still the hottest man you've ever seen. Don't put that in the past tense." He forced laughter into his voice when a part of him didn't feel like laughing. She was with Elie Archambault all the time. The man was very good-looking. When he was in France, he'd been featured in dozens of magazines as an eligible bachelor with money and the world's most beautiful models on his arm. Val brought her hand to his mouth and bit down on her fingers.

"I stand corrected. You *are* the hottest man I've ever seen. I couldn't stop staring at you that night. I knew I shouldn't have been there. My friend asked me to go, and then she wandered off and I was afraid to move. Everyone was way older than me, and I knew Stefano would lose his mind if he found out I was there."

"When I went over to you and our shadows connected, that first sexual jolt was electrifying, even embarrassing. You were underage, and I was a grown man lusting after you. People were surrounding us, and I had no way to hide the fact that I was desperate for you. I didn't even know you, and I'd never wanted a woman more. I looked up at the wall and just like in the mythical story I'd always laughed at, my shadow was binding your shadow to me as fast as it could."

He would never forget that moment, either. That first time it actually registered that there might be hope. That he might have a chance at a life. That the bleak darkness already consuming him, swallowing him whole, might not get him after all. Because of her. That scared, beautiful teenage child of the enemy, looking up at him with the most devastatingly gorgeous blue eyes. He knew he wanted to look into those eyes forever.

Emmanuelle had turned her head slowly toward the wall. Toward their shadows. He wanted to stop her. He didn't want her to see. He didn't want anyone to see. She broke the light. Told him it was an accident, that she was clumsy, but he knew better. She'd been terrified when she saw those ropes wrapping around her shadow, trying to imprison her.

"I knew, when I saw our shadows together, that my life wasn't going to be all blood and torture and ugliness if I could just have you. You were going to be my heart. My soul. There could be beauty in my life. Something worthwhile. A treasure to protect and fight for. So, no, for me, it wasn't just about the best sex in the world. I needed to know I would be coming home at night to a woman who loved me the way I loved her."

She softened him. She gave him back his humanity. He waded through the grime of Miceli, Angelo, Tommaso and so many others. He was no angel. He reeked of dirty crimes, but he drew lines. In his clubs, the women were protected. They did only as much as they wanted to do, and if they were touched when they didn't want to be, the customer paid for it with blood. They were paid fair wages and were hired if they applied for the job. They weren't coerced into working, or forced.

The women entertained in clean back rooms, and yes, some of them were into providing whatever customers liked, but again, they had panic buttons, and help would come the moment they asked for it. They were paid well and could leave at any time. They weren't working off "debt," and they certainly weren't trafficked. The family had many other businesses, some legitimate, some not, and he paid close attention to all of them. Now all of those businesses were in his hands, not Giuseppi's.

"You wanted to know what else the myth had to say. I had to research it. Most of the families quit telling their sons the story at all. Originally, it was told in Sicily so long ago that I believe over the years, shorter and shorter versions were made up. No one ever recorded seeing such an event actually happen. That doesn't mean it hasn't happened. Part of the mythology is you can't tell anyone. If you find such a woman, you don't tell any other family. She is your secret alone. You protect that secret with your life."

"That makes sense if she's spying on the other families for you."

"It's more than that. The hope is that you have children with her and your children can do what she can. In the shadows, the children and your wife can always escape if they are attacked. Even if you can't enter with them, they'll always be safe. If you can keep this secret and instill in your children the need for secrecy, their children and wives will always be safe as well. The horror of having your entire family murdered will never happen if you continue to be vigilant, but with the knowledge that they can escape."

She was quiet, and he didn't turn his head to look at her, knowing she had to process the idea of a Saldi family, a crime family, being able to move in the shadows the way her family did. Would she feel as if she had to inform Stefano? Probably. She told Stefano anything that might someday affect her family. Val respected her for that. She was loyal. He wanted that intense loyalty to burn for him as well. There was more, and it would be even more difficult for her to handle. He wasn't looking forward to telling her, and it was possible this was as far as he would go if she couldn't accept this much.

Emmanuelle sighed. "It's a scary thought that members of crime families can use shadows to move around, Val. They kill each other as well as other people. I don't know if I want to be the one responsible for the start of providing that to others. If we had a daughter and she was able to go into the shadows and another family saw her shadow and bound her to them . . ." She trailed off.

He kissed her fingertips. "Baby, we would educate our children. Teach them the danger of what could happen. That first time can easily be broken. I would stop anyone who would try to take our daughter like that."

He felt the shiver run through Emmanuelle's body and knew his voice had grown too cold. Dropped too low. The thought of his child being taken and imprisoned against her will brought out the monster in him. He'd done that to Emme. She'd been sixteen. He wanted to think it was different with him, but he wasn't all that good of a man. He tried to be for her, but deep down, he knew he had to work at it hard. And then there was Dario. If Dario ever found the woman he wanted, Valentino wouldn't hesitate to do everything in his power to help him acquire her, just as Dario had done for him.

"Going into the shadows isn't easy, Val. I had a younger brother, Ettore."

"I remember."

"That was how he died."

He turned back to her, wrapped his arm around her waist and pulled her tight against him, hearing the sorrow in her voice. "Baby, I thought he had a respiratory illness. Pneumonia maybe."

"He had bad lungs. Asthma as well. He worked out all the time just like the rest of us. He trained hard. The shadows require stamina. It can take a toll on your body and can cause brain bleeds. It isn't easy."

"What? What the fuck, Emme?" Anger ripped through Valentino. What was her brother thinking, sending her into the shadows if it could kill her? Brain bleeds?

"I'm just warning you, it isn't a picnic. Ettore went in, but he died in there. Stefano was able to find his body and bring him out. Even that was sheer luck. There are feeder tubes everywhere going off the main ones. Some are greased lightning. You have to know what you're doing and be able to find your way around. You have to be able to keep maps of cities in your head and find them at lightning speed while it feels like your entire body is being pulled apart, all the skin is leaving your bones and there is nothing left of you."

"Why would you go into them?"

She was the one who was silent for so long he didn't think she would respond. "I'm an assassin. That's my job, Val. The woman you want for the mother of your children kills people."

Valentino wasn't shocked. It had been long suspected that the Ferraros were contract killers. No one knew how they did it, or how they got away with it, but it was known in the neighborhoods how someone could get an audience with them. Once, Greta had gone to visit Emmanuelle's grandparents when they were alive. They'd shared tea and Greta had told them how the son of one of the dons from one of the five ruling families wouldn't leave her alone. He touched her inappropriately every chance he got. If she told Giuseppi, he would kill the man and there would be a war. She didn't know what to do, and could they give her advice? She didn't want anyone to know. She'd only told Lucia Fausti, one of her closest friends, who had encouraged her to go to the Ferraros and just tell them her troubles. That was all. Just tell them.

Valentino retold the story to Emmanuelle. How her grandparents had listened attentively without saying a word, encouraging Greta with a smile or a reassuring touch. They had thanked Greta for coming and said they would be in touch with her. Five weeks later, the man who had been harassing Greta had been found in his own home, sitting at his desk, his neck broken. There had been no sign of forced entry. No fingerprints. No forensic evidence at all to connect anyone to the crime. His neck had simply been broken. He'd been alone in a locked house.

Greta hadn't been able to say if the Ferraros had anything to do with his death, but she had slipped them an offer of money, a very generous one. A few days before the man's death, she received a text to transfer the money to an account. She had done so immediately. No one had ever contacted her again. The account hadn't been traceable; at least she hadn't thought it was. She had waited five years before she confessed to Giuseppi because she'd known he would be furious with her for not telling him. The story had been repeated more than once, within their household only, and Valentino had watched the Ferraros. Dario had as well. At first, they'd bought into the playboy image, but after a while, that hadn't made much sense to them—especially not Stefano. He was a killer. Just looking into his eyes, one could see that. It took one to recognize one.

"Why would Stefano allow you to become an assassin?"

"That's what we do. Who we are. That's our family business, just as you have yours. You train from the time you're a child; so do we." Emmanuelle rolled away from him to sit on the edge of the bed.

Elusive. She slipped off the bed and padded on bare feet, naked, to the windows. Graceful, her body feminine. Flowing across the large room until she stopped, and then she was completely still again.

"You didn't come here alone, did you, Val? Dario is somewhere close sharpening his knives or cleaning his guns, right?"

"What are you worried about? Do you see something?"

She shook her head. With their wild lovemaking, her hair had come loose from her braid, and part of it tumbled down her back, snaking in waves to her bottom like a dark, sensuous waterfall.

"No, I'm just uneasy all of a sudden. And I wish you'd take your bodyguards with you."

"Dario has always been my bodyguard."

"You need more than one now."

He didn't answer her.

She wrapped her arms around herself and rubbed up and down on her forearms as if she was cold. "Tell me the downside of the Saldi myth. What you haven't told me. The upside would be the two of us together, our children better protected, but how is it I couldn't leave if I wanted? What is the downside you don't want to talk about, Val? How you can control me, keep me imprisoned?"

He sat up and shoved both hands through his hair. His body hurt like a son of a bitch, reminding him he'd taken a couple of bullets. The wounds hadn't been that bad, but the bullets had penetrated and they still didn't feel that good and he'd exerted himself quite a bit.

"Baby, do we really have to do this? It's a damn story. I already have enough sins, don't I? You were a fucking teenager when I took advantage of your shadow. I still use sex to control you—in fact, come over here now. I'd like to take advantage of your hot little mouth. My dick feels like it's going to shatter any minute."

She turned toward him. "I think you're insatiable. I want you to tell me, Val. All of it. Stop stalling."

"Then do what I tell you. You love sucking my cock. You always have. I loved teaching you. There's something about your eyes looking up at me, Princess, and your perfect lips wrapped around me, stretched to the limit, your mouth working hard to take me down. I love watching that. Come here, baby."

He slid off the bed and stood, feet planted wide, fist circling the base of his thick, needy cock. His balls hurt they were so tight. He'd always been big, but his dick felt like a monster, a steel rod, throbbing, the blood pounding through it with such urgency it felt like a fire raged. He'd gone that fast into a storm of need just at the idea of having her mouth on him.

It was this way every time. He wanted to be gentle. He wanted to be loving. She deserved both. He *felt* both emotions for her, deep inside. Then his body took over and he couldn't think straight. He became some primitive caveman claiming his woman.

He never seemed to intimidate Emmanuelle the way he should have, not when it came to anything sexual. The fire only blazed hotter in her. She matched him flame for flame, desire for desire, in the bedroom. She made her own demands. If he made her wait, drawing out her pleasure, she allowed it and then turned the tables on him. Emme liked sex and was a willing partner, no matter what he wanted to try.

"You look very tempting, but you aren't saying the things I want to hear. Tell me about the ropes on the shadows and I'll make you very, very happy."

"Woman, you'll make me very, very happy no matter what."

She laughed. "That's true."

She knelt at his feet, looking neither shy nor submissive. She looked powerful and sexy although a little battered with her black-and-purple breasts. She placed her hands on his thighs and leaned into him, her tongue licking at his balls, as if she might feast there. The way she did that, lapping with her tongue, stroking caresses, swirling them and then moving to the base of his cock, sliding her tongue right up his shaft to the underside of the broad crown where the sensitive vee was, nearly took the top of his head off.

Emmanuelle took her time, working his cock, getting him wet her way, teasing him, making him so hot for her he nearly took over, but then her mouth engulfed him, her lips stretching wide and he lost his ability to breathe for a minute. She was incredible.

He loved her. It was that simple. He fucking loved her. He had to give her something before he couldn't think straight, and that was happening fast.

"The more the ropes go on, supposedly the more we're tied together on a molecular level. I thought that was silly until I realized our nerve endings were tied together. There was the music in our bodies. Then I started experimenting, calling to you. Thinking about calling to you. I know you heard me a few times. You refused to answer, but you did tell me to shut the hell up very emphatically. Every time I saw you no matter how far away you were, if I could position my shadow near yours, I went after it."

She lifted her head, his cock sliding out of her mouth. She glared at him. "You're such a selfish bastard."

He was. He fisted her hair and yanked her head back. "Open your mouth."

She kept glaring. He caught her jaw in his other hand and applied pressure, pulling her head back even more by her hair. Still glaring, although there was a hint of laughter in her eyes, she opened her mouth, albeit slowly, making him very aware it was her choice. He pushed his cock deep. She closed her lips around his wide shaft and sucked hard, her tongue lashing him.

He nearly went up on his toes. His eyes wanted to roll back in his head. Hot flames licked down his spine. There was no way to think. To tell her anything. Not when her mouth was taking him to another world, where blood and death didn't exist. Where he hadn't been created to be a monster.

Emmanuelle made him feel like a man. A good man. She worshiped him. She worshiped him with her body. Her mouth. That mouth. No one controlled her. Not even him, as much as he wanted to think he could. Emme made her choices, and *he* was her choice. This was her choice. To love him. To give him a reason to survive in the middle of a world of blood and violence. A reason to keep going.

Val managed to open his eyes just enough to look down at her. On her knees willingly. Lips stretched around his cock. Willingly. Eyes looking up at him. So blue. Filled with love. For him. His gut twisted. His heart came apart. Went from his chest into hers. She took him deep. So deep. Eyes on him.

Liquid. Struggling to breathe. Giving him that. Giving him her surrender so he could have paradise.

He could feel the rumbling through his body like a fucking volcano, a boiling in his balls, the roaring of hot blood rushing through his veins just like lava. "Emme." He had to warn her. He'd already taken her three times, yet he knew he was going to blow again. He shouldn't have been able to, but her mouth was driving him insane, creating an insatiable lust he couldn't control.

Instead of pulling off him, she took him deep, the tunnel constricting the hard length of him. Unable to resist, he gripped her hair on either side of her head and let himself push deeper, watching her eyes. Thrusting. Feeling the euphoria. Letting it take him as he detonated. Letting her take him. Rockets went off. He held her there while she struggled to take every last drop for him.

She pulled back, and he let her go, his hands gentle, massaging her scalp. He could barely stand, his legs shaky. Only Emmanuelle could do that to him. Thankfully, the bed was one step behind him, and he could lean against it. She continued to kneel on the floor just looking up at him. His hand cupped the side of her face, his thumb sliding over her soft skin because he couldn't resist.

"Everything about you is beautiful, Emmanuelle. Everything. I missed you so much. I especially missed how you make me feel."

Her lashes swept down. "Great sex?"

His fingers traced her lips. She had the best mouth and she knew how to use it. She'd asked him to teach her how to give him a blow job, and they'd spent so many wonderful hours at the lake house practicing. She had taken their lessons very seriously and knew exactly how to please him in so many ways. She'd added a few little tricks of her own here and there.

"I do love the sex, but no, I didn't mean that," Val said. "You make me feel as if I'm a human being. A good man. You make me remember how to laugh. How to feel emotion. Real emotion. I like to just look at you. Sometimes, when you're asleep, I stay awake and watch you breathe. When you're away from me, I want a camera on you so I can see you're still there and I know you're alive and well. Breathing."

He wasn't explaining very well. He could see the confusion in her little frown.

"Val, you are a good man. You don't need me to know that."

He shook his head. "You saw what I did to Parisi. I didn't feel a fucking thing. He was a traitor to my family. He was my father's best friend. Did you know that? Best man at his wedding. Sat at our table for dinners. We sat at his. He was my father's advisor. He was the one who told the assassins how to find the safe rooms in the house to get in. How to use the passageways. Miccli didn't know. Parisi did. He led the killers straight to my father. A good man cannot do what I did and feel nothing, Emmanuelle."

His thumb continued to slide back and forth across her lips. His woman. Soft as hell, even inside she was soft, yet she wasn't. Her body was firm. Fit. The body of a warrior. Muscles ran under all that soft skin. She'd admitted she was an assassin. She killed. She had trained from the time she was a child. She didn't have a killer's eyes, not the way Stefano or her other brothers did.

Valentino caught her chin and tipped her head back so she was forced to meet his eyes. He stared down at her, looking for the killer in her. She didn't look away. She met his penetrating stare calmly. As hard as he tried, he couldn't find that killer, yet she killed. Emme was extraordinary.

"Let's shower again, Princess, and rest for a little while before we have to face the world." Maybe if he took enough showers, he could wash some of the filth off of him.

"You have the rest of the story to tell me."

"I'll tell you." He would. He wasn't going to lose her because he had already ensured she couldn't leave him. One way or the other, they were both trapped. Damned. He wasn't a good man, and if she hadn't heeded his warnings before, she would after he told her the rest of the story. He held out his hand to her.

Emmanuelle put her hand in his and allowed him to pull her up. Val pulled her into him. He needed the closeness with her. His elusive woman. She was so peculiar, always thinking he didn't love her as much as she loved him, yet she was the one ready to run. He was fully committed to her. He always had been, almost from the moment he'd spotted her sitting across the room from him, even before their shadows had connected. Those eyes of hers.

He wrapped his arm around her and fit her under his shoulder, wincing a little because his wounds hurt like hell. He probably shouldn't have been expending so much energy, but his dick was making all kinds of demands, and it had gone without for a long, long time. He owed it.

Emmanuelle burst out laughing and brushed her fingers over his semihard cock. "I think that connection you were talking about in your mind really is working. I caught a little bit of that. Owing your cock? Really? Maybe you said it out loud?"

"Two years was a long time to just masturbate to my memories and pictures of you, Princess. It isn't like I let the monster have any real action. And I was investigating Miceli's ring by that time, which took me to strip clubs. Too many to count."

He was leaving out the part that he had to check on his family's strip clubs or that some clubs included some darker fantasies. Had his body reacted? Hell yeah. Had he wanted another woman to get him off? To touch him? Not for one second. The thought was abhorrent. He knew those ropes wrapping around her shadow had done that to him. He hoped they'd done the same thing to her—imprisoned her shadow, but *both* of their bodies. He knew Emmanuelle hadn't considered that consequence for him yet.

A little shiver went through her body as her arm went around his waist. "Did the doctor say it was okay for you to get those dressings wet?"

"No, but I brought more gauze. You can change them for me."

She tilted her head and rolled her eyes at him. That would have to stop if any of his men were around, but he liked when she was so damn sassy all the time.

"You take a lot for granted, Val."

"I know I do, Emme. I have to. I have to believe you love me enough to choose to stay with me. I need to believe that." He didn't even care if she heard the ache in his voice. She already had seen him totally vulnerable. How many ways did he have to lay it on the line for her?

The water was hot and felt good on his sore body. She was beautiful standing next to him, using some subtle-smelling gel over her body. He noticed she winced when she soaped her breasts, so he took the gel from her and cleaned her himself. "Let me, baby. I really wish I could wake this man up from the dead and kill him myself slow." He'd had no idea he could be tender until he touched Emmanuelle's dark bruises.

She had gorgeous curves—her breasts and hips. Her assailant had punched her deliberately on the soft tissue to inflict the most pain. The bruising was spread from the sides of her breasts, across the nipples, almost to the top of the curves and along the underside. Down lower, in the valley between her breasts, he'd gotten in at least one, maybe two more shots, spreading a dark purplish black over her skin that reached toward her ribs on either side.

"I hate that he did this to you."

"You were shot, Valentino. These are a couple of bruises."

Her voice. A caress, smoothing over him in that way she had. Getting inside him. Taking him apart. She had no idea that her "couple" of bruises made him want to spend hours, maybe days even, using an IV, keeping the perpetrator alive so he could make him suffer for hurting her. No, he wasn't a good man, but if that meant sending a message to the world that no one ever lay a hand on her, that was all right with him.

"The bullets didn't hit anything worth mentioning, Princess. I value these breasts of yours." He tried to inject humor into his voice when he felt such rage swirling too close to the surface. They were too connected. She might feel it as well, and sometimes she looked afraid of him. He didn't want her to ever think he would hurt her.

"I value every inch of you, honey, so try not to get shot again. Although Dario did say you were very heroic, insisting he drag your father out while you fought off an army."

He swore, embarrassed. He might have to kick Dario's ass, although it was damn hard to do. And he'd been shot. Maybe he'd have to give himself a little time to heal. "Don't believe anything Dario says."

She laughed, and he loved the sound. He caught the wet tangle of her thick hair and pulled her head back, taking her mouth. Usually fire raged between them the moment their mouths fused together, but this time it was all about tenderness. Love. Melting together. Giving her something to hang on to when he knew she would need it.

He lifted his head and stared into her eyes. "Love me back the way I love you, Emme. Enough to stay and live my life with me. It won't be easy. I know that. I know what I'm asking. This life, my life, what you would have to put up with, but love me enough to want to stay with me. To have my children and protect them with me."

There, with the water pouring over them, with his fucking heart hurting so bad he thought he might not survive the next few minutes, he asked her. He'd come to her knowing he had to take the shot, do his best to lay his heart on the line for her. Let her see what she was to him. If she didn't choose him on her own, he would still have her, but it wouldn't be good. It would hurt both of them like hell. It would turn into war. War with Emme would end in disaster.

Emmanuelle's face went soft. Her eyes were all about love. She reached up and cupped the side of his face. "Valentino." His name. A whisper. "You know I love you more than life itself. I would do almost anything for you."

He heard that little word in there. *Almost.* She was all about loyalty. He needed that loyalty to be all about him. To belong to him. If he could show her that the Ferraros and his family, *his* family alone, would make tremendous allies, then she might understand there would not be conflict within her loyalties. He didn't have all the details of what she did. He needed them to understand her dilemma. She needed more details of the Saldi story binding her as well as what he did in order to make an informed decision. Neither wanted to be too forthcoming without a full commitment. They seemed to be at an impasse.

He turned off the water and stepped out, reaching for the warm towel to dry her off first. "Keep talking, Emme. You said 'almost.' I want to know you're with me. I need to know you are. We can find ways to make up our own rules. To live our lives as best we can, that way we both can be happy."

She wrapped the towel around her, going to the sink to brush her teeth while he dried off and then wrapped the towel around his hips. He'd brought a small case with him. Brushing teeth together in the bathroom felt almost domestic. He'd never had that experience before, and it made him want to smile.

CHAPTER TWELVE

Emmanuelle bandaged Valentino's wounds, acutely aware of his dark gaze fixed on her the entire time she worked on each of his wounds. She knew what she was doing. It was part of her training. All members of her family were required to know how to stitch up their own flesh, let alone someone else's.

It was just, Val's gaze never wavered from her face, not for a second, and she felt it like a physical touch. He'd always been able to do that to her. Her skin reacted with goose bumps, and her stomach did that silly, slow somersault that made her feel like such a fool. No one else had that effect on her. She had such composure, with the exception of when she was with Valentino.

She wished he'd cover up. His body was beautiful. Truly beautiful. All muscle. The scars he had didn't detract in the least from his beauty. Neither did the tattoos he wore, and she couldn't say she was all that fond of tattoos. But Val's, yes. He was so comfortable in his own skin. He always had been, and he'd taught her to be as well. She was grateful to him for that, but with that came the continuous need for physical, sensual contact. Emmanuelle knew they weren't going to be given much more time to work things out between them.

"Stop looking at me like you're going to chain me to the bed and start talking, Val. Seriously." She avoided his gaze by glancing out the window, the one with the view overlooking the lake.

It was impossible to say why she was so uneasy, but she was. Perhaps it was the fact that shadow riders never disclosed what they were to anyone else. If someone else found out about them, it was a death sentence. She'd been so careful to keep her family away from Val for that very reason. Now, Stefano knew Val was aware of all of them. She had no choice but to tell her brother that Valentino Saldi knew the Ferraros could slide into the shadows and that they were assassins, although by now, she was certain Stefano already was aware. There was very little that got by her brother.

"I like that you're so efficient with wounds. We always employ our own doctor, but having my wife able to handle gunshots and stabbings might just come in handy."

She lifted her lashes and looked him directly in his dark, beautiful eyes. "I'm also handy with guns and knives, just so you know."

"I find that incredibly sexy, Ms. Ferraro."

"I'm sure you do, Mr. Saldi. Where exactly is Dario? Please don't tell me he's in my living room."

"Why would he be in your living room when you have several very comfortable bedrooms?"

"My house should have told on him." It hadn't. She hadn't caught one single vibration. Even her brothers and mother gave off energy that sent alarms radiating through her body. She felt it through the floorboards of the house. The walls. Sometimes the windows. She understood why she wouldn't with Valentino, they shared a physical connection now. Dario? No way. There were no ties whatsoever to him. "Both of you went all through my house, didn't you?"

"Only I did. We needed to know all the entrances, exits. Anywhere an enemy might get to us. I mapped out your home and sent the information to Dario. He's on the roof. I couldn't convince him to act like a human being and come inside. He's up there with a sniper rifle. Said you always know when someone gets too close. Better me taking a chance than him."

That made her feel better. At least Dario wasn't somewhere in the house and her radar had let her down.

"I like your home, Princess—it suits you."

Emmanuelle couldn't help the warm feeling his praise of the house brought her. She'd taken her time finding the perfect property. "I really love it." She drew her knees up and rubbed her chin on top of them. "Val, I get that you would want to protect your wife and children. I'm going to reiterate that it isn't as easy as you might think to go into the shadows, and not everyone can do it. Not even those born specifically for it, or those trained from childhood for it. That aside, you said when the man first ties the woman to him, those ties can be broken. That's when he has to be close to her when she's spying on his enemies. What's the second phase, when the ropes are heavier? When he's managed to put more of them on her shadow?"

She kept her gaze fixed on his face. She'd decided to go one step at a time, not jump straight to the endgame. Val clearly didn't want to go there with her and kept stalling. She needed to know each phase of the Saldi myth just in case. If not for her to get out, then to pass on to Stefano so he could relay it to the council to protect all female riders—and so she could protect any daughters she might give birth to.

"There's still time for the two to part ways, although it is much more difficult," Val said. "At least, according to the original source I translated. It was old, Emme. It took a while for me to find it. I was lucky in that Giuseppi had insisted I learn multiple languages, Sicilian being one of them. Depending on how strong the bonds are, the knots can be untied, but both parties have to cooperate, or the male can kill the female or the female can kill the male. Those are the only ways to break the bond at that level."

"Lovely. So he knows he can kill her, but she is unaware of that fact, I suppose. You certainly didn't enlighten me."

He gave her a faint grin. "You most likely would have gutted me without a second thought for trapping you."

"Very likely. A nice, slow death would make up for the trouble you've caused me. What kinds of things would your prisoner do for you?"

"Emme, you're not my prisoner."

"I am, though, Val."

"If you're my prisoner, Princess, then I'm just as much yours."

"Perhaps. What does she do for you?" He hadn't asked her to do anything for him.

"She can spy from a much longer range. The tether between the two is longer, but he still has to be fairly close to her. I'm uncertain how close. I never put it to the test. I wasn't looking for a spy. The idea of me ordering you to put yourself in danger to spy for me never entered my head. I want to protect you, not have you somewhere an enemy might kill you."

Emmanuelle wasn't going to point out to him that she couldn't be killed so easily. She believed him. His voice rang with sincerity. At no time had he asked her about her family secrets, and he'd never once suggested she look into what Miceli, Angelo or Tommaso were doing. In fact, he'd told her to stay away from them. Often. He wanted to put bodyguards on her. That had infuriated her since her brother already had put them on her and she continually had to find ways to elude them.

"After that stage? When the ropes and knots are really being packed on. When the knots are intricate and nearly impossible to sever. Ricco is especially good with knots, and he said it would be extremely difficult to undo those knots."

"That's where things get very dicey with this myth, which isn't a myth. It seems to be reality. You know how the original fairy tales always seemed to be very dark and grim? This one is as well. The couple can live together happily ever after if they stay together and cooperate, but if not, really sinister and bad things begin to happen."

A chill slid down her spine. Valentino wasn't saying things to frighten her. Not only was he repeating the old myth, he believed it—and seemed to have reason to.

"The more we're connected, the better the chances are that you can take me into the shadows with you, but I can't go in alone. So, if there is danger, you could choose to save me." He gave her a faint grin. "Worst-case scenario, we have a couple of kids, we're under attack, we go in together, me holding the children and you holding my hand or however it works, and we escape through the shadows." He waited a heart-beat. Two. "Most likely scenario, I tell you to get your ass in the shadows with our children while I stay behind and try to kill every fucker who threatened you and our children."

He would do that, too, she knew it. He hadn't trapped her so he could be a shadow rider. This wasn't about that. A tiny bit of relief allowed some of the tension coiled in her stomach to ease. "Naturally, I'd have to fall in love with a badass. Not a smart one, either. A smart one leaves and comes back to fight another day. He doesn't stay and get riddled with bullets."

"He does if he's giving his wife time to get to safety."

"His wife is safety." She glared at him. "Valentino, if I do this with you, I'm not going to be like Greta, or Parisi's wife, or any of the other wives. I'll be a full partner. I will know your business, whether you like it or not. I'm not a trophy. I'd never be happy in that role. I understand completely that this is a man's world and they would never accept me. That's fine. I'll stay in the shadows when you have your stupid meetings, and I'll listen and catch all the undertones. I'll find their weaknesses, just as you did when you were a boy. If you can't see who I am and what I'll be in the relationship, then there is no need for us to continue moving forward with these ex-planations."

She knew whatever he was going to tell her was bad. It didn't matter. She couldn't live with him if he intended to

give her just a part of him. "You have to be in all the way
with me. One hundred percent or nothing. That's what you're
asking of me. Maybe that's the secret of this myth and why
you can't tell another soul even within the family. You have
a vow to them. A blood vow. Parisi said never put a woman
first. He was adamant that it was wrong. Miceli feels the same
way. Anyone dealing in human trafficking feels that way.
Giuseppi didn't feel that way and neither do you. So think
about that, Val. You can tell no one, not even to benefit your
organization, your *famiglia*. You have a sworn blood oath to
them, and yet you can't tell anyone in that *famiglia*, according to the myth. There has to be a reason that loyalty is first."

Val leaned his head back against the headboard, crossed
his arms over his chest and regarded her with his dark green
eyes. He could look very ruthless. Unforgiving. Hard. Merciless. Or, like now, soft and tender. He rarely got that look
for anyone but her. It melted her every single time, but he
couldn't change what she knew about herself—what she
would need to be happy. A lifetime of unhappiness was not
something she was willing to settle for.

She waited for that to sink in. Valentino had always been
good at reading her body language as well as her facial expressions. He knew she meant what she said. She would never
be a pushover. She loved him. She absolutely couldn't be
around him and not want to have sex with him. She'd fall if
she was close to him. That was a given. She was too weak. She
knew that about herself. But she wouldn't marry him. Be his
wife. Be a part-time partner, a doll for him to come home to
and play with at night. That would never be her.

"My world isn't safe, Emme."

"Do you think mine is? Do you think my bodyguards go
through the shadows with me when I'm sent out on a job? I
go alone. When it's my turn, I take the assignment, go where
I'm told and I don't have any backup. I enter a house, sometimes surrounded by enemies, kill my assigned target and
leave the same way I got in. I will continue to take rotations
whether or not I'm married to you."

His eyes went from soft to hard with dark, merciless fire building in the depths. She wouldn't back down, it was too important, but he had a way of making her heart accelerate too fast when Stefano couldn't even do that. It wasn't like she thought he'd ever hurt her, so she wasn't certain why she got that little thrill of fear chasing through her, but Val could do it.

"When you're my wife, Emmanuelle, we'll discuss whether or not you'll continue to work for your family." His dark eyes stayed on hers. Steady. No blinking. A predator's eyes. "You want to be my partner? Full time? How do you think you can do both? Work with me and work for your family? That isn't feasible, and you know it, especially when we have children. Or do you expect someone else to raise them? Do you want full-time nannies? Others feeding them when they're babies, or getting up with them at night? What role do you see us playing with our children?"

Her stomach dropped even more. She pressed a hand to it. She knew what he was doing. He knew all about Eloisa. She'd never taken care of her babies. She'd brought them home from the hospital and abandoned them until they were old enough to be trained as riders. That training began at the age of two. Emmanuelle hadn't told Valentino about shadow riding, but she had told him about her mother's style of parenting.

"You know I'll take care of any child I have and will expect you to as well. We had this discussion. We both agreed we wanted to be hands-on parents, no one else raising our children. You don't have to bring my mother into this, and I won't bring up the fact that by being with you, there's constant danger to our children every second of every day."

"I think you just did bring up that little fact, Princess."

Now his voice was devoid of emotion and his eyes had gone as cold as ice. A chill crept down her spine. She wrapped her arms around her middle, shivering. She'd rather have a fiery fight, storming at each other in a flash of heat, than the ice he could produce. She wasn't capable of that cold demeanor—not toward him, not even pretending.

"Babe, put on a robe. Something warm. As much as I detest you covering up your body, I don't like you cold."

At least he didn't realize she was affected by his arctic reaction. She slid off the bed and made her way to the walk-in closet, grateful she could keep her back to him. She needed the respite. Why was it that she was the one so distressed and he seemed so in control? Pulling the longest, thickest robe she owned from its hanger, she slipped into it.

As she came out of the closet and approached the bed, she noticed the wall where the night-light shone. A single shadow danced there. When she looked closer, she realized it was two shadows intertwined. Her shadow. His. The two shadows were bound together by a million threads. Not threads. Veins. Arteries. Something else. She couldn't quite figure it out. Even so, more ropes seemed to be knotting around both of them, rapidly tying them together.

She stared at the strange phenomenon for some time, long enough that Valentino turned his head to look as well.

"Weird, isn't it?" she finally said. "People are bound to notice that."

"It will eventually fade," he said. "With enough ropes, according to the story, it will fade if we both have an absolute commitment to each other."

Emmanuelle sat on the bed again, studying his face. He sounded like he was telling the truth, but really? That was insane. "That can't be true. Our shadows will fade from the wall and not be seen by others if we both equally commit to our relationship." She did her best to keep the sarcasm out of her voice.

"I'm only telling you what I translated, baby. I thought it was a crock of shit, too, but so far, everything that damn thing said has been right on point, so I would venture to say the shadow fades if we both commit."

She tapped out a rhythm on her thigh, keeping her focus. "What else, Val? What is the dark part of the fairy tale? What happens if I try to run? How do you keep me in line?"

He sighed. "I don't. I wish it were up to me. I'd drag you

back and put you in my bed. Keep you there until we figured it out. You don't like something I do, baby, you tell me, we fix it. That's how it works. We talk about it. You don't run from me."

"Val." She tried to sound stern when for some inexplicable reason she wanted to laugh. She pushed her knuckles into her mouth to muffle any errant sound. He really would chase her, drag her back and think they would find the answer in bed. Maybe they would. They talked about important things better in bed than anywhere else. "If you aren't the one keeping me in line if I run, who is?"

There was a long silence. His features darkened. He turned his head slowly toward the wall where their shadows were tied so tightly together. There was something about the way Valentino turned his head, slow, stealthy, almost as if he didn't want to be noticed, a predator watching a predator.

Emmanuelle frowned as she observed the shadows. What was it Val was trying to point out to her? The shadows weren't in any way normal, but then this entire Saldi mythology with the capture of her shadow with ropes hadn't been from the start. She narrowed her eyes and watched intently as the two shadows interacted. They mimicked Val's movements as well as hers, yet there were a few spontaneous movements of their own, as if they were separate entities.

She blinked rapidly. That wasn't possible. She kept her gaze fixed on the shadows as she inched closer to Valentino for comfort. This time a chill encompassed her entire body. Something very sinister was happening right there in the sanctuary of her home. In her bedroom. In the haven of her shadows. Her lip trembled, and she bit down hard to stop it.

Val reached over and pulled her right onto his lap. He often did that, so she cuddled into him, never taking her gaze from the shadows on the wall. She realized every movement she made, her shadow followed, same with Val's. Once they settled together, so did the two shadows. That was when the spontaneous movements began again. It wasn't her shadow moving by itself; it was his alone. Each time the shadow jerked or took a step on its own, it seemed threatening. Menacing. Evil, even. She didn't know why, because when the shadow interacted with hers, it was just the opposite, loving and sweet.

"How can it do that? Why is it doing that?" She whispered the question, reaching up to hook one arm around Valentino's neck. She wanted to climb inside him. The thing freaked her right the hell out.

"I told you those early fairy tales had nothing on the Saldi one. You're looking at how they kept the poor woman trapped. That thing right there. I can't go into the shadows to find you or the children, but it can. It can find your family, or anyone you love. It isn't human. It's a killing machine. How the hell do you kill a shadow? Something not alive? Something not real? Unseen? Unknown? You'd have to kill me, Emme, and I don't know if killing me would kill it, because that thing has separated itself from me."

He ran his hand up and down her arm soothingly. She wasn't certain if he was soothing her, or both of them.

"It isn't detached completely yet."

"I keep sending more rope in and binding it to your shadow. That's holding it, but I don't think I can do it for long."

"Does the Saldi myth say that you can use that shadow as an assassin against your enemies?" She tipped her face up to look at him. She didn't know how she wanted him to answer. Yes or no. Neither was a good answer. A shadow that had no one to answer to was a loose cannon. For all she knew, it could become a serial killer.

"No, not my enemies in the sense of anyone such as Miceli. Only those to whom my wife would run away to. Those she would seek shelter from. Her family. Friends. Even grandparents. And I can't send it or direct it. I can't even stop it."

"Oh my God!" She tried to throw herself out of his arms, away from him. The answer shocked her. Horrified her. It was the last thing she expected him to say.

Valentino's arms tightened around hers, holding her to him. Rocking her. Soothing her. Cradling her to his chest as if she were a child. "I know. I'm sorry, Emmanuelle. I didn't know. I had no idea until it was too late. Dario and I were both researching, trying to find ways to get rid of the thing without harming you or me, but there is nothing, absolutely nothing, written about killing that thing."

"That is the most hideous thing I've ever heard. How do you know it doesn't get worse? How do you know it doesn't turn on us?"

"I don't. I'm still looking for answers. This thing with Miceli heated up fast and suddenly took precedence."

"Why does the woman have to take all the punishment? Maybe the man cheated or was so mean he drove her away. Maybe he did something that hurt her so much she had to leave him. Did that creepy shadow ever think of that?"

Why did women always get the short end of the stick? At least it seemed that way to her. She knew women cheated on their husbands. She knew they could be abusive, but in the majority of cases, it seemed it was the other way around. This grim fairy tale the Saldis had was skewed toward the men.

"I don't think the shadow can be reasoned with. I'm pretty certain it doesn't have a conscience or feelings, Emme." Val brushed kisses along her temple. "And it will go after everyone I love if I were to leave you once the commitment is made."

She pulled back to look at his face. "Could we not make a commitment? Would that save us and everyone else we care about? At least until we know how to get that thing back under control?" She didn't know why she blurted out the last line, but she did. The look on his face? The hurt in his eyes? She wasn't rejecting him. She loved him with every cell in her body. Heart. Soul. She was bound to him. Already committed. But that thing . . . She didn't want to endanger her family any more than she already was.

"I think it's too late, baby. That's what I've been trying to assess for the last few weeks. Each time I saw you, I was stupidly allowing my shadow to connect with yours. You didn't seem aware of it. Or that shadow was covering it."

Valentino rubbed his chin over the top of her head. Back and forth. She could feel her hair getting caught in the stubble on his jaw. She'd always liked when that happened. To her, it felt as if that connection, no matter how small, mattered. Emmanuelle pushed closer to him. He winced, and she immediately pulled back, annoyed that she'd forgotten his wounds when he'd been so careful of hers.

"I'm sorry, Val." She tried to slip off his lap. He liked her there. He always had. It had taken some getting used to. Stefano had held her when she was a child, but it wasn't like she'd had a million cuddles. Valentino was affectionate. He showered her with touches, with kisses, and he liked her close.

"You're fine right where you are. As for the creeper shadow, he isn't discriminating one way or the other. I get out of line or you do, doesn't much matter to him. He will go after the ones I love or you love. I think he was created so we stick it out no matter what. Maybe that's so the Saldi line has a chance to continue. Who knows? There was a portion of the myth cut off in the place I found it, an old library. The keeper of the library wouldn't give me any more. I was considering making a trip to Sicily, but I couldn't leave Giuseppi. I had to deal with Miceli and then strengthen our position in the organization again. And I had to get you back."

The way he said that he had to get her back, his tone low, shimmering over her skin like velvet, his lips in her hair, sent the familiar weakness through her body. A fist of dark desire low in her belly, a melting sensation in her chest, around her heart. It was so difficult to love Valentino Saldi and know he had only to look at her a certain way, use a certain tone, and she would be hard-pressed to resist him.

"We have to show that to Stefano."

He gave a little groan. "I knew you were going to say that. Your family has its own secrets, Emmanuelle. I know that women like Grace or Nicoletta don't come along every single day. Vittorio told the world he was engaged to Grace after she was shot and he went to the hospital with her. There were many instances of him being photographed with other women over the year he claimed they were in a relationship. He said that was to throw the press off so they could have time alone. I didn't believe it for a minute. He claimed her once he realized her shadow was different. Clearly, your family doesn't claim their women in the same way, but it is still a claiming. A taking."

Emmanuelle was silent. He was absolutely correct. They didn't imprison other riders with ropes, but they were tied together, and if broken apart, the consequences were severe. Not death and destruction, but still severe. The difference was the consequences were severe for the riders; they didn't affect the loved ones. There was no death sentence hanging over their loved ones. Was it wrong to expect Valentino to expose his family secrets to Stefano when she wasn't about to tell him the Ferraro family secrets? At least not all of them? That was so unfair. And if she was with Val, shouldn't he command her loyalty?

"This is so complicated, Val." She heaved a sigh. Valentino and Stefano were both powerful men, and both ruled powerful, dangerous families. "We could use help figuring out that evil force of mayhem and destruction."

"I'd like to see what the little fucker does when you make your full commitment to me, Emmanuelle. Maybe he'll stop trying to get loose. I throw ropes on him as fast as I can, tying him up along with your shadow, but I can't always get to you. You make it difficult."

"I don't know if I can live your life, Valentino. You haven't said what kind of wife you want. Not really."

"I have told you, woman. You're just not listening. I don't expect you to be anything you're not, Emme. Stop stalling. You're afraid. That's why you ran in the first place. Initially, you may have believed I was cheating, but then it was an excuse because you didn't want to face leaving your family and joining mine."

He was right. That was true. From the time she was born, she'd been taught the Saldi family were the enemies of the Ferraro family. The feud dated back well over a hundred years, when the Saldis, corrupt with power, had tried to massacre the Ferraro family.

"It's just that you're offering me so much, Valentino. A war. The wife of the head of one of five crime families in Chicago. A creepy shadow that may want to kill every member of my family and yours and we don't know how to stop it. Women throwing themselves at you all the time. I've got to pretend around your men that I'm some piece of fluff. Not certain how you're going to treat me in front of them, but I have experienced your icy-cold don't-give-a-damn mask more times than I care to count. On top of that, you've made it pretty clear you don't want me riding shadows in my rotation for my family, which is what I do. What matters to me. I don't know, honey, why I'm hesitating committing to all that goodness stacked right in front of me. Must be the riches you've dangled in front of me because I'm such a material kind of girl."

"You didn't mention Dario. He's always a plus to have around," Valentino pointed out. "Did you make your pro and con lists? You always make out lists, Emmanuelle. Surely, there were some pros."

"You're a great kisser. And the sex is off the charts. I thought about making you my number one sex companion. Just spend nights with you and then head home. We could be like the Hollywood glam couples who never get married but go everywhere together and look gorgeous. You are gorgeous. That was on the plus side. Dario was *not*. Your bodyguards weren't on the plus side, either. I have enough of those of my own."

"I don't want you to want me for sex, Emme, but I'll take that if that's all I've got on the plus side."

"You do annoy the crap out of my mother. That was up right at the top." She laughed softly and then tipped her face up to brush kisses along his jaw because she detested the note of hurt in his voice. "No one is sweeter to me than you when you want to be. No one. No one listens to me or knows me better than you in spite of the fact that I complain that you don't listen. I know you do."

His arms tightened around her, holding her to him. "I'm still hearing that 'but' in your voice, Princess. You've got to tell me what's really holding you back. Why you didn't come to me. Why you would rather contemplate an arranged marriage than be with me. Don't give me bullshit this time, Emmanuelle. Fucking be honest so we can work this out."

She *detested* looking so childish in front of him. He was always so strong and confident, and she was back to being that silly teenage girl. She wasn't. She was Emmanuelle Ferraro. Everywhere she went, she had confidence in herself—or so it looked. She was wealthy, beautiful, poised—she had that act down to perfection, but who could keep it up night and day?

"Emmanuelle." Valentino caught her chin and turned her face up to his, forcing her eyes to meet his. "Baby, talk to me. This is me."

"That makes it worse, not better." She wished she could take back the admission as soon as it escaped. He was too intelligent. He knew her too well, and there was nowhere to hide from him. His dark green gaze moved over her face, seeing too much. She tried to veil her expression with her lashes, but she knew it was far too late when his features darkened and he swore softly.

"Talk to me, Emme."

That was an order. Pure Valentino Saldi, head of the Saldi family. He sounded just as scary as Stefano, if not more so. She was used to obeying that tone. There was comfort in hearing that particular tone, weird as that sounded.

She shook her head, and she looked away from his eyes. "I don't want to be with you when I know I love you so much more than you love me, Val. I hate that you can control me through the way I feel about you. I do everything wrong. Living with me, you're going to see that. Because you don't have the same crazy feelings I do for you, it's going to matter down the line. All my shortcomings are going to annoy you until you won't be able to stand looking at me, even being in the same room with me. That shadow won't deter you from having affairs. Nothing will. In the long run, I'll never be good enough."

She blurted out her worst fears. The truth of Emmanuelle Ferraro. She'd never been good enough. It had never mattered that she'd had a perfect scorecard in every subject. There had been fault found with some performance. Her language skills weren't perfect, even though her instructors had deemed them so. Her accents weren't right. Her instructors were just babying her as usual. Her mother had gone so far as accusing her of sleeping with them in order to maintain her good grades.

Training in hand-to-hand skills and weapons, she never was good enough, no matter how many extra hours she put in. No matter how often Stefano and the others praised her and told her she was every bit as good as they were, her mother sneered and told her they were just making her feel good, that she lagged behind their skills by miles.

As a woman, she was too heavy and needed to diet, her hair wasn't glossy enough, her skin needed to glow more. Her eyes were too big, her mouth too generous. Her lips too puffy. She sounded like a neighing horse when she laughed. Men rarely stayed faithful to the women they loved, let alone women who failed them. And if they weren't good in the bedroom?

She told him every single thing her mother had said to her, over and over, almost daily since her childhood. Val heard her out, staying silent while the tears ran down her face. She hated that shame and embarrassment were so impossible to hide from him. When she finally stopped, when she couldn't remember any more of the litany of her sins, Val groaned and dropped his face into her shoulder.

"I played right into your insecurities when you overheard the crap I said to Marge, didn't I, Princess? Your fucking mother. She set you up to always feel inferior, and I just beat you down right along with her. I'm so sorry, Emme. I really am. You're not anything like Eloisa has made you feel. Nothing like that at all. I don't see you that way, and no one else does. Only you, because she wanted you to look at yourself that way. I have no idea why a woman would want her daughter to be so insecure."

Emmanuelle had never understood why her mother despised her so much. She'd tried telling herself Eloisa had been hard on her because she was afraid for her and wanted her to be the best shadow rider possible. But why would she constantly belittle her looks? It was never-ending. She was hard on the boys, but not like Emmanuelle.

She kept her head down, refusing to look at Valentino. She'd never permitted herself to break down like this, even when she was alone. But a marriage of convenience, with eventual cheating by a man she didn't love, was far better than having Val cheat on her. Or having Val look at her with the same disdain her mother held for her. She couldn't bear that.

It was humiliating to confess it all to him, that she'd hidden away and made them both suffer because she'd been too much of a coward to face the truth. She'd been too ashamed to tell him. She hadn't wanted to face the truth herself, let alone tell the man she loved.

Valentino rocked her gently, never once reproaching her. He didn't force her head up or make her look at him, he just held her close to him as if she were the most precious treasure in the world, letting her cry until she couldn't cry anymore.

How could she ever live without him? There was no way she could give him up, not when he reacted to a complete breakdown like that. Hiccups. Ugly crying. She was a mess. It didn't seem to matter to him. He just held her, rocked her and stroked her hair or brushed kisses through it.

Emmanuelle began to focus on the things he murmured against her temple in his low, velvety voice. Soothing. Gentle.

"I love you so much, Princess. We can make it through anything together. We can. It's going to be all right. You'll see. I know this woman, owns a store down in New Orleans, third generation, makes voodoo dolls, the real deal. Unless you'd let me let Dario loose on her. I mean, I'd do it myself, but down the line, I know you, you'd get all sentimental and you'd be mad at me. You're not a woman to withhold sex, but I'm not taking chances, so it's the voodoo chick or Dario if we're going in that direction."

She rubbed her wet face on her sleeve and blinked rapidly to try to clear her eyes. "What in the world are you talking about?"

Val kissed her temple and sat up straight, his arm sliding around her neck. "Your mother. I can't exactly pay my respects myself, so I'm considering our options. The woman needs a serious kick in the pants. A wake-up call. If I could control that creepy little shadow, I'd send it, but I can't, so my options are limited. I can't do her in as much as I'd like to— she's your mother—although, if she messes with you, that option may go back on the table."

The low note in his voice warned her he wasn't joking. She pressed her head into his chest hard. "Don't threaten my mother. We can decide not to see her, but you can't harm her in any way. I'm serious. She's my mother."

"Miceli's my uncle. He's Dario's father. That doesn't mean he doesn't deserve to die. He absolutely does. No one hurts you, Emme. Stefano should have been protecting you. All of your brothers should have been. Eloisa is a bitter, vicious woman. I don't care what she went through, so don't defend her. You always do. She made your childhood a living hell. She's not going to continue to make your life that way, and she won't do it to our children."

"No, she won't," Emmanuelle said decisively. "I tried very hard to be everything she wanted in a daughter, but I couldn't measure up."

"You measured up, Emme. She didn't want you to feel beautiful or to succeed where she failed. You are beautiful. You walk into a room and no one can take their eyes off you. It took me a long time to get over a very childish reaction of jealousy with so many men's eyes on you all the time. You always felt like you were slipping away from me, and I wanted to hang on to you so much tighter. That was my insecurity, not yours. You're beautiful inside and out. My looks cover a monster. I have to own that."

She turned her face up to his. "That isn't true. Those women and children you're risking your life to find say differently, Val." She cupped the side of his face. "You always made me feel beautiful. You were the only one. I saw that in your eyes. Felt it when you said it. Believed it. Until that night."

"You knew better, Emme. We share the same nerve endings. I can't lie to you. You heard the lie I told her. You hear the truth when I say how beautiful you are. When I say I love you and you're the only woman I'll ever love."

She reached behind her and hooked her arm behind the nape of his neck. "All right, then, Valentino Saldi. I'm making my full commitment to you. I'll stand with you, be loyal to you, work this thing out with you and probably hit you over the head quite often. What do we do first?"

"We get married."

That was the last thing she expected him to say. It felt like a punch to her gut. Her breath rushed out of her lungs in a long exhale so there was no air. None. At. All.

CHAPTER THIRTEEN

"Breathe, Princess. You know how. You're just having a little panic attack." Valentino was wise enough to keep the
amusement out of his voice. His princess, at the mere mention of marriage, every single time, suddenly couldn't find a
way to breathe.

He held her, nuzzling the top of her head. Rocking her.
Loving her. She was going to marry him. Just by the way she
couldn't breathe, he knew she was going to do it. He didn't
push her, because that was a sure way to disaster. He just held
her and waited, breathing with her, watching the shadows on
the wall, watching the creepy one settling back where he
should be. There were no more strange, independent movements, which meant Emmanuelle had finally committed
fully to him.

Peace settled into him. Strange when he'd never felt it
completely encompass him. She'd brought moments to him.
Little reprieves when they were together at the lake house,
but then she would slip away from him and he'd feel even
more alone and desperate to get her back. Sometimes he

thought of just taking her. Imprisoning her like his damn shadow had done. He was a ruthless man, and not a good one. He wasn't above using any means possible to get his woman, but he wasn't going to do that. He wanted her to choose him. Emmanuelle was a fighter. One misstep and she might really cut his throat.

"All right. When?"

"We have to go immediately. We'll take one of the jets to Vegas, get married and get back here. I'll ask your brother to keep watch over Giuseppi while we're gone. No one will know we're even away from here. I swear, Princess, when this is over and we've found Miceli's trafficking ring, we'll have a decent wedding."

"I don't care about that. I was never the girl that dreamt of a fairy-tale wedding."

He caught her chin then and lifted it so her eyes met his. He wanted her to see him. "I was the boy that dreamt of one. I wanted to watch you come to me wearing that dress, looking like my princess, Emmanuelle, on Stefano's arm, with the church filled with our families."

Her blue eyes moved over his face for what seemed an eternity, and then she smiled. Slow. "I guess I'll have to wear a dress that makes me look like a princess, just for you, Valentino. We'll have our church wedding, if that is what you really want. In the meantime, if we're going to Vegas, I can call Franco Mancini, our pilot, and ask him to have our jet ready. Miceli will never suspect you're on it with me. Stefano might insist on going with us."

"Do you want him there?" Val would give her the world if he could. He had no idea if Stefano would approve of them rushing off to Vegas, let alone going with them. The idea of even telling him before it was done was daunting. He knew Stefano had a tremendous influence on Emmanuelle. Her oldest brother's word had been law for too many years.

Emme's teeth tugged at her bottom lip, her blue eyes steady on his. She nodded slowly. "Yes. No matter what he says, Val, I'll go with you to Vegas."

"Then contact him and let's get ready." He hesitated. "I have a ring, baby, one I commissioned some time ago from Damian Ferraro, one of your million cousins. He talked to me at great length. I have to say, the man is very unnerving. He looks right through you. He told me he didn't understand how I could end up with a woman like you. I didn't tell him who you were, but he seemed to know. When the rings came, they weren't anything like I asked for. He told me to trust him. That only these rings would do for you. If you didn't like them, he would make the rings I asked for free of charge."

Emmanuelle's breath caught in her lungs. "Damian is a genius when it comes to making jewelry. Only certain elements can safely go into the shadows. He would make rings that would go into the shadows with me."

"How would he know you can go into the shadows if I never said who my fiancée was?" Val asked. Her family was plain freaky.

"That's his gift, besides making the most beautiful custom jewelry."

Valentino could tell she wanted to see the rings. That made him relax a little more. He hadn't been happy when Damian had given him rings that hadn't looked anything like he'd ordered. He wanted Emmanuelle to have the very best, to look down at her hand and know she belonged to him and he loved her. The excitement on her face told him maybe her cousin knew more than he did after all.

He tipped her chin up and took her mouth. Gently. Tenderly. No matter if he started out that way, and he tried to, their kisses always turned into something else. Hot. Wild. Burning out of control. He poured love into her. Saying it with everything he was, wanting to reassure her after the insecurities she'd revealed to him. That had taken courage on her part and he'd always take the greatest care to remember how her mother had torn her down. He vowed only to build her up, to support her.

Valentino lifted her off his lap before it was too late. They were never going to get to Vegas if he didn't stop. "See if we can use your family's plane. If not, I'll call for mine. We both need to get dressed and I'll let Dario know we're going. If your brother is coming with us, we need to arrange protection for my father."

"Stefano will do that and let you know immediately," Emme assured him. She slipped off the bed, her phone in her hand. "I'll text Franco first. If he's a go, I'll text Stefano while I'm dressing."

There was determination in her voice and she was already texting the pilot, he could see her thumb flashing over the keyboard. He moved more leisurely, although it wasn't because he just wanted to stare his fill at Emmanuelle. There was that, of course; he could look at her all day and it would never be enough. Watching her move across the room, he could see the sensual woman and the predator. It was sexy as all get-out. He moved slowly because his body protested every small movement he made.

The sex had been often and rough. Sex between them usually was. It had been a long time, and they'd both needed it for a variety of reasons, but his body let him know he wasn't quite as ready for that kind of out-of-control workout as he would've liked. His muscles protested every movement, making him feel like an old man.

He texted Dario that they would be heading to Vegas. He wanted two men they trusted on Giuseppi along with Stefano's guards. Giuseppi was still in the suite at the Ferraro Hotel, in the lap of luxury, and would most likely be visited by the Ferraro women and their men and treated as an honored guest. His father would eat that shit up. Stefano had assigned two very grim-faced and clearly competent guards to him, Drago and Demetrio Palagonia. His father would be safe, high up in a very secure hotel with the Ferraro guards as well as his own.

Suppressing a groan, he set his feet on the floor and forced his muscles to stretch out. The leg wound was the worst. He made himself stretch more, until he knew he could move quickly if necessary. Liquid glue or whatever the surgeon had said he used wasn't staying with all the running around Val had done. The wound continued to leak. He'd changed the bandage multiple times. He most likely shouldn't have gotten it wet. Dario had changed it as well, and now Emme.

"Stefano is meeting us at the plane. He didn't even object, Val." There was a slight note of suspicion in her voice. "Did you warn him we might be getting married?"

Valentino knew that little note. His woman had the famous Ferraro temper, whether she wanted to admit it or not. She kept it under tight control, but she had it. She didn't like her brothers knowing her business—unless she decided to tell them. She definitely wouldn't like her man going behind her back and informing them of anything without her consent or knowledge first.

"Princess, who is the head of your *famiglia*? Who raised you? If I am to get consent to marry you, I ask permission from the head of your family. It is tradition. Stefano is the head of your family."

"And if he'd said no?"

"Then we would have eloped. He knew that. He knew I had already compromised you."

She came out of the master bath, her expression murderous. "*Compromised* me? What century are we living in, Valentino?"

He burst out laughing as he gingerly stepped into the trousers of the suit he'd hung in her closet. "Not sexually compromised, you little hellcat. I compromised your shadow. Get ready before you make me so hard, I can't zip up my pants and you have to take care of my cock all over again."

Her gaze swept down his chest to his groin and stayed there, a dark, hungry mixture of lust and desire in her expression. Her tongue moistened her lips. "It's not like they'll put the plane in the air without us."

His cock jerked hard. Throbbed. Burned. "Emmanuelle." He poured a warning into his voice.

She raised her gaze to his. There was amusement there, daring him to share laughter with her at their predicament. The way they were with each other every time they got close.

"Get out of my sight, Princess." He put a growl in his voice.

She burst out laughing as she disappeared back into the bathroom. He couldn't help but join her, even though he was as hard as a rock. It didn't matter. Emmanuelle Ferraro had agreed to become his wife. That was what truly mattered to him. He loved her with every breath he drew.

S urrounded by the enemy.

Val glanced down at Dario's text and smirked. The Ferraro family had shown up in force for Emmanuelle. He was happy they had. At first, not so much. Thinking about it, though, the way she'd been treated all of her life by her bitch of a mother, having her brothers and their women show Emme they loved her and wanted to see her happy mattered.

She had her hand firmly in his, and she'd leaned into him to read the text. He hadn't shielded the screen from her. Dario knew she could see it. She took the phone.

Allies now, you dolt.

Val looked around the plane. Stefano had his woman with him. Francesca seemed to be the center of the Ferraro family, just as Stefano was the leader. The others all looked at her with tremendous love and respect. Emmanuelle treated her as if she were the greatest treasure on earth.

Valentino was an observer. He rarely missed a single small detail. That was what allowed him to find strengths and weaknesses among all the capos his father worked with. It had allowed him to see through lies and to know who stole from them within their organization. He read men's characters. He saw into women's motivations. He needed to do the same with the Ferraros, and this was one of the best opportunities he would ever have. Stefano was a born leader, and not one of his brothers, all true alphas, all dominant men, challenged a single decision. That said a tremendous amount about his leadership and the respect they had for him.

Stefano clearly loved his wife. He didn't try to hide the way he felt about her. He was protective, concerned, relaxed in her company, laughed more, and was very attentive to her needs. He clearly watched her, even when he was engaged in a conversation with his brothers. If she needed anything at all, he would break off in the middle of a sentence and order it for her.

Ricco was much quieter than the rest of his brothers and appeared more dominant, but only because his wife, Mariko, appeared to be submissive. She was blonde, although part Asian, a gorgeous woman who sat close to her man and spoke in a low, sultry voice. Val knew Ricco was considered a true rope master, one of the few who could make that claim, studying under Master Kin Akahoshi for years both in Japan and then the United States. Val knew the two men still worked closely together.

Ricco and Mariko seemed very in tune with each other, moving as if a coordinated team. When Mariko would get up to do anything at all, Ricco's gaze was on her. Val found himself studying the woman. It didn't take long to come to the conclusion that unlike Francesca, whom they all guarded and watched over carefully, including Mariko and Emme, this woman was a warrior. She was part of the guard. She might have looked totally feminine, but looks were deceiving in the Ferraro family. Mariko Ferraro could strike one down as easily as one of the men. She went into the shadows and was an assassin as surely as Emmanuelle was.

His phone vibrated. Emmanuelle laughed.

Since I can't ever go to sleep now that Val's got you back in his life because I expect you to cut my throat the first chance you get, I suspect I am on your family's most wanted list.

Valentino loved the sound of her laugh. He glanced over at Dario, who was in the seat next to Emilio. Evidently, most of those on the plane, including Dario, loved Emme's laugh.

They all glanced up and smiled. She had that kind of infectious laugh. It was melodic. Dario rarely smiled about anything. Val had never been certain if he could smile, but once in a while, something Emmanuelle did would bring that little half smirk onto Dario's face, and Val would want to kiss Emme for it.

We not only have a list in Stefano's study but all the faces are up on the board above their names. Yours was #2 but I think it was moved to the #1 spot now that Val is marrying me.

Emilio snorted and coughed. Enzo pounded his back helpfully. Dario shook his head as he studied the text. He didn't look across the aisle of the luxury plane at Emme.

Val took his eyes off his cousin to study the next Ferraro pair, Giovanni and Sasha. Giovanni was notorious for his temper. He was quiet one moment, burned hot, out of control and then it was over in a flash. Brilliant, quick-witted, funny, he was crazy about his wife, Sasha. She was a little bit of an enigma. She moved like she could handle herself. He knew quite a bit about her, because he made it a point to always know everything he could about his enemies, and in this case, Emmanuelle's family. She was from Wyoming and had grown up on a cattle ranch with her parents and older brother, Sandlin. Blue-eyed with curly blonde hair, she'd come to Chicago because Sandlin had suffered a traumatic brain injury in a car accident that killed their parents. The Hendrick Center was reputed to be one of the best places to treat brain injuries. She also looked as if she could handle herself, but Val honestly couldn't tell if she was at the same level of lethalness as Mariko was.

Then there were Vittorio and Grace. Vittorio had always appeared to be the peacemaker, the quiet, soft-spoken Ferraro. He was the tallest of the brothers and broad-shouldered. Although soft-spoken, his voice was very compelling. His eyes were an intense green, and Val knew from experience that he packed a hell of a hard punch. He was like a damn oak tree. He designed race car engines and played the piano. It was difficult to define him.

Grace, Vittorio's wife, was a partner in an extremely successful event planning business. A couple of years earlier, she had taken a bullet in her shoulder and had since had several surgeries to repair it. Val had made it his business to find out and knew the surgeries hadn't been nearly as successful as anyone would have liked. She had suffered through infections, and the last surgery had been a complete replacement shoulder, in the hopes that her body wouldn't reject that.

He understood why not only Vittorio, but the rest of the family, was protective of her. She was a very sweet woman, gentle and kind. She didn't seem to ever complain. Emmanuelle clearly thought the world of her. Where Mariko and Sasha were reserved around him, which Val didn't blame them for, and Francesca was open but wary, Grace was friendly and willing to like him because he was Emme's choice. She was an unusual, rare woman.

Vittorio's attention was centered on her in the way Stefano's was on Francesca. Maybe even more so. These men were strong and deadly, every one of them, and yet they had a tremendous weakness. He looked to the last of the brothers.

Taviano. Taviano had claimed Nicoletta almost immediately, from the first time that she had come to live with her foster parents, Lucia and Amo Fausti. She'd been a broken teen, wild and out of control. The Ferraro family had protected her, claimed her as their own and built a circle around her to keep anyone else out.

Taviano was a replica of Stefano in many ways. He had the same build, those same blue eyes. Emmanuelle said he was an excellent chef. Val knew he designed engines for race cars along with Vittorio. He seemed to be quite brilliant, a trait the Ferraro family shared. His choice had always been Nicoletta. She'd grown into a woman, much more confident and much like Emme and Mariko. Val guessed she could go into the shadows and was trained in their work as an assassin as well.

Stefano came over to them and dropped into the luxury seat on the other side of him. He gave Valentino a wolfish smile. "You're studying the members of the family as if they're your enemies. Sizing them up for weaknesses."

Because he was holding Emmanuelle's hand, Val felt the instant tension coiling in her, the sudden rigidness in her fingers and the pulling tightness in her tendons. He stayed relaxed and used his thumb to brush caresses over the back of her hand, trying to convey to her that all was well, not to worry.

"It's a habit I'm afraid I'll never be able to break. I developed it after my parents died in a car bombing." He gave a casual shrug. "Perhaps before that. I don't remember. It feels like I've always done it."

Stefano held out his hand to his sister, palm up, indicating he wanted Val's phone. Emme looked up at Val for permission, and he wanted to kiss her. She'd never done that before. She'd always obeyed Stefano's commands without thinking about it, at least around Val. He gave a slight nod and she placed the phone in Stefano's palm.

"I do the same thing," Stefano admitted. "That's what keeps us and our families alive. In this case, marrying Emmanuelle makes you *famiglia*. We take that very seriously. I would imagine that you do, too. Until you prove disloyal to us, and we would take that very seriously as well, we are *famiglia*. That means something, Valentino. So when you study us, do so through the eyes of *famiglia*. We will do the same."

He typed in a message and then handed the phone back to Val. "Francesca is very excited. She hasn't been out of the house for a while. We left Crispino with a sitter, Velia, another cousin of ours out of LA. You'll meet her soon, I'm sure. She and her brothers will help when needed. In the meantime, Francesca can have a bit of a well-deserved breather."

Val liked that they all took such good care of their women. "When you're out in the open, at clubs, the races, charity events, do you act the same with your wives?"

"You mean in front of the cameras?"

"In front of your enemies?"

Val continued to brush his thumb back and forth along the

back of Emmanuelle's hand. If he showed the bosses of the other crime families that he felt the way he did about Emme, he would be putting such a target on her back. Most of the families felt the way Parisi did, that women gave them children, heirs, but they weren't part of the business. They took mistresses and went to the clubs to play.

A couple of the families were like Giuseppi's, believing family was off-limits and wives were sacred. They were careful and didn't allow others to know how they felt, afraid of kidnappings and even torture or rape if they failed to cooperate with demands. Val knew if anyone had Emmanuelle, he would give away everything he had to get her back. He'd put a bullet in his own head if it would guarantee her safe return.

"We're . . . more cautious. We do look like playboys. Our former images have given them some protection. They go nowhere without bodyguards. Francesca doesn't always like it. Neither does Grace. Both feel it stifles them at times. Francesca does quite a bit of the work in the neighborhood for our *famiglia*. Going to an elderly woman's home with several intimidating bodyguards can be irritating. I get that."

"But it doesn't change a thing," Val said. It wouldn't change it for him.

"No. It has never stopped me from sending them with Emmanuelle, either, even though she is perfectly capable of protecting herself. It hasn't stopped Emilio and Enzo from sending bodyguards with me. Or, I imagine, Dario from sticking close to you."

Valentino gave a derisive snort. "Nothing can stop Dario from doing anything his mind is made up to doing. I think if you killed him and he was already in hell, he'd just come back and do it anyway." He glanced down at his phone to see what message was sent to his cousin.

I was forced to take you off the most wanted list. Reluctantly. You are now famiglia. You will be expected to come to all family dinners and socialize. That means more than grunt.

Val did his best to keep a straight face. He couldn't look

at Dario. He passed the phone to Emmanuelle. Who knew Stefano had a sense of humor?

"You know it can't work that way in my circle. The moment I show a vulnerability, the sharks circle. They'll be out for her blood."

Stefano nodded. "Perhaps that is true, but if that is so, Valentino, they are not your allies. She will bring out your enemies faster than anything else."

Val's temper swirled hotly. Anger burst through him. "I don't use my wife as bait any more than you would use yours."

"Emme isn't Francesca. Emmanuelle has certain abilities that Francesca doesn't have. Her allegiance is to you. Do you plan to keep her in your kitchen? She's your partner in the same way our women partner with each of us. She's what you need. You're what she needs. Don't be a prideful fool because you've been taught women should have one place in your home. You'll ruin the best thing you've ever been handed if you do that."

Val knew what Stefano was telling him was the truth. Emmanuelle had already told him that. He'd listened. He'd tried to let her idea of a true partnership sink into his brain. His first step had been to acquire her by any means possible. Marry her. Get her commitment. Emme didn't go back on her word. Once she took her vows, she would bend over backward to make things work between them.

He didn't want Emmanuelle in danger. That was the bottom line, but just by marrying her he was putting her in danger. The marriage would give him so much. He would be strengthening his position in the five families immediately. He would be allies with the infamous Ferraro family. The other bosses would fear going up against him. He had already sent a huge message to everyone that he was in charge, and he wasn't fucking around, sitting on his ass, waiting for Giuseppi's murdering brother to come at him again. He was going after Miceli.

He had also signaled it was business as usual. He had insisted his capos pay their debts to him and do it immediately or tell him why they couldn't. Even in the midst of a war with his uncle, he ran the Saldi empire with an iron fist. He'd weeded out the traitors and was still looking for others. He was bold, merciless, ruthless, and considered one of the most lethal but fair in the business.

He looked at Mariko and then at Nicoletta. Clearly, Ricco and Taviano didn't love their women any less. Stefano would never encourage him to put Emmanuelle's life on the line. He would want her happiness. He knew her better than anyone else.

"We haven't talked about her skills. I never asked her specific questions about what she could or couldn't do. We were always very careful not to get into each other's family's business. I loved and wanted her for her. I know she loved me for me. I studied your family just as I do everyone coming in contact with us. I guessed at what you did, but I never asked her, and it seemed rather preposterous."

"It does, doesn't it?" Stefano said. "Emmanuelle will be an asset to you as a full partner, Val. She's brilliant. She's intensely loyal, and you can talk to her. She'll see things you'll miss, but if you try to relegate her to a place where she feels she's nothing but a trophy on your arm, you will eventually find that she's going to take you down faster than any of your enemies."

"Emmanuelle is right here, in case anyone notices," she said, looking up at Val. "I thought we discussed this. Are you having second thoughts? If you are, you should say so now, before we get married, not after. I mean it, honey. A full partnership is all I'm accepting."

Valentino pulled her hand to his mouth, pressing her knuckles to his lips, and then scraped his teeth back and forth over her skin. His heart accelerated. He knew she was fully aware of it because they were so connected by the way their nervous systems were entwined together.

"I'm trying, Princess. The thought of anyone kidnapping you, putting a sniper's bullet into you, or torturing you because of me makes me sick. I think I'm on board, and then it's like my worst nightmare and I find myself backing away from the idea and wanting to wrap you up in a little cocoon somewhere safe."

Val wasn't even embarrassed to confess to her in front of her brother, not after seeing the man with Francesca. Val knew he sounded as raw and vulnerable as he felt.

She cupped the side of his face and looked into his eyes. His heart immediately had that curious melting sensation it sometimes did around her. It was the intensity of her blue eyes when she gazed into his. Her slow, sensual smile.

"I'm so in love with you, Valentino Saldi. I know you see me as gentle and soft. I've trained since I was two years old to be anything but. I'm good with any weapon. Hand to hand. I can fly helicopters, planes. I'm hell on wheels in a car, motorcycle, any land vehicle, boat, whatever you need. I can spot a tail and I can lose them. I can build a bomb or take one apart. I'm not as good at that as some of the others, but in a pinch, I can get it done. The point I'm making is, I'll be a good partner. I know when to keep my mouth shut if you need candy on your arm. If you need a badass, I'm your girl. If you need someone watching from the shadows no one can detect, you have that, too. I can coordinate your safety with Dario and intend to whether you like it or not when you go to any meeting. I'm good, baby. Better than good. You hit the jackpot when you fell in love with me."

"She's right," Stefano said before Val could reply. "You did hit the jackpot. Because aside from the fact that she's not bragging—every single thing she stated is a fact—she's our baby sister." He swept his hand around to include his brothers.

They all looked up, alert.

"You're Emmanuelle's choice. She's made that more than clear. I know she loves you and I can see very clearly that you love her for herself. So the biggest part of the jackpot is Emme and her abilities and how much she loves you, but the rest is her brothers and their women and how much we love her. That means we include you. We back your play and keep you alive. So she's right: you did hit the jackpot. Don't fuck it up by being overprotective."

"What did he just say?" Francesca asked.

A ripple of laughter went around the plane. Stefano frowned at his brothers.

"He told Valentino not to fuck things up with Emme by being overprotective," Vittorio said. "Great advice. I concur wholeheartedly."

"You do?" Grace asked. She looked up at her husband as if she couldn't quite understand what was being said. "You don't think a man should be too protective of his wife? Is that what I'm hearing from the two of you?"

"Yes, do explain, Stefano, Vittorio," Francesca said. She got up from her seat and began to make her way to the empty chair on the other side of Stefano.

The moment she was standing, nearly every man in the plane was up, reaching for her, as if she were fragile and needed help. She glared at them, but they ignored her. It was Giovanni who had his hands on his sister-in-law's waist, guiding her to Stefano.

"You mean like that?" Francesca demanded as she took the seat beside her husband. "The kind of thing that makes a woman want to pull her hair out?"

"If there had been any kind of turbulence, you could have fallen," Stefano said, leaning down to brush his mouth gently over hers. "Your brothers are just careful with you. Don't be upset with them because they care."

She rolled her eyes. "You told them I was pregnant again, didn't you?"

Emmanuelle gasped and turned toward Francesca. "You are? How far along? What did the doctor say? Should you be on the plane? Stefano? Should she be on a plane?"

"I would never allow her on a plane if the doctor hadn't given permission, Emmanuelle," Stefano assured. "Seeing you married was important to Francesca, to all of us."

"I've made it past the first trimester. I'm surprised you haven't noticed I'm wearing looser clothing."

"You still look thinner to me," Sasha said with a little frown. "How can you be pregnant and lose weight, not gain it? I'm at your house nearly every day. How come I didn't know?"

"I get sick. Sometimes I'm so sick the nurse comes and has to give me an IV with fluids. It's really quite horrible, but at the same time, if that's what it takes to have the baby, I'm willing to be sick," Francesca said. "We didn't tell anyone until it looked like I might be able to carry this one."

"What did the doctor say about the delivery?" Vittorio asked. "Are you going to have to go on bed rest?"

Immediately, Valentino noticed the tension rise on the plane. Emmanuelle's hand gripped his tightly. Already, he'd gleaned from the conversation that Stefano's wife had lost at least one baby, most likely others, and that when she had delivered, it had been life-threatening. Why the hell had Stefano allowed her to get pregnant? Was he so determined to have heirs? Val would have to ask that question when he was alone with Emme. He could see Stefano loved his wife and wanted her safe, yet she was risking her life carrying a baby. There were surrogates. What the hell!?

"He said maybe bed rest as the baby grows. We're having a girl. I'm very excited about that. Stefano is sharpening all of his knives."

A heavy sigh went around the plane.

"Stefano, really? You had to do that to us? A niece?" Ricco glared at his older brother. "More sons, yes; daughters, no. We all agreed on that. We don't need more girls in the family. They're stubborn and want equality."

Valentino noticed that Francesca hadn't answered the question of her delivery and neither had Stefano. He decided to test his initiation into the family. "Weren't you all just instructing me on how I should make absolute certain that I give Emmanuelle a full partnership and not fuck up my relationship by being overprotective? The next thing I know, you're handing Francesca down the aisle like she can't walk on her own and declaring no female children are allowed to be born because they demand equality. I'm getting whiplash from the constant back-and-forth."

"I am as well," Grace said in her quiet voice. "Vittorio, you were going to give me an explanation of what you meant. How a man shouldn't be overprotective of his woman because that could ruin his relationship."

Vittorio unsnapped his wife's seat belt, lifted her right onto his lap and flipped Val the bird behind Grace's back. Val's phone vibrated.

Famiglia at work. Nice one, Val, Dario pointed out.

I thought so.

Someone is bound to take out a gun and shoot you.

Might be worth it, Val fired back.

I have to admit beating the Ferraros at their own game feels satisfying even if you do get killed. I promise revenge.

Thx.

"The thing is this, Grace," Vittorio said. "Francesca is pregnant again, and we have to look after her. She's very fragile in that condition. We all love her very much and don't want anything to happen to her or the baby. You can't tell me you don't feel just as protective of her. I love you for that." He nuzzled her neck.

Val watched Grace lean back into him, her lashes falling as if her eyes were heavy. Even so, Vittorio was very careful of her artificial shoulder and how unstable it was. Valentino needed all the techniques he could get to handle his woman. Emmanuelle was a little wildcat when it came to sex. If he wasn't careful, she was going to get the upper hand far too soon.

"I'm not pregnant," Grace murmured, her voice so low Val barely caught the little thread of sound. "And I think you're overprotective of me."

Vittorio kissed his way over her neck to her ear. "Do you think that, Grace? That I'm overprotective of my most precious treasure? What is overprotective? You're not tied to my bed the way I would prefer. You're not confined to the house with guards at every door. I'd like that as well. You aren't stripped naked and cuffed by the ankles and wrists to the St. Andrew's Cross looking out over the lake, where I like you waiting for me, unable to move. That's overprotective to me. You have a successful business out in the public, and I give that to you even though I worry every damn minute you're exposed."

His voice was velvet soft. Again, if they weren't so close, Val doubted if he could have heard a word Vittorio said to his wife. The brothers acted as if they didn't hear. He knew Dario listened, but he wouldn't care. He was the kind of man who would do the things Vittorio threatened his wife with.

"You have a shoulder that refuses to heal. Your health is fragile." His teeth bit on her earlobe and tugged and then scraped down her neck. She arched her head back to give him better access. "I'm careful with you, Grace, not overprotective, but that's coming. Should you ever get pregnant, you'll be seeing that side of me, and you'll be fine with it, won't you?"

She turned her head to look at him, one arm sliding around his neck. "Yes."

Emmanuelle threw her arms into the air. "That is so not me, Valentino. I hope you *never* think that's me."

He laughed. His little wildcat was so far from Grace's or Francesca's personality it wasn't funny. He liked both of the other women, but he was madly in love with Emmanuelle.

"I'm well aware, Emme. Have no worries on that score."

You are so pussy-whipped.

Ouch.

You are. You have been since you met her. You should be ashamed. She's cut your balls off.

"Dario thinks you cut my balls off."

Emmanuelle raised an eyebrow. She took his phone from his hand and stared down at it for a few long minutes while overhead a voice told them to prepare for landing. In a few minutes, they would be getting married. Emme would be his wife.

He watched as she carefully sent his cousin a new text.

Val's going to have the best sex of his life. Anytime, anywhere. That's what shadow sex can get you. Thought to help you out with that but seeing how you view what loving a woman does to you, I know finding even the right shadow woman for you would be doing her a disservice. Too bad because there's nothing like it in the world.

Hearing Dario groan was very satisfying.

Emme grinned at him. "I do so love revenge."

CHAPTER FOURTEEN

Emmanuelle stood in the mouth of the shadow tube watching each of the men in the room carefully. These were the men her husband would have to trust with his life. If they betrayed him, there was a better-than-average chance that he could die. He was giving instructions. Laying out the raids to them, in what order. They were going to hit Miceli's main businesses and shut them down.

She knew he planned on killing Miceli's key people and taking prisoner anyone who might be able to give them information on where the children were being held. It wasn't in the warehouses. They had the ability now to stop the auction, but they needed to know where everyone was being held and also how each pipeline worked. They were separate from one another. It wasn't only little girls brought in, it was also little boys. It wasn't only teen girls, it was also teen boys. However, it was always women if they were older. As far as Val had found out, there were no men brought in over the age of seventeen.

The idea of human traffickers made Emme sick. She

couldn't imagine how Val and Dario felt. They'd been on the trail of this ring for over two years. They knew Miceli, Tommaso and Angelo were involved, but they needed to know all the players. They needed to know which of the other families were providing children, teens and women. There had to be one or two very powerful figures that stayed behind the scenes and ran everything. Those were the men Val and Dario were ultimately after. Even if they shut down Miceli, it would only cause a brief disruption, not halt the business.

Emmanuelle had spent a great deal of her life in the pull of the shadow tubes, but this was the first time she was responsible for the man she loved. That was a terrifying thought. If she missed something, if one tiny detail escaped her and she overlooked a sign of treacherous intent, Val could be ripped from her in an instant.

Her heart accelerated. Her lungs burned for air. The beginnings of a panic attack. Valentino's dark gaze shifted toward her for one second. A hot, dangerous lick of heat sweeping past the shadow they'd created for her. He took a deep breath of air into his lungs—her lungs. Let it out. He knew. He always would know. They were that connected.

She was ashamed that she'd let herself panic. That wasn't her style. She breathed on her own, feeling the flood of warmth surging through her veins. She didn't want to be distracted, but she knew he was reassuring her that this was his life. He was used to the danger just as she was used to the danger of her life.

Emme kept her gaze from straying to her gorgeous husband and, one by one, inspected each of the men who would go on the raids with him. Normally, a man of his stature would never lead the raids, but Val insisted that if his men were going to put their lives on the line for him, he was going to direct the entire operation with them. Miceli wouldn't expect them. He would never think that Valentino would dare to raid his lucrative businesses himself. He might hit one, but all of them? In a single day?

"We don't leave anyone behind. If you're hit, shout out.

We have partners. Your partner is responsible for pulling you out of the fire. If he doesn't get you out, he'll answer to me. We let civilians go. His key people die. I want one prisoner taken from his people. Dario will select that person ahead of time and appoint who will take him. We'll pass him off, and he'll be brought to the interrogation site. It's that simple. We take Miceli's money and we burn his buildings to the ground. We strike fast and we get out even faster. Anyone hurt, we treat at the rendezvous point. We have a clinic set up if surgery is needed. Any questions?"

When there were none, the men moved quickly, drifting through the hotel's lower structures to the garage to enter cars. Valentino waited until it was only Dario, Severu Catalano, Luca Amato and Quintu Noto, three of the other men they trusted the most.

"Let's get this done, gentlemen," Val said, slipping on his gloves. "We've got a tight schedule."

"I'm still not happy with you going, Val," Severu said. "We can't afford to lose you."

"We can't afford for any of the families to think I'm above spilling blood myself," Val countered. "I want you to stay back, Severu. I can't afford to lose you. You're the man I count on to think things through. We need to figure out our next step."

Severu shook his head as they made their way to the garage through the underground tunnels. "Not on your life. You go, I go. We agreed to clean the shit up first, and then it would be don and advisor. That was the agreement."

Emmanuelle suppressed a smile. Valentino had more than his rebellious wife on his hands. It seemed some of his men were just as loyal to him. She saw his face darken. He got that look, the one that said he was the king and the world had better bow to his will. Deliberately, she stepped out of the shadows close to him, scaring his entourage, so that all but Dario pulled weapons on her.

"Damn it, Emme, you could have been shot," Valentino

snapped as she fell into step beside him, walking toward the car.

"Sorry, honey. I needed to give you a message from my brother before you went. It was important."

"Next time, make some noise," he groused.

She avoided looking at his men. They would see the woman in the pinstriped suit with her hair in a tight braid woven in a crown around her head. She always braided it as tight as she could possibly get it to keep from feeling as if she were being scalped. She kept her eyes down, the errand girl, the wife delivering a message from one of her powerful brothers. It was an illusion they wanted to keep up as long as possible until they knew who their enemies were.

Dario had fallen into step on the other side of her, shielding her from the others. When had he taken to doing that? She could have texted the information to Val's phone, but Bernado Macaluso, Val's resident hacker whiz, had cautioned them against doing just that. He could hack phones, said it was too easy.

She matched her steps to Val's as they approached the car that would take him to the first of many of Miceli's businesses. "Stefano says for certain, Marge is holding women somewhere in her strip club beneath her underground dungeon club. Ricco is looking with him, but he says no doubt she would let them burn before she would give up their location."

Her voice was pitched very low so only he could hear. His gut twisted. He knew Marge was hard, but to allow innocent women to die a horrific death sickened him. The worst of it was, he could see her doing that. Not just because she didn't want to get caught, but because she enjoyed hurting others. She would want Valentino to know he had killed those women. She would taunt him with the knowledge.

Marge was one of the pieces of Miceli's trafficking ring, a huge part of it. She had knowledge of it, but she wouldn't easily give it up. Val could take men apart, compartmentalize, but he couldn't do the same to a woman. His father could, but he wasn't built that way. He didn't like inflicting pain on women.

Not being able to extract information from a woman was a weakness Giuseppi had tried hard to stamp out of him, but had never managed to do. Dario had covered for him time and again. Now, facing the possibility that he would have to take Marge to the interrogation room made him feel sick all over again.

"Wait for me at home, Emme," he said suddenly, cupping her face between his hands. He looked into her blue eyes. The world was there. His world. He needed something fresh and clean to come home to. "You don't need to see me like this." He hated the pleading in his voice.

He bent his head and kissed her. Taking her mouth, not caring if his men waited on him. Not caring if they saw he had a weakness. He held her face between his hands and kissed those perfect lips of hers. That perfect firestorm that seemed to cleanse him from the inside out. When he lifted his head, he traced her swollen bottom lip with his thumb.

"I see the man I love, Valentino," she whispered. "I'll always see the man I love. Get going. The others are waiting for you. And stay safe. I mean it." She turned her head to look at Dario. "You, too. I don't know why, because you're an ass who thinks he's superior to all women, but I've grown fond of you, so come back safe."

She didn't wait for either of them to reply. She walked away, again without looking at the other three men who stood by a car, doors open. She felt their eyes on her, so she kept her head up. Valentino could break her every time. She rounded the corner and stepped into the first shadow that would take her out of the underground in the direction she needed to go.

Valentino was hitting Miceli's smallest restaurant. It laundered more money for him than businesses ten times its size. It was very popular and stayed open nearly all night. The back room had a narrow staircase that led to a wine cellar with a variety of Italian wines in tall racks. The staircase was narrow for a reason. It allowed the security people to see anyone coming at them that shouldn't be downstairs. The illegal gambling was extremely lucrative for Miceli because his very wealthy patrons were allowed to bet on various opportunities, which he provided through closed-circuit screens.

They could request shows and pay for them. Everything from raping women to raping children. There were fights to the death between men and between boys. Miceli provided anything his patrons wanted. Valentino wanted a list of those patrons, but he knew shutting down the ring was the most important thing he could do first.

Valentino had a secret crew in the Ferraro brothers. They would enter the gambling pit through the shadows. He didn't want Emmanuelle anywhere near those depraved screens. She didn't need to see helpless men and boys when they couldn't get to them. That would break her heart and give her nightmares. It was impossible to unsee what one saw. He knew because he'd tried.

His men would go in through the front and back doors, taking over the restaurant, herding any innocents out and closing and locking doors before they proceeded with their grim task. He'd chosen the early morning hours, when the fewest people frequented the place, but the gambling hall beneath was still heavily occupied.

He walked right up to the front door, smiling at the man on the door, who looked bored as hell. He was busy looking at his phone and just reached out to pull the door open without even looking up. Valentino recognized him from his childhood. He'd been in Miceli's organization a long time. He often had a different woman on his arm every month attending parties and charity events. Growing up, Val hadn't understood why the women kept their heads down and didn't respond when anyone spoke to them. Biff would laugh heartily if anyone said anything and say they used their mouths for other things.

Val walked into the cool, dark interior of the restaurant, Dario on his heels, sliding in front of him, giving him a glare. Behind him, Luca wrapped his arm around Biff, putting a knife to his throat, while Quintu casually jerked the gun from under his jacket. They rabbit-walked him inside.

"Do you have any idea who you're fucking with?" Biff demanded, his eyes trying to adjust to the lighting.

Quintu moved around the room, stopping at one table only, then snapped his fingers. "Wallet." He had pulled up a scarf that covered half his face.

The man handed it over without protest. Quintu took out the license, made a show of studying it and turned to the woman, snapping his fingers. She gave her wallet to him as well. He did the same thing and then handed both back and pointed to the door.

"Leave while you can. No cops or we come calling and wipe out your entire family. We can find you anywhere, anytime."

The couple instantly got up, and without looking at anyone else, keeping their heads down, they hurried out of the restaurant. Quintu trailed after them and locked the door, turning the sign to closed. The moment he did, Luca shoved his knife through the back of Biff's skull and dropped him to the floor.

Valentino had leaned over the counter to watch the woman at the register, making certain she didn't hit the panic button that would tell those in the gambling room they had unwanted visitors. He smiled at her. "Hi, Alice. Do you remember me? I talked to you a few months back. You were dating Angelo, hoping for a ring, I believe. You would do anything for him to get that ring on your finger."

He reached out and took her hand, stroking her tense fingers. "I don't see a ring, Alice. Did you discover he had so much pussy available to him that he didn't need a wife? He likes to play in his dungeon. You were too accommodating. He wanted you to bring him other women, women who weren't so accommodating, didn't he? You did that for him, didn't you?"

Her gaze shifted away from his, and she nodded. He already knew the answer.

"Val, it isn't my fault. I love him."

"No, Alice, you really didn't love him. You don't now. You wanted out of the trash life you lived and thought grabbing onto Angelo would give you that. How many of your friends did you deliver to him?"

He kept his voice low. Soothing. He already knew the answer to that. She was sick. She didn't care about anyone but herself and what she wanted. Again, her gaze shifted from his.

"Don't lie to me, Alice. I'll know if you lie."

"Seven."

"He tortured them down in the dungeon after hours, didn't he? With you there. Your friends. Women you grew up with. Women who trusted you. He tortured and raped them with you cheering him on. He recorded those sessions and sells them to his sick patrons, making money off the suffering and death of those women."

"I didn't know."

"You knew. You helped set up the recording equipment. You can be heard telling one woman to smile for the camera as she was dying. Where are these women held before Angelo uses them, Alice? If you don't tell me, you'll be taken to my interrogation room and I'll let Dario loose on you. You won't like what he does. It can last for days. Weeks. The pain never stops. Body parts disappear."

She went white beneath her beautiful olive skin as she shook her head desperately. "I don't know. He never told me. I would bring my friend to the club and when we were laughing and dancing, they would drug her and take her away. We were upstairs, not even in the dungeon. I never was told where they held her."

Her voice resonated with the truth. Valentino sighed. He glanced at Dario as he pulled out his gun. Dario knew as well as he did that Alice couldn't tell them anything they needed to know. Valentino began screwing on a suppressor, not wanting to alert those down below, but Dario simply pulled the trigger twice and then turned toward the interior with the other four men who had been eating there. They were part of Miceli's guard. He lifted his gun again. Luca and Quintu added their bullets and all four men went down.

Quintu immediately cleared the register, but then went into the back office to the safe. He dropped down on his knees on the plush red-and-gold carpet and began to work on the combination lock. Valentino's men crowded behind Val and Dario as they started toward the wine cellar.

"Everyone in place?" Val asked, using the wire in his ear.

"Back door has been breached. We're in," Romeo Vitale answered. "Sir, this room is filled with money. Stacks of it. We've got about twenty sinners."

"Anyone that is a significant player?"

"I don't think so," Romeo said, but there was a question in his voice.

"Tore Vitale? You have an opinion?" Val had to rely on those there.

A small silence followed the question. "There is one man both of us are considering. He's sweating like a pig and keeps looking down the stairs toward the wine cellar like he thinks someone is going to save him," Tore said. "But none of them are giving much away."

"Kill everyone but him." Val gave the order.

He wasn't going to wait for one of the Ferraro family to second-guess his men. He had to be able to rely on them. Stefano and the others couldn't always be with him. His crew needed to be discerning. Romeo didn't trust his own judgment, but he felt the same way Tore did. Tore laid it out there. Neither man had a lot to go on, but at least they made a decision. Val was looking for leadership in his capos. Both Tore and Romeo were young, but he saw good qualities in them.

He started down the staircase, avoiding the narrow one that led to the wine cellar. This one led to the offices and the storehouse where all the walk-in refrigerators were, the giant shelves for breads and pastas and whatever else Miceli wanted stored. Behind the pantry doors was his real operation, the counting and bundling of his money.

Dario opened the pantry doors and went through to the back room first. Dead bodies lay on the floor in a river of blood. It should have bothered Val, but it didn't. These men knew where that money came from and they didn't care. As long as they got their cut, they were happy and kept their mouths shut. He glanced around the room. There were seven long rows of tables that went across the room, a chair every two feet for these men to sit and count the money, stack and band it for Miceli.

The money went into a floor-to-ceiling vault behind an iron gate, both of which were open. The vault was already neatly crammed with banded bills.

"Holy fuck," whispered Luca. "This is going to hit Miceli hard." He grinned at Valentino. "Really hard."

"Start filling those sacks." Val indicated the deep white canvas bags stacked to the right of the vault, clearly used to transport the money to other places. "Move fast. We're running out of time here. Get as much as you can. I'm going downstairs to greet our good citizens. If there's anyone of interest, we'll nab them up and take them to the room; otherwise, we'll just kill everyone and burn this place to the ground. You'll only have about five to seven minutes so work fast or the money goes up with Miceli's restaurant."

"You got it," Tore said. "Move, boys, you heard Don Saldi. Clean out the vault and everything off the tables. Put the sweaty pig in the car. Make sure you gag him. He seems to like ball gags. He's got three of them in his pocket. Use one of them."

Val was careful as he picked his way through the war zone, not wanting to get blood on his shoes. "Coming down, Stefano. You have them covered?"

"Yes." Stefano's voice was clipped.

Yeah. He'd seen the fucking bets being placed and what the filthy, vile creatures were betting on. Stefano was like him. He just wanted to end them.

"Did you keep Emmanuelle out of there?" He hoped her brother had done a better job of controlling her than he had.

"Unfortunately, she was running point. She saw the closed circuits before I did. In a way, Val, it was a good thing. She needs to know what you're fighting. There's going to be some things that you, me or Dario have to do that she may object to, and seeing those sick images will help her be understanding."

"I don't want her understanding if it means she has night-mares. Would you allow Francesca to see that shit?"

"I can assure you, Emme is not Francesca."

Val made his way down the narrow stairs toward Miceli's patrons, the wealthy men who were so bored they liked to be as depraved as possible, feeling as if they were entitled to do anything they chose simply by virtue of their bank accounts.

"No, Emme isn't Francesca, but she still could use a little protection. A little care. Her mother fucked her up royally. Did you know that? She doesn't believe in herself. Doesn't see herself. That woman painted such an ugly picture of Emmanuelle, that Emme sees herself through those eyes, so much so I can barely get her to believe I love her. I can barely get her to believe anyone could love her. She might be ca-pable of being a badass assassin, Stefano, but she's my woman, and I want to treasure her the way you treasure your woman."

Valentino was pissed—really pissed—at Stefano. It was there in his voice. In the set of his broad shoulders as he strode through the door in his immaculate suit. His features were hard, his dark eyes glinting with rage. This was the same bullshit Stefano had used on the plane when they headed to Vegas.

Don't fuck things up with Emmanuelle by being overpro-tective, when it was clear, his woman was protected from everything by everyone. That just reinforced to Emme that she wasn't worth as much to the family—not as a woman. As an assassin, she had value; as a woman, none at all. He'd like to kick the shit out of Stefano and his brothers, but mostly, he wanted to spend a few minutes with Eloisa. He'd make an exception on hurting a woman for her.

The men sitting in front of their now-black screens came to attention, backs straightening as they tried to appear important in the suddenly bright room. Their eyes were riveted on Valentino. He was an imposing figure, and he knew it. He looked the epitome of power and danger. He wore the mantle of a man who decided the fate of others with the snap of his fingers. These men, with their wealth and their buying and selling of human beings, used to getting whatever they wanted when they wanted it, stirred uncomfortably when his dark, merciless gaze touched them.

One decided to bluster, to demand he be released immediately. "This is preposterous. You have no idea who you are dealing with. I could crush you and everyone you care about . . ."

Val took his time pulling his gun from his immaculate suit. He lifted it and shot the billionaire between the eyes. Then shot him again twice through the heart before he could fall. He pushed the gun back into the harness and walked around the room slowly, flicking his cold, empty gaze over them, dismissing them, recognizing most of them. He wasn't surprised at who was there.

Bernado Macaluso needed time to get into the phones of each of the men betting in Miceli's underground world.

"Four minutes," Ricco said.

"Tracing multiple accounts." Bernado was calm.

Valentino was determined to drain as much money from these men as possible to use it for any victims they could recover now and in the future. He hadn't discussed that aspect with Emmanuelle yet, but he would. They would find someone to put in charge of the best way to help the victims find safety in homes and counseling. That wasn't Val's forte. He dealt in blood and death.

"Is there something you want?" Senator Moralison asked. He sounded bored. He sat back in his chair and folded his arms across his chest.

Val flicked his gaze toward Dario and then raised his eyebrow at the senator. "Cutting out your tongue would be a start. Not hearing the sound of your voice."

"Spare me your moral lecture, Saldi," Moralison sneered. "That ten-thousand-dollar suit doesn't cover up the Sicilian reeking underneath it."

Dario caught the senator's head in a firm grip and yanked it back, placing a knife to his throat. His eyes were flat and cold. There was no mercy in the dark depths. No feeling at all. He made the cut slowly, giving him a happy smile, letting the senator feel the very sharp blade as it penetrated the skin and went into the artery. Blood ran down his neck onto his white collared shirt. Dario stepped back, wiped his blade between the senator's shoulder blades and then walked away.

"Need Douglas Patrick's account encryption code. He's the only one with any kind of decent security. I don't have the time to break it," Bernado said.

"Douglas." Val stood in front of him. "Would you be so kind as to write down your encryption code immediately for your offshore accounts? If you don't, Dario is standing directly behind you."

Douglas Patrick, a young billionaire who had inherited his grandfather's fortune from the diamond mines in South Africa, quickly wrote down what Val required and handed it to him. He shrugged. As far as he was concerned, there was far more money where that came from.

"Got it," Bernado said. "I'm out. We're done here."

Val went to the door and pulled his gun. He shot Douglas Patrick first. He had a folder on the man four inches thick, and everything in it was depraved. They killed everyone in the room. Val walked out with Dario while his men set up explosives to take down the building and burn it to the ground.

Marge's beloved strip joint was next on the list. There were several smaller businesses like this restaurant that had secrets, and big money exchanged hands, but Valentino was interested in stamping out the human trafficking pipeline in his territory. The more he had investigated, the more he realized how widespread it was. It wasn't just a few women or teenage girls: Miceli had an entire business built on young children. Boys fighting to the death in rings. Teens being auctioned off, both boys and girls. Little girls and boys being auctioned off. This was far bigger than what Valentino had ever expected when he'd first begun.

His uncle hadn't been the one to put all of this in place. Someone else had. They'd gone to Miceli knowing his weakness for women, his cruelty and his obsession with money. He hated being second to Giuseppi. This trafficking operation had been up and running long before Miceli had joined. Valentino could take down Miceli, but he wouldn't know which of the other families was involved if he simply shut down Miceli and his cousins' involvement.

Val slipped into the back seat of the car that was to take him to the next raid. Once the door was closed, he pressed his fingers to his eyes. His temples were pounding. The headaches were coming back. They'd started when Emmanuelle had left him, and he'd felt as if he'd lost her for good. Now he knew it was because he felt as if no matter what he did, it was never going to be enough. He couldn't stop the flow of children from getting to the depraved wealthy, those above the law who could buy them.

"Miceli's going to be pissed." There was satisfaction in Dario's tone.

"Yeah. We have to take the victories where we can, I guess," Val said without opening his eyes. "I don't want Emme to be at the club."

"You know she's going to be there, Val." Dario's voice was back to no expression. "She's tough, and she won't hold you responsible for anything she sees there. She knows you're not into the shit she'll see in the dungeon. Her job, her family's job, is to find the women and hopefully the kids so we can burn that place to the ground."

Val stayed silent while he thought that over. He felt for Dario. Sometimes there was no talking to him, no reaching out. Dario had been fucked over by Miceli. It didn't matter that the man was his father; Miceli didn't give a shit about him. It hadn't occurred to him that his son would become hard and dangerous and would have been an asset to him. Now it was too late.

"We'll shut them down, won't we, Dario?" Val murmured.

"Damn straight we will," Dario answered. "And find out who's behind this. We'll shut them down, too." He gave a little snicker. "Who would have thought we'd turn into the fuckin' good guys?"

"That is a little ironic, isn't it?" Val opened his eyes to look at his cousin. "And a bit on the scary side."

"I don't know how to do 'good guy.'"

He grinned at Dario. "There's no 'good' for you. That's just taking it too far."

The car pulled to the curb, and Val and Dario looked out the window. The strip club was across the street. In the early morning hours, the building appeared deserted. There were few cars in the lot. Marge's vehicle was there, but she had an apartment on the premises. Valentino and Dario had the complete layout of that luxury apartment. It looked like the replica of a penthouse suite at one of the finest luxury hotels in Chicago, which was such irony given the stark contrast of the conditions the women were taken to when kidnapped and sold at auctions.

Those women had a concrete floor with a drain to relieve themselves, a tiny cell, barely large enough to turn around in, no blankets, no warmth or air-conditioning, no clothes, no privacy, and they were beaten, subjected to electrical shock, raped, brutalized in every way, while Marge lived above them in luxury, listening to her music and entertaining her friends with the finest wine and the best food money could buy.

"Marge has a tremendous amount of security in her clubs. Cameras everywhere. She thrives on blackmail," Dario said, his dark gaze on her car.

"The Ferraros are good at what they do. Once they're in, Bernado will do the rest."

"Did you ever think the Ferraros would be our allies?" Dario asked.

Val shook his head. "Honestly? I thought Stefano would try to kill me, not help me. He loves Emmanuelle. I'm not nearly good enough for her."

"You're good enough for her."

Dario startled him with the proclamation. It wasn't something Dario did often. They didn't show their affection toward each other often. They weren't like that, even though they were closer than most siblings. Val didn't make the mistake of looking at Dario. He kept his gaze fixed in the parking lot.

"Emme heard what I said to Marge that night. About her not knowing anything about sex. Her mother had already done such a number on her, making her feel worthless. Marge has experience and confidence. She could so easily tear Emmanuelle apart. This entire scenario is fucked up, Dario."

He let the worry show, even though both Luca and Quintu were in the front seat. The privacy screen was down, but they still might have overheard. He usually was more cautious. He wanted Dario's help with Emme, just in case something went wrong. His gut was telling him things could go south in a heartbeat.

"Emmanuelle's strong, Val. Tough as nails."

"Not when it comes to being a woman. She's vulnerable."

Dario was silent so long, Valentino pulled his gaze from the hot red sports car in the parking lot to look at his cousin. Dario was looking down at his phone, studying an image on the screen. He handed the phone to Val.

There was a photo of Marge with her blond hair falling around her face. Her features were beautiful at first glance, but when one really looked, they were hard. Her lips thin, her green eyes sharp and jaded. There was a multitude of lines around her mouth from smoking. The continual Botox injections had taken a toll by showing the sites, with tiny brown pinpricks looking like raised freckles above her upper lip and around her forehead. Her smile was fake, not lighting her eyes, but drawing back her lips to show her whitened teeth while her eyes stared straight ahead in a predatory way.

Beside Marge's photo was one of Emmanuelle. Her hair was all over the place. Pulled back in a ponytail, so much had escaped the way it often did, showing his wildcat. The thick silk fell every which way around her small heart-shaped face. She was definitely Italian, with her skin and curves and that glossy hair. Her eyes laughed along with her generous mouth. She was so beautiful, she took Valentino's breath away.

Dario took his phone back. "You can see."

"I can see. You can see. God knows, any man can see, but I doubt that Emme can see. Her mother made certain of that, and I played right into Eloisa's hands. I don't understand why a mother would want to undermine her daughter's self-confidence like that. It makes no sense."

"Any more than a father forcing his son to fight for his life and the life of his mother just for the pleasure of other men like the ones in Miceli's basement tonight?"

Valentino took a deep breath. Dario's tone hadn't changed in the least. They could have been discussing the weather. "Yeah. I don't understand that shit, either."

"Or forcing a son to witness him torturing a man for days, one who'd sat at his dinner table and who he'd known from his childhood. Forcing him to participate, including delivering the killing blows with a hammer?" Dario continued.

Val refused to turn his head. He couldn't imagine telling Emmanuelle he was going to teach his son the way Giuseppi had taught him. The end of an empire. He pressed his fingers to his temples. What kind of legacy did he give his children? On the other hand, how did one stop the kinds of things that needed to be stopped?

The cops couldn't stop human trafficking. The FBI couldn't do it. The special task forces set up couldn't stop them. They tried. It wasn't that they didn't. These rings had so much money. So much. They bought and sold human beings. The wealthiest in the world were above the law. They made their own laws. They were the law. The politicians. The religious leaders. The bankers. Valentino knew because he had the money and the ability to look into that world. He could supply whatever was wanted. He saw the depravity. Someone had to stop it all or at least slow it down. Save as many kids as possible. To do that, he had to be in the dirt with the filthiest. That meant he had to ask Emmanuelle to do so.

"Don't think about it," Dario said. "At least you're a good man. You've got something to offer Emme. I can't offer a woman anything but heartache and pain. I find the right one, I know I'll take her, but it won't be right. It won't turn out like you and Emme. That fuckin' shadow thing, it will be doing its job, working to keep us together."

A chill crept down Valentino's spine. "Don't even kid about that, Dario. That creature is dangerous. Hell, if you get out of line, who do you think it's going to come after? You have one family you care about. That would be me. Emme. Our children if we have them."

"It won't be me that steps out of line. I choose a woman, she's mine for life. I don't cheat. I keep her. She's the one who will want to run from the monster." Dario's voice turned hard. "It will be the ones she loves in jeopardy, not my family."

"Shit, Dario, give her a reason to stay if you find her. Bind her to you so she's at least loyal." Valentino glanced at his watch. Time seemed to be crawling by. What the hell was taking so long? The entire Ferraro family was searching the club, the dungeon beneath it and every passageway they could in order to find where the women, the teens and hopefully the children were being held. If they couldn't find them, they would have to take Marge and break her. The thought made him sick to his stomach.

"Only women in cages, Val," Emmanuelle reported softly in his ear. "No children. No teens. I questioned them. They haven't seen or even heard any others talking or crying.

Their captors never talked about others. They're in . . . bad shape. Need medical attention. They've been brutalized severely. Have thirteen of them."

"We've gone through the underground passageways thoroughly." Ricco took up the report. "We're all convinced no one else is down here, nor have they been."

"We had to kill five guards," Vittorio said. "I was able to open the cages, but three of the women can't walk. You will have to tell us when it is safe to bring them out."

"Planting charges," Giovanni added.

"Planting charges," Taviano echoed.

"Ten men inside main club. Six in dungeon," Stefano reported. "Two bartenders, both male, both armed, in the dungeon club. Have semiautomatics behind bar. Two bartenders in main club, one woman, one male. Both armed, both have semiautomatics behind bar. Six strippers in main club working on their acts, staying as far from the men and bartenders as possible. All have phones. No women in the dungeon club working at present. Marge, the woman you were looking for, is in the dungeon, in the back office, going over books."

"Safes?" Dario asked.

"One is in the main club in the back office there. A small safe behind each bar. That money is bagged from the bar safe and transferred to the main safe in the club office. The dungeon and club money seem to be kept separate. The dungeon setup is the same as the one for the main club. Marge has the code, retinal scan and thumbprint to get into each of the office safes. They make a great deal of money. There are cameras everywhere. Bernado is already into her security and has taken over the cameras. He has her video feed. She does like her blackmail, particularly from the dungeon club," Stefano continued.

CHAPTER FIFTEEN

Valentino made his way across the parking lot to the front door of Miceli's prize strip club. He walked with his usual confidence, his men flanking him, and all around the parking lot, an army in suits, gathering, to pour into the club after him. At least they were getting the women out of here. It wasn't the teens being auctioned off. It wasn't the children. But it was something.

Luca shot the doorman in the heart twice and pulled open the door. Dario stepped through, gun drawn and shot the two guards as they spun around. One in between the eyes, the other in the heart.

Stefano snapped the neck of the male bartender as he reached for the semiautomatic. Emmanuelle did the same to the female. Both enemies dropped to the floor. Emme didn't look at Val; instead she spoke quietly into his earpiece.

"Mariko is helping the women get ready to be transported to your medical unit. We don't have clothes for them."

"Severu, take care of it," he ordered his advisor tersely. "Need transport as well for thirteen."

"On it." No hesitation.

Valentino had no doubt Severu Catalano would get them everything they needed immediately and ask all the right questions of Mariko about each woman so the medical unit would have an idea what they would be dealing with. Severu was intelligent and more than fast at computing a problem and coming up with solutions. That, as well as his fierce loyalty, was the reason Val had named him as his underboss.

Several of his men rounded up the strippers, who looked very frightened. His men pointed to a corner and told them to sit and not speak. They nodded. Val left them with their phones deliberately. Any stupid enough to try to call the cops would be identified quickly, but more than that, he wanted to know if any of them would try to inform Miceli. It was virtually impossible for them to get a message out. They didn't know that, of course.

Val and Dario went through the room looking over the remaining men. These were soldiers. None of them would have answers for him. None of them would be able to lead him to the teens or children. He shook his head in frustration and headed for the stairs, flicking his finger toward Romeo and Tore.

"Keep the girls quiet, but treat them gently. They haven't done anything wrong. When we're finished downstairs, we'll let them go," he said to the two men.

They nodded their understanding. It wouldn't be so easy to keep the strippers quiet when they killed Miceli's soldiers in front of them, but that was their problem now.

Val and Dario entered the club called the dungeon. It was called that for a reason. Those women locked in cages were the entertainment while men brought their women to play—and they played rough in this club. They paid a lot of money to do so.

Miceli charged a yearly fee just for the privilege of being a member. He charged an exorbitant amount for drinks and food. There was an astronomical price for the use of private rooms with tools. Not private meaning that others couldn't see in. You could put your woman on display any way you wanted to. You could have others join in. You just had the use of the room and the toys and furniture in it. The charges piled up from there, but it didn't matter because only the wealthy played in the dungeon. They played rough and dirty and any way they wanted. There were no restrictions whatsoever.

Stefano and Emmanuelle disposed of the bartenders as Dario killed the one guard trying to draw a weapon against them. Marge was already out of her office and had planted herself on a barstool when she found herself staring at Emmanuelle instead of the bartender.

Emmanuelle dropped the dead man onto the floor and smiled at Marge. "I really suggest you don't pull that silly little gun you keep hidden in the harness on your right thigh. I'd kill you before you ever got it out, and we have so much to talk about."

"We do?" Marge deliberately looked over the bar at the dead man on the floor. "I didn't even see how you got back there."

Val watched through the mirror as Marge glanced across the room to the other bar and saw the very handsome man who stood behind the bar where her bartender had been. He looked like Stefano Ferraro, but the lighting was so dim, he knew it would be difficult to tell. Marge preened, sitting up, facing toward the bar and crossing her legs. She never looked in the mirror to see Val or Dario behind her. She'd just watched Emme kill a man, but already she was distracted by the thought of Stefano Ferraro in her dungeon club.

Marge had no regard for human life at all. Men, women or children. She was that selfish. Right now, ignoring Emmanuelle, she flashed a smile at Stefano and batted her fake eyelashes at him.

"Honey, get me a drink," she ordered. "Coffee. Splash of whiskey. Top shelf." She waved her hand toward a bottle without looking away from Stefano.

Val knew Marge was putting Emme in her place by

showing her she didn't matter, relegating her to the service of bartending. Waiting on her. Emmanuelle was already gone. She'd quietly removed the bartender's weapons from Marge's reach and slipped away.

Valentino's men were in the room. They'd disarmed Miceli's men. These were the men Miceli trusted with his merchandise. He reached around Marge, slid his hand up her skirt and removed the little revolver she liked to keep in the harness there. "Just making certain you don't do anything rash, Marge. Not that I expect you to do that."

Her eyes went wide when she realized he was there and he was that close. She looked around the room and saw her men surrounded by his. For one moment her thin lips quivered and then she lifted her chin and smiled at him.

"Aw, Valentino. Are you angry with your uncle?"

"Just a little bit, Marge. Everyone upstairs is already dead, but they couldn't tell me anything I wanted to know. The women in those cages, downstairs, they can't tell me anything, either. I suspect you might be able to, but you're going to hold out for a little while."

She smirked. "You're not the kind of man who likes to see a woman in pain, Val. I'm not too worried. You can threaten me all you want, but I know you'd never really hurt me. You might kill me, but you wouldn't hurt me."

One of the men on the floor let out a scream, and Val and Marge turned their heads just as the guard's intestines slithered across the floor toward them. The gun he had in his hand dropped from nerveless fingers. Dario smiled at Marge, his eyes dark and scary. There was no humor in his smile. No compassion. No humanity.

"I'm not going to take you to our interrogation room, Marge," Valentino said softly. "Dario asked to take you. I'm afraid he likes inflicting pain, and it doesn't bother him in the least if it happens to be on a woman."

Marge's gaze jumped past him to Dario, and then she swallowed hard and looked away, lifting her chin.

"I will ask the question again, gentlemen. Where are the

teenage girls that are being sold at auction being held? All the little virgins?" Val didn't raise his voice. He kept it low. Gentle, even.

He paced away from Marge to walk in front of the four remaining soldiers. He studied their faces. They all looked defiant, still not believing he meant business, or that he could possibly defeat their powerful boss.

"Romeo, have you collected the money from the main safe?"

"Yes, sir, and all access has been granted to every account. Soldiers deceased. Ladies are waiting for exit plan. Charges planted and ready to blow when you give word."

"Thank you. Severu? Mariko? Have you transported our guests to our clinic for medical care?"

"Two more to move out, sir. Am assured all charges in place. Will advise when last one is safe," Severu answered.

"Thank you." Val glanced at his watch. "No takers?" He lifted the gun he'd been holding against his side and shot the most defiant of the lot in the head, deliberately at close range so his brains would splatter all over the man in line nearest him.

"Again, I'll ask the same question. This time I'm not waiting as long. I'm looking for information on the young virgin teens that were to be auctioned off. Where they are being held. I will also accept information on any children being held. Young boys or girls or who handles them. I'm being generous. That's a broad scope."

One of the men shifted nervously in line, but another glared at him and muttered a single name. *Marco*. Instantly, everyone was quiet. No moving. Blank faces.

Val wandered over to the third man in line, pressed the barrel of his gun between his eyes and waited a heartbeat so it would sink in that he was in charge.

"I'll ask again, gentlemen. You can see that I'm not playing games. Marco may be a scary badass, but he's not here right now, and I am. I suggest you play nice with me. If you're worried that Marge is going to rat you out, she will not survive her time with Dario. No one survives their session with Dario. The only choice they have is to decide if it will be short or if they will prolong the agony for hours, days or even weeks."

Valentino had no idea who Marco was, but the name seemed to inspire fear in everyone. It was possible he was behind the human trafficking ring, or at least one of the bigger connections. Val simply played it off as if he knew who Marco was.

He glanced at his watch. "Five seconds and another one of you dies."

The man on the end cleared his throat. The one next to him glared at him. "Don't you dare. You took an oath."

Valentino shot him through the throat and then through his eye. When he fell, Dario spit on him.

"He took an oath first to the Saldi name. To Giuseppi Saldi first before all others, as did Miceli, and he turned traitor. That oath is binding. Any oath that comes after is not binding," Val said. "That is our world."

The man on the end nodded. The second man looked confused. Valentino shot him, reloaded and holstered his weapon. "Give me the information you have."

"Don't you dare," Marge screamed. "I'll kill you myself."

"You're a dead woman walking," Val said quietly. "You can't kill anyone."

Quintu came out of the back office. "All of the money has been transferred from the safe to the cars. Also, from the bars to the cars. The accounts are open."

"No." For the first time, Marge looked really scared. "Val, you can't take the money. It isn't just Miceli's. He'll kill me if it disappears. You can't take the cash. You know how Miceli is about money. He'll hunt me down."

"Marge," Emmanuelle spoke gently for the first time. She stood near the woman, but just out of arm's reach. "You really don't seem to understand. You aren't going to live through this. You're part of a human trafficking ring. You sold women and children into sexual slavery so you could have whatever luxury you wanted. They need information you have."

"Well, I'm not giving it to them unless I get something out of it. I want ten million dollars, all the money I already have in my bank accounts, a new identity and a place free and clear where Miceli and his people will never find me. I might consider cooperating with Val then." She looked at the man in front of Val. "Don't be such a fool, Aldo: Bargain. Get something back before you give them what they want."

Val smiled. "He is getting something, Marge. He doesn't die by being burned alive with his intestines scattered across the floor."

Aldo paled and let out a groan, looking as if he might vomit any moment. Valentino ignored him.

"As for you, you can say whatever you want, make any demand you want, scream, beg, cry, yell—none of that matters now. I have no say. I have turned your interrogation over to Dario. He is solely in charge of you. You killed two women in this dungeon one night with a smile on your face, Marge. It seems Dario took great exception and asked for this favor. I granted it to him."

It was Marge's turn to pale. She looked between Dario and Val and then at the dead men on the floor. She raised her head and looked around the room, taking in the silent army of men watching her. Watching Aldo. Some silently moving out of the back office. Behind the bar. They were cleaning out the stacks of cash from the vaults. She sagged as realization hit. Val found some small satisfaction in seeing Marge finally get it: That no one was coming to her rescue. That she would be turned over to Dario for interrogation. That there was no out for her no matter what she threatened. Dario would extract the information.

She would tell him lies to begin with, but in the end, she would give him the truth. They always did. Valentino didn't find it to be true, that torture didn't work. Pain won out. You just had to be good enough to know the difference between what they thought you wanted to hear, what they were programmed to tell you and what was the actual truth. In other words, you had to be able to hear those lies. He was adept at it, and Dario was particularly good at it as well.

"I only know that Miceli likes to keep the little girls close to him. He's afraid the men might get crazy and ruin them before he can sell them," Aldo whispered hoarsely. "His sons control the kids. I don't know nothing about that."

"Where does Miceli keep the girls?" Valentino pushed. These were thirteen- and fourteen-year-old girls sold as virgins in an auction. He knew that Miceli had them already because the auction had been slated to take place. Word had gone out. Val had pushed his investigation in order to find a way to rescue the girls.

"I don't know exactly." Aldo's gaze shifted to Marge. "She knows."

Marge shrieked at him, something unintelligible, and then tried to fly at him. Two of Val's men stopped her. She fought them, kicking and twisting. Val glanced up to see Ricco Ferraro standing behind Aldo. He was a silent wraith. Val moved away, allowing the attention of the room to stay on Marge as Ricco caught Aldo's head between his hands and delivered the killing break to his neck, murmuring, "Justice is served."

"Get some control, Marge," Val advised. "Did you believe you'd never have to pay for your sins? Or did you think Marco would suddenly materialize and protect you?" He gave her a cruel smile. He threw the name out there in hopes that she would give him more information. "You let Miceli lull you into a false sense of security. Didn't you remember what Giuseppi was like in the old days, when he killed entire families? When he left bodies on doorsteps in pieces? Each of the families has an army to call on, and they're large, but no one has what we have. They can't do what we do. That's why we've been around for hundreds of years."

He heard Aldo's body drop to the floor. He didn't turn

around. Marge had gone still, her body between the two large men who held her prisoner.

"You can't go to war with everyone, Valentino. Miceli has turned half of your own crew against you."

He smiled at her again, his shark's smile. "They're already dead. It wasn't hard to find them. Money trails are easy, Marge. So are pussy trails. The ones who like to play usually frequent your playhouse right here. Men break easily enough with a little persuasion."

"You think you can fight both your uncle and Marco Messina at the same time? Marco will eat you alive."

Valentino didn't allow his shock to show on his face. Tibberiu Messina was the head of the very prominent Messina crime family with a large territory. They didn't wage war. They didn't need to. Marco, his youngest son, was well educated, ran in prominent circles, was engaged to his college sweetheart, an heiress to some kind of candy fortune. By all accounts, the two were very happy. Tibberiu had four sons. The other three were balls deep in the family business, hard as nails. Val could see one of them involved in this mess, maybe even branching out on their own, but not Marco. That made no sense at all. Even so, he kept every thought locked up tight behind an expressionless mask.

Marge's venomous gaze swept past him and locked on Emmanuelle. *"You."* She spat the word. "Do you have any idea what he truly thinks of you? Val uses people. He uses women to get what he wants. They all do. Do you really believe he's any different than his uncle is? He spent weeks cultivating me, flirting, sweet-talking, until all I could think about was him. I did anything and everything he asked me to do. Hours and hours of fucking. I knew he was seeing you. I asked him about you. He told me you were nothing to him, that his father told him to get information from you. I believed him."

Valentino didn't dare glance over his shoulder and look at his woman—his wife. Marge was telling enough of the truth that it was the truth to her. Her voice rang with it. Worse, it would play right into Emme's insecurities as a woman. Those terrible insecurities her mother had worked so hard to instill in her from the time she was a toddler. He wanted to wrap his hands around Marge's neck and squeeze until there was no life left.

"He cast me aside just the way he'll cast you aside the moment he has no more use for you. Right now, he's got your family as allies, and he needs them, doesn't he? Don't you see? He's desperate for allies. He can't trust that many people, and your family is considered the sacred gold mine. I can't believe he actually brought it off. The big investment. He hit pay dirt, didn't he? Oh my God, Valentino, you did what no one else managed to do: you caught the elusive Emmanuelle fucking Ferraro."

"Four minutes," Luca said in his ear.

Valentino wasn't certain he could last four minutes without strangling Marge. Maybe he should have one of the men put her to sleep. Vittorio had come up behind her. Mariko had also. Vittorio didn't have an expression on his face, but Mariko was looking at him with open suspicion. He couldn't blame her. Every word Marge said made sense.

There wasn't the slightest stirring behind him as if Emmanuelle held herself very still. Damn it, they were past all of this. She knew how much he loved her. She had to know. Marge was striking out, trying to rip them apart, trying to find a way to hurt him, because she knew she was going to die and there was no way out for her.

Dario appeared out of nowhere. He walked with that predatory, jungle-cat way he had, stalking Marge, his eyes focused completely on her face. Val could see her attention instantly switch to him. Every hair stood up on her body. She looked scared to death. If the two men hadn't been holding her up, she might have fallen. As it was, the smell of urine was suddenly strong in the room.

Dario's eyebrow shot up. "Marge." He said her name softly. Gently. Almost tenderly. "I don't like the things you're saying to Emme. You're deliberately trying to hurt her. She's someone I like, and I don't like very many people. I'd watch what I say because I'm taking note and adding on to your days and nights of excruciating pain. You already deserve so much. Do you really want more?"

Marge shook her head over and over, sagging between the two men. Dario patted her cheeks and indicated the door. "Go quietly, Marge. Don't give them any trouble. If they have to sedate you, the drug they use will make you very ill. That will just compound how you will feel when we have our little chat together."

He stepped back.

Marge's eyes were wild. She looked as if she was on drugs, her pupils blown, bouncing all over the place. "Emme. For God's sake. Do you know what he'll do to me? I don't know where these girls are being held. I don't know anything at all. I managed Miceli's club for him. That's all I did."

Val nodded to the men holding Marge, and one produced a syringe. She screamed and tried kicking, but he avoided her swinging foot easily. The other man held her head while the first one plunged the needle into her neck. The drug didn't take effect immediately, but her guards continued walking her to the door.

"One minute, sir," Luca said.

"Everyone out," Valentino said. "We're going to blow the place, so make sure you're all clear. Get out."

Dario waited, eyes meeting his. Both men knew he was afraid to turn around and look at Emmanuelle. She was still there, right behind him. She hadn't moved a muscle. Hadn't changed position. All around them, the building was emptying, but his woman, Mariko, and her brothers remained. He knew her brothers were waiting to ensure Emme left.

Stefano was in front of him. He put one hand in the air and turned his finger in a circle. Instantly, the Ferraros were gone. Including his wife. He felt her absence. Technically, she was supposed to stay in the shadows. She was part of Stefano's crew, not his. She wasn't riding in his vehicle with him. They were raiding Miceli's many businesses, and the Ferraros were going ahead of them. Emme was part of them.

Valentino cursed under his breath as he walked out of that hellhole with Dario. He just wanted to check in with his wife before she left. Make certain she was all right. Make certain *they* were all right. Was that too fucking much to ask? He walked across the parking lot, not in the least upset that they were going to take down the monstrosity of a club. The women had been removed from the cages and taken to the medical facility where they'd be taken care of before Val could send them into the rehabilitation programs. He would have to know who had families and who didn't. Bernado would check into it.

The regular strippers had been told to go home after Bernado checked out their phones. None of them had ties to Miceli or Marco. They just wanted out. They'd gone to the club in the hopes of making a living and had ended up working for practically nothing. They had been treated despicably by Miceli's sons and men. Marge or her bouncers hadn't protected them from the customers or clients. They were pretty miserable and seemed happy enough to lose their jobs.

Valentino slid onto the leather seat and pulled out his phone, staring down at it. Emmanuelle didn't carry her phone into the shadows. She did wear a wire made of some kind of natural element her brother Giovanni had come up with. He liked to "tinker" with electronics. Still, it didn't afford them any privacy.

They were three blocks away when the series of explosions went off, and they were massive. Orange, red and black smoke and flames rolled high into the sky. There was satisfaction in knowing that the dungeon and the cages hiding their vile secrets were gone for good. Miceli and his sons had no way to use the club again for any purpose.

He took a deep breath and tried to relax as the car took him toward their next location. He would give anything to have Emmanuelle in the car beside him. No, on his lap. He always liked her curled up on his lap. She never started out that way, but she ended up that way.

Emme. Princess. He'd spent hours at night when he couldn't sleep reaching for her. Visualizing the pathway of their shared nerves together. To him, that center was like a heart with arteries and veins flowing in every direction, carrying their life's blood to each other. *I need you right now.* He was so used to her eluding him. Slipping away.

He rubbed the wedding band sitting on his finger and then twisted it back and forth, aching for her. For a whisper of an answer. He detested that she'd had to hear anything Marge had to say, or be anywhere near the woman.

"Oh, for fuck's sake, Val. You look like some lovesick bull who just got his balls whacked off."

"Shut the fuck up, Dario," he snapped at his cousin. "You know you're capable of falling in love, whether you want to believe it or not."

Dario stared at him for a few minutes and then nodded slowly. "I'm not going to deny that it is a possibility. A slim one. It would take the right person, but I'd fall hard if it happened. The difference, Val, is I'd be damn careful not to let her see that shit. And I'd *never* let anyone else see it. You know how vulnerable she makes you? Someone sees the way you look at her, or sees the way you do that . . ."

Dario leaned forward, glancing toward the front of the car, and then he indicated the way Val had his hand wrapped around his wedding ring. Dario sat back on the seat again and shook his head.

"Not planning on giving any woman of mine the upper hand, which you handed to Emme on a platter. She's already going to give you enough trouble without that. Now we both have to watch her like a fucking hawk. Add to that, you put a target on her back. Not happy about it."

Valentino had to agree. He wasn't happy about it, either. "She was never going to sit on the sidelines, Dario. She wasn't born for that."

Dario sighed. "I get that. It's called negotiations. You don't just hand her the win."

"We're married. It isn't some kind of game, with one of us winning and one of us losing."

"You don't think so? I can just about guarantee it is."

"You have a strange view of marriage."

"Not marriage. The battle between a man and a woman."

"Dario." Val hit his head on the back of the leather seat three times. "There's no hope for you. You have such a skewed view of relationships. Why should it be a battle?"

"Because it is. Because if she gets the upper hand the way Emme has, she could die, Val, and then you've lost everything. You're going to die. You and I, we don't do anything by halves. When we take down a fucking enemy, we rip out their heart and soul so they don't have a chance of ever coming back at us."

Valentino knew it was true. They were loyal to a fault. And they loved with everything they were. And he loved Emmanuelle Ferraro Saldi.

"When we were on the plane going to Vegas and Stefano made the comment about not fucking up my relationship with Emme by being too overprotective, at first I thought he was giving me advice because she's trained as an assassin and isn't ever going to be happy sitting at home. I already knew that. It doesn't make me happy, but I thought we could use that. Take her to the meetings with us, have our ace in the hole, so to speak."

Dario nodded, his dark eyes serious. "Yeah, there're a lot of ways Emmanuelle moving around in the shadows can be an asset as long as she stays there."

"Then I thought about it. Emme's had bodyguards on her, serious ones, her entire life. You've seen them. I'd give anything to have Emilio and Enzo training our people. They don't leave anything to chance. They don't make mistakes. The only way Emmanuelle ever got away from them is moving through the shadows. That's how she came to me at the lake house, or any of the other places we met. She didn't outwit her bodyguards, she slipped into a shadow and disappeared. They can't follow her into them."

Dario nodded again. "So, what are you saying about Stefano's comment?"

"Well, first off, he directed that comment not at me, but at his wife. He wanted to get a rise out of her and the other women on the plane. And he did. He might have been telling me it was okay to have fun in the family. Outside of it, we can look like cruel bastards, but when we're alone with them, we can be family men."

"I can see he might have been doing that."

"Stefano expects me—us—to be just as vigilant watching over Emmanuelle as the Ferraros are over their women. More so because she will be out in the open. He expects us to put bodyguards on her and even ask for Ferraro bodyguards if the need arises."

"The hell with that," Dario said. "We can protect her."

Valentino found himself laughing. "You can't have it both ways, Dario. Either Emme's in danger and she has to be guarded every second by whatever means are at our disposal or she's not. I say we have our most trusted guards on her, but when we feel the danger is especially high, as it is now, we use the Ferraros as well, and that includes her brothers if necessary."

Dario doubled his fist and pressed it to his heart. "At least they know better than to look smug. I still might not survive having to work with them."

"We're the ones who should be feeling smug. We pulled off what no other outfit in Chicago ever managed to do. I married the Ferraro princess and officially have an alliance with her family. That not only makes us stronger than anyone else, but it has put even more fear into our enemies than I ever could have with what we're doing. When word leaks out—and we'll make certain it does—that Stefano himself may have been along on one of the raids, that will solidify our place as the strongest family in Chicago."

Dario relaxed against the seat. "There is that. If they help us find out who's behind bringing these kids into this hell . . ."

Valentino eyed him warily. They were on touchy ground now. He glanced at his watch. They were still several minutes out from their next target. "Do you believe Marco Messina could be behind all of this? We found out about it only a few years ago. He would have had to have started into it when he was pretty young. He's what? Five years older than us?"

"He's a Messina. He was raised in the life. He runs the legitimate side of their businesses, but he's still running their businesses," Dario pointed out. "I don't trust anyone, Val, other than you. The men we have in place in our inner circle are the most I'll ever trust anyone else, and I'll be watching them all the time." He hesitated.

"What is it?"

"Bernado. We're putting a lot of faith in him. A tremendous amount of faith in him."

"We saved his life, Dario. We took care of his mother when she needed it." Val was patient. He understood his cousin. He understood Dario's fear. Bernado had a particular skill that was unmatched by either of them. If he betrayed them, neither of them would be aware of it until it was far too late. They had no real way to watch over the man.

Valentino trusted his instincts. They'd never steered him wrong. Even as a child, he'd been aware Miceli was two-faced. He had been certain, even then, that his uncle had something to do with murdering his birth parents, but there was no proving it. Nothing but his gut reaction. Bernado was devoted to Valentino and Dario. He wasn't the kind of man to wield a gun, but he could go after any business with his keyboard.

"Have you ever asked Bernado to look into Stefano Ferraro?" Dario asked.

Something in Dario's voice had Val looking up sharply. Suspiciously. He looked at his cousin through narrowed, hooded eyes. "No, I made it clear the Ferraros were off-limits."

"I did." Dario showed no remorse. He might have played

second to Valentino when they were in public, and there was no doubt that he would have taken a bullet for him, but when they were alone, they were equals. "With all the skills he has, Bernado couldn't get anything on Stefano or any of the other brothers aside from regular shit that meant nothing at all. Worse, he said, he was immediately flagged and had to shut everything down before he was identified. Whoever is in Stefano's corner was coming after him fast, and Bernado says he's buried deep."

Valentino rubbed the bridge of his nose. "I don't pretend to understand the first thing about what he does, but if he needs help, maybe we should try to find someone to help him."

"I thought of that. Asking him to find someone means we have to trust him entirely, and we can't have that person report directly to us anything Bernado might be doing wrong," Dario said. "And we don't have the expertise to find someone with his kind of genius. Nor can we indebt someone to us unless I maneuver that situation."

Val sighed. He knew what that meant. The Saldi family, under his father's regime, had resorted to that kind of manipulation on more than one occasion. Giuseppi had always claimed to be fair with his men. Yet, when he needed a certain person with a skill set completely loyal to him and felt there was no other option open to him, he'd taught Val and Dario that "saving" that person's life and family after first sacrificing a few family members in a bloodbath would give him the required devotion. That had never sat well with Valentino. Fortunately, he hadn't had to resort to that type of false rescue. He truly had helped Bernado, as well as a few others.

He met Dario's gaze steadily. "You would do that?"

Dario sighed. "No. I can do a lot of things, Val, but that's not one of them. I don't kill innocents, not even for you, at least I never have. Who the hell knows what I'm capable of? I don't, these days. Now that Emme is on board, I could go a lot further than I thought I could to protect her."

Valentino couldn't help the smirk. "She got to you."

"She gets to everyone. Yeah. She got to me a long time ago. I wanted to beat you to a bloody pulp for laying a finger on that girl. On the other hand, I knew what it would do for you. For us. She's different. She's no coward, Val. She'll be fierce when it comes to protecting your children."

Valentino nodded.

"And you," Dario added.

Val studied his cousin's dark features for a long time before he decided to give him the truth. "And you as well. You're family to her, Dario. She regards you as a sibling. She'll protect you just as fiercely."

"Don't you think I know that? I wanted to slice Marge into a million little pieces for trying to make Emme doubt you and herself. She did it deliberately. She wanted to hurt you and hurt Emmanuelle. Everything Marge does is calculated, even when she's scared out of her mind. She thought Emme might turn on you and fight for her."

Valentino nodded. "I was aware of that. Marge figured if Emmanuelle switched sides, her family would follow suit, that she could manipulate the situation in her favor. I just hoped Emme would be aware of it as well. That damn mother of hers undermined her confidence in herself as a woman so much, and I didn't help with what I said to Marge that night Emme overheard. I was terrified she might just walk out on me right there. I knew she wouldn't help Marge. Emme had already seen the women in cages below the dungeon club, and she knew Marge was part of that. She wants us to stop the trafficking. But . . ."

"But she might believe what Marge said about you using her to firm up your position with the other families."

Valentino glanced down at his watch. They were only two minutes out now. "Because part of it was true. That was the beauty of what Marge said. A mixture of the truth and lies. Mariko bought into it. I did benefit from marrying Emme. I did form the alliance with the Ferraro family that every other one of the families wanted. I married the princess. I even call her 'Princess.'" He looked out the window. Shit. She still hadn't reached out to him.

The car pulled to the curb. Stopped. The unassuming offices of Farsighted Logistics looked as if they comprised a very small business. Behind the suite of offices was a larger garage housing a fleet of trucks and vans. The company had started out small, handling the details of transporting their customers' freight and merchandise, booking all the details and tracking them across the United States. Eventually, the company grew so large and made so much money they began to acquire their own trucks along with those first smaller vans until they had a presence in nearly every major city. What wasn't known was that Miceli transported more than his customers' freight in his vans and trucks. This was just one of many of the businesses that would be destroyed before the day was over.

CHAPTER SIXTEEN

They had raided seven of Miceli's businesses in a single day, taking several men and Marge from the first four. After that, there was no one they thought could give them information needed to find the children or the teens held for sale. Nor were they any closer to moving on the pipeline itself.

Breaking another human being down, destroying him completely so he was willing to give up anything in order to stop what was happening, so he was willing to believe the pain would end, was long, exhausting work. It required stamina and the ability to disassociate completely.

Valentino had spent hours on the first two, who he was certain weren't going to have much for him. They didn't, other than to confirm that Angelo and Tommaso were up to their ears in the muck. His two cousins sent closed vans to collect freight in the dead of night and drop it off at the back of one of the auto repair shops, switching vehicles. More than once, one of the men had heard crying. The voices sounded very young. He hadn't gone to investigate because it wasn't his business.

The auto repair business looked legitimate but was a front

for high-end stolen cars. The list of specific cars was brought in every fourth Thursday night, quickly turned over and taken by trucks to be shipped out to buyers. It was nearly impossible for anyone to catch on to what was happening in the shop as every other day of the month, the shop and workers did legitimate repairs and their work was impeccable.

Bernado had already discovered the illegal business in the way he had everything else Miceli did: by tracking the money. He had moved it from Miceli's accounts, and when they raided the garage, they found the secret vault in the well beneath what appeared to be an oil reservoir in the cement. They took that as well.

In the corner of the shop, with a bundle of old dirty rags, Dario uncovered a threadbare blanket. It was clearly a child's. Purple and green with a monkey in a tree. There were oil stains on it now. Dario retrieved the little square of material, swearing under his breath, his eyes going colder. Folding it, he looked around a little helplessly, as if he wasn't certain where he could put it. Valentino held out his hand. With some reluctance, Dario gave it to him, and Val tucked it away until they got into the car and he could lay it on the seat so neither would forget it. They would do their best to clean the damn thing and find its owner.

They hit business after business and found the same thing. Extra cash. A ton of it. All bundled and ready to be sent out. Rumors of children having been in one or two briefly, but only for a few minutes, never seen, only heard by a couple of those they spoke with before they killed them. Miceli lost the majority of his soldiers, and they came up empty-handed with no real information to show for their work.

They had prisoners, key members of Miceli's inner circle, ones Valentino hoped would give him what he needed to find the girls and children before Miceli and his sons could sell them. He spent long, hideous hours interrogating the two men just to find out they'd heard the children, confirming what that little blanket had told them—the children had been at the auto repair shop.

The other place the vans had been where someone had heard crying was a paint and body shop. That had surprised Valentino. The shop was located, not in one of the warehouses known to be used as a cover for Miceli's dirtier work, but in the business district near Ferraro territory. Not in it, but very close to it. The shop was owned by two brothers who hadn't had any affiliation with the organization.

Bernado had looked into them. Their books had been easy enough to hack. Valentino and his crew had raided the shop and found no evidence of the children or teens, but they had found the brothers. After four intense hours, Severu had gotten it out of them that they had actually seen children, both boys and girls, but no teens. The children had been there briefly, a pit stop only, and then they had been taken away.

Valentino was done for the night. Exhausted and discouraged that he hadn't gotten any closer to getting to those children. He'd seen the look on Dario's face. He felt the same. He took the private elevator upstairs to the suite Stefano had given him, ignoring his bodyguards, not wanting to talk to anyone.

It was late enough that he knew Giuseppi would already have gone to bed. He was normally good about giving his father updates, but not tonight. Not after the raids and interrogations and coming up empty. He should have tried to focus on the fact that they'd managed to free the women they had from the cages beneath the dungeon, but for him, it just wasn't good enough. He'd failed those children yet again.

Time was running out for the girls—the little teenagers being auctioned off. Val pressed his fingers to his eyes. He'd probably made it ten times worse. Now Miceli really needed the money from a sale. He would probably accelerate the timetable, not postpone it as Valentino had hoped.

He stopped halfway across the large sitting room when he saw Emmanuelle sitting in one of the extremely comfortable chairs in front of the window. Her large blue eyes were dark with suspicion, and her expression told him she was closed off to all explanations. He was tired. So fucking tired. He let her open the conversation. The accusations. He'd heard them all before, and maybe she even had a right to them after the bullshit Marge had spewed, but he was just too tired to care.

He let his gaze travel over her, take her in, because he'd waited all damn day just to see her. Just to take her inside.

"It was impressive learning so much today in front of everyone, Valentino. Your reasons for wanting to be with me. They're all good. They work. I know in mob families arranged marriages are common. You even said if we had a daughter that might happen."

"Could happen with a son," he bit out, trying not to clench his teeth. His head hurt. His chest did. Those wounds. Or maybe it was his fucking heart.

She narrowed her eyes. "You should have just told me why you really wanted to be with me instead of pretending you loved me, Val. I can respect marrying for allies."

Valentino stared at Emmanuelle for a long time, his heart contracting. His gut twisting. His head pounded with the force of a fucking freight train. He let out his breath in a long, slow exhale to keep from swearing at her.

"Any other time, Princess, we'd have the same fucking conversation we have over and over to reassure you, but I'm too damn tired. If you prefer to believe your bitch of a mother and a woman who gladly sells other women and children to keep herself in luxury instead of your man, who is selling his fucking soul to the devil to get those women and children back and shut that shit down, well, you're just going to have to do it tonight. I tell you I love you. I tell you you're my heart and soul, and you still choose not to hear me. I can't do a fucking thing about that tonight, baby. There's not much left of me at the moment."

He walked over to the bar, shrugging out of his jacket and tossing it on the back of a chair. Splashing whiskey into a glass, he tossed it back and then dragged the tie from his collar. He didn't look at her again. He couldn't. His head hurt almost as bad as his heart. Neither hurt as bad as his soul. He just had to lay it down for a while.

Unbuttoning his shirt with one hand, he started to pour himself more whiskey and then decided the hell with it and just tightened his grip around the neck of the bottle and lifted it to his mouth.

"Where is he?"

Val paused with the whiskey bottle halfway to his lips and turned. Emmanuelle stood a few feet from him. "Who?"

"Marco Messina. You want to know if he's involved. I can find out where he is, but if you tell me, it will save time. I'll get the information for you, not because I think you wanted me for that purpose but because we need to know."

He turned away from her, carefully placing the whiskey bottle on the bar. "I don't want you going anywhere near him."

"He won't see me, Val. That's the point of being in the shadows. You're never seen."

He didn't give a damn. He'd considered having her spy for him more than once over the last few years. He'd be a fool not to. In all that time, when he'd considered it, he'd been her backup. Dario had been right there. But now he realized he didn't want to risk her.

"I don't want to do this with you tonight, Emme." He pressed his hand to his head and then looked down at his shoes. He always made it a point to keep his shoes immaculate while questioning a prisoner. There was a psychological advantage that occurred when he remained immaculate and the prisoner was reduced to blood and guts and shards of bone. He saw it happen time and time again.

He sank down into the comfort of the chair and bent to remove his shoes. Just tilting his head that angle made his head pound worse. Black spots danced behind his eyes, and a groan escaped. He righted his body, tipping his head back, grateful he hadn't turned on lights.

To his shock, Emmanuelle crouched down and took care of his shoes, sliding them from his feet and setting them aside. "When did your headaches start getting so bad, Val?"

"You know I get migraines." He always saw them as a weakness. Giuseppi certainly did. He'd never allowed Val to stay in his room when he'd had them, nor was he to mention them to Greta. He wasn't to flinch or act in any way as if he had a headache. Headaches were for women. Headaches were not something men ever got unless one was shot in the head and brains were leaking out.

"They seem worse." There was worry in her voice.

He glanced down at her. She was looking up at him, a frown on her face, speculation in her blue eyes. "What is it, Emme?"

"I told you shadow riding can cause brain bleeds. I had a brain scan, and I'm perfectly fine, but . . ." She broke off, looking scared. "We're just learning about the effects, Val. We don't know anything at all about what happens between two people tied together the way we are. Suppose I'm not affected by being in the shadows but you are." She sat back on her heels. "Maybe you should go in and have a brain scan just to be safe."

He couldn't help but smile, even if movement of any kind hurt like hell. "Woman, you know you're getting a little paranoid, right? It's a migraine."

"Did you bring your meds?"

"No. We left the house on the run, remember? People were shooting at us." He closed his eyes, feeling sick, wishing he could blame the nausea on the fact that he'd spent hours trying to extract information from two different men who really didn't know shit about where Miceli was holding his victims. Val's biggest fear was that Miceli might decide to kill them out of pure spite. It was something his uncle might do.

"Let's get you in bed, Valentino. I'll get your medicine and be right back."

Just the sound of Emmanuelle's voice was soothing. He allowed her to help him up. She stripped him of his trousers and, with one arm around his waist, got him to the master bathroom.

"I'll be back in a few minutes, babe."

"Don't go, Emme. Stay with me."

He didn't want her leaving, certainly not to go anywhere

near his father's home. Miceli would have eyes on it. He hadn't destroyed it for a reason. His uncle easily could have had his men burn the estate to the ground, but he'd left it intact. He was sure Giuseppi would feel the need to show everyone he was strong enough to go back to his home and rule from there. Miceli would be certain to have his assassins ready to kill his brother.

"Do that thing you do." There were some people who couldn't stand to be touched when they had migraines. Valentino had always been one of those until Emmanuelle had worked her magic on him. She had a gift with massage. She had a way of knowing the exact amount of pressure to use on his neck and scalp. Even his face.

She didn't argue with him. When he came out of the master bath and slipped into bed, she took off her shoes, climbed onto the bed, sliding easily behind him, adjusting the pillows there in the dark. He found it shocking how comfortable the Ferraro Hotel's bed was. It wasn't as if Giuseppi had shit beds. They had money and hadn't spared any expense getting the best; Greta had insisted on it. She'd wanted to ensure Valentino and then Dario, both, had the best start with their growing spines and joints—whatever that meant to her.

He nearly groaned aloud when Emmanuelle's fingers began to massage his scalp. Soft circular motions at first. He kept his eyes closed and let her scent envelop him. It carried him away from the scent of blood. She had a natural fragrance to her skin that even took the coppery flavor of blood from his mouth, where sometimes it seemed to soak into him.

Her fingers were strong and the pressure increased steadily on his scalp and then down his neck and into his shoulders. He held death there. Not just a clean death. This kind of death was ugly. Dark. A slow, torturous assault on the body that crept up in pain and true suffering until the excruciating agony was impossible to bear even by the strongest of men. Until that dark, ugly death was welcomed, even begged for.

Emmanuelle's fingers were firm, fighting for him. Going

to battle with the devil. His angel versus Satan. Only she dared to take hell on for him.

"I'm sorry I was ugly with you, Princess. I should have been more understanding." It wasn't her fault that Eloisa was such a fucking bitch or that he was too tired to take that bitch on.

"Don't, Val. You were right, and we both know it." Her voice was soft with love. Tender. "I'm a mess. I always have been. I try very hard to give everyone, including me, the impression of self-confidence, but it isn't true. It wasn't only Eloisa. Phillip, my father, wanted nothing to do with me, either. I tried so hard to be perfect for them. I don't know why it was so important to me to get them to notice me when I was little, but it was."

He kept his eyes closed. Her fingers never stopped that perfect massage. Never faltered in the steady pressure. She knew exactly what he needed and where he needed it.

"Children need their parents' approval, baby," he murmured softly. "Some more than others. It's natural."

"I had Stefano. He was the one who got up with me in the middle of the night when I had nightmares. We weren't allowed to have bad dreams or to be afraid of monsters under the bed. Eloisa and Phillip would be furious if I woke them up, especially as I got older. I would be afraid to go to sleep because the nightmares were so real and I'd get trapped in them. If I screamed and woke them up, Phillip would stand in the doorway swearing at me, and Eloisa would . . ." She broke off and very gently moved her hands to the knots on his shoulders.

She'd rarely talked to him about having bad dreams or what her mother might have done to her in the middle of the night.

"Keep going, Princess. You're safe with me."

He wasn't certain Eloisa would be safe from him, however, based on what Emme was telling him. He felt powerless to save those young girls from an auction. He knew they were somewhere right at that moment, being held in cells or rooms, or even cages, terrified out of their minds, being treated as less than animals, waiting to be sold to someone who would do whatever they wanted to their bodies. He couldn't do one thing to help them.

The terrible pounding in his head increased. Somewhere little boys and girls were being held. They'd been snatched off playgrounds, taken from their parents, maybe their beds, held the same way as those hapless teens. Small children needing to be rescued and he was lying in bed, useless, with a fucking migraine of all things.

He had been trying to find out who really was behind grabbing the kids, find the actual pipeline so he could shut it down, and yet no matter what he did, what he sacrificed, it was never enough.

Now Emmanuelle, his beautiful Emme, the one child who should have been a pampered princess in her home of luxury and so much wealth, was telling him in her soft voice that she couldn't even have a nightmare without fearing her parents. What the fuck was wrong with the world? He sure as hell didn't know.

"Val, you're tensing up. I'm supposed to be helping you relax." Emmanuelle leaned over him and brushed a kiss on his forehead. "Just lie here quietly."

He still hadn't opened his eyes. "Only if you keep talking about your childhood. I was listening. I was thinking about the auction and how I didn't get any information. What a fucking failure I was yet again. You were distracting me. I need that." It was the truth, and yet it wasn't. He hoped it was enough of the truth that, mixed with the very real pain of his migraine, she would buy it.

"Honey, there's no doubt in my mind, you'll find these people. You can't take on the world by yourself, Valentino. None of this is your fault."

"Those teenage girls sitting in cages waiting to be bought, scared out of their minds—that's going to happen in the next day or two. If I don't get information fast, those girls will be gone, and I won't get them back. Not ever, Emme. You know why? Because I didn't move fast enough. I didn't want to take men down to a room like the one under this hotel and do what I did today—what Dario's down there doing right now. What I'm going to have to do tomorrow."

Even he could hear the self-loathing in his voice. He didn't feel it. He danced with the devil and had resigned himself to what he was a long time ago. He hadn't known a part of him still resisted the grime he was covered in and could never rid himself of.

"Valentino, stop." Her fingers moved on his neck, finding those hard knots that made him feel as if someone had driven spikes into him. "Breathe deep. I'm talking to you."

She had her soothing voice back, that soft sound that sank into him and somehow, in spite of the filth that covered him, sank deep, right into his soul, where all those dark ugly deaths resided. Her voice, her hands, her love found a way to allow those restless deaths peace, freeing him, freeing his soul. That sounded like poetic crap to him, but it was the fucking truth.

"Stefano would always be there when I was a toddler long before Eloisa, but when I was older and still had nightmares, he was away training. He wouldn't have allowed Phillip and Eloisa to come near my room. By that time, Stefano dealt with all of us pretty much exclusively in the parent department. Eloisa still made most of the decisions when it came to training us. I'll give her respect when it comes to riding. She is an excellent shadow rider, and she definitely wanted all of us prepared for the severities of riding. Stefano is just as tough on us but in a different way."

She was silent, her hands back to working on his scalp. He loved that feeling when she would start over, fingers soft again, moving in those slow circles, massaging every inch of his pounding skull before taking on strength and finding pressure points.

"Princess." He prompted her with one word. He felt a little guilty. He'd convinced her she needed to talk to him in order to keep him from thinking too much about his failures. He wanted to hear about her childhood. Things even her older brother didn't know.

She sighed. "Once Stefano left, things didn't go well for me. Ricco was gone as well. Giovanni left on and off. They weren't really supposed to leave until they were a certain age, but Eloisa didn't like to have to deal with them, so she sent them away without Stefano's knowledge."

"Leave for where?"

"There are other rider families, so we're often trained by other riders. I'm younger, so Eloisa and Phillip were stuck with me. I kept having nightmares and I'd scream bloody murder in my sleep. Eloisa's preferred method of waking me was to slap me silly or throw ice-cold water in my face, drag me out of bed onto the floor and dump more water on me. I was disoriented and would start to fight. She would immediately fight back as if we were in the gym and I'd get my ass kicked. Then she'd leave the room and tell me to clean up the bed and myself."

Valentino lay perfectly still, listening to the air moving through his lungs as he breathed. Blood rushed through his veins. He didn't make any effort to contain the anger sweeping through him. He just let the sparks move from his body to hers along all those nerve endings they shared in much the same way they shared sexual need.

"Val." She breathed his name. "That was a long time ago."

"It was yesterday."

"She viewed nightmares and screaming as weakness."

In the same way Giuseppi viewed his migraines. "You disturbed her perfect world." He reached his hand up and laid it over hers, stopping the way her hands soothed his terrible pain. "I don't know how she managed to give birth to a perfect woman like you, Emmanuelle. Everything about you is beautiful to me. Everything. That little stubborn streak. That fiery temper of yours. You kiss like sin. Your laugh is pure magic. I wouldn't change one single thing about you. Even when you fuck up, when you decide to make things right, you just do it, no messing around."

"I wanted her to see me, Val. I always felt so invisible. I am invisible to her. She'll never see who I really am."

He hated that she sounded so lost. If he could have moved, he would have pulled her down over the top of him. He liked her sprawled out on him, straddling him. Right now, the best he could do was just try to let her know she was his world. He saw her.

"She doesn't want to see you, baby. You have to accept it and move on."

"I've already done that. Finally. I chose you. The moment I did, I knew she would never accept that choice. I'm no longer a rider to her. She'll do whatever Stefano decrees, but she'll disown me as a Ferraro and a rider."

"She might come around." He knew Eloisa never would.

"It's too late as far as I'm concerned." She kissed his hand and then let go of it. "You need to go to sleep. You have work to do tomorrow, and you have to get rid of this migraine."

She was right, Valentino knew: no matter what, he had to be on his feet in the morning. There was no stopping his woman. She would be going to find his medication. He knew her.

"If you do go to get my meds, Princess, take backup with you." He didn't open his eyes. She had him floating. Drifting. He was already sliding away, not remembering if she gave her promise or not, but he thought she did. He did feel her kiss on his forehead and then his lips.

Emmanuelle didn't want to ask one of her brothers to go with her to get Valentino's migraine medicine, but he needed the shot. Sometimes, when he got a migraine, he would get a series of them. The shot would break the cycle, but if it didn't, he could take it the moment he felt one coming on and prevent one.

She was certain interrogating the prisoners had brought this one on. She could tell it was far worse than any of the others she'd witnessed. Once he was asleep, she was determined to go back to his house and get the medicine. She messaged Dario and asked him where it was kept, explaining that she was going to find it and get it for Valentino.

The medicine couldn't go through the shadows, but she should be able to have a car waiting to get it back to the hotel fast. That meant she would need to find the medicine. While she looked, she'd be safe, but once it was in her possession, she'd be in the open. If there was anyone watching, she'd have to either dispose of them or sneak her way through the house to the street, where she could meet the car that would carry the shot back to the hotel.

Emmanuelle considered which of her brothers to call. Ordinarily, she wouldn't bother, but she had been an idiot again, practically accusing Valentino of marrying her so he could use her for spying. How many times was he going to have to reassure her? A million, probably. He was normally so patient with her. The moment he wasn't, she knew he was hurting. She felt so low that she would for one moment believe anyone but him.

Valentino looked at her with love. He touched her with love. He spoke to her with love. Had he been a shadow rider, he would have claimed her partially because she was also a rider. What really was the difference? Nothing at all. She was the one with the self-confidence problem, thanks to Eloisa. She had to get over that before she ruined everything with her husband. It was a small thing to do—swallow her pride and bring along one of her brothers as Val asked.

Emme briefly played with the idea of calling Elie but knew Valentino wouldn't be happy with that decision. Sooner or later she would have to talk with him and reiterate the truth— that Elie and she felt nothing but sibling affection for each other. He probably really knew that, but wasn't quite ready to acknowledge it yet. As much as she'd heard the honesty in Valentino's voice when he'd tried to explain about Marge, she hadn't been willing to listen to it; the hurt ran too deep. If she was being totally honest with herself, her own fears had played a big part in keeping them apart.

Need to get meds for Val from his home tonight. Can't go without backup. You free or should I ask one of the others?

It was very late. The raids had taken up most of the day.

Part of her had been appalled that so many cops had to have been on the payroll to get away with so many raids. They had gone directly from one business to the next. Granted, they were on the clock, and the Ferraros had gone in first, mostly to make certain none of the women or children they were looking for were being held captive in any of the places before they were burned to the ground, but there were several dead bodies in each of the businesses. Most had looked legitimate. Emmanuelle supposed they might have been on the FBI's radar, or at least the local cops, but somehow, Valentino Saldi had never been questioned.

It had to be known that the heir to the Saldi empire was staying at the Ferraro Hotel, but the police had never questioned him in the terrible raids on his uncle's businesses. The reporters speculated all sorts of wars between families, but no one spoke out against Valentino. When the report did come, she knew it would be orchestrated by him and worded in such a way to make his enemies afraid and yet ambiguous enough that it would seem as if he had nothing whatsoever to do with any of the raids or deaths to the outside world.

Mariko and I will be happy to be your backup. We will meet with you at the back entrance to Giuseppi's home. Do not enter until we are with you.

She rolled her eyes as she glanced down at the text. Already, Ricco was taking over. Telling her what to do. She was used to being bossed around by her brothers. She couldn't imagine how Mariko felt. Her sister-in-law was a shadow rider of immense talent. She took her own rotations, and yet, when she went with her husband, she always followed his lead. It was impossible not to love Mariko, with her combination of lethal and soft, but sometimes, Emmanuelle just wanted to see her, one time, lose her temper with Ricco. Did Mariko have a temper? If she did, Emmanuelle had never seen it.

Will arrange for a car to be waiting to take the meds to the hotel for us.

Let me do that.

Emmanuelle burst out laughing. It was laugh or pull her

hair out. Did Ricco think she was incapable of arranging for a car to meet them at Giuseppi's home? She glanced in the mirror, making certain her hair was in a tight weave and her suit was locked down. She was tired, but getting Valentino's medicine shouldn't take long.

Dario hadn't answered her yet. She considered texting him again. He always answered. He was in the same suite, in one of the bedrooms close by. Or was he? Had he come back from the interrogation room? She hadn't stayed down there. Both Valentino and Stefano had asked her to leave. Had they ordered her, she might have resisted, but seeing the man tied to a chair and having been with her brothers before when they questioned someone for information, she had decided to comply. Dario hadn't been in the room.

Just as she stepped outside the suite into the hallway and the guards outside the door came alert, her phone vibrated.

You have someone go with you. Meds in top drawer of walk-in closet in black storage container. You've seen them. Do not go alone. Miceli will have someone there. I can't get there to protect you.

Ricco and Mariko are going with me.

Be safe. I want to know the moment you get back.

Yes, Dad.

She got a bird emoji. That made her laugh. "I have a sick sense of humor from growing up around too many men," she explained to the bodyguards. "I'm heading out, but Ricco and Mariko are meeting me, so no worries. You can text them if you need confirmation, Drago."

"I'll have to confirm with Emilio. He'll text Ricco."

She looked at the two men waiting by the elevator. They were both in suits. Both Valentino's men. Both assigned to protect Valentino and Giuseppi, although they didn't look as if they were going to step aside.

"Mrs. Saldi? I have to get a confirmation from either your husband or Dario that it's okay for you to leave the suite," one said.

This was one of several recruits Dario had trained himself. She remembered him talking to Valentino about it a couple of years earlier at the lake house. They hadn't wanted anyone to know. Dario had been on the lookout for men he believed would be good to make up their own personal soldiers, men they could count on, not recruited or made by Giuseppi or his capos. Dario wanted a small group of trained men he believed would be loyal to Valentino and him, with no ties to Miceli or any other crime family. Dario was suspicious of everyone, but these were the men he'd trained in secret and the only ones he allowed to guard Val if he wasn't around. Even then, he was very aware Emmanuelle and her family were watching over him as well.

She remembered the two guards' names—Lando Regio and Pace Detti. Neither was married. Both were in their thirties. It was clear they were ex-military. They held themselves the way Drago and Demetrio did—as if they could handle themselves. Lando was busy texting, as was Drago.

Emmanuelle decided to do a little texting of her own to Mariko. Not only do I have to answer to my husband, Dario and every one of my brothers, but also a set of Saldi bodyguards who have to check with either Val or Dario and a set of bodyguards who have to check with either Emilio or in this case Ricco. Testosterone much? The dark ages appear to be alive and well in our family.

She couldn't take her phone into the shadows. She tapped her foot in front of the elevators, waiting for permission from a multitude of men, vowing she would just grab shadows from here on out. She would be honest and take back any promises she might have inadvertently made to her husband because this was ridiculous—hilarious, but still ridiculous—and she knew herself. She didn't have the patience for it.

"Dario gave you the okay," Lando said.

"How very generous of him," Emmanuelle said, flashing Lando a smile. She looked up at Drago as the elevator doors slid open. He stepped on with her while Demetrio stayed behind. "I suppose you got the okay as well, because I'm not grown-up enough to make decisions all on my own."

"Emme," Drago reprimanded. "I do my job. I'm thorough. I keep you alive."

"I told you Ricco was backing me up."

"You're a wild card, woman, you always have been. It isn't like we all don't know that. You get pissed and you go your own way. Every one of us knows you're the most difficult detail."

"I am not. Stefano is."

Drago shook his head. "You are. By far. Emilio purposely trains the newbies with someone experienced on you because you're going to give them hell every time. You're going to give them the slip so many different ways. You're the best training tool we have."

Shocked, she stared at him. That just couldn't be. "I'm not as bad as Nicoletta. She's the wild child."

"She doesn't have near your imagination."

Emmanuelle didn't know whether to feel complimented or insulted. The elevator slid smoothly to a halt just as her phone vibrated. She glanced down at the text from Mariko.

Laughing emojis. I had no idea what I was getting into. They don't tell us before they get us to fall in love. You were born into it and then fell for Val. He'd better treat you right. Are you truly happy with him? Do you know he loves you with all his heart?

Mariko had been there when Marge had spouted her poison. She didn't know Valentino. She didn't know Marge. She only knew the things Emmanuelle had told the family two years earlier, that Valentino had been with a woman and told her he had been ordered by his father to get Emme to fall for him so he could learn the Ferraro family secrets.

Absolutely he loves me. He would do anything for me. I should have told you the truth about that night. I was so afraid to be with him. I know Ricco had to tell you about how the shadows react differently. I was so terrified of loving him and what it might mean between our families. And he's like Stefano in a lot of ways.

Emmanuelle stepped off the elevator into the private

alcove built into the shadows for the family. The dim light threw the tubes in many different directions. Emme was careful to stay out of any of them.

I see that, Mariko admitted.

Coming to you now, Emme texted.

She locked her phone and handed it to Drago. "Take good care of him for me and don't let anything happen to you. I refuse to believe I'm the worst in the family for cooperating with the bodyguards, even if that means including Elie." That was said as a last resort.

Drago slipped her phone into his pocket. "Even including the daredevil. Be safe, Emme." He stepped back onto the elevator, but didn't allow the doors to close until she chose a tube and stepped into it. At once, the force pulled at her, ripping at her flesh and bones, threatening to tear her apart. She was so used to the sensation, it barely registered anymore.

The Saldi estate was impressive. Giuseppi had purchased it for Greta, claiming his bride needed a home befitting a queen. He had managed to secure a property that had been built with the finest materials and craftsmanship. The end result provided living and entertaining areas, nine full bathrooms and two partial baths, and five very large bedrooms with sitting rooms and walk-in closets. There was a panic room in the main master bedroom and hidden passageways for Giuseppi and his family to escape into if they needed to. The walls were thick to keep the house cool from the heat and warm from the cold. Greta's favorite room had been the sunroom overlooking the vast gardens.

The entire estate was surrounded by two acres of trees and landscaped gardens. The wrought iron fence was high and surrounded the entire two acres. There were four points of entry. The front gate was always manned, while the other three had a code that had to be entered in order for the gate to open. The code was changed daily. Cameras were everywhere. The grounds were patrolled with armed guards and dogs.

When one entered through the back, the drive wound

through an impressive riot of flowering trees and shrubs. Fortunately, there were plenty of low lights on the shrubs and trees to throw shadows. The detached garage was behind the main house. The garage was extremely large, with radiant heating not only on the floor but on the covered walkways leading to the garage. It was an eight-bay garage, with each bay holding up to four very large trucks or cars. It could hold a collection of cars, at least that was what Val had told her.

Ricco and Mariko waited just outside the garage. Ricco had a frown on his face, which immediately gave her pause.

"What is it?"

"I'm glad you called for backup, babe. Something big is going on here. I don't think they're waiting for Giuseppi to come home. They've got men everywhere, Emme. There are patrols on the grounds and in the house, and they have two shooters on the roof. That was just a cursory, very quick look."

Mariko nodded. "On the street, they've got cameras as well as patrols, both in cars and walking up and down on both sides of the street from one end to the other. They're heavily armed."

Emmanuelle shook her head. "That really doesn't make any sense. It sounds as if they've been here for a while, not just since Val's been raiding their businesses."

Ricco nodded. "Exactly my thought."

"Did you check inside the garage?"

Ricco nodded. "Two large vans and a truck along with several of Miceli's SUVs. I'm not certain we can safely get Val's meds out, Emme. How important are they?"

They were pretty important, as far as she was concerned, but it wasn't like they didn't have pull with doctors. They could get the medication in a safer way. Just not tonight. "I would like to get it for him tonight, so he's good to go for certain tomorrow. That could be important, but if we can't, we can't."

"Here, use one of the burners Henry stashed outside the gates for us. Text Vittorio the information. Tell him it's imperative we get the meds. Ask him to get on it, ASAP. I'm letting Stefano know we have a situation here." Ricco handed her a phone.

Emmanuelle took a deep breath. She couldn't very well tip off her family, without letting Dario and Valentino know as well, even if technically her family was allies. She detested waking Val if he was asleep, but he had to know. She sent a group text to Dario and Val apprising them of the situation and that Ricco, Mariko and she were going to investigate further. She added that Vittorio would be getting the much-needed meds just in case there was a problem that had to be dealt with immediately at the Saldi estate. She thought that was a very tactful way to put it.

It didn't surprise her that Henry had managed to stash a few burner phones right under the noses of cameras and guards. He would have been driving the car taking the meds back to the Ferraro Hotel. No way would Emmanuelle have asked him. She had made up her mind to cut all ties with her mother. Sadly, that meant cutting ties with Henry as well. She had planned to ask Emilio to send one of the bodyguards. Henry was like a shadow though. He might have been getting up there in age, but he'd worked for the CIA at one time, and he clearly hadn't forgotten his training. No doubt he was close by, several streets away, waiting to make certain all three of them made it out safely before he left.

Keep us informed, Dario returned.

Get the fuck out of there, Emme, Val texted.

On it, Vittorio said, no questions asked.

Emmanuelle took a breath, stashed the phone under a scooped stone, gripped her brother and sister-in-law's hands and then chose a shadow that would take her into the large, gorgeous house. She'd been in it on several occasions. She knew her way around. Ricco and Mariko would each choose a different way in. All of them had studied the blueprints. They knew what to expect with the layout. They just didn't know what to expect from Miceli or his sons.

CHAPTER SEVENTEEN

Greta's beautiful great room, the one she had always been so proud of when she entertained large crowds of their friends and relatives, had been transformed. Valentino barely recognized that it was the same room. He stared at the screens, his gut churning, for the first time almost grateful that his adopted mother was dead. This violation of everything she had ever created for her family was an abomination.

Giuseppi and Greta had always wanted children. They'd dreamt of having a large family. Giuseppi had often told Val and Dario that they had talked of having as many as a dozen children. Greta had had multiple pregnancies, but she had lost every child, some early, some later, some at term, when they were stillborn. Eventually, when they were barely thirty, they had realized she couldn't have children, and they gave up trying. They both had been heartbroken. Greta had urged Giuseppi to divorce her and find another woman who would give him the babies and family he deserved. Giuseppi told Val and Dario he would give up his life before he would give up Greta.

Greta had created a world of beauty, a home, for Giuseppi

and eventually for Valentino and Dario. This house, with this great room, with the stone fireplace and overstuffed sofas and chairs that invited company to sit and stay to visit: she had done that for them. Everywhere one went in Greta's home, there were loving touches that said she welcomed you there. There was none of that now.

The great room was enormous, and it had been transformed into a cold, unfeeling den of pure debauchery. There was a makeshift "stage" with stairs leading up to it from either side where a teen could be brought up and displayed to those waiting to bid on her or him. The teens were clearly being held in rooms near one of the master rooms that had access to a passageway that led to the great room. The prisoner would then be escorted to the stage via the passageway.

Those doing the bidding had tables on the floor below the stage, with waitresses serving them drinks, drugs and food from trays. The waitresses were topless and wore tiny miniskirts with nothing underneath. Several of those that were waitressing had already been manhandled and abused, forced to their knees, their breasts slapped with hands or crops, while others at the table laughed and sneered. No one tried to stop anything done to them.

On the stage, for the entertainment of those in the audience, men and women were brought in to perform all kinds of sexual kink. The audience members were invited to participate if they desired. Several took part as the evening continued and more drinks were consumed. Val understood what the idea was. If Tommaso could get the clients totally uninhibited, feeling as if they were entitled to do anything they wanted, they would pay any amount of money to have their own sex slave in the form of an untouched teen that they could train to do anything they wanted. Eventually, when they tired of her or him, they'd simply sell the teen to someone else and come back for more.

Valentino could barely stand to watch the abuse of the waitresses, but they needed all of the clients inside. Once Tommaso closed the doors and had the outside gates locked, that would signal that the bidding would start soon. The Ferraro family was in the shadows looking for the teens, trying to get numbers and what kind of shape they were in. They needed to know how many guards were on them as well.

Tommaso was taking no chances that he would be hit here at the Saldi estate. They needed the money from the auction desperately. They were sparing no expense to get the clients to feel safe and comfortable. The streets were patrolled outside the gates. The guard stations were manned at all four points of entry. Inside the gates were roving patrols. Inside the house were soldiers dressed in suits, but obviously armed. They stayed to the back, but the walls were lined with them.

The security screens Bernado had pulled up showed armed men in every room of the house. Some were seated at tables, eating, but most were on alert. There were more on the rooftop, the balconies, even in the sunroom off the main verandah. Tommaso was leaving nothing to chance. He had dim lights on outside in the gardens, not wanting to draw the eyes of the police or security in the neighborhood. He might have done better to create the atmosphere of a party since he had numerous cars arriving throughout the evening.

"Stefano's people will be clearing a way for our people to get in through the rear. As soon as they locate the teens and have their numbers, they'll let us know," Valentino informed Dario. "We want Tommaso to lock the place down before we go in and take over."

"I don't understand how they can get through that many soldiers without anyone knowing and we can't," Severu said, looking closer at the screen. "Doesn't make any sense, Val. I've tried watching that family for a few years now, trying to learn something from them. I know they work out a lot, meaning they beat the hell out of anyone that's stupid enough to ask to train with them, but we do that, too."

Valentino was uncomfortable with his underboss asking. Next to Dario, Severu was the most intelligent—and the most lethal—of all of his men. He was also the man he trusted with his shit—if he did trust. He lived in a fucked-up world where he had to question everyone's motives. He didn't want to have to kill Severu, but he didn't want the man to get too close to the Ferraro family secrets.

"Their skills are renowned. Right now, I don't care how they do it, just that they do."

Fourteen girls. Six boys. All of them are bruised but in relatively good physical condition. They've been beaten, some more than others. Boys in the worst condition. They aren't being held together. They can't see one another. He has them scattered throughout the house with handlers for each of them.

Valentino could feel Emmanuelle's anger coming right through her text. She was safe, or she couldn't be texting him. That meant she was no longer in the house, but back with her family, ready to start the assault, ready to open the way for him and his men. They were just two streets over, in a house that his family owned—one Miceli knew nothing of. Few did.

William Gibson had died years earlier saving Giuseppi's life. He'd left behind his wife of forty years. He wasn't a soldier. He wasn't a made man. He was a gardener. A gentle soul who happened to be in the wrong place at the wrong time. He loved roses. So did Greta. His wife, Clara, often accompanied him to have tea with Greta, when he came to trim the roses. She had come that day, and the two women were in the gazebo together when gunmen had burst onto the property.

Giuseppi had been leaning against the outside of the gazebo talking with William as the two men admired their women. Giuseppi told Valentino he had just been laughing, feeling happy. The sun was shining, the day beautiful, and his Greta was happy with her friend over. He liked simple, uncomplicated William. William didn't ever want anything from him. He was happy with his life. He worked for his money and went home to a woman he adored. They had no children and went through their life loving each other. Giuseppi and Greta considered them a guiding light when they learned they couldn't have children.

The two gunmen opened fire without warning. William flung himself at Giuseppi as Giuseppi yelled at the two women to get down, to get on the floor of the gazebo. William took the bullets meant for Giuseppi. The bodyguards killed both assailants, but it was too late for William. He was dead immediately. Greta held Clara in her arms, rocking her back and forth while Giuseppi looked up at his underboss, a man at that time he could count on, vowing to find out who was behind the attack.

Giuseppi took care of the funeral expenses, and he bought the house around the corner outright, paying cash. Clara was moved in so she could visit Greta easily. The two women remained close. Giuseppi paid for Clara's private nurse when she needed one, and Greta visited her daily right up until they lost her. The house remained empty, but was cleaned regularly. Now, Valentino and his army waited in it until Stefano said they had a clear point of entry to the Saldi estate.

Bernado had enough feed to loop the security cameras, particularly to the garage and grounds. They needed the garage for the dead bodies. It wasn't like they could just leave them piled up in the rose garden for Tommaso to spot.

"I want complete stealth. Use knives or a suppressor on your weapons," Valentino said. "And I want kills. Don't bother to take prisoners. Make certain you are wearing gloves. You don't want evidence traced back to you."

As far as the clients went, Val didn't care if they would be valuable to him, he wanted them dead. All of them. They had come to buy young teens, and they deserved death—a slow one—not the quick kill they'd get, but one couldn't have everything, and he was going to get the teenagers home to their families. If they had no families, he was going to make certain they were taken care of.

"Bernado, last chance. You make absolutely certain there are no undercover operations going on. Stefano's people are checking as well. We don't want any mistakes." No one wanted a cop killed, especially a fed, but if they were in deep in this fucked-up operation, that was on them. Who could sit by and watch this happening? He certainly didn't have the stomach for it.

His phone vibrated again. He noticed Dario had his in hand as well. Be safe. We're going in. Switching to wires.

It was starting. "Loop the feed, Bernado. Be extremely careful. I don't want Tommaso tipped off by a rookie mistake."

"I don't make rookie mistakes," Bernado snapped, his voice an outraged hiss in Valentino's ear. Everyone would hear the wires and his commands.

"Let's hope not. Let's hope no one does." They were outnumbered. On the other hand, Tommaso didn't have the Ferraro family of assassins or Elie Archambault.

Emmanuelle was grateful Stefano had called in their cousins to help when she saw the size of the force they were facing. Tommaso had not just taken over the Saldi estate in order to hide his teenagers for auction, he was hiding an army, determined not to be thwarted in making back the money his family needed to pay their soldiers and keep face with the other families.

She'd gone through the house, sickened that Tommaso had taken Greta's home and turned it into something so vile. Nearly every downstairs room was being used for something sinister and disgusting by his men. The waitresses were fair game to any of his soldiers. If they walked past them, they were shoved into walls or thrown over tables, or pushed to the floor. The moment the soldier was done with them, no matter how roughly used, they were expected to carry on with their work. These women had to be part of the trafficking ring as well. They looked defeated. Hopeless. Fearful. They did whatever was ordered immediately, without hesitation.

Stefano had an army of his own he was about to let loose. There were all of her brothers, Mariko and Nicoletta as well as Elie, and three of her cousins from New York, Geno, Salvatore and Lucca. Including Emmanuelle, twelve experienced riders were a huge number of silent assassins to have in one area. Stefano hadn't stopped there. Like Valentino, he wanted to wipe out the human trafficking ring from their territory once and for all. The two men seemed to take it personally that someone had managed to slide such a depraved operation under the radar on their watch.

Stefano had also called in the LA cousins. Emmanuelle had been shocked. She wasn't even sure it was legal as far as the council went. She knew Eloisa would never approve, and most likely, the council wouldn't, either. Elie hadn't protested, but then Elie liked a fight, especially a dangerous one. The worse the odds, the better he liked it. He also loved Emme and her family, and this one was for her. He detested traffickers, so adding that all together, even if later, his family called him on the carpet, he would still side with Stefano.

She had seven cousins, all excellent, experienced riders from LA. Severino, the oldest, ruled his family with an iron hand, much in the way Stefano did. There were six brothers and one sister. Velia, like Emmanuelle, was the youngest, and her brothers tended to watch over her. Stefano directed them up to the roof to get rid of enemies above them, first on the garage and then on the house. From there, the seven would work their way down to the balconies and kill all guards who might spot Valentino's army moving on the house. They would then enter the rooms from the upper balconies and kill anyone in the rooms, room by room, upstairs. Their job was to ensure everyone on the upper story was dead.

Emmanuelle, Nicoletta and Mariko were to secure the girls and boys. They were to first kill the guard in the room with each girl or boy, then calm and assure her or him that they were there to rescue them but they had to stay where they were until the signal was given that they could be safely brought out of the mansion through the rear exit.

Stefano and Emmanuelle's brothers would aid Valentino's men inside as much as possible, but Giovanni and Vittorio would break off at Stefano's command and help Geno, Salvatore and Lucca clear the street of Tommaso's men.

Valentino was responsible for getting the teens checked

out medically and turned over to the authorities he could trust to get them safely back to their homes. Bernado would check backgrounds as soon as he could identify who the teens were, in case they were taken off the street and had nowhere to go and no family to take them in.

"Going in now, need your four," Stefano said softly, using the code agreed on ahead of time with Val.

"Four" meant Dario and Severu, two of the men Val put his faith in. The other two were Levi and Axel Carson, brothers, two more of the ex-military, ex-mercenaries Dario had found and trained. They were Valentino's men, not part of the family in the way Severu was, but dedicated solely to Valentino and Dario. Stefano wanted the four men to deal with the bodies in the garden area the Ferraro family would leave behind.

"Street is not clean. Street cleaners have not yet been employed. The roof is still dirty." Stefano continued with his report. He meant there were still enemy eyes on the rooftop and on the streets, so the four would have to be very careful.

"Copy that," Valentino replied.

Emmanuelle's heart reacted to the soft sound of his voice. She'd kissed him. Told him she loved him. Tried to prepare him for what Tommaso and his uncle had done to Greta's home. There was no way to prepare anyone for this kind of depraved nightmare. There was an army in the house, and he was going in. That was just terrifying, because Valentino wasn't a man to hide behind his bodyguards.

"Be safe, everyone, in twos, watch each other's backs. They're armed. We need to do this in silence. Fast. We're out-numbered," Stefano reiterated. "Go."

Emmanuelle stepped into the shadow that would take her past the guard at the gate and up the drive to her designated starting point. She was to take out every roving patrol in the section of acreage in the rose garden—gazebo, fountains, the flowering shrubs and trees that formed a beautiful arching tunnel she'd secretly hoped to get married under one day. This was one of the many places that anyone in the house could easily view from the windows and balconies. The way the house was built encouraged those inside to do just that. Having an auction taking place with food, drink, drugs and anything goes with the waitresses might have meant fewer guards watching the grounds from above.

She stopped just inside the mouth of the shadow tube, allowing her brain to acknowledge that her body was in one piece. Normally, riders would have studied the pattern and timing of patrols in an estate they were going to penetrate, but there was no time for that. There was also no real discipline to the way the guards were behaving.

Stefano told them, in the briefing, that it appeared Tommaso was using most of his own men inside, but had hired others for the guards outside in the street and grounds and even some in the house. It wasn't a brilliant move when any of those men could have gone to the cops and told them who was peddling young teens—unless Tommaso planned on killing them all afterward. She wouldn't put it past him to do so.

Three men stood just outside the back of the house, staring into one of the wide, curved windows of the kitchen. There was a bank of windows surrounding the kitchen, making it light and airy and giving those inside views of the flower gardens as well as the vegetable and herb gardens just around the curving landscape.

One of the men stepped closer to the window, breathing heavily. "Damn, that's hot. Wish I was assigned inside. How did they manage to get that assignment and we got stuck out here?" He lifted his hand high and flipped whoever it was inside off. "He's fucking her face and flipping me off. What a dick."

The other two guards moved closer to the window to see the show. Emmanuelle shadowed them. She made certain her image didn't appear behind them so their buddy couldn't see her as she moved into position. She caught the head of the third one, the one not so eager to see, between her hands and jerked, breaking his neck, murmuring "Justice is served" as she lowered him to the ground and immediately was on the second guard.

They were so intrigued by what was happening in the kitchen that they weren't paying attention to anything else around them. The first guard had unzipped his jeans and was stroking his cock. She broke the second guard's neck, lowered him to the ground and waited a moment until the man in the kitchen was fully engaged in what he was doing, too far gone to care or know what was happening outside, before she killed the first guard. She left them for Valentino's trusted crew to put in the garage where no one would find the bodies until everyone was far away from the premises, with alibis that couldn't be broken.

Hearing voices, she stepped into a shadow that was wider and longer, an easy one that was more like a highway, one she could leisurely navigate, allowing her to take a look at how many guards were in the section of the grounds she had been assigned to clear. Mariko had started on the other side of it. They would meet in the middle. It was a large section.

Emmanuelle counted five more guards just in the area around the kitchen and vegetable garden. Thankfully, they were spread out. Two had met near the tomato plants and were talking in low voices, warning her someone was close, but these men were taking their job much more seriously than the other three had.

She left them to their conversation, giving them time to say whatever they thought was important. Hopefully, they would split up, making her job easier. She went after the other three who were patrolling alone. She took them, one by one, softly reporting where she dropped each body, giving the location to Dario, although not using names, only a coded location of the bodies. She went back to locate the other two chatty guards. They had separated. She needed to get to both before they came upon the three bodies she'd dropped.

She had to depend on her cousins to do their jobs and get rid of any eyes on the roof and balconies. Not wasting time looking up took discipline. She had to use every ounce of her radar for her immediate section of the grounds to be cleared. The guard she stalked was closer to the street than she would have liked. The street wasn't cleared yet and wouldn't be for some time. That wasn't a priority yet. They needed the rear entrance clear, the roof and balconies and then the house. At the same time as the house, the street would be cleared. It was all a matter of precise timing. She sighed. Anything could go wrong.

"With you," Valentino's voice whispered in her ear on their private channel.

He'd heard that sigh. She was never certain their channel was really private. Giovanni had assured her it was, that no one, not even Val's geeky, techy, whiz-kid friend could penetrate the encoded channel, but she still worried. She didn't want Valentino to look less than he was in front of his men. She was coming to understand that appearances of strength were everything in his world. They could even mean the difference between life and death.

She came up behind the guard and killed him easily, lowering him to the ground behind several wide shrubs, whispering the location and a warning that it was close to the street. She switched back to the private channel. She felt Valentino close. He was no longer in the safety of that house just two blocks away. She didn't like that he was close. The streets weren't safe. This was how it felt to him when he thought she was in danger.

"Just so you know, you are the love of my life. The one and only." Before he could reply, she stepped into a shadow tube and let it take her back to the highway tube. She needed to find that last roving guard before she proceeded toward Mariko. They had to get into the house and start looking for the girls.

The gardens flashed by, and she forced herself to look all around her, catching glimpses of guards in other sections. They weren't her problem. She had only to find the ones she was assigned to and exterminate them to keep Valentino and his men safe as they got into the house to take down Tommaso and his men. They had to put an end to this inhumane idea that one could take young children from their homes, shelters or off the street and sell them to the highest bidder as if they had no value other than for their bodies.

She spotted the guard with one foot on the steps to the gazebo, his hand on the door. He looked around surreptitiously, and then stepped inside and closed the screen door. The gazebo was beautiful, mostly white, the door made of heavy-gauge mesh with panels of carved wood painted white. Each window was screened with that same heavy-gauge mesh. One could push up the windows or open the door and allow the fresh air in, still safe from all insects, or keep the gazebo cozy with heaters on and use it through the winter.

Emmanuelle couldn't imagine what the guard was doing in the gazebo unless he planned on taking a break. She needed a good shadow that would take her inside the large structure. At night, from this distance, it was impossible to tell if the shadow she chose would take her inside, but she didn't hesitate. She stepped into one of the smaller feeder tubes, a little ugly one that was crooked and zigzagged but went right up the steps and under the door. She prayed it continued even for a few inches on the other side.

Several times, she had registered the reports of other riders reporting to the "Four" the location of the "dirt." She hoped Mariko wouldn't be reporting her body, or that the sound of gunfire wouldn't alert the enemy and the entire mission wouldn't be blown because of her mistake.

Emmanuelle had always trusted her instincts, and she had to now. She stopped herself before she was spit out of the mouth of the narrow tube into the interior of the gazebo. She'd had tea with Greta here more than once. Now it smelled of fear, blood and sex, drowning out the scent of the night-star flowers that William had planted around the building so long ago to give Greta and Giuseppi a beautiful, all-encompassing experience even after dark.

When one looked down at the flowers from the balconies, they appeared like stars. Looking up at the night sky, the couple had the constellations and real stars. Looking down, they had the flowers that appeared to be stars glowing at them. If Giuseppi and Greta sat together late in the evening, in the gazebo, they were surrounded by that beauty and the scent of the flowers. Now that beauty was destroyed by three men who had a naked woman shoved up against the screen of one of the windows.

"'Bout time you got here, Lyn," the one holding the woman snapped. "We started without you. Do you have any idea how difficult it was to smuggle her out here?"

"Shit, Pat, didn't want anyone to see me. She looks great. Turn her around. You know how I like big tits."

"She's got 'em, don't you, honey?" Pat spun the woman around to face the other two men. "Barry couldn't help himself. He whipped her tits while I fucked her ass. She's gonna like taking all three of us, aren't you?"

The woman was bruised from head to toe. She'd clearly fought them, but had given up completely and just stood with her head down and her hair hanging around her face.

"She doesn't seem very responsive," Barry said. "Rosy, thought I told you what would happen if you didn't answer when we asked you questions."

Emmanuelle had had enough. All three men were totally focused on Rosy, surrounding her like wolves about to devour prey. They had their backs to her. The latest to join, Lyn, stepped close and grabbed Rosy's breast cruelly, squeezing hard and slapping at the other.

She took out Barry first. He was just one step behind Pat, laughing, tapping his thigh with a wicked-looking strip of leather. Snapping his neck, she moved immediately to Pat and did the same to him before Barry dropped to the floor, crumbling like a ton of bricks. Lyn started to turn at the sound, but Rosy clawed at him, launching her own attack, hitting him with her fists and then raking at his face with her nails. He swung back around, punching her in the face. Rosy dropped to the floor of the gazebo as if she were a stone, clearly unconscious. Lyn swore. It was the last sound he ever made.

Emmanuelle let the "Four" know where to find the "dirt" but added that there was a live, unconscious friendly in need of medical help, but she would not stay unconscious long. She rode a shadow to meet Mariko at the designated spot and wasn't surprised to find her sister-in-law was already waiting.

The two entered the house cautiously through the kitchen. Pat had brought Rosy out the door, and it wasn't locked. Tommaso was so focused on getting his clients drunk or drugged, and in the mood he wanted them in, with the performances on the stage becoming more and more depraved, that he wasn't paying much attention to his newly bought mercenaries. His own men were spread thin, and couldn't cover the streets, the grounds and the entire huge house, plus watch over the teens that he'd insisted be kept apart as well as watch the auction room and guard him. It was no wonder no one was overseeing the mercenaries.

Emmanuelle discovered a young girl being held in a small bathroom just off the master bedroom. She'd been fairly certain they would need access to the passageway if they were going to escort the teens to the stage using that method. She looked to be about thirteen and wore only a thin blue wraparound robe that barely covered her bottom. Her hair was pulled back from her face in a high ponytail, and her face was devoid of any makeup. She was barefoot. She sat on a towel on the floor with her knees drawn up, her arms hugging her legs and her head down on top of her knees.

A man talked to her in a low voice with the door cracked open. "You know I've been good to you, never steered you wrong."

"You hurt me."

"Only when you wouldn't obey. I had to teach you to obey for your own good. These men are going to offer to buy you girls. You want someone nice to buy you. If you get someone bad . . ." He trailed off. "Some of these men are really cruel. They'll share you. Hurt you. They'll use you and then sell you to other men. That will happen to you over and over. You don't want that. You want someone nicer to buy you. I'm trying to help you."

The girl looked even more scared. "What should I do? What if one of the mean ones buys me? I couldn't stand that. You have to tell me if that happens."

"No. It's best you don't know."

Something in his voice made Emmanuelle look at his face sharply. He was smirking. Why would he be smirking? Was he deliberately trying to scare the child even more before she went on the auction block?

"I have to know. You said after they bid and purchase me, you'd bring me back here to wait while the others are bid on. You could tell me then." The girl was pleading with him.

"Are you sure?" He made her beg, the smirk even bigger.

Emmanuelle wanted to kill him on the spot, but she needed to wait to understand what he was doing.

"Yes. Please. I have to know. If he's one of the really cruel ones, you have to tell me and what I can do."

The man gave an exaggerated sigh. "I'll tell you, but honestly, there isn't much you can do except . . ." He trailed off.

"What? Tell me."

He swore. "I'm not going there. Just accept what you have to do. Obey him in everything and hope for the best. Hope he isn't one of the cruel ones or married. Hope he doesn't share you or pass you around or sell you. Or doesn't like to whip you until you bleed. Some of them like that. If he does, just endure it."

The girl began to sob. "You have to tell me what I can do if he's like that."

There was silence as if he was reluctant, but he was smiling as if he had accomplished exactly what he'd set out to do. "You can never tell anyone I said this to you. And if you have to do it, you need to wait at least one month or more after he's had you. Swear to me."

"I do. I swear it."

"You could kill yourself. That's your only out. You get in the bathtub and open your veins. It won't even hurt. Or if he gives you drugs, you just take way too much. But you have to wait at least a month. Do you understand me, little pet? If this comes back on me, they'll kill me for trying to help you."

She was nodding her head. "Yes, I understand. Thank you. I'll wait. I will."

Emmanuelle would bet her last dollar that no matter who bid on this girl, when she was brought back, her guard would tell her the buyer was cruel and would do something terrible to her, not that it was likely to be a lie, but there was something more going on here.

The next girl was located just down the hall and around the corner in a full bath. Like the first girl, this one was very young, dressed in a similar wraparound robe, looking seriously miserable. She might have been a year or so older, her hair chestnut, cut shorter and falling around her chin and neck, making her appear vulnerable.

Just as in the first case, her handler sat outside the bathroom with the door cracked, his voice soothing as he spoke to her as if he was trying to guide her through the upcoming ordeal. She appeared to be listening intently. Emmanuelle had ridden the shadow nearly right up to him and stood in the mouth of it so she could clearly hear every word he was saying. To her shock, it was nearly word for word what the first guard had said to his prisoner.

This was a script. The handlers were going off a script they fed to the young girls or boys. Obviously, during the time they had the teens, they broke them down by in turns being good to them or hurting them. The children had no one else and clung to the only one that fed them or took care of them in any way. Now the abuser was scaring them more by pretending to care, to warn them. At the same time, they were encouraging them to take their own life after a month, although this man specified six weeks. Why?

Emmanuelle turned that over in her mind. The bidding

brought in as much as five hundred thousand or even more per virgin. There were fourteen girls and six boys in this group. That, apparently, was the usual number Tommaso auctioned off at a time. Not all the teens would kill themselves, but it was likely some of the younger ones would, especially if they did end up with a crueler buyer. There seemed to be some pretty depraved men bidding, although the majority of those accosting the waitresses were Tommaso's mercenaries or his soldiers. He let them because he wanted a show for the audience.

Emmanuelle, Nicoletta and Mariko had the locations of all fourteen girls and six boys by the time the bidding had started. As each teen was brought back to their designated space, it was easy enough for them to ride the shadows and be there waiting.

"I'm so sorry," the guard told the little sobbing thirteen-year-old. "You know what to do." He patted her head. "He'll be good to you that first month. You'll see. Just hold on, and when you get your chance, take it." He all but pushed her into the half bath and stepped away from the door after locking it.

As he turned, he died, his smirk still on his face. Emmanuelle and Nicoletta dragged his body out of the hall into the sitting room and closed the door, taking his keys. They couldn't let the young teenager know she was going to be free until the last moment. They couldn't take the chance she might make a sound or try to make a run for it. She wasn't hurt and didn't require medical attention, so they rode the shadows back to the auction.

As each young teen was brought out to be bid on, they followed him or her back with their handler to their assigned "cage." It was very clear all of them had been given the same story—that they would be told if a cruel man had won the bid for them. Each had been informed they'd been bought by the worst man imaginable and their only out was to kill themself. Each had been given a specific time period to do so. Tommaso had certainly thought of everything to keep his business profitable.

Once all the teens' handlers were taken down, Mariko

and Emmanuelle reported they were ready to bring them out as soon as the streets were cleared and Valentino's crew was ready to take over the estate.

Valentino gave the go-ahead to his army of men, reiterating that the Ferraro family members were part of their family and were wearing distinctive pinstriped suits. Under penalty of death, none of them were to be harmed. His men swept in through the back entrance, Dario, Severu, Levi and Axel surrounding Valentino along with Luca, Quintu, Romano and Tore, which Emmanuelle knew Val would detest. Those were the men that would no doubt put themselves in the path of a bullet for Valentino.

She hurried as fast as she could, taking her charges out to the van rigged with medical equipment to transport the young teens to the clinic Val had set up for them. There were doctors, nurses and counselors waiting. It hadn't quite set in that they were actually rescued. The older teens were suspicious, not quite believing, the younger teens not comprehending, still terrified after what their handlers had told them.

The moment the vans had safely pulled away with their escort, Emmanuelle turned back to the house. She caught the largest shadow transporting her through the yard, which was completely clear of all of Tommaso's mercenaries, to the inside of the mansion, where gunfire was erupting in a steady thunder that was terrifying to her.

She knew Val would be looking for Tommaso. They had all exits blocked. The clients couldn't leave. They had sealed their fate when they'd actually bid on the teenagers, buying them as if they had the right to purchase human beings. Tommaso couldn't count on any of the men outside or upstairs. They were already dead. The teens' handlers were dead. He had only his soldiers and the mercenaries that were assigned downstairs. Those men were utilizing every bit of cover they could find, suddenly finding themselves fighting for their lives.

The clients were already dead or dying, caught between the two armies. Stefano and his brothers did their best to get the waitresses out a side door to the sunroom and then outside.

One was still trapped and was lying on the floor with her hands over her head. Emmanuelle beckoned to her. The woman lifted her head up a few inches, and then a look of determination came over her. Staying on her belly, she crawled to Emme.

"Stay low," Emmanuelle cautioned. "Don't move until I say."

The woman nodded. The room was trashed, with tables overturned and bodies strewn on the floor like bloodied mannequins. Emme spotted Dario in the far corner, near one of the massive pillars, steadily firing his weapon, his eyes tracking the room as he did so. Valentino was on the other side of the pillar, picking his targets, but he, also, was looking for one man.

Emme stretched her arm out, fingers managing to snag the barrel of a gun from a fallen enemy. She pulled it toward her. The movement attracted the attention of a man just off to her left. He was crouched down in the sunken conversation area, protected on two sides by floor-to-ceiling marble fountains and a stone fireplace. With him were five others, surrounding him, clearly trying to shield him. Their ultimate goal was to make it to the door just behind her, the same exit she was trying to get the waitress safely out.

Tommaso gave her a wide, evil grin as recognition settled over him. "Valentino's little bride." He indicated her to the others.

There was no cover between her and the men. None. Emmanuelle didn't hesitate. "Get out. Go now." Firing the gun rapidly at Tommaso and his crew to give the waitress a chance to get out of the building, Emme rolled away from her, hoping to find a shadow to disappear into.

Valentino came out of nowhere, striding right through the bodies, the death and destruction, as if he were invincible, as if no bullet could possibly touch him. He was grim-faced, a dark demon rising from the very pits of hell, his weapon spouting bright orange and blue flames with each thundering pull of the trigger.

Dario, Severu, Levi and Axel moved with him, keeping

the firepower steady on Tommaso and his crew, forcing them to turn toward the new threat. Two of Tommaso's men went down. Tommaso crawled on his belly away from his circle of protection, toward Emme, as the Saldi men approached without once breaking stride. He stopped abruptly, cursing, his head swiveling from side to side as he tried to see where she could have gone.

Then Valentino was standing over him, kicking away his weapon, kicking him in the ribs, his gut. He crouched down beside his cousin. "Where are the little kids?" he asked, his voice low. Quiet. Velvet soft. "Angelo's got them, but you know where they are and you're going to tell me."

"Fuck you, Val," Tommaso yelled. By contrast his voice was shrill.

Val shot him through his left hand. Tommaso screamed and rolled back and forth, looking around frantically for help.

"I asked you a question."

"I don't know."

Valentino calmly shot him through the top of his left foot. Tommaso's screams rose to new heights.

"I'm tired, Tommaso, it's been a long day. Your entire crew is dead. Your mercenaries are dead. The teens have been rescued and taken to a hospital. There's no money for your father to send up the food chain. I imagine his partner is getting a little impatient by this time. Just like I am. I want those kids. The next bullet goes into your right hand. We'll start on that side of your body."

"Wait. Wait, Val." Tommaso held up his left, bloody, shaking hand. "I don't know specifically, but he and Marge have several places they would take them." His voice shook, and he kept rolling from side to side as if he could get away from the pain.

"I'll need to know where those places are, Tommaso," Val said, his voice exactly the same: Patient. Calm. Almost soothing.

Tommaso rolled toward Valentino and suddenly lunged at him, the blade of a knife going straight toward his heart.

Simultaneously, Emmanuelle emerged from a shadow to the right of Tommaso's head, hands gripping hard and wrenched, breaking his neck. Dario fired three shots, two between the eyes, one into his left eye. Levi shot him in the heart twice, and Axel shot him in the throat twice. Valentino's gun also spit out three bullets, one through the palm holding the knife, two to the gut, because he wanted the man to die slowly and suffer. It seemed like that wasn't going to happen.

He went back on his knees and glared up at his wife. "You could have been killed. Dario could have shot you."

"You could have been killed, and Dario would never have shot me. He knew where I was."

"The others didn't know where you were."

"I want to go home. The cops will be here soon, and we can't possibly control the situation," she whispered. "Hurry, Valentino." She looked at the men surrounding him. "Please get him out of here. Clear everyone out of here, Dario."

"We're on it, Emme," Dario assured. "We'll meet you as soon as possible."

CHAPTER EIGHTEEN

I'm sorry, Val," Emmanuelle said softly, from where she lay sprawled over the top of him. Naked. Her head on his chest. Her knees on either side of his hips.

Valentino kept one hand on her bare bottom, that smooth skin, rubbing the curve, drifting in a sea of peace. Sheer peace. He didn't get that often. His body completely sated. His woman wrapped around him. His mind still, not looping at warp speed, trying to drive him insane. This was his kind of paradise. His personal version. He didn't give a damn where he was, as long as he had this woman with him.

"For what, Princess?" He murmured it, without opening his eyes, letting himself rest. Needing just a few more minutes with her before they started the insanity all over again.

"When I was so ridiculous with you the other night. Listening to Marge. To my mother. To anyone but you. I won't do that anymore. Even if I'm totally insecure sometimes and don't feel beautiful or sexy, I promise it will be you I listen to even when Eloisa's voice is in the back of my head whispering that I'll never be good enough."

She rubbed her cheek on his chest and then pressed her lips over his heart. "I love you so much, Val. Sometimes it hurts, I love you so much. It scares me to love someone the way I love you."

His hand crept up her spine to the nape of her neck to massage the tension knots there, easing them out of her. "That's exactly how I feel about you, Emme. Maybe we're supposed to feel that way about each other, so over-the-top crazy we can't bear to be apart. We tear each other's clothes off the second we're alone. All that so the shadow creeper doesn't get loose."

A little shiver crept down her spine. "Don't even think about him. It might make him real again. I haven't noticed him when our shadows are on the wall together, and I deliberately looked for him."

"I looked, too. That's why I think maybe we're supposed to be as wild about each other as we are. We feed each other's desire and emotions."

She moved in a suggestive little glide down his body. "You could feed my desires anytime, Valentino. My emotions would do a happy dance."

He had no choice but to watch her through hooded eyes. They needed to be up and moving. They'd already stolen time for themselves this morning. He'd woken her with his mouth between her legs. He loved the taste of her. How wild it made her. How wet. Those moans of hers. Her body so responsive. She liked his tongue and teeth. His fingers. He gave her multiple orgasms before he took her hard, determined to prolong his time, his pleasure with her as long as possible.

They fell asleep again, woke and he put her on her hands and knees, intending to take her fast, but he couldn't resist playing. Teasing her. Making her wait. Bringing her to the brink of an orgasm over and over until she was pleading with him. Begging him. Demanding. Threatening him. He loved when she got to the point of threatening him. They collapsed together, and Val had pulled her on top of him, while they rested, just because he needed to feel her surrounding him the way she did.

There was something decadent about watching his woman crawl down his body with such purpose, her eyes hungry, wanton, the blue so dark with desire for him—for his cock. She worshiped his cock. What man didn't appreciate that? He loved her wild hair, but he bunched the thick mass in his fist, sweeping it out of his way so he could watch as she kissed the insides of his thighs, taking little nips with her teeth, driving the blood, the fire, straight to his groin.

It didn't seem to matter that he should be drained dry, that her body had milked every drop of seed from him, there was always more when she was like this. She brought him to life with very little trouble. Stroking his thighs, kissing, nipping. Making his heart stop with the way she took her time. Her tongue tracing his sac, lapping, sucking, pressing kisses over his balls while her fingernails ever so gently raked down.

Emme was his undoing. She unraveled him every time. She cupped his sac, jiggled, her fingers dancing over him, even as her mouth and tongue branded his shaft with fire. It was the way she gave his cock such attention. Every little detail that stole his breath, made his lungs burn for air. Watching her brought him to his knees figuratively or literally at times. She paid complete attention to his every signal. Worshiped him. Loved him. Swallowed him whole. Lavished such utter devotion on him.

She never seemed to think of herself or what she would get in return. When she took his cock in her mouth like this, she was all about Valentino. About making him feel good. More than that. Sending him to paradise. Shooting rockets to outer space. Hell, he didn't know, only that the expression on her face, in her eyes, the way her lips stretched around the wide girth of his cock, added to the fantasy she gave him that sent him to another planet.

Emmanuelle spent time on his body, and when she was through with him, he couldn't move or think for far too long.

He could only lie there, his heart beating like a fierce drum, while she lay with her head in his lap, her arms wrapped around his hips and her hair everywhere. So much silk over his cock and balls, tangling there, on his thighs, along his legs. It should have made him crazy; instead, he fell asleep again, one hand burrowing deep into all that hair, holding her to him as if she might escape him while he slept.

How are we going to find where the children are, Valentino?" Emme asked. "Tommaso didn't tell us."

"Dario got it out of Marge."

He couldn't help the drop in his voice. The grimness. Dario had worked on the bitch for two days. Two nights. He'd been relentless. Merciless. He knew exactly how much blood a body could lose before they would die, and he didn't allow that to happen. By turns he was cruel and harsh and then he'd switch, attending to her needs, giving concessions, giving hope.

Dario was good at making a woman believe anything he wanted her to believe, especially when she was in pain. Val wasn't going to tell Emmanuelle that. Marge had been completely broken, telling Dario everything she knew and then some before she begged for death. She'd begged a long time before she got her wish. Val wasn't going to tell Emme that, either. There were things about Dario that were his to share, and maybe someday he'd get to the point that he would with Emmanuelle, but until then, Valentino felt it was necessary to keep some things to himself.

Emme spun around, nearly tripping as she pulled the pin-striped trousers up her legs and over her hips. The material molded to her curves, making his heart contract and the blood rush through his veins. Her hair was still damp from the shower, but now braided tight in preparation for their task ahead. "Does Stefano know?"

"Of course. I would never leave him out. We're partners in this. He's been a man of his word and then some. Why would you think I wouldn't tell him?"

"Valentino." She nearly wailed his name. A clear reprimand. "You didn't tell *me*. I'm your partner. You're supposed to tell me before you tell anyone else."

He couldn't help the smirk. She stood right in front of him, barefoot. Those sexy trousers molding to her perfect body, showing off the curve of her hips and that perfect ass. Her tits jutting out toward him invitingly, nipples hard and tight. He was a breast man, and she had them. The perfect rack. That sexy hair. That sinful mouth.

"I'm very serious, Val."

She narrowed her eyes at him, but he could see the goose bumps rising on her skin. The heat. If he stepped close to her and opened that pinstriped suit, there was no doubt in his mind, if he swiped his finger between her bare lips, he'd find her slick. The taste of her was in his mouth just like that. Just thinking about her.

"It's a little difficult to be serious when you're standing there looking sexy as sin, baby. Just thinking about you going into battle with nothing under that suit makes me hard as a fucking rock. I can't hear your lectures if you don't cover up, so put your jacket on and start again, for me. I'll try harder to concentrate."

He ran the pads of his fingers very gently over the swell of her breasts. Those sweet curves. Her nipples. He couldn't resist holding the weight in his palms and leaning down to taste the soft flesh in the heat of his mouth.

"I thought we were already late."

She cradled his head to her, hands in his hair. Not once did she try to pull away. She was right: they were late. They needed the early morning hours to set up their attack on Angelo and Miceli and retrieve the children before Angelo could ship them out of Valentino's reach.

"We're going to have to take prisoners with this one, hopefully Angelo or Miceli. I have to break them, Emmanuelle. I don't have a choice." He poured steel into his voice. Resolve. He would find that place of darkness in him, that hole that allowed him to do unspeakable things he never wanted Emme around to see. "If I don't find out who is behind this, we saved these kids but didn't do a thing to stop it from happening to others."

She reached up to cup the side of his face with her palm. Her blue eyes stared intently into his, as if she knew what he was saying to her—and she probably did. "We'll find him. The one behind all of this. We'll find him and we'll stop him. I have every faith in you, Valentino."

"I'm sorry I'm not a decent man, Emmanuelle." His hand came up to cover hers. He pressed her palm tight against his skin. It hurt to know he wasn't and never would be. "You deserve better, but I knew I could never be without you. You give me peace when I didn't think I could ever have it."

"I love you so much, Valentino. More than I can possibly ever express to you. I wouldn't want to be with anyone else. Just love me back the same way, and that will be enough for me. You be whatever you have to be to get to this man. Selling children has to stop. It has to. There is no doubt in my mind that you will find the way to stop this particular trafficking ring. Whoever this person is, man or woman, behind it, had better be worried, because you're going to get to them."

She made him weak. He couldn't afford to be weak or vulnerable and she made him both. It didn't matter. She was also his greatest strength. He bent his head and took her mouth gently. Sometimes the fire raged between them. Sometimes it was a slow burn of a promise, like now. He promised her everything he had to give. His heart. His soul. His complete loyalty.

"Angelo has several places he hides the children, according to Marge. We have to check them out without them knowing. Stefano offered to do that."

"He didn't contact me."

"I asked him not to. I wanted you with me," Valentino admitted. "I *needed* you with me," he added before she could voice a protest. He glanced at his watch. "Let's go, baby." He buttoned her suit jacket, enclosing her breasts. The bruises were still there, standing out starkly against her otherwise flawless skin. "Ride with me. You're a Saldi. My wife. Stefano and his crew can use their own cars, but I want you with me."

She framed his face with both hands, her expression one of regret. "We'll use the shadows. You told Stefano where the places to look for the children are. He will have sent my brothers and cousins hunting. Once they're found, he'll report back to you and then call for us to set things up and be ready for you. I have to be part of that. I'm a shadow rider, Valentino. I work best in the shadows. That's where I'm an asset to you. It was okay to ask Stefano to have me spend the night with you, but I need to be with them when we take down your cousin and uncle. It's the best way I can help you."

Valentino knew he couldn't protect her as he wanted to. Maybe staying in the shadows was more of a protection for her. He didn't even care if Elie Archambault worked as her partner, as long as he protected her.

"You have your wire?"

She nodded. "I'll put it in when we have to give up our cell phones. Stefano will contact my bodyguards and let them know where I need to meet him. Until then, I have to stay with Drago and Demetrio."

"And my men, Emmanuelle. You have to get used to Levi and Axel. They're going to be assigned to you at all times. When they aren't with you, Pace and Lando will be."

"Honey, I have to disappear into the shadows. What then?"

He hated the gentleness in her voice. The way she spoke to him as if he wasn't quite thinking things through. Dario knew about the fucking shadows. Maybe he'd take her four bodyguards into his confidence as well. If they said one word of it to anyone, he'd slit their throats. They knew what he was. They knew he'd do it.

"We have to go." He'd discuss it with her later. There were going to be quite a few discussions later, apparently. "When did you get so stubborn?"

She burst out laughing, slung her arm around his waist and looked up at him with soft, glowing eyes. That look always melted him. He shook his head and looked away, putting his stone face on. Letting the cold settle into him. Giving the outside world nothing of what he felt. As far as anyone was concerned, he was Valentino Saldi and he would end a life on the slightest hint that someone had betrayed him or the *famiglia*. He was ruthless and merciless. His reputation was already rising fast, and it had only been a couple of days.

They entered the elevator and rode it down together with the bodyguards. Dario was waiting, leaning against the wall, looking bored, just inside the lower parking garage. His gaze slid over Valentino and then Emmanuelle. There was no expression on his face whatsoever, but Valentino felt the little shiver that went through Emme. She knew Dario almost as well as he did, and she knew something was up. He was going to have to tell Dario that his bored indifference tipped Emme off to the fact that something was wrong.

His phone vibrated. Emme's must have as well. She pulled it from inside her jacket as she stepped close to Valentino, under his shoulder, but not so close he couldn't get to his weapons. He liked that about her. She had always been aware of the space between them in public. He had put it down to taking care not to let others know they were a couple. Now he realized it was more than that. Emmanuelle was just as careful as he was about being in a position to utilize all weapons.

One last piece of information before Marge died. She witnessed Miceli meeting with Marco Messina on two occasions.

That was bad. Really bad, if Marge confirmed Marco met with Miceli on two occasions. Valentino couldn't imagine Marco, the youngest son of crime boss Tibberiu Messina, setting up and carrying out a large human trafficking ring that had to encompass more than just the Saldi territory. The rot had to have spread to other families. Marco would need his father's backing. Going to war with Tibberiu was next to impossible. Valentino didn't have the manpower. Not yet. Maybe never. Even with the Ferraro family as allies, he couldn't touch the Messina family. He stopped the flow of traffic in his own territory, but he wouldn't be able to cut off the head.

He swore softly, his eyes meeting Dario's. He and Dario had sworn a blood oath. Even Giuseppi didn't understand their full commitment to stopping Miceli. For Giuseppi it was a matter of a traitor going against the *famiglia*. Worse, Miceli was his brother. Giuseppi was now convinced, as Val had been all along, that Miceli was behind the car bombing that killed their youngest brother and his wife. It was important to stop him, but for Val, the most important thing was to crush the human trafficking ring at the very heart, to cut off the head. If that head was the very powerful Messina family, they would not do so easily or soon.

He felt Emmanuelle's eyes on him and steeled himself to meet her gaze. Dario had sent her the message as well. Her family would have to check out the information and could do so much faster than Valentino could. That meant he would have to allow her to go without his protection. He knew that would become the scenario over their years together. His woman was so unafraid of risk, while he would always be terrified when she was out of his sight. He knew she felt the same for him.

"We have to go, Val. We can't take a chance that Angelo and Miceli will move those kids. It's rare for both the female and male children to be held together," Dario said.

"Take all the men with you, Valentino," Emme said softly. "Demetrio and Drago are here, and I'll be leaving to meet my brothers and cousins shortly."

Val knew she was right. As much as he wanted to leave his men to protect her even for those few minutes before Stefano sent word where she was to meet him, they couldn't watch her disappear into the shadows without some kind of explanation. He cupped the side of her face, ran his thumb over her cheek and nodded.

Abruptly, he dropped his hand. "Let's go, Dario." He indicated the cars. They would tell the drivers the location once they were close to it. They weren't going to take chances that Miceli or Angelo would move the children before they could get to them. Valentino had an army moving on the location, but he was sending his men there from various sites.

All drivers were sent to the highway in the general direction that could take them anywhere. If they had a traitor among them, he had no chance of tipping Miceli off that Val's men were coming for him. In the meantime, Stefano and his crew could get there first and hopefully stop them from leaving should they be forewarned.

The neighborhood was old and run-down. Emmanuelle could see why Angelo had chosen to hide the children here. No one would care in this desolate place if they heard the sound of children crying. It was a common sound, along with adults fighting and women screaming from the beatings they took. The smell of alcohol was prevalent, along with urine and rotting garbage.

Dogs, ribs showing, snapped at one another as they searched through the trash on the ground. Broken glass was strewn everywhere in the unkept brown grass that dotted the yards behind tumbling fences long in need of repair. Houses, paint peeling, squatted like sad memories to the past, broken stairs leading to sagging doors.

There were no new shiny cars on the dirty, narrow roads. If one drove onto them, they would be spotted immediately by all residents. The roads throughout the neighborhood had large pits and potholes in them as if this part of town was so forgotten even the way in and out had long since been lost to the city.

Emmanuelle was certain Stefano had let Valentino know his men couldn't bring their vehicles close to the neighborhood without letting Miceli know he was being raided. Miceli didn't need sentries of his own, not with this pitiful place. She had spotted three snipers on the roof of an old apartment building that she was fairly certain no one could possibly be living in, but she'd seen the homeless take shelter in all kinds of buildings. This one seemed as if it might collapse at any moment.

The walls of the abandoned apartment building actually sagged in places, or appeared to if one looked at it too long. She squinted her eyes, studying it from the mouth of the shadow she'd taken to arrive at the location Stefano had given her. He was waiting, along with her brothers and cousins.

"There are children inside," Stefano said, the lines in his face grim. "Part of the roof has caved in. There's mold on the walls, meth labs in two of the apartments on the second floor and a dead body in an apartment on the first floor. It's been decomposing awhile."

"This is where they bring little children?" Mariko asked softly.

"They are selling these children to pedophiles, Mariko," Ricco said. "They couldn't care less what kinds of nightmares or poisons they expose them to."

"What shape are they in?" Vittorio asked.

"Most of them are thin, bruised, terrified. The littlest ones are curled into little balls," Stefano said. He was back to using his flat, expressionless tone, the one that gave nothing away, but told his family he was at his deadliest. "They are kept in dog crates of various sizes. Most are dirty, and they aren't kept together."

There was a moment of stunned silence. Stefano gave that to them before he continued in that same flat voice.

"We need to keep Miceli and Angelo alive. They have to be able to be interrogated. If not by Valentino and Dario, then I want to be able to do so. This has to be stopped."

Emmanuelle had always known what her brothers were capable of. She'd seen it, although they'd always sent her away, so it was more truthful to say she'd seen the beginning of their interrogations. Were the families the same? She had always thought of the Ferraro family as the family on the side of good and the Saldi family as evil. It wasn't as black and white as that. Stefano had never made it out that way. He just hadn't wanted her with Valentino. She knew why. It would be dangerous for the wrong people to learn to ride the shadows.

"We can't touch those children or attempt in any way to get them out before we take out Miceli's soldiers. The entire neighborhood is riddled with his people. He's got them everywhere. He expects Valentino to find him. He wants him to. He intends to make this his last stand. He's laid traps for him, and we have to find those traps and disarm them before Val gets here."

"Traps?" Emmanuelle echoed.

"Land mines. If we don't find them and get rid of them when they leave, they won't get rid of them, and they could blow up any child walking between the houses," Ricco said.

"Do you think Val has a traitor talking to Miceli?" Emmanuelle asked. She didn't want someone Val trusted to suddenly whip out a gun and shoot him in the back when he least expected it.

"It's possible, but more likely, the moment Marge was taken prisoner, Miceli knew they would make her talk. She knew too much. They didn't have too many places they could take the children fast and prepare for war. No cops are going to bother them here. No neighbors are going to interfere. He had enough time to set his traps for Val and his men. There's most likely a minefield outside. If you notice, not a single person in the neighborhood is walking around. That just doesn't seem right, not even in a place like this."

In the dilapidated apartment building, condemned and falling apart, the children, taken from their parents and about to be sold by greedy men to line their pockets for more money, were now being used as bait. Soldiers with guns were on rooftops and waited in windows and behind doors for the rescuers to show up to save the children so they could kill them. In the yards and between houses, those same soldiers had planted explosives, which would kill not only the rescuers but, when everyone left, the residents living in the homes in the neighborhood.

Emmanuelle shook her head. When was it ever enough

money for some people? What was all the money needed for? Why did some human beings get the idea they were so superior to others? She didn't get it, yet she had believed her family was "good" and the Saldi family was "bad." What did that make her?

Stefano broke them up into teams. They had to first take out the eyes on top of the buildings. Once they did so, they had to study the way the roving patrols on the ground worked. That would help to show where any of the minefields were buried. All of them were well versed in noticing details. Looking for freshly dug earth or scattered garbage would be easy enough, but when lives were at stake, they couldn't be too careful.

Emmanuelle and Vittorio were paired together. Stefano sent them to cover the west side of the neighborhood, with two of her cousins from LA, Max and Tore. They took the rooftops first, trusting that whoever had the apartment rooftop would get their job done fast. The apartment building was the highest point and therefore was considered the "eagle's nest." Those eyes had to be taken out first so all of them could take out Miceli's sentries without his knowledge.

She chose a shadow that took her to the western tip of the subdivision, if one could call the neighborhood a subdivision. Even the trees reminded her of the scary Halloween movies she'd seen where half-dead creatures climbed out of the twisted trunks and assaulted the living with sticklike limbs. What once had been picket fences were broken, shattered sticks, either missing or lying in splinters, mostly long buried in rotting vegetation. Broken windows were boarded or left with large shards of yellow glass hanging. Dirty sheets attempted to keep the cold or heat out. The houses were small, but at one time, they had been nice. Now the porches sagged and boards were cracked on stairs and floors.

Emme stepped out of one shadow into the next to ride up the side of the house to the roof. She couldn't imagine the roof faring any better than the porch. A man lay on his belly facing the narrow street, looking completely ridiculous in a three-piece suit. He looked so out of place she wanted to laugh. She might have, but she saw that he had laid a child's blanket down to prevent his precious suit from getting dirty while he waited to kill the rescuers. That blanket had to belong to one of the children held captive.

Emmanuelle didn't hesitate. She rode the shadow right up beside him, straddled him, snapped his neck and left him lying there with his semiautomatic in his arms because damn him to hell. Stepping back into the mouth of the shadow, she stood for a moment, studying the ground below her, looking for roving patrols. Once she spotted three different pairs of men walking covertly through the narrow housing, she studied their movements carefully, committing them to memory. All riders had to be able to have a photographic mind for maps and grids. Really, everything.

She observed the men for a few more minutes as they did a second circular pattern, overlapping with a fourth pair of men from a different grid, making their rounds stealthily through the neighborhood. Another brother would be memorizing that pattern. She didn't find one instance of anyone so much as pushing a curtain back to peek out and look from any of the surrounding houses.

Emme caught another shadow that took her down to the ground, across the yard and up to the next house. She went building to building, removing the sentries that Miceli or Angelo had placed on the western end of the subdivision, waiting for Valentino's arrival.

Once she had cleared those on top of the houses, she went to the ground. That was a little trickier. She had to avoid any of the traps set for Val's soldiers as they swept through. She carefully marked the land mines she found or suspected for her brothers to dismantle as she followed her prey. The shadow tube she chose was fast. She stopped only to place the little mark her brothers would recognize before once again proceeding after the first pair of roving sentries.

She came up on the two men and waited until one dropped back just a little before coming out of the shadows. She gripped his head to administer the wrenching break and then was on his partner before the first body dropped. She dragged them against the side of the house so the bodies lay in the deeper unkept grasses, appearing part of the debris building up around the crumbling buildings. As always, she had calculated where to find the next pair of roving sentries and she'd already chosen her shadow. Calmly, she stepped into it.

Emmanuelle never thought about how many men she might have to kill in order to make it safe for Valentino's men to enter the neighborhood. She had pushed Val out of her mind. The only goal was to save the children kept in the dirty dog cages Stefano had told them about. Not once had her brother's expression changed. Not one single time. His voice hadn't changed when he gave them their orders.

Stefano had seen a lot of things in his life. He had grown up fast and had to make very tough decisions at a young age. She knew her brother could be counted on no matter what. She also knew he was ruthless and every bit as merciless, and then some, as Valentino. She'd often wondered if that was why she had been so drawn to Val in the first place.

Stefano was dangerous, but he was loyal, and he would protect what was his with everything he was, no matter how difficult the decision. She knew she was tough, and she could do what was necessary to defend those she loved, but she had a soft heart. Bringing murderers and rapists to justice didn't bother her, but she could never do what Stefano or Valentino did to get answers fast in order to find out where innocent children were being held. She knew that would tear her apart. She couldn't watch or hear it or think about it. Sometimes she tried to be like her brothers and put on her stoic face when they had to cast a vote on prisoners living or dying, but somehow, her family seemed to know. The moment she voted, her brothers escorted her out.

This was different. This was about saving children and stopping the monsters who sold them without a qualm. She dropped the last pair of sentries and carefully patrolled every inch of the ground around the houses, marking any place she found that could hold a hidden trap for those walking. Already, the cleanup crews were working to remove any of the lethal bombs hastily placed in the ground.

The good news was Miceli's men didn't have a lot of time to build the bombs. The subdivision was small enough, and there were still people living in the run-down area. It might be old and dilapidated, but those people called it home. Miceli couldn't order them all killed. That meant those living in the houses had to have a way to safely leave to go to work or get groceries. It would be stupid to place a bomb that would go off in their path and tip off Valentino that Miceli had prepared traps for him.

"Moving into the neighborhood now," Valentino's voice whispered softly in her ear.

Her heart instantly accelerated. The outside sentries were taken care of, but there were so many in the three-story apartment building. And what about the other side? She and Vittorio had ensured the sentries were down on the western side and Giovanni and Max along with two others had taken apart the bombs—a much longer and tedious process. That had to happen in three other quadrants. *Now* she worried about Valentino.

"We're moving into position to back you up in the building," Stefano's voice answered. "Tell your men to look sharp and avoid any area on the ground marked with a small check formed by something natural such as a twig or grass blades. A bomb will still be live. My people are still dismantling them."

There was a small silence. At once, Emmanuelle felt Valentino's concern. Not just his, but Dario's as well. She knew that concern was for her.

"Sir."

Emmanuelle didn't recognize the voice, but it was familiar.

"Your wife. She's out there. We need to get her back here with us."

That was definitely unprecedented. No one spoke on an open channel to the head of the family about his wife that way. There was genuine worry in the voice. The man didn't seem to care that he might be taking his own life in his hands. She realized that had to be one of the bodyguards assigned to her. Levi or Axel. They were brothers and sounded a lot alike.

Again, there was a short silence. Stefano broke it. "She's safe."

"Sir. The threats are credible."

"One thing at a time." That was definitely Val.

"She's safe." Stefano's voice was flat. Cold. That shut-the-fuck-up voice that demanded instant obedience.

Wait. What? Threats? Credible? Were they talking about threats to her? She took a deep breath and let it out. Valentino had worried about that. In fact, it had been his number one concern. He'd said showing any kind of emotion for her made him vulnerable. By marrying her, he'd put a target on her back. He was stirring up trouble taking over as head of his father's organization. They hadn't been married that long, but it was no secret they'd been seeing each other on and off for years. She wasn't going to be surprised or concerned.

"First concern, those children. Second, I want both prisoners alive," Valentino continued, this time with an edge of steel to his tone.

His men looked like a pack of wolves as she watched them from her vantage point. They came into the subdivision from every direction, guns looking like extensions of their bodies, showing all too much familiarity with those weapons. They were in good shape, moving fluidly, stealthily, straight toward the three-story apartment building.

Her eyes automatically sought out Valentino, the love of her life. Her heart did that curious melting sensation that annoyed her, but she was coming to terms with it when she saw him striding in the middle of the men trying to surround him, trying to cover him. Dario was there. She hadn't started out liking Dario. In fact, she had regarded him with open hostility, but now he was family to her. She worried about his safety as much as she did about Valentino's. Maybe more.

Dario took terrible risks. He didn't seem to care whether he lived or died, only about getting the job done. This job definitely was personal to all of them.

Vittorio ran his hand down the back of her head. "You all right, honey? You ready for what you might see in there?"

"As long as those children are alive, I'm good with what has to be done. Stefano said they were alive. Let's get them out of there."

"He's a good man." Vittorio stood for a moment, his gaze on Val. "We didn't want him for you, Emmanuelle, because he's hard as steel. He's never going to bend when it comes to taking care of you. He'll be like Stefano with Francesca or like me with Grace. You're his world. His entire world. We look like we have different worlds, but really, they aren't. You know that, right?"

She nodded slowly. "He is a good man. We have to be careful though. I know that we do. The shadows work differently for our families."

"There will be times when he'll have to make hard decisions you won't always agree with, honey, but you have to back him up. You have to love him through them even though it hurts like hell to give up your freedom or choices. Promise me if you have trouble with that, you'll come to me or Grace. We'll help you. You can talk freely to us. I give you my word of honor. I'll always be for your union, your marriage."

She wrapped her arm around her brother's waist, her gaze on her man as he got closer to the apartment building. In another minute, she would be in the shadow tube, taking that shadow right inside with the first wave of her family to dispense with as many of Miceli's guards as possible at the entry points to clear the way for Valentino's army.

"Thank you, Vittorio. That means the world to me." It did. Having her brother give his word was huge. She'd never forget it, and more, she knew she'd need someone to talk to occasionally. She didn't try to fool herself into thinking marriage to Valentino would be easy.

"Let's do this," Vittorio said and stepped into the shadow.

She followed him in, and the little feeder tube wrenched her apart, seemingly pulling her skin from her bones and her hair from her scalp. If she wasn't careful, it would pluck her eyes from her head. How could she ever explain the sensations to Val, tell him what it was like inside a shadow, traveling at a high rate of speed? Explain that it was dangerous for a child, yet if he wanted his child to learn, that was exactly when it was best to teach them, when they were very, very young.

She barely had time to put the brakes on or she would have slammed into Vittorio's broad back as he stopped in the mouth of the tube to orient himself before he chose his targets and another shadow inside the apartment in order to best help the coming army. The moment her brother was out of the way, Emmanuelle did the same, all business.

She removed three guards, one at a door, one at a window and one roving. She moved on to the next room. Her family went room by room, floor by floor. Already, Valentino's men were inside, engaging with the enemy. She tried not to think about the sound of gunfire and the screams of dying men as she moved through the building.

The stench of mold and urine was sickening. The idea of young children being subjected to this horrible place disgusted her. The dog crates were on the second floor. The children had been put in various rooms, including bathrooms and closets, throughout the second and third floors. She counted nine boys. The oldest appeared to be ten, the youngest perhaps four. The conditions of the cages and the floor beneath them sickened her. Some of the boys had bottles of water inside the cage; others had none. The boys had bruises on their bare cheeks and legs and their dirty faces. Her stomach plummeted.

There were eight girls locked in individual dog crates. These children all seemed to be very young, no more than six to three. They seemed eerily silent to her. Their little bodies were dirty, bruised. One or two rocked back and forth, staring sightlessly. She turned away, her heart pounding.

Vittorio reached for her, but she avoided his hand. She couldn't bear to be touched right then. She didn't want any act of kindness, not when babies had suffered so long without hope and the perpetrators were right downstairs. She felt that she could forgive Valentino anything for the rest of their lives. He had been working on trying to follow this trail for years. She could see why. Who did this kind of thing? Monsters. True monsters. They had to be stopped in any way possible.

Emmanuelle went down to the first floor, trying to keep her body from trembling and the rage under control. She'd experienced anger, she had a temper, but she'd never felt anything remotely like this emotion in her life. She wanted to plunge a knife straight through Miceli Saldi's heart. Not once, but over and over. Not deep, but shallow, so he felt each strike, once for each of those poor little children locked in those crates.

For the first time in her life, she thought she was capable of going into one of those secret rooms deep under the ground Stefano had where he locked away a prisoner to extract information needed to find a hostage fast. She wanted to be the one to slice through Miceli or Angelo's skin and do it over and over until they suffered what these children had suffered.

Valentino looked up as she walked toward him and the two prisoners. She stepped over bodies, not even looking at them as she approached. Levi and Axel closed in on her from either side. Vittorio was behind her. She felt him at her back, and the two men at her sides, but she kept walking with determined purpose.

Miceli and Angelo had been attempting bravado with Valentino and the others, but something in her expression wiped the smirks from their faces. Stefano suddenly moved to intercept her direct path. He positioned himself just to the right of the prisoners. Ricco stood to the left of them. She kept walking, covering more than half the room at exactly the same pace.

As she stepped over another dead body, she saw a knife on the floor inches from a hand. She bent and smoothly palmed it, never breaking stride. Valentino moved to intercept her.

"I need them alive, baby," he murmured softly as he came up to her, standing directly in her path, his fingers very gently settling around her wrist.

"I'll leave them alive." She lifted her gaze to his. "I promise."

"I know you would," he said, his voice still velvet soft, as gentle as ever. "I need you to give me the knife. I'll do whatever you want me to do, but I have to do it. Or Dario. It's a matter of a promise we made." The pads of his fingers trailed over her lips and then down her chin. He caught her chin and tilted it. "I swear to you, baby, I'll do what you ask me to do, but this is something I can't give you."

"Those children, Valentino." She didn't want her voice to break. She didn't want Miceli or Angelo to see her break down. "What they've done to those children. That trauma will never go away. Never. The scars will be there for life . . ." She broke off and raised her gaze to Dario, who watched her impassively with his dark, dark eyes.

They stood in silence for what seemed forever. She allowed Valentino to take the knife from her. "Find out who is behind this, Val. Don't let either of them die until they tell you."

She had to blink several times to keep water from her eyes.

He brushed his lips over hers. "We're taking them to the interrogation rooms now. I give you my word, they won't go easily, and we'll get a name."

"And we find a way to help those children."

"Stefano will help as well. They'll have the best care." Val looked over her head at his men. At her brother.

Emmanuelle felt a touch on her arm, and her brother escorted her out, with Levi and Axel on either side of her.

CHAPTER NINETEEN

"Marco Messina couldn't possibly be the brains behind such an organized and extensive network of human trafficking as you've uncovered," Geno Ferraro announced.

They had arrived in New York in the private luxury jet. Emmanuelle, Valentino, Dario and a host of bodyguards, as well as Stefano and several of her brothers. Taviano and Nicoletta hadn't made the trip, but Ricco and Mariko were there. The paparazzi had followed them from the airport to Geno Ferraro's enormous condo, with its private garage and security elevator.

Valentino and Emmanuelle were keeping up appearances as a newlywed couple, jetting with the family to New York to visit her cousins. The Ferraros were notoriously close, and it would be expected that the couple would be seen out with her cousins if the family accepted her husband. They wanted it to be known that he was accepted.

"Marco is the youngest of the Messina brothers. He has a good head for numbers and runs the family's legit businesses. He makes damn good money doing it. In fact, so much so, that his father is always threatening to retire and make him head of the *famiglia*. That is the last thing Marco wants, by the way," Geno continued with his report, delivering the news to the others in his direct way, with a slight New York accent.

He was a big man, with wide shoulders. Valentino could see why he was often described as intimidating by every reporter writing articles about the infamous Ferraro family. This man was the head of the New York Ferraro family. He was soft-spoken, but his voice carried complete authority. With his cousins he seemed as relaxed as perhaps he would ever get—which wasn't much.

Geno snagged a handful of peanuts from a bowl on the table and ate them, narrowing his eyes at Emmanuelle. "The least you could have done was learn to cook like Francesca."

"If I had skills, you barbarian, I wouldn't waste them on you. You're bossy, and I already have too many bosses." She turned and included Levi and Axel in her glare.

They were playing cards with Lando and Pace at a smaller table behind them, seemingly not paying attention, but Levi smirked.

"You want to eat, we should go to that Italian place just down from your condo. The one that serves those little salty breads that look like the middle of a doughnut," Emmanuelle continued, her voice hopeful.

Valentino settled his fingers around the nape of her neck. He was getting used to her brothers and cousins and the way they were with Emmanuelle. All of them were very protective of her, and he liked that. He wanted them to be. He wanted her to be surrounded by love. To feel that all the time. The more protection she had, the better. They liked to tease her. It was one of the many ways they showed their affection for her.

As days went by and the news of their marriage traveled to the other *famiglias* in Chicago, as well as whispered rumors of Val's utter ruthlessness when it came to managing the business, more threats had been made against his wife. He'd known it would happen. He hadn't realized just how crazy it would make him feel. He'd shared every one of them with Stefano, just as he'd promised her brother he would.

He'd met her three New York cousins in Chicago very briefly, but he hadn't spent time with them. Geno was much like Stefano, aloof and impossible to read, other than the cold promise that if anyone harmed a single hair on Emmanuelle's head, he would hunt them and never stop until he found them.

"You are such a heathen, Emme," Geno said, but he stood. "How do you think you're going to keep that man happy if you don't cook for him?"

"Sex, Geno," she retaliated without even blushing. She didn't even blink with her brothers and cousins or the bodyguards in the room. "Awesome sex."

Geno just stood there for a moment, very still, his face an expressionless mask while his gaze swept over her. "Never say the word *sex* again, Emme. You're five. You shouldn't even know that word."

Laughter swept through the room. Emmanuelle took pity on him. "I can cook, Geno. I was just hoping we could eat out, but let me look and see what you have in the fridge."

His hard features didn't exactly soften, but his eyes did. "We've got a reservation already. I know it's your favorite place, and since this is your celebration, you can have anything you want."

Valentino held out his hand to his wife. The moment she put her hand in his, he pressed his thumb over her rings, rolling them back and forth. He liked the feel of them. Solid. Real. He found, as he followed Geno and Stefano through the condo toward the elevators, he liked Geno far more than he'd thought he would.

Stefano watched over Emmanuelle like a hawk. Her brothers did. Now her cousins. That was all right with him. As far as Val was concerned, there couldn't be enough eyes on her. He was more than grateful for the army of ex-military men Dario had acquired and trained. Dario had been conscious of keeping the men they could bring into the *famiglia* Italian so if any of them should ever want to move up in the organization, they could. These men were dedicated and loyal to him—to Dario and to Emmanuelle. The four he had appointed as her bodyguards were extremely detail-oriented, and they didn't take a lot of shit off his beautiful wife. She teased them, but when she tried to misdirect them, it didn't work.

"Are you spoiling her?" Vittorio asked as they prepared to leave the condo.

Geno glanced at his watch. "My brothers are meeting us at the restaurant. We have the entire back room to ourselves. They wanted to get there first and do a sweep to make certain we can safely talk. We own the place, but you never know. And no, absolutely not, Vittorio. This was Salvatore's idea, not mine."

Valentino didn't believe him for a minute. Evidently, neither did the bodyguards. They had gathered up their cards and put them away. One of them gave a little snort of derision, but when Geno flicked them a cool gaze, there was no expression on any of their faces.

Emmanuelle rolled her eyes. "See, Geno, no one believes you. You made your first mistake when I was a baby and you let me crawl in your lap and sleep on you at all the family events."

He rubbed his hand over the top of her hair. "I just did it to annoy your mother. She detested when I picked you up. It was fun watching her get that pinched look on her face. Then she'd have the big dilemma. Did she take you off me? Or let you stay?"

Geno showed Val's men to the elevators. Valentino liked that Levi and Axel were hesitant to leave Emme's protection to others. They didn't step onto the elevator until he gave them a subtle signal. Both he and Dario would ride down with Emmanuelle and her brothers and cousin in the other elevator to the garage and meet them there.

"There was no way she would have taken me off your lap," Emmanuelle guessed.

"Nope, so I held you until Stefano came and got you,"

Geno confirmed. "See, wasn't being nice or spoiling you. Get in the damn car and stop bothering me." He leaned down and brushed a kiss on top of her head, ignoring the four bodyguards that had been waiting, and moved a little closer to her, as if he might suddenly decide to shove a knife in her ribs.

Valentino pulled her close to him on the back seat of the town car. Before she could say anything to him, he took her mouth. Kissing Emmanuelle in front of her family was always a risk. It could get out of hand fast. There was no holding back, and fire flared hot and bright the moment they came together. He preferred to do so when they were alone, so whenever he had the opportunity, he didn't waste it.

Geno had arranged for several cars, so Valentino had his wife all to himself, although the restaurant was close—too close, as far as he was concerned. "Want to get you back home so I can be alone with you, baby—too many around us all the time."

She laughed softly. "I agree, but you will love everything about this place."

The car pulled up to the front of the restaurant, and Emme slid out, Valentino right behind her. She stood on the curb a moment while the others also got out of their cars. Val looked cautiously around, being subtle about it. The bodyguards did the same, taking in the rooftops and surrounding buildings. Dario walked a few steps from them, looking at the restaurant itself.

The building was large and made of stone. It looked on the outside as if it had once been a warehouse sandwiched between other warehouses. The city had crept into the district, overtaking the boho lifestyle, claiming the large buildings, turning them into smaller boutiques or larger galleries so that shops were flourishing all along the streets.

Emmanuelle's hand slipped out of his as she tipped back her head to try to get a better view of the front of the restaurant. "This is so cool, Val. It really was a warehouse before Geno, Salvatore and Lucca had it renovated. Salvatore is really interested in design. He came up with the idea and kind of sold it to his brothers. He found the warehouse, and they bought it. Lucca found the architect to work with them. According to Salvatore, he was quite brilliant. Wait until you see the inside. You'll agree completely."

As she spoke enthusiastically, indicating the front of the building, she moved around Dario to step back from the shrubbery so she could gaze up where the scrollwork was etched into the stone.

Val turned to look where she indicated, but the sound of tires screeching and catching had Levi and Axel both spinning and moving fast, and him turning back toward Emmanuelle. A car lurched, boring straight at them, then jumping the curb, heading right at Emme. She had her back to it. He reached out for her wrist, his heart in his throat, intending to yank her to safety.

"Emme, get out of there," Stefano yelled.

Dario slammed into her, sending her into Valentino's arms. Dario landed on top of the two of them, with Levi and Axel over the top of them, weapons drawn, aimed at the car. The driver managed to get control before he hit the restaurant. He turned off the car and got out, crouching down to put one hand over his face.

"Is everyone all right? The accelerator got stuck. I tried to stop it with the emergency brake. I thought I was going to kill all of you." He started to stand, and his legs gave out. "I'm afraid I'm going to get sick. Tell me everyone's all right."

"We have a few questions for you," one of Geno's bodyguards said smoothly. "We'll have the car towed as well. Don't worry, we'll get you home."

Levi and Axel stepped back to allow Dario and Valentino up so they could help Emmanuelle off the ground. She was immediately ushered into the restaurant.

"Do accelerators really get stuck, Val?" she asked.

"Sometimes, but not that often," he answered honestly. "We'll find out. Geno's men are on it. Right now, we're going to have a really nice dinner and hear what your cousin has to say about the Messina connection to the trafficking ring.

Miceli was adamant that Marco was the brains behind the entire network. He met with him and got the details from him. He was told his father was not involved, nor were his brothers. This was his baby, and he'd developed the idea while he was in college. Angelo backed him up separately. They weren't in the same room and were interrogated at different times. There was no way Angelo, in particular, would have held anything back."

Valentino felt the little shiver that crept down Emmanuelle's spine. He rubbed her back as they followed the hostess through the restaurant toward their private room. Salvatore's concept was unique and quite beautiful. The floor was cobblestone. The warehouse had been utilized by bringing in intriguing archways of stone to define the various spaces. The tables were covered in bright red-checked cloth. The chairs were comfortable-looking, sporting black legs and high backs. Overhead, rows of glass lights lit the restaurant spaces.

As they made their way through the very spacious restaurant, he glimpsed two bars, both boasting racks of wines. There was a space designated for a family area, with more booths and a bar that held sparkling drinks rather than those catering to adults. Valentino had never seen that before.

They went through several stone archways to the back room where Salvatore and Lucca waited for them. After greeting them and waiting for their hostess to leave, Salvatore announced the room was clean. They made small talk until the bread and hors d'oeuvres were on the table with wine.

"I spent time following Marco," Geno said as he put several pieces of bread on his plate. "I'm absolutely convinced it isn't him. Salvatore was assigned Tibberiu, the father, and the oldest brother, Alessandro." He looked expectantly at his brother.

Salvatore shook his head. "If either of those two are involved, they certainly aren't talking about it to anyone. One would think if part of their pipeline went down in a big way, they would be all over that, but these two never so much as mentioned it. They talked about Val, and how strong a leader he was. Tibberiu hoped he could keep the entire Saldi territory in line. He said with Miceli out of the way, the territory was huge under one man. He was worried about that, and Alessandro agreed with him. They talked about possibly bringing up the idea with the other families of cutting that territory into two and putting someone else in as the head there."

Val shook his head. "That's not going to happen." He looked at Dario. A Saldi, heir to that empire. A man he trusted and a leader. Dario returned his look with a deadpan stare. So far, that was a complete no, but he wasn't giving up.

"It doesn't make sense that both Miceli and Angelo named Marco. They met with him. Saw him face-to-face." Val took another bite of the bread. Emmanuelle was right. The bread was delicious. Salty. Buttery. He glanced at Emme and saw her watching him. He nodded at her and smiled. She gave him her sassy little grin. "Marge as well."

"One of his other brothers? Do they look enough like him to pull off a deception?" Vittorio asked.

Lucca shook his head. "I checked both of the other brothers, Giovi and Vincenzu. Like Alessandro, they're as hard as nails, like their father, but no way are they involved. Nor do they look like Marco. They couldn't pass themselves off for him at all. I'm sorry, Val, but this is a dead end. The Messina family is not who you're looking for."

Val frowned, exchanging long looks with Dario, and then Stefano and Vittorio. All of them had taken part in the interrogations of Miceli and Angelo over several days. None of it had been pretty or nice. All of them were certain the information had been correct. Marge had also named Marco. One of the lower-level informants had also given Marco's name.

"It isn't that difficult anymore to impersonate someone," Emmanuelle said. "Actors do it all the time. You study their mannerisms, the way they walk, the kinds of language they use, the tilt of their head when they talk. You need a lot of video, and you watch it over and over. You listen to the sound of their voice. You have to have the same body type, obviously."

A waitress came in and no one spoke while she took their orders. She was very familiar with the family and clearly wouldn't have repeated anything, but no one would take chances or put temptation in her way.

Valentino turned the idea of impersonation over and over in his head. If someone was using Marco Messina's identity, they were definitely risking the wrath of his father if they were found out. If Val could prove such a thing and take it to Tibberiu, that would solidify his position even tighter with the Messina family. That couldn't hurt anything.

The deception had to have been planned very carefully, years earlier, by someone who knew Marco very well. Someone he was close to. Friends with. When he was in college or before? Theater. People changed appearances in theater.

"What are you thinking, Val?" Stefano asked.

"Emmanuelle could be on to something. If someone has been impersonating Marco, they probably know him. Most likely they've known him a long time and either are still close friends with him or were very good friends with him in the past. To put a network like this together takes time. Years. It has to grow. It started small somewhere. My guess, in a school. Whoever started this maybe pimped out his girlfriend for unpaid debts or just for kicks to see if she'd whore for him. He started a little side business and made money."

If his family was involved in organized crime, he might feel entitled to sell drugs or women, even in high school, if they did that sort of thing and he was aware of it. Most of the families flew under the radar these days, not wanting to look like they did in the old days.

Valentino texted Bernado to have him start hunting down any connection between Marco Messina and anyone around his age from any of the other families that might be considered a possibility. He could see that Stefano was setting his investigators on the trail as well. He found it a little disconcerting to be sharing information with the Ferraros, but Stefano was equally as generous with him. As long as that continued, he would use every resource and try to come to terms with having a larger family than he'd expected.

He glanced at Dario who was frowning, watching the interaction with Stefano and Geno as they both were as busy on their phones as the two of them were. He had the feeling they would be expected to go to the Sunday dinners at Stefano's penthouse with Emmanuelle's family. That would be interesting. Dario might lose his mind.

"Let's say Marco has a friend in high school or college who gets the bright idea of impersonating him and using his identity to set up a human trafficking ring," Stefano said. "Why? Why would he determine from the get-go that it would be better to use Marco's identity rather than his own even at the start of the endeavor?"

"That's easy enough," Vittorio said. "The Messina name carries the most clout. If you're young and you want to impress people much older, get them to listen to you, you choose the heavy hitter. In our family, we have all kinds of cousins. Someone young wanting to make an impression isn't going to throw out the name Greco, they'll use Ferraro."

There were nods of agreement all around the table. That made sense to everyone.

"Now, he's got a good start and he doesn't want to get caught." Lucca took up the narrative. "All suspicion is going to fall on Marco, not the imposter or his family. It's win-win at this point. He's been at it a long time now, and the money is good. He's not going to stop."

"Val took down an arm of his pipeline and crippled part of his territory. He's going to want to get that back. That means he has to eliminate you. He'll look to see who takes over Miceli's territory, and if he thinks he can, he'll approach him with a proposition, but he'll have to kill you, Valentino," Dario said.

"*We* did," Valentino clarified. "Everyone in this room."

"He's only looking at you, Val," Stefano said. "He'll be looking to hurt you. That includes getting at you through Emmanuelle."

Geno glanced at his watch. "My people are taking apart that car right now. My investigators can't find any ties to any kind of crime by the driver. He's definitely not a hit man. No money trail that they could find. He looks clean."

"My guy came up with the same information, although he's going to continue to dig," Val said. "Just to be on the safe side."

"I was looking at his face," Emmanuelle said. "And really listening to him when he was talking. I can hear lies." She turned to look at her bodyguards. "Just remember that, Levi and Axel. I hear lies. The driver was telling the truth. It was a simple accident. They happen. I was grateful nothing happened to him or any of you or the restaurant. I love this place so much, Salvatore. It's really quite unique and beautiful."

Valentino wrapped his arm around her shoulders. "We're just making certain, Princess."

"In any case, if it wasn't an accident, I was hardly the target. Everyone was standing there. Most likely you were, Val." Her eyes darkened, and for a moment she looked anxious. "Dario, he needs a million bodyguards around him all the time. Don't listen to anything he says."

She sounded brave enough, almost like she was joking, but there was very real fear in her eyes, and that turned his heart over. It always did. He captured her hand again, his thumb unerringly finding her rings.

"Nothing will happen to me, Emmanuelle. We'll find this person and take him down. Everyone in this room is dedicated to that purpose. And Dario doesn't need any more encouragement when it comes to being a watchdog. I think he shot me with ten trackers and has some kind of satellite surveillance hooked up in his eyes." He said the last to make her laugh.

The waitress rolled a cart filled with plates of food into the room. Behind her, a second waitress followed, that cart loaded as well. The two began to place the plates in front of them while two men served wine or a sparkling beverage to them. Once everyone was served, the waiters and waitresses left and closed the doors behind them.

Talk turned to other things, and laughter spilled over. Valentino let himself enjoy the company of the Ferraro family for a short time. He didn't share Emme's opinion that the car jumping the curb had been a random accident. He didn't believe in coincidences. Maybe the target had been him. Maybe not. But if it had been Emmanuelle targeted because she was married to him, he wanted to know and put an end to whoever was trying to intimidate him by using his wife. He glanced at Dario. Dario's eyes met his. He felt the same way.

Over coffee and outstanding tiramisu, Bernado got back to him. Jason Caruso went to the same private school the last year of high school with Marco Messina. Same college. Roomed together. Took theater for 2 semesters the first year. Caruso continued to take theater while Messina focused on business. Messina has master's. Father pulled Caruso out, didn't like the direction he was going. Both work for their family.

That fit with what Emmanuelle had said. Caruso had spent time with Marco, and he'd taken several theater classes. Val shared what Bernado had found with the others.

"Ask him what he means by the direction Caruso was going," Stefano said. "Never mind. Rigina is getting back to me. She's giving me the same information but added a little more about his history with theater."

Caruso has amazing reviews in off Broadway plays. He was really good in every performance he was in, no matter how small or large. He was beginning to make a name for himself but was suddenly pulled out of the business in his last year of performing arts by his father. Word was, his father frowned on such an impractical career.

The Caruso family had a small portion of a waterway they acquired in a business deal, from Giuseppi. They controlled two ports on the lake, bordering Saldi territory. That made sense if they were involved in human trafficking. There were five families in Chicago, and the Caruso family had arguably the second-smallest amount of territory, businesses and clout. It would seem much more likely for one of the larger families in the middle of Chicago to be the big spider sitting in the web branching out across the city. Yet the more Val thought about it, the more he was certain they had hit on the right answer.

The second name came in: a member of the Russo family. Of the five ruling families in Chicago, the Russo family held the third-largest territory. The Russos had a very large family, with six children—four sons and two daughters. All business, Valentino could believe any one of the sons or their father were shrewd enough to carry out such a plan, but it seemed unlikely. Nevertheless, he would follow up. They would check out the new information because they had to, but Valentino would bet every last dollar he had, and it was considerable, that the man they were looking for was Jason Caruso.

"What do you know about Jason Caruso's father, Val?" Lucca asked.

"Arsenio Caruso has three sons and one daughter. They have a portion of territory along the waterfront. We held the entire waterfront, but Arsenio came to Giuseppi some years back and they made a deal giving the Carusos a small section with two ports on it. It's quite lucrative, and they've always upheld their end of the deal. We've never had any problems with them, and they've never encroached any further into our territory," Val said.

"There are clear lines for territories." Vittorio made it a statement.

"Absolutely. Each of the five families in Chicago has their territory, and they rule that area. The Messina family holds the biggest territory, and they definitely are the most powerful. My family holds the second-largest territory, and we have the water and ports, so it is extremely lucrative. The Russo family might be next in terms of holding a sizable territory. The Caruso family would sit about here, right in with the

Russo family or just under it in terms of territory. The small-est territory belongs to the Savoca family. Cristiano Savoca is a shrewd businessman, and everything he touches turns to gold. He has a reputation for keeping his word. He has two sons, and like their father, they have good reputations." Valentino summed up the other men holding territories in Chicago.

"So not all the same in terms of how much money and power each family has," Salvatore said. "You don't all share."

"Not with one another, no. We do make deals occasion-ally, but we stay out of one another's business unless it is necessary to work certain details out between us, or smooth over a dispute. No one wants to go to war, such as what hap-pened with Miceli and Giuseppi." He smiled at them—the smile he might give that inner circle, the smile of a predator. No one was ever going to stop him from going after his ene-mies if they struck at him as Miceli had at his father. If he found a traitor in his organization, he would take him down hard and fast. There would be no negotiations if he found the Caruso family had betrayed their deal. That had been bro-kered in good faith. The deal had been more than generous.

"We need to get back to Chicago, gentlemen," Stefano said. "Thank you for your hospitality."

It had been necessary to keep up appearances. Both the Ferraro family and the newlyweds needed to look as if they were staying at the Ferraro Hotel, carrying on with their lives in front of the world, had alibis, and weren't caught up in the bodies dropping all over the city. There wasn't a single cam-era shot of the cars carrying those raiding the Miceli's busi-nesses. The dead bodies didn't have any evidence on them.

The victims couldn't tell anything other than that they were rescued and grateful and wanted to go home. Miceli Saldi and his sons had mysteriously disappeared and were nowhere to be found. The evidence had piled up against them as the ones committing the crimes, but if they were alive or dead, no one knew.

Once back in Chicago, Valentino wanted to take his

woman home to the lake house, but they were still making repairs to the property. He wanted to make that his permanent home. That meant security had to be much tighter and all damage and any memory of it gone so Emmanuelle never had to think about it again.

Stefano had taken his own car, anxious to get back to Francesca, which was fine with Valentino. Emmanuelle fell asleep, head on his shoulder, and he had the chance to just spend time alone with her on the ride back from the airport, looking at her without having to worry about anyone thinking he'd lost his mind. It seemed like, in the time since he'd coaxed her back to him, too much had happened too fast, and they hadn't had time to slow down and just breathe each other in. He wanted that time with her.

The driver pulled up to the private entrance of the hotel, and Valentino gently woke her. "Emme. We're here. At the hotel, Princess. Let's go up and get you in bed."

Her feathery lashes lifted, and her blue eyes were looking at him, doing crazy things to his heart. She got to him every single time. He smiled at her. "I love you." He brushed his lips gently over hers. "Never doubt that, Emmanuelle."

"I don't, Valentino." She hooked an arm around his neck as he helped her slide out of the car and set her on her feet. For a moment she swayed unsteadily, as if she wasn't quite awake.

Val had always loved seeing her that way. Emmanuelle wasn't a light sleeper, and when she woke, she needed a moment to adjust to the world around her. He liked that moment. His woman still drifting a little. He had his eyes on her, the disheveled, sexy hair falling around her face and down her shoulders and back like a dark waterfall. The silken strands were wavy, looking wildly unruly—bedroom hair for certain. She could crawl in bed, but she wasn't going straight to sleep, Val decided. She could try, but he had plans. Wicked ones. But she'd like them.

Levi, Axel and Dario arrived in the second car. Ordinarily,

they would have taken two separate cars, one leading his car and one following, but it was late and they decided to head home. No one knew they were making their way back to the hotel. The two bodyguards and Dario exited, and the car pulled away. Valentino turned toward them as Emmanuelle leaned against the side of the hotel as if she couldn't stand up on her own.

"I might just sleep right here," Emmanuelle declared, and started to slide down the wall just as a shot rang out.

The bullet hit right where her head had been. Two more shots followed the first one, following Emmanuelle as she dropped all the way to the ground. Valentino dove for her, throwing his body over the top of hers, pinning her beneath him. Levi and Axel faced the shooter, weapons out, bodies in front of the couple.

"Move, move, go to your left," Levi said sharply. "There's cover to your left, Mr. Saldi. Can you get her moving?"

Dario had disappeared. Val knew what that meant. He was actively hunting the shooter. Emmanuelle was already heeding Levi's commands with Val. Neither wanted Levi or Axel in harm's way, and it was clear the shooter was willing to kill them in order to reach Emmanuelle. She was definitely the target.

Valentino and Emmanuelle immediately rolled toward cover as quickly as possible. The alcove was small, but a thick wall would block the shooter's sight to them. Emmanuelle hadn't made a single sound. His anger was back. The idea that someone would want to kill her because of him was almost more than he could stand. The sidewalk had little pebbles on it, and they dug into their backs. He couldn't protect her from that, and it seemed a silly inconvenience to even consider when they were being shot at, but he couldn't help what went through his mind.

He managed to pull out his phone to text Stefano. He wanted the shooter. Between Dario and Stefano, they would get him. They remained in the alcove for what seemed like hours. In reality, it was only twelve minutes, but it was twelve minutes too long. He got the all clear the same time Levi and Axel did from Dario. Then he got a second one from Stefano.

"You can't say life with me is dull," he said as they stepped into the elevators. He found himself holding his breath. Waiting. Beside him, Levi and Axel seemed to do the same.

For the first time since the incident, Emmanuelle looked up at him. He should have known better. Her eyes were bright. Clear. Shining. Her smile lit up his world. She leaned into him, fitting her body against his.

"I never did like dull, honey. You know that."

Jason Caruso wanted his own money in order to get out from under his father's thumb. Emmanuelle discovered his secrets easily enough because he wrote his story down like a movie script, determined one day to produce it for the big screen. He was going to not only produce it, but play the leading role. He had started off small enough, exchanging his identity with Marco's to see if he could pull it off. He didn't want to get in trouble when he was talking a girl into paying off his debts for him with her body. Marco had so much more pull than he did. It amused him to think that Marco might wonder why a girl would be so angry with him later when he didn't call her again after she did so much for him.

In college, he began really thinking about how he could make his own money without relying on his father for support. There were always assholes who wanted women, or younger girls or boys. He had his ear to the ground. They just needed the right supplier. He had to be careful, and he couldn't ever get caught.

Emmanuelle read through the script that Jason so meticulously worked on, detailing with excruciating care how he'd built himself an empire in sex trafficking to rival anyone. It was slow going, cultivating and developing the various networks. He always used Marco Messina's identity if he had to meet in person. It was so much more powerful to be a Messina than a Caruso, and those he spoke with were both impressed and scared.

He hadn't left his father's employ because he could use the shipping lines and ports. The trucking companies. It felt good to be putting one over on his father, who thought him weak for wanting to be in acting. Acting turned out to be his greatest asset. Even now, his family still made fun of his dreams of acting in theater and movies. Little did they know that he had amassed a fortune of his own, one he had no intention of sharing with them—and he'd done so through his acting.

Emmanuelle was shocked at how detailed Jason's script was. She supposed anyone finding it would never guess it was real, that rather than being an actual documentary, they would believe it was pure fiction.

Jason wasn't doing business with any family other than the Saldis in Chicago. He had partners in New York, Ohio, Texas, Florida, Alabama and Kentucky. He had been very busy. It took Emmanuelle days to find the various ties to each of those places and who they were. Jason's script was right on his desk. She had to follow him, staying in the shadows, changing places with her brothers at times to take breaks. Eventually, they pieced the entire network together on a large board in Valentino's suite.

They had to get proof for Val to supply, first to Arsenio Caruso and then to the heads of the families. He would give Arsenio the evidence against his son just before he would deliver the proof to the heads of the families. Dario would have already taken Jason into custody so Arsenio couldn't find a way to warn him. The Ferraro family would do the rest, spreading out like the assassins they were to go after Jason's entire network. Valentino wanted the ring dismantled and all key players dead, from the kidnappers to those driving the children across state lines.

Strangely, an obscure church was involved in the acquiring of the teens in one state, and a teen club in another. A motorcycle club, a massage parlor, even a pet shop and an ice cream shop all were involved. One by one, they sifted through the various places that lured children in. The parks parents took them to, swimming places, anywhere that was crowded and a parent could lose sight of a child even just for a moment. Sports games, shopping malls. Parents looking at cell phones. It was all so easy for the kidnappers. They had perfected their strategies.

Valentino and Dario were patient, working it all out on a board, untwisting the lines until they were smooth and they knew every route. They knew the trucks and vans that picked up and dropped off. The recreational vehicles and boats transporting and who they belonged to. The two men recognized the codes given to each trafficker and what the supplier wanted or needed.

When they were ready, the first thing Valentino did was visit Jason in the early morning hours on the day he'd called a meeting of the heads of Chicago. Jason was drinking his coffee like he did every morning, sitting back in his favorite chair on the dock with his iPad. He looked up when Valentino, Dario and Emmanuelle came striding up to him, their bodyguards moving with them.

He put his iPad down and stood, smiling in welcome. Valentino knew the fact that Emmanuelle was with him would immediately take away any worry.

"This is a surprise. And an honor." Jason gave a charming little bow toward Emmanuelle. "It's lovely to meet you."

"Emme spent a great deal of time getting to know you, Jason," Val said. The men with him kept walking right up to Jason. "She was with me when we found all the children Miceli and Angelo had in dog crates. All the teens Tommaso had locked up. All the women Marge had below her dungeon. She spent a great deal of time in your room with your script and then following you to all of your meetings with the people you work with. Of course, you dress up like Marco Messina, but it's you, and we have the proof."

The men had surrounded Jason, and now they had him bound and gagged.

"I'm meeting with the heads of the families in a couple of hours to show them that proof. I'll give your father the heads-up so he won't be blindsided, just out of respect. As we speak, your network is being taken down. You will be taken to a location where no one can help you, not even a higher power. I'm afraid the devil is after you, wanting you to pay for your sins, and you have quite a bit to pay for."

He stepped back, and the men took Jason out of his sight. It was a good thing, because he wanted to sink his fist into the man's gut. He had quite a bit to do. They'd worked hard to take this ring down and show the proof to the others. He needed to do that, not suddenly get caught up in the petty satisfaction of striking out at this poor excuse of a human being.

He glanced at his watch. The Ferraros were moving on the various branches in each state, targeting those in the highest positions and leaving enough evidence to convict others in lower positions. Once he told the other families, this was done. His position as head of the Saldi family was solidified. His task to bring down the trafficking ring was completed, and his promise to Dario and himself had been kept.

Valentino could have his life back, and he could have it with his wife.

CHAPTER TWENTY

"Henry and Eloisa are at the gate asking to be let in," Dario announced. "Do you want to allow it, Valentino?"

Emmanuelle spun around, glaring at her husband. She opened her mouth to snap at Dario, who was safe in the control room, but Val laid his palm over her mouth, one arm locked just under her breasts, holding her back to his chest.

"Sure. I'll handle them, Dario." He kissed the side of Emme's neck, blazing a trail of fire all the way to her ear, where he tugged with his teeth on her earlobe. "You're such a little spitfire, woman." There was amusement in his voice.

It was impossible to resist him when he was like this, and Emmanuelle didn't bother to try. She turned in his arms and linked her hands behind the nape of his neck, leaning her body against his. "Why would you want to allow Eloisa into our world?"

"I think it's time I make it perfectly clear she isn't the one running your life anymore." He sank his teeth into her bottom lip and then her chin.

Her heart accelerated. He made her weak so easily. She

liked it though. Before, she was always terrified of losing herself in him. Now she found strength in loving him. In being a part of him. "Who is running my life now?"

"Me. It's always going to be me." He kissed her, pouring the familiar fire down her throat. "Go ahead and protest, but it won't change a damn thing. It's still going to be me."

"You tell yourself that, Valentino Saldi."

His laughter was warm against her skin when he kissed his way down her throat to the tops of her breasts, spilling out above her tank top. Before, if her mother was anywhere within a hundred miles of her, Emmanuelle would have never worn anything showing cleavage. Now, when she was with Val, she preferred to wear clothes that showed off her curves.

"I do tell myself that. And I tell you. I figure if I tell you often enough, you'll listen."

He pushed down her tank top and the lacy bra that didn't do much more than showcase her breasts for him. His hot mouth latched on, and she cried out, throwing her head back as heat rushed through her veins. His fingers stroked relentlessly at her other nipple, not hard, just gentle brushes that threatened to undo her because all of a sudden she needed so much more.

Dario's voice came over the intercom. "Pulling up to the door now. Whatever you two are doing, you'd better stop and pull it together."

Emmanuelle cradled Valentino's head to her, fingers in his thick hair, hating to give him up. Her hips rocked against his thigh. "If I were wearing panties right now, Val, they'd be soaking wet for you," she whispered when he lifted his head.

He groaned and pushed his forehead against hers. "That's not very nice, Princess."

She tugged up the hem of her long, flowy skirt, inch by inch, prolonging his agony, baring her thigh slowly. Taking his hand, she pulled his palm to her bare mound and then curled a finger into her wet heat.

"That's all for you, honey." She pulled his hand away from her body, let her skirt drop and brought his fingers to her mouth, deliberately curling her tongue around them. "Too bad we don't have the time. If you'd wanted to talk to Eloisa, we could have met her somewhere else, not in our private home."

She hated the idea of her mother setting foot in her house. Eloisa would turn up her nose at everything. Nothing would be good enough for her—especially Emmanuelle's choice of husbands. She would find a way to try to cheapen what they had together and make Emme feel small and ugly, a traitor to her family. She would be horrible to Valentino.

"I can meet alone with them outside on the patio."

"She'd really like that." Emmanuelle stuck her chin in the air. "I refuse to allow her to intimidate me. I just don't want her in our home." Her mother had managed to ruin everything Emme had ever loved.

"We'll ask Lando to bring them around to the courtyard. They don't have to come inside," Valentino said. Before she could reply, he was already issuing the orders to Dario and then holding out his hand to her. When she tried to tidy her hair, he caught her wrist and pulled her hand down. "Leave it, baby. You look so damn sexy. This is our life, not hers. Fuck her if she doesn't approve. We're not asking for her approval. She came to see us, not the other way around. You sit close to me and keep your hand in mine. You want to end the charade, you dig your nails into my palm, and they're gone. Just know, if I don't like anything she says to you, she'll hear about it."

Emmanuelle had been terrified for so long, afraid Eloisa would find her way into Val's home and murder him to keep him away from Emme. She hadn't wanted Valentino near her mother. She knew he would never tolerate the things Eloisa said to her if he knew. Even back then, when she'd been so young, Valentino had been protective of her.

She nodded her head. He would throw Eloisa and Henry out without thinking twice about it. She'd made certain none of her siblings—or her mother—could use the shadows to enter unwanted into her home. Ricco had invented a small device to put in the doorway to prevent a shadow from sliding under the door. She used them at every entryway and in every door. She had them in her vents. She took no chances at all. She would always be vigilant.

No matter how much she told herself to relax, that this was her home, her beautiful lake house, and Valentino was holding her hand, walking with his casual, lazy panther stride beside her, Emmanuelle found herself tensing up as she always did the moment she spotted her mother sitting in the comfortable lounge chairs beneath the umbrellas.

Tall frosted glasses of lemonade sat on the little table between Henry and Eloisa. Henry smiled at them in greeting. Eloisa scowled, her gaze sweeping over Emmanuelle in disapproval.

Valentino held the back of her chair as he took the one across from Henry. "Nice to see you both," he greeted.

"Val," Henry said. "You both look good. Married life suits our girl."

Eloisa rolled her eyes. "Let's not pretend we came here for pleasantries, Henry."

Henry's gaze swung to her. "We didn't? I thought you said you needed to visit your daughter, Eloisa." His tone was mild.

"Needing to visit my daughter means I have to talk to her about something important. It doesn't mean I *want* to sit here and pretend we're all going to be friends. I wish to speak to my daughter alone." Eloisa's eyes bored into Valentino.

Val lifted Emmanuelle's hand from his lap to his chest, his thumb sliding over her wedding ring, back and forth, mesmerizing Eloisa, until she scowled at him. He appeared completely unaffected by her scathing look. "That's not going to happen. If you want to say something to my wife, say it. Otherwise you should leave."

Eloisa switched her venomous stare to Emmanuelle. Emme refused to flinch under her black gaze. She'd seen it enough times. "What is it you wish to speak to me about?"

"If you insist we do this with him present, then fine. You can't possibly have children with him. You need to make certain, Emmanuelle. Have a hysterectomy right away." It was a clear command.

Emmanuelle nearly fell out of her chair. It was the last thing she'd expected her mother to say. She looked up at Val because he was her only sanity in that moment.

Valentino leaned toward Emmanuelle. "Baby, is there something you didn't tell me about your health?" He looked straight at Eloisa. "Is she at risk in some way if she has a child?"

Emmanuelle looked at Henry, the taste of betrayal in her mouth. He looked as shocked as she felt. Clearly, he really hadn't known why Eloisa had wanted to come to see her.

Two bright spots of color dotted Eloisa's cheeks, and she tilted her chin up. "No. She knows why she can't have children with you."

"I'm done here." Emmanuelle stood. "Please don't come back to my home. I don't want to see you again ever, Eloisa."

"I will take this above Stefano's head, Emmanuelle."

Emme didn't turn around. She walked straight into the house, very aware Valentino didn't follow her.

Eloisa, we should go," Henry said.

"Not quite yet, Henry," Val said. He reached out and lifted a plain manila folder that was lying on the table on the opposite side of where his wife had been sitting. "I think both of you will find this interesting. It's a report on an incident involving Emmanuelle. Someone tried to kill her. As you can imagine, I take that kind of thing very seriously, as do her brothers. An investigation was launched by the Ferraro family as well as my people. We also found the would-be hired assassin. You'll be happy to know Dario and Stefano interrogated him to ensure that there were no mistakes. Both families came to the same conclusion."

He handed the folder to Henry. Eloisa tried to take it from Henry's hands. Henry frowned at her. "What is this?"

Eloisa shook her head. "Don't read that, Henry. Let's just go. We have to hurry."

He flipped open the folder and scanned the pages inside fast before lifting his gaze slowly to Eloisa.

She brought her hand defensively to her throat. "Don't look at me like that. Someone had to do something. She's a traitor. She can't be with him. Stefano will never do what's right."

"She's your daughter, Eloisa," Henry said. "Your *daughter.*"

She lifted her chin, her eyes going hard. "I have a duty to do what's right." She pointed to Valentino, and her hand shook. "She cannot marry this man and have children with him. You know that. She knows it, but she's always been willful. She cares nothing for duty. She's selfish. Stefano is too weak to do what's expected of him."

"Stefano is the head of the riders, not you, Eloisa," Henry said softly. "He makes all decisions."

"Henry," she hissed. "Stop. We aren't alone."

"Only an Archambault can do what you contracted outside the riders to do. They are the only family that can make the decision to put another rider to death. You know that. What you've done is punishable by death. What were you thinking?"

She shook her head. "No. I did the only thing possible. There was no time. I have to stop her before she can hurt the riders any more than she already has."

Valentino reached out and took the report from Henry's shaking hands. He had noted immediately that Eloisa had said *have to stop her.* She didn't intend to ever stop, not that it would have mattered to him. This woman had paid money to have someone kill Emmanuelle. There would never be forgiveness in him. It didn't matter to him who she was. Dario had advised caution. Dario had even said he would take care of it for him, just in case Emme ever asked him directly. In case she ever became suspicious.

Val was unapologetic about who he was. Emmanuelle had

married him knowing she would always have his full protection. She might not like it, and might not always agree, but no way would someone get away with blatantly putting a hit out on his wife. He didn't give a damn who it was. In fact, it was far worse that it was her own mother.

He sat back in his chair and, with cold, merciless eyes, regarded the woman who had given birth to his wife. "I don't understand how someone like you could have actually had a hand in the genetic makeup of someone as beautiful and incredible as Emmanuelle. She's an angel, and you—you're something that crawled up from hell. I understand that, Eloisa, I do. I think I originated from there myself. The difference between us is this. I recognize when someone is good and I protect them. You, apparently, don't care. You have no moral code. How that happened when you're a fucking Ferraro, I don't know."

"Valentino," Henry said softly. "I'll take her to Europe. We'll go away from here." There was a plea in his voice.

Val didn't have enough compassion in him to understand how Henry could want to be with a woman like Eloisa.

"You and I both know that will never stop her. She's fanatical. And she's been obsessive and abusive toward Emme since the day she was born. Only Eloisa knows why."

Eloisa's features contorted into a mask of hatred. "The first time my parents ever came to see her, my mother actually picked her up. She never held a baby in her life. Not one time, and she had several children and grandchildren. But she held Emmanuelle. The *princess*. So beautiful. So perfect. Everyone thinks she's so perfect. Even now, when she's betrayed her family. Betrayed her heritage. The great trust she was given. She still is considered perfect. Something has to be done."

"Eloisa, stop talking," Henry pleaded. "You don't know what you're saying or doing."

Eloisa stood up, hands on her hips as she glared down at Valentino. "You don't scare me. You never have. Try and come after me. She can't protect you any more than you can protect her." She spun around and stomped off.

Henry closed his eyes and shook his head before he pushed himself heavily out of his chair. "She never had a chance at life, Val."

"I'm sorry. I only care about Emmanuelle, Henry." Valentino told him the truth.

Henry nodded and followed Eloisa to their car. Valentino remained sitting in his chair. It took a few minutes and then Stefano and Elie Archambault appeared out of the shadows and sank into the chairs next to him.

"I didn't think she would admit it," Stefano said. "She just came right out and told you she put out a hit on her own daughter. She made no apologies for it."

"And she wouldn't stop," Elie added. "Stefano, it has to be that her brain has been affected by the lesions. She isn't thinking right."

Valentino flicked a quick glance in Archambault's direction. If either of them thought for one moment Eloisa was going to live through this, they were sadly mistaken. No one put out a hit on his wife and got away with it. He said nothing. There was no reason to.

Stefano sighed. "I knew she hated Emmanuelle. She was always abusive toward her."

"You don't know the half of it," Val said.

"I have no choice," Stefano said. For the first time he sounded old. Tired.

"The report was sent to the council, Stefano," Elie reminded. "Only an Archambault can be sent after a rider. You know that. Let them handle it. This is one you don't want to touch."

"She will continue to go after Emme," Stefano said. "You heard her. If they don't act fast, she might hire someone else. Or worse, try herself and force Emmanuelle into a situation where she has to kill her own mother in self-defense or let her mother murder her."

Valentino sighed. "Really? Do you think I'm going to sit by and let this woman get away with trying to murder my wife? I'm not a shadow rider, and there's no love lost between us. In fact, the things Emme has told me that her mother did to her when Emmanuelle was just a little girl make me want to strangle her with my bare hands. People think I'm a monster."

He shook his head, trying to hang on to his temper, trying to remember that Eloisa was also Stefano's mother. At some point he must have one or two good memories of her.

Elie leaned toward Valentino. "It's precisely because Emmanuelle is your wife that you can't be the one to do this, Val. I know you thought I was a threat to you, but Emme is like a sister to me. I love her dearly. What I do know is she loves you with every single breath she takes. The last thing she ever needs is to find out her husband killed her mother. It doesn't matter if Eloisa deserved it. You can't be the one."

"She has to go now, before she contracts with another killer. The last one got too close."

Elie nodded his agreement. "Eloisa committed a crime against a shadow rider. She has indicated she will continue on that same path. Both Stefano and I have sent reports to the council indicating time is of the essence. Neither of us wanted to come to that conclusion, but we had no choice. Emmanuelle has had too many terrible things in her life that she's had to cope with. Don't make this yet another one. Give her your life together, free of any of that. If you kill her mother, you and I both know it will eat away at her. This will be taken care of."

It went against everything he was to have anyone else protect his wife—remove his wife's would-be killer. He was that man. He would always be that man. But Stefano and Elie made sense. He knew Emmanuelle. If for one moment, she sensed he had something to do with her mother's death and she asked him, he would have to tell the truth. That would always lie between them. Emmanuelle wouldn't want to let it. She would understand, but it would still come between them.

Val rubbed the bridge of his nose. "I know you're right. I just don't want to take any chances with Emme's life. I feel so damn bad for Henry."

"He knew what he was signing up for," Stefano said, pushing out of the chair. "All of us have tried with her, over and over. You have no idea the things she's done and the chances she's had. We'll take care of Henry if he lets us." He stepped into a shadow and was gone.

Elie stood as well. "Take good care of Emme, Val. I've put in for an arranged marriage. I got word from the council that I have a match. I won't see my bride until the day of the wedding. She'll be coming here to marry me. I don't want to return to France. I hope Emmanuelle will become friends with my wife."

Valentino lifted an eyebrow. "You did what? I read those bullshit papers Emme filled out. They were so detailed it was unbelievable. You could be blackmailed for the rest of your life if someone got ahold of those."

"According to the council, no one is supposed to ever see them. It's a new program. You answer the questions online. The program matches you, and then it is erased. Emme wasn't supposed to print them out."

"She's such a perfectionist she didn't want to make a mistake, so she printed the questions out and answered them. I think she changed her answers several times." Valentino had to smile in spite of the fact that he'd been so angry when he'd realized that Emmanuelle was really contemplating allowing herself to be partnered with another man—one not him. "Go after the woman you know you're supposed to be with, Elie."

"She doesn't want me, and I can't blame her." Elie shrugged and stepped into a shadow.

Valentino stared after him for a long time before walking into the house.

Dario met him inside. "How did it go?"

"They say the riders will take care of it. I'll give them a couple of days. They don't want me to be the one to do it." Val shoved a hand through his hair and looked toward the kitchen. Emmanuelle had taken to trying out various recipes, and the house always smelled good. Today was going to be no different in spite of her mother's visit.

"I'll do it if it comes to that. They're right: it shouldn't be you."

"Or you. You're family to her as well. And stop being so fucking stubborn. You're taking over Miceli's territory. You have no choice, and you know it. We don't want anyone else in that position."

"I'm not some leader. I stay in the background."

"Stay in the background, but you're still going to have to take over. It's done. I already told the others, so don't whine. You just have to stand around and look tough. That shouldn't be too hard for you."

The two made their way into the kitchen. Valentino hid a smile when Dario went straight to the sink and washed his hands before picking up a knife to begin chopping the mountain of vegetables waiting on the center island.

"I'm doing it, Valentino, but I'm still staying here. Not giving up the food."

Emmanuelle tossed them both a quick grin from over her shoulder as she cut up chicken. "Seriously? Are you two still arguing about Dario taking on his new role? Dario just doesn't want to wear the suit. You look totally badass in it, hon."

Val came up behind her, pressing his body tight against hers, arms around her waist. She was armed with a knife, and he was always respectful when his woman was armed with any weapon. "Don't give him compliments. He's already full of himself."

He couldn't help himself: he bit down gently on that sweet spot between her neck and shoulder that always brought goose bumps. He loved that sound of her laughter. Evidently, her bodyguards, a staple in her kitchen, did as well. The four of them, Levi, Axel, Pace and Lando, had been put to work also, coring and slicing apples for the deep-dish cinnamon apple pies they all loved.

"You could hire a chef, Dario," Val said. "He doesn't want

his own territory because he wants to live here. He doesn't like missing out on your cooking."

He was rewarded with Emmanuelle's laugh. She put her head back on his shoulder for a moment. "It's a good thing you never started eating at Taviano's house, Dario. He's a way better chef than I am. I watch the cooking channels to improve. Poor Val has to pretend he likes some of the stuff I make for him." She turned her head and pressed kisses into his jaw.

Just getting that from her made the cold, dark place inside him that was an abyss of hell, marking him a monster, burn with a hunger to find even bigger monsters and take them into that fiery pit with him, just to protect her.

At once she lifted her head, half turning to look into his eyes. "Valentino? Are you all right?" Her voice was whisper soft. Her eyes drifted over his face. Saw too much. She always knew when he was disturbed. "Honey, I told you not to let Eloisa come here. Whatever she said to you, let it go. I love you. You're my choice. We'll have children together, and the hell with whatever weird problem she's decided she has with us. It isn't her business, it's ours."

Naturally, Emmanuelle would believe Eloisa had upset him, and she would try to reassure him. That was so like his woman. He didn't know how he'd gotten so damn lucky, but he vowed to himself he was never going to fuck it up.

"I'm good, Princess."

Valentino made sure his woman was absolutely good with three orgasms before he drove her up again, listening to her gasping pleas. Her little denials that she couldn't possibly when she was able, and would, because he could feel her body coiling tighter and tighter around his, already practically strangling his cock. Being in Emmanuelle felt better than anything he could imagine, and he wanted to stay there as long as he possibly could.

Deliberately, he slowed his pace, wanting to give his

woman as much pleasure as possible before he allowed himself his own release. He didn't want the time to be over. There were times, like now, when he looked into her eyes and felt like they were touching each other's souls. It shook him every fucking time. He never wanted those moments to end. It wasn't just about the physical, the insatiable lust he felt for her, but the lust infused so deeply with so much love it was a part of every cell in his body.

Her body coiled tighter and tighter around his cock, locking down, a tight friction that sent fiery streaks rocketing from his thighs straight to his balls and down his spine to lash at his cock. Molten lava churned, roiled, threatening to erupt.

"Catch up, baby. Fast," he ordered.

"I can't. Not again," she whispered. Staring into his eyes. Loving him. Her breath ragged. Her legs around his waist. Tight. Wrapping him up. Fingers threaded through his.

"You can."

Her orgasm rushed over her hard, taking her like a wild storm, a crowning fire, sweeping through both of them, robbing them of all air. Her silken sheath clamped down like a vise. A thousand flames surrounded his cock, burning over him, branding him. Milking him. Dragging every drop of his seed from him. Over and over, his cock jerked and pulsed, a mindless pleasure consuming him, sending him orbiting, burning like a fucking phoenix until he lay on her, a dead weight, nothing left but utter peace—the way she always gave it to him.

I've been doing quite a bit of research," Emmanuelle told him, massaging his scalp, her voice a soft murmur, when they could talk again. When he had moved enough to lie on her belly, arms around her hips. "It's tough going reading the books in the earlier languages. There isn't much information to find on the Saldi creepy shadow creature, Val."

He caught the little hint of worry in her voice. "I get the feeling as long as both parties cooperate, everyone is safe. It's only when one decides to try to divorce or cheat that the vengeful shadow creature comes into play and straightens them out."

"That's a pretty big motivator to keep your marriage together," he murmured.

"I have to meet with the members of the International Council of Shadow Riders tomorrow morning, Valentino. They're trying to make it as informal as possible, but I know it isn't. They'll be at the hotel, and I have to explain to them how our union came about and what the Saldi shadow legend means to the Ferraros. I've really studied it and tried to make sense of it, but in such a short time, with most of it lost, I don't feel prepared."

"I'll be with you." He made it a statement.

She continued to massage his scalp in silence for a few minutes. He knew she was uncomfortable with him going. "Stefano will be there. You're not a rider, and some of them may be resentful. I don't want them to treat you with less than respect. I'm not saying that they would, but if they did, I'd be upset, and so would Stefano."

"You're not going to face them without me. We're in this together. If they have questions, I may be able to answer them better than you. In any case, I think they'd have less respect for me if I left you to face them alone. We don't have all the answers they want. I wish we did, but we don't. They'll just have to accept that. They aren't going to tell us we can't have children. They can't dictate anything to us."

"They can tell me I can't be a shadow rider."

He rubbed her bare thigh soothingly. "For your family, no, if they're that vindictive. I don't know how that would serve them, but they could do it. They can't stop you from going into the shadows when you think it best for us or for our children. They no longer have any say over you unless you continue to be a rider for them, Emme."

She sighed. "That's true. I wish it didn't matter so much to me. I don't want to think my self-esteem is tied up in what I do."

"Babe." He turned his head, his chin on her belly, eyes on her face. "You trained from the time you were two years old. You were never supposed to be anything else. You are a shadow rider. You'll always be a rider, whether you work for your family or you choose to work for us—and, baby, it will always be your choice. *Always*. That fucking creepy shadow can't make you do anything you don't want to do, because I'll never ask it of you."

He watched her eyes. He knew how to read people. He was fucking brilliant at it, but especially at reading his wife. His declaration meant something to her. A whole hell of a lot, especially since she could tell he meant every word.

"I'm your partner, Val. Even when I know I have to pretend to stay a couple of steps behind you and look like the little wife in the background, I'll be in the shadows listening to every word our potential enemies—or Dario's—have to say."

When a smile lit her eyes, he knew it was safe to put his head back on her belly. Naturally, she would include Dario. He was family. She would keep him just as safe as Dario intended to keep her.

"That's good, baby. No matter what the council tells us, we stand together."

Valentino knew the council wanted to hear about the Saldi myth. They wouldn't be any happier than he was that they didn't have all the information, but they would understand. They would most likely put their best historians on attempting to find the portions lost.

The Saldis had attacked the Ferraro family, nearly wiping them out. Those remaining, mostly riders, had scattered, leaving Sicily and separating to make it much more difficult to be tracked down and murdered. It also made it more difficult for any Saldi to ever find a woman who had a particular shadow that matched with the myth handed down from father to son. In a millennium, it was easy, over all those years, to change the wording, for the story to become twisted and even forgotten.

Valentino was aware that the council was in Chicago because an Archambault sat on it. With the members came others to look after them. In the case of Marcellus Archambault, head of the International Council of Shadow Riders, several family members had come with him. They had supposedly come to speak with Elie about his application for an arranged marriage. They were there for other, more important reasons, and it was a relief to him.

Elie had made a promise to Valentino, and he was keeping it. In the last week, Stefano had made it clear to Henry to watch Eloisa every minute—that she would attempt again to put a contract killer on Emme's trail. Val wasn't certain Henry was up to that task, and waiting that week had been endless, especially since he couldn't stay home, which meant there was no keeping his wife home.

He was head of the Saldi *famiglia*. It was necessary to carry on with business as usual. He had to support Dario in weeding out the worst of Miceli's supporters and bring his capos back in line. Dario was as tough as nails and ruled with an iron fist. If anything, he was much scarier than Valentino, and no one wanted to cross him. Dario, however, made it clear he didn't want to oversee the territory. He continued to push Valentino to appoint someone else to the position.

Val had a bad feeling he might have to give up and allow Dario his way, which meant he would have to take over completely. He had explained his reasoning to Dario a hundred times, but Dario just shrugged and walked off. Valentino could swallow the entire territory—it was his right; it had belonged to Giuseppi before he had given part of it to his brother—but it would be easier if Dario stepped up.

Val and Dario met with all the capos and went over the businesses, legitimate and not. Fortunately, they had Bernado to check the books of every business before each meeting to ensure everyone was paying what they owed. Traitors met with the same fate that Valentino had bestowed on those he found in his father's organization. Dario was the one who took care of those considered traitors in Miceli's organization. They had sworn a blood oath to Giuseppi first. They were his men before his brother's.

The businesses that had been destroyed needed to be rebuilt from the ground up, and that had begun immediately. Men loyal to the *famiglia* were placed in positions where the most money would flow to them. The others had to work harder to earn their place. Women who had been treated badly were offered jobs with good wages, benefits and protection in place.

Through it all, Emmanuelle stood in the shadows to make certain those saying they were swearing allegiance to Valentino and Dario meant what they said. She could hear lies and before and after the two entered a room, she listened to the conversations that took place. She made it much easier and faster to weed out those who had been working closely with Miceli and his sons. There were few of those men left. Most had tried to stay away from Miceli and had kept their heads down, working at their businesses and paying the money owed as quickly as possible to keep Miceli from demanding they join his newer ventures.

Valentino wasn't willing to wait longer than a week before he would indicate to both Stefano and Elie that he was done waiting. He couldn't take a chance that Eloisa would put out another hit on Emmanuelle, so he was more than happy to hear that she had been summoned before the council the following day at her brother's hotel. Nothing would keep him away.

Representatives came from all over the world to attend the passing of a shadow rider. Eloisa Ferraro's funeral was held in the church where her children were christened and married. The building was huge, and right now it was filled to capacity with mourners. Her sons sat in the front rows, dressed in their immaculate suits, their wives beside them. Her daughter was there, husband on one side, his cousin on the other. Henry sat with the family, looking grief-stricken, not looking up through the entire service.

Eloisa's siblings and cousins made up a number of pews and then some kind of honor guard that came from various countries followed the large family. The locals sat in the church knowing Eloisa had known many people, but they were shocked at just how many.

She had died unexpectedly from a brain aneurysm. It was a tragedy, and one that couldn't have been prevented. She had been working hard to bring awareness to brain injuries, pushing the use of brain scans when talking about injuries occurring in car and motorcycle accidents. She wanted people to understand how important it was to take brain injuries seriously. It seemed so ironic that in the end, she would succumb to a brain aneurysm.

The entire family wore suits, as did her honor guard, those representing other countries. Relatives, even those coming from other states, wore pinstriped suits, the signature of the Ferraros. Cousins wore suits with various colored ties, but it was clear from their features they were related, even if they were from San Francisco, Los Angeles or New York. It was tradition for all Ferraros to be cremated and laid to rest in a private crypt in a fenced and locked section of the old cemetery.

Eloisa Ferraro's ashes were escorted around the block to the old cemetery in the Ferraro territory, the local mourners walking behind the honor guard as they walked in silent formation straight to the cemetery. It was an oddly silent procession. There were so many people, and yet they made little more than a whisper of sound as they moved behind the small golden container holding the ashes of Eloisa Ferraro.

Her children were directly behind her. Stefano pushed his wife in a wheelchair, his son riding on her lap. The others walked in complete silence, their heads up, no one shedding a tear. That was expected. Ferraros rarely showed emotion in public. Only the family were allowed once inside the gates. The locals left to mourn together, gathering at their private businesses. The honor guard went to the hotel to wait for the family.

Once they were in the town car, Emmanuelle between Valentino and Dario, Val wrapped his arm around his wife. There were no prying eyes to watch her if she broke down. Her body seemed abnormally cold to him, although she wasn't shivering.

"Are you all right, Princess?" He rubbed her shoulder gently.

Dario moved closer to her, as if his warmth could help in some way. He exchanged a long, worried look with Valentino over her head.

"I don't know how I'm supposed to feel. I have regrets that I was never able to repair the damage to our relationship. I don't know what the damage was, or how it even happened. From the time I was a child, my memories were mostly of her attacking me at night. During the day she was sweet to me in front of everyone. I clung to that. I would respond to her and try to do everything she said to make her happy."

She leaned her head against Valentino's shoulder. "She terrified me. I didn't know what was wrong with me, what I did to make her act the way she did toward me." She pressed her fingers to her eyes. "I tried, I really did. Now I just feel empty."

Dario heaved an exaggerated sigh. "I know this is her funeral and she was your mother. I should have sympathy. I'm only going to say this once and you better not be recording this. Either one of you." He caught Emmanuelle by the shoulders and turned her to face him. "I love two people in this world. Valentino, like a brother, and you, like a sister, because you both are worth loving. So fuck her, Emme. Fuck her for not seeing how damn beautiful you are. And never make me say that again." He let go of her, pulled out his phone and stared down at the screen as if he hadn't said a word.

Emmanuelle looked up at Val, blinking back tears. He grinned at her and brushed her upturned mouth with his. Dario detested showing emotion. They had already grown into a tight family. That was good for Dario. He needed Emme's softness as much as Valentino did.

"I love you, too, Dario. Thank you."

Dario didn't respond or look away from his phone.

Emmanuelle leaned into Val and looked up at him again, her blue eyes filled with love, that look that turned him inside out. "To answer your question, Valentino Saldi, I'm perfectly fine. I love you very much. I have no regrets for the choices I made. Or that you made either when you decided to send all those little ropes to bind my shadow to yours."

That was the first time she'd ever acknowledged to him that she had come to terms with the fact that he had all but taken her prisoner. At first, he hadn't realized what was happening any more than she had, but later, when he realized she was terrified of loving him, that she really was going to run from him, he'd taken every opportunity to seal her to him.

"I didn't know about the creeper." He felt compelled to admit that to her.

Dario made a rude sound.

Valentino scowled at him. "What does that mean?"

"Are you telling me, even had you known, you wouldn't have gone for it? Because I can tell you, if I find my woman, I don't give a damn about a creeper shadow; in fact, I'm all for it. Anything to keep her in line if she's trouble like yours."

Emmanuelle rolled her eyes. "He's all talk, Val."

Valentino was grateful he didn't have to answer the question Dario had posed because the fact of the matter was—he would have done anything to secure Emmanuelle. She was his peace. She'd given him so much more than he'd ever expected, including this huge family he was going to have to learn to maneuver his way around.

He brushed a kiss in Emmanuelle's hair and ran his thumb over her wedding rings as the town car pulled up to the front of the luxurious Ferraro Hotel. He looked out the window as his bodyguards came up to the car, moving into position to block sight from either direction so when his wife exited the car no one would be able to get to her. He didn't think there was a threat at the moment, but he wanted her to get used to security. She would always have to live with it.

He exited the vehicle before her, took her hand and wrapped his arm around her waist. With Dario, they walked together into Stefano's penthouse, where the rest of the family waited to welcome them.

Keep reading for an excerpt from
Christine Feehan's thrilling new mystery

MURDER AT SUNRISE LAKE

Available Summer 2021

M ommy, Daddy's doing the bad thing again.
  The child's voice very clearly said the words she'd
said to her mother when she was four years old. When she
was five. When she was seven.

Stella Harrison knew she was dreaming, but she still
couldn't fight her way to the surface. This was the fifth night
in a row she'd had the dream, and the camera had widened
the lens just a little more, as it had every night, so she saw
additional pieces of the hideous nightmare she couldn't stop.
The man fishing. He wore denim bibbed overalls tucked into
high olive-colored waders. A blue cap was pulled low over
his eyes so she couldn't see his face. There were boulders
among the heavy reeds and plants that grew thick along the
shore, creeping out into the lake. He'd made his way through
the boulders to get out from under the shade of several trees.

She tried to warn him. Yelling. Calling out. *Don't cast.
Don't do it.* Every night she saw his line go into the same
spot. That little darker area that rippled in rings like a little
round pool, so inviting. The fisherman always did the same

exact thing, like a programmed robot. Stepping forward, casting, the lure hitting perfectly, sinking into the middle of that inky spot, dropping beneath the water into the depths below.

The camera switched then and she could see beneath the water. It should have been tranquil. Peaceful. Fish swimming. Not the man in the wet suit, waiting for that hook, waiting to tug and enter into some kind of terrible game with the fisherman above the surface. The fight for the fish became a real life-and-death battle, with the fisherman lured farther and farther from the safety of the shore and into the reeds and rocks—closer to the threat that lurked beneath the water.

The mythical fish appeared to be fighting. He seemed big, and well worth the exhausting battle. The fisherman paid less and less attention to his surroundings as he reeled the fish nearer to him and realized he was close to winning his prize.

Without warning, the killer, beneath the water, rose up right in front of the unsuspecting fisherman, slamming him backward so that his waders couldn't find traction on the muddy floor of the lake. He hit his head hard on the boulder behind him and went down. Immediately, the killer caught his legs and yanked hard, dragging him under the water and holding him there while the fisherman thrashed and fought. He was weak from the vicious blow to his head from the boulder.

Stella could only watch, horrified, as the killer calmly finished the scene by yanking the body to the surface for just a few moments so he could drag the bottom of one wader along a boulder before pulling the fisherman back into the water and tangling him in his own fishing line just below the surface, in the reeds and plants close to the shore. The killer calmly swam off as if nothing had happened.

The lens of the camera snapped shut and everything went black.

S tella woke fighting a tangle of sheets, sweat dripping, hair damp. She sat up abruptly, pressing the heels of her hands to her eyes. Rubbing, scrubbing her palms down her face over and over. Trying to erase the nightmare. Not again. It had been years. *Years*. She'd made a new life for herself. New friends. A place. A home.

Now the nightmare was back and reoccurring. This was the fifth time she'd had it. *Five* times in a row. It wasn't like she lived in a big city. Usually if murders were happening everyone would know, especially in a small town, but this killer was brilliant. He was absolutely brilliant and that was why he was going to get away with it—unless she brought attention to the murders. Even then, she wasn't certain he would get caught.

She hadn't realized she was rocking herself back and forth, trying to self-soothe. She forced herself to stop. She hadn't done that in years, either. All those terrible habits she had developed as a child, that came back as a teen, she'd managed to overcome. Now she found they were sneaking back into her life.

There was no going back to sleep even though it was still dark outside. She'd planned to sleep in. She'd taken a few days off even though they were winding down. She owned the Sunrise Lake Resort and had for several years, turning it around from a dismal losing business to one that not only made large profits but helped out the local businesses as well. She loved the resort, loved everything about it, even the hard work—especially that. She thrived on solving problems, and those problems changed hourly, keeping her mind constantly active. She needed that, and first managing and then owning Sunrise Lake provided it.

When the owner decided it was time to retire four years earlier, he sold the resort to her. They'd kept the transaction quiet, and he continued to stay on the first year as if he owned it. Over time, his visits became fewer and fewer. She renovated the main house but kept a special cabin for him, so he had a place whenever he came back.

The property was beautiful, high in the mountains surrounding a good portion of Sunrise Lake. Knightly, the nearest town, was located an hour's drive below them on a fairly winding highway. The town was small, but that just made the community close-knit.

Stella had made good friends there. She liked living in the backcountry. She felt grounded, connected, alive there. There were all kinds of things to do, from skiing to backpacking to climbing. She fit there. She wasn't throwing it all away on a few nightmares. That would be so foolish. It was just that the nightmares were so vivid, and now they were reoccurring, becoming more detailed.

It wasn't like there was even a body—yet. She shivered. There was going to be. She knew it. She just knew there would be. Somewhere, a fisherman was going to be murdered in the next two days. There would be no way to prove that he was murdered. She had to stop thinking about it or she was going to go insane.

She rolled out of bed and headed straight for her shower. She had overseen the renovations to the main house herself, paying particular attention to the bathroom and kitchen. She loved to cook, and more than anything, after a long day of work, she wanted to know she had plenty of hot water for showers and baths. Her spacious bathroom was a work of art.

The stand-alone tub was deep, and the shower larger. She liked space in her shower and lots of jets coming at her from all sides, since she was often sore from the work she did or from climbing, skiing, backpacking, or any of the other outdoor activities she chose to do. Even dancing with her friends sometimes went on all night. Her shower was perfect for her.

She'd designed the renovations of the main house for two people, although she didn't believe she would ever have a significant other in her life. She was too closed off. She didn't share her past with anyone, not even her closest friends. She didn't really date. The minute anyone started to get too close, she backed off.

The hot water poured over her as she washed her thick blonde hair. Her hair was the one thing she was a little vain about. She didn't wear it down often, but it was almost silver in color, thanks to her Finnish grandparents on her mother's side. She had inherited that light, light hair color from them, along with her crystal-blue eyes. The thickness of her hair and her darker lashes were a gift from her father's side of the family. He was originally from Argentina. Her mother had met him in college in San Diego where they had both attended. Her father was from a wealthy Argentinean family. Between her two parents, she had been lucky to get amazing genetics.

The hot water helped to dispel the last of the nightmare and the bile in her stomach. Unfortunately, her uneasiness persisted. She just wasn't certain what to do. She had only had those dreams twice before and both times had ended up being worse than her nightmares. Sighing, she squeezed as much water out of her hair as possible before winding a towel around the mass, and then she dried her body off slowly with a warm towel.

Dressing in her favorite pair of jeans and a comfortable tee, she pulled on a sweater and her boots before braiding her hair. She didn't dry it if she could help it, and since she actually had a day off and she rarely wore make-up or dressed up, she was ready to go in minutes.

"Bailey, I can't believe you're still sleeping. Get up, you lazy animal." She put her hands on her hips and tried to look stern as she regarded the large Airedale still curled up in his dog bed right beside her bed.

Bailey's eyes opened and he looked at her and then around the room, noting the darkness, as if to say she was out of her mind for getting up so early. Heaving a sigh, the dog got to his feet and followed her through the spacious house to the front door. On the porch, she hesitated at the door. She had stopped locking her door or setting the alarm some time ago, but lately, that crawling feeling down her spine was back. The churning in her stomach started all over again. Bailey waited patiently for her to make up her mind.

Stella knew it was ridiculous to stand in front of her door like a loon. She made decisions all the time. It was just that giving in to her fears was like going backward, and she'd promised herself she would never do that. She stood there indecisively, staring at the thick carved door for another full minute before making up her mind.

Locking the door, she set the alarm, furious with herself for giving in to the nightmares and unrelenting terror that consumed her when she was asleep. Fear crept up on her unawares, and slowly but surely took over until she was caught up in things best left alone. If she was going to actually acknowledge that a murder was going to take place in her beloved Sierras, no one was going to help with investigations this time. The killer would make it look like an accident. She didn't have dreams unless the murderer was a serial killer, which meant he would kill again. Accidents happened all the time in the Sierras.

There would be no gossip, no whispers or rumors. Before, she'd hated that, the way everywhere she went murder had been the topic of conversation. Now if she wanted to stop a killer, she would have to ask the right questions herself. Several of her friends were involved with search and rescue. She knew the medical examiner. Maybe she could figure out a reason to ask questions that would make sense and, at the same time, raise suspicion that the death wasn't an accident.

Stella deliberately avoided the marina and walked in the dark to reach the family pier. This dock was not one that the original owners drove their boat to—they used the marina's piers for that. It was private, a dock for enjoying the sunrises and sunsets, just as she was doing now. The dock had been positioned perfectly to catch the beauty of the mountains mirrored in the lake as the sun rose or set. She never got tired of the view.

She was so familiar with the layout of the grounds that she barely needed her small penlight as she maneuvered the narrow path that took her away from the main buildings, the small grocery store, the bait shop, the collection of cabins, the play areas designated for children and the game areas for adults.

The trail took her behind the campsites and RV sites to an

even narrower path that led through a pile of boulders and into a heavy forested area. Once through the trees, she was back to the shoreline. It seemed a ridiculous place to put a pier, but she liked the peace when she needed it most—like now. Tourists didn't know the way to the pier and that meant precious solitude when she had a few hours—or a day—to herself.

Fall had arrived, and with it the glorious colors as only the Eastern Sierras could cloak herself with. She loved every season in the Sierras, but fall was definitely a favorite. The cooler weather after the summer heat was always welcome. There was still fishing, and tourists were still coming, but things were slowing down so she could take a breath. Climbing was still a possibility and she loved climbing.

Then there was just the sheer beauty of the blazing reds, all the various shades from crimson to a flat almost purple-red, on the leaves of many of the trees. The oranges were the same, all the varying shades. She hadn't known there were so many shades, subtle to brilliant orange, golds and yellows, the colors vying for attention even among the varying greens, until she came to the Eastern Sierras.

The mountains rose above the lake, containing forests of trees pressed together so tightly they seemed impenetrable from a distance. The mountains stretched for miles, with canyons and rivers, amazing forests and beautiful scarred rock found nowhere else. This was the place of legends, and she had come to love it and the ever-changing landscape.

Stella sat on the end of the thick planks making up the pier and stared out over the water of the icy lake. Fed by the high mountain rivers and snowpack, Sunrise Lake was a huge bowl of deep sapphire-colored water. A light breeze ruffled the surface, but for the most part, the water gleamed like glass. Sometimes the incomparable beauty of this place stole her breath. It didn't seem to matter what time of year it was; the lake and surrounding mountains always had such elegance and majesty to them.

Bailey curled up beside her, close, the way he always did when she sat on the end of the pier. He went right back to sleep, never knowing how long she planned to sit, waiting for the sun to come up. She wished Bailey could talk, so she could at least have someone to sound important things out with—like murder—but when she'd tried, the dog gave her a look like she'd lost her mind and shoved his face in her lap, inviting her to scratch his ears. Taking advantage. That was her beloved Bailey.

There was no warning. A hand touched her shoulder and she nearly threw herself forward off the dock into the lake. Bailey didn't even look up or make a sound. The hand caught her in a firm grip before she could tumble off the pier. She turned her head to glare up at the man towering over her. Sam Rossi was one of those men who could walk in absolute silence. Sometimes, like now, he freaked her out. He was too rough to call gorgeous, with his chiseled masculine features, all angles and planes. His jaw was always covered in a dark shadow that was never a beard yet never shaved. He rarely smiled, if ever, and when he did, that smile never quite reached his arctic-cold eyes.

He had a body on him. Wide shoulders. Thick chest. Lots of muscle. He was strong. She knew because she employed him as a handyman and he had to do all sorts of jobs that required unbelievable strength. He had to have knowledge of boats, carpentry, fishing, climbing and most outdoor activities, and so far he hadn't let her down once.

He had scars. Lots of them. He took his shirt off when it was hot as hell and he had to work outside. Not so much when there were others around, usually only her, or when he was a good distance from others, but she'd seen the scars and those scars weren't pretty. They weren't the kinds of scars one acquired in a car accident. He looked like the skin had been flayed from his back. He'd been shot more than once. He had a few knife scars for certain. She hadn't looked closely. She'd made it a point not to stare, although she'd wanted to. She'd never asked and he'd never volunteered an explanation.

"Quit sneaking up on me," she snapped irritably as she

reached for the coffee he had in his other hand, which was clearly meant for her.

He pulled the to-go mug out of reach and sat down, Bailey between them, ignoring her outstretched hand.

"Sam." She practically growled his name. He couldn't bring the aroma of her favorite brew and then withhold it.

He quirked an eyebrow at her. Evidently, he thought he could. He set the mug on the opposite side of his body so there was no way she could lunge over the dog and grab it. Ignoring her, Sam calmly drank from his mug and looked out over the lake. Bailey didn't even help her by biting him. Or lifting his head and growling.

"Did you come out here just to annoy me?" Stella demanded.

He didn't answer. She knew he could keep up the silent treatment forever. It was like his *annoying* nickname for her. He called her Satine in that silly voice—Satine, the lead character in the movie *Moulin Rouge*. Well, not that he had a silly voice exactly; he had a low, mesmerizing, sexy-as-hell voice. Fortunately, he didn't call her Satine in front of anyone else. He didn't talk much, so it never came up when her friends were around.

She was not one to be embarrassed by much, not even when she was caught in a ridiculous situation, but because she harbored a slight crush on Sam she found things she normally would laugh at nearly humiliating.

She loved the movie *Moulin Rouge*. Loved it. It was her go-to movie when she was in a funk and wanted a pity party. She didn't have them often, but when she did she played that movie and cried her eyes out. When she wanted to watch something that made her heart sing, she played *Moulin Rouge* and ate popcorn and cried and laughed.

Stella didn't even know how it happened that Sam had come in once when she was having a pity party, but he had. He'd sat down and watched the movie with her. After that, he'd joined her more than once and seemed to watch her more than the movie. As usual, he didn't say anything; he just shook his head as if she was a little nutty and then walked out afterward. She didn't even know if he liked the movie, but if he didn't, he had no soul, which she shouted after him. He didn't even turn around.

She knew every song by heart, and every single morning when she did her exercises she played the songs, sang to them and danced. At night she did her fitness routine to them and did a little burlesque show. Naturally, Sam once walked in just as she was kicking her leg over a chair and she didn't quite make it and landed on her butt. That was the first time.

She loved to do aerial silks as a form of exercise. Because the house was two stories and open, she had her own rigging in her home and she practiced some nights. Of course, once when she'd gotten tangled for a moment and found herself upside down, desperately trying to get her foot unlocked from the silks, music blaring, he had walked in.

The third time she was doing a very cool and sexy (if she did say so herself) booty shake to the floor and back up again. Naturally, he would be leaning against the doorjamb watching, arms crossed over his chest, those dark eyes on her. She could never tell what he was thinking because he had no expression on his face.

He took to calling her Satine in a low, dramatic movie voice every now and then. She wanted to glare at him, but it always made her laugh. He didn't share the laugh with her, but his dark eyes sometimes went velvet-soft and her stomach would do a strange little roller-coaster loop, which irritated the crap out of her.

"Seriously, Bailey, what kind of watchdog are you?" She sighed as she sank her fingers into her dog's curly fur. There was no getting around the fact that now that coffee was in her reach, she needed it. "Sam, thank you for thinking to bring me coffee. I appreciate it *so* much."

Since she did appreciate him bringing coffee, it was easy to keep the sarcasm out of her voice, although a part of her wanted to be sarcastic. Maybe push him off her private dock into the snow-fed freezing-cold water. He'd no doubt find a way to drag her into the water with him so she couldn't even get satisfaction that way.

Without a word Sam handed her the to-go mug. She gratefully took her first sip as they both watched the breeze play with the surface of the water. She stole a quick look at Sam's face. Fortunately, Sam never smirked. He was a restful person in that he never demanded anything from her. Sometimes she was so exhausted at the end of the day she didn't want to have to give one tiny bit of herself to anyone.

Those days, Sam would be on her deck grilling vegetables and steak or whatever, as if he knew she'd had a terrible day and didn't want to talk. He'd indicate the cooler and there would be ice-cold beer in it. She'd grab one for herself, hand him one and go sit in her favorite swing chair hanging from the overhead ceiling covering the porch. He never asked anything of her. She never asked anything of him. That was the best part of their strange relationship. He just seemed to know when things were bad for her. She didn't question when he showed up and made things better or how he seemed to know she needed a little care.

She sighed and took another sip of coffee, her hand moving through Bailey's fur. She'd found a few things that made life great. This place and its beauty. Her dog. Coffee. Her five friends. Her favorite movie of all time and maybe Sam Rossi. She wasn't certain what category to put him in. They didn't exactly have a relationship. Sam didn't do relationships. Neither did she. They both had too many secrets.

The leaves on the trees closest to the pier were yellow and red, some orange, and they swayed with the breeze, creating a frame on either side of the wooden planks at the shoreline. Many of the leaves had dropped on the boulders where the lake's waters lapped at the shore. On the pier, where the breeze sent the leaves spiraling down over the wood, it had turned into a carpet of blazing color.

The sun was just beginning to rise and the colors shifted subtly. Rays began to spread across the water. They were low at first. A golden globe barely seen reflected in the deep pools of the sapphire lake. The sight was pure magic, the reason Stella lived here. She felt connected to the real world. Humbled by nature. As the golden sphere began to rise, the trees took on a different look altogether. The ball looked as if it grew in the water, spreading out across the lake, shimmering beneath the surface like a golden treasure.

Stella kept her gaze on the sphere. It appeared to be moving as if alive. Each sunrise was different. The colors, the way it presented in the water. The magic. She couldn't always get to her favorite spot to watch the dramatic entrance, but she tried. There were always the sounds of the morning accompanying the sunrise. The melodies of the early birds. Some were the songs of the males defining their territories. Some birds had beautiful musical qualities, while others seemed to be raspy.

She listened for the way the birds sang. Some ended on high notes, while others let their notes trail off low. Some called out in a single coarse pitch as if they were just greeting one another or calling out to say, *I'm here!* She enjoyed her early morning solitude before the sun actually rose and she could see which birds were up with her.

She noticed the hum of bees and the skitter of lizards in the leaves. There was always the drone of insects, the cicadas calling. It was all part of the nature she could count on there in the Eastern Sierras. It didn't matter what time of year it was; there was always something that gave her that connection she needed to the earth itself instead of to the insanity that made up a world she didn't seem to fit into or understand.

"You gonna talk to me?"

Stella's stomach was already in knots. She needed to talk to someone. If she was going to talk to anyone it would be Sam, but what was she going to say? She sent him a look from under her lashes, hoping he wouldn't see fear in her eyes. That was the thing about Sam. He was far too observant. He noticed everything. Details everyone else missed.

She wasn't the talking type. What did she really know about him? She wanted to trust him. He was the only man who came and went from her home, but she didn't know him. She didn't know a single thing about his life. She didn't even know if he was married or had children. She didn't know if he was running from the police, although looking at him, she knew instinctively that if he was on the run, it wasn't from something as mundane as the cops. Sam would be hiding from some international crime he'd committed, one the CIA or Homeland Security would know about and no one else.

As a rule, Stella knew everything there was to know about her employees, but not Sam. When she'd asked him to work for her, he had been a little reluctant. In the end, he had said he'd work for cash only. Under the table. She didn't usually go for that. She kept everything strictly legal, but she was desperate for a really good worker who knew the kinds of things Sam knew. At the time, nearly every cabin needed renovations. Electricity, plumbing, walls crumbling. So much work. Motors on the boats. She needed him more than he needed her. She'd hired him thinking it would be for a short period of time. That short period had turned into more than two years.

She stayed silent. Took another drink of coffee. Kept looking at the lake. What was there to say that didn't make her look as if she was losing her mind? Nothing. There was nothing she could say. Even if she revealed her past, blew her carefully constructed lie of a life, what would be the point? There was no proof, and she doubted if she could get any proof that accidents weren't going to be accidents and a serial killer was on the loose. As of that moment, even the fisherman hadn't been found dead, because no crime had been committed—yet. The killer would strike in two days. She needed to drive around the lake and look for the location.

"Been here over two years now, Stella. You never once locked that door. You don't snap at the workers, especially if they make a mistake. That's not your way."

She didn't look at him again. Instead, she kept her eyes on

the lake. The tranquil lake that was so deep and could hold countless bodies if someone weighed them down. Above the lake the mountains rose with all the beautiful trees. So many places to bury bodies no one would ever find. Hot springs. Some of the hot springs were hot enough to decompose a body.

Without thinking she pressed her fingers to her mouth the way she'd done when she was a child, to keep from blurting out anything she shouldn't say. A habit. A bad habit she'd worked to get over, and now it was back. Just that fast. Her fingers trembled and she wanted to sit on them. She hoped he didn't notice, but he saw everything. She knew he did. Sam was that type of man. She dropped her hand back into Bailey's fur. Buried her shaking fingers deep.

"Satine, you want help, I'm right here, but you gotta talk. Use your words, woman."

"Did I really do that? Snap at someone because they made a mistake?" She did turn her head and look at him then. "Did I do that to you, Sam?"

His tough features softened for just a moment. Those dark eyes of his turned almost velvet, drifting over her. Unsettling her. "No, it was Bernice at the boat rentals the other day."

Stella pressed the heel of her hand to her forehead. She had done that. Not yelled. But she'd definitely been snippy. Okay. More than snippy. She was not a boss to be snippy or short with her employees. Bernice Fulton was older and had worked for her for over five years. She would take it to heart. "I'll talk to her."

That day was unusually hot, though everyone had been expecting the cooler fall weather. Because it was so warm, those in the resorts had rushed to rent the boats, wanting to be out on the lake. Unfortunately, that included people who didn't have the least idea of how to run a boat, or dock one. Both Sam and Stella spent the better part of the evening rescuing very drunk parties of two, four and six, as well as a single mom and her two very young children, who, thank heavens, were wearing life vests.

Fishermen had been complaining all day, a steady stream of grouchy, irritable or downright furious people, mostly men, acting superior, although most of them knew her now. They'd come to respect her over the years. Still, they weren't immune to the unexpected high temperatures. Humidity when there was usually dry heat, and all the crazy tourists who didn't have the first clue about how to navigate boats on the lake. Nor did those tourists even seem to have any manners when it came to sharing the lake with those fishing.

Stella had been yelled at, called names and insulted so many times, mostly in reference to her IQ and ability to run a fishing camp, which Sunrise Lake was *not*, but she didn't correct anyone. She merely hung on to her polite smile, listened to every concern and complaint and assured them that it would be taken care of—unless they went too far.

Stella had learned a long time ago when she first signed on as the manager that if she wanted the respect of the fishermen, she had to stand up to them. She wasn't shrill, she didn't yell, and she looked even the oldest, most hardened man in the eye when she spoke to them. She knew her facts, fought for their rights, but refused to allow them to push her around, no matter how upset they were.

Still, at the end of a very long and trying day, after going out to boat after boat mostly to retrieve drunks who didn't know how to dock, she wasn't in the best of moods, and she had snapped at Bernice Fulton. Sam was right. She didn't do things like that. He'd kept his cool. He always did. Sam didn't snap at anyone. Of course, he didn't talk to anyone. He didn't have to. He turned that stare of his on anyone giving him a bad time and they stopped.

When he got aboard a party boat with five women in bikinis, all of whom were throwing themselves at him, he barely glanced at them. He simply brought the boat in, tied it off and didn't even gallantly help the drunk women onto the pier. He just walked off, leaving them to Bernice. Stella knew because she'd been watching. It had been the only thing she'd laughed at the entire evening.

Stella was having nightmares every night now. She wasn't able to sleep afterward, which meant she was getting very little sleep. That certainly contributed to her growing crankiness. Not being able to discuss her uneasiness and the alarm she felt with anyone added to her irritability. She had no idea what to do in order to protect her friends or those she knew living in the area.

"Bernice will be happy you're clearing the air, Stella, but you aren't telling me why you're upset. What's going on?"

She took another sip of her coffee and regarded the glowing surface of the lake. A little shiver of apprehension went through her. There was no talking to anyone about this. Not even Sam. She had to figure this out on her own, at least until she knew Sam wasn't involved in any way. He'd arrived two years earlier. He didn't talk to anyone. He was a complete loner. He could shove his belongings into a pack and be gone in minutes.

Sam was good at every outdoor activity. He was extremely strong. He had scars all over his body indicating something terrible had happened to him at some point in his life. Psychologically, what did that do to a person? She'd tried to find out about him on the Internet, looking him up, but there was nothing that she could find. She couldn't imagine Sam being a killer of innocent people, but she had to know before she trusted him enough to talk to him.

She could feel Sam's eyes on her and knew he wasn't going to let it go. She was acting differently. She'd snapped at an employee. She'd locked her house. She was obviously upset.

"What made you decide to bring me coffee this morning, Sam?"

He didn't bring her coffee every morning. He didn't make her dinner every evening. He didn't stop by her house to watch movies every night. She never invited him. He just showed up. When he did, he always cooked dinner. He brought beer. He never asked for anything. Never. He never once stepped over the line to try to do so much as kiss her. She'd been tempted to kiss him more than once, but she never crossed that line with him, either. She was afraid he'd just walk away, and she wanted him in her life however she could have him.

Sam liked to both boulder and trad climb. He showed up to climb in the area like so many others. He had taken a four-wheel-drive rig containing his possessions and stayed at one of the local campgrounds. He didn't ask anything of anyone. He seemed to live off the land for the most part, but he wasn't afraid of work and he was good at almost everything. She'd noticed him right away working in town for Carl Montgomery, the local contractor. Well, the only real decent one. If Carl hired him, that meant he was good.

It was impossible not to notice him. Stella noticed everyone. She was detail oriented, which was why she was so good at her job. Sam was a loner, even in the middle of a busy jobsite. He rarely spoke to anyone, but that didn't stop him from doing any job asked of him. In the end, she decided he would be perfect working at the resort as a handyman. He could do just about any type of job she required.

She offered him a good salary, a cabin year-round and a four-wheel-drive vehicle upgrade. He hadn't jumped at the offer. He'd taken his time, thinking it over. He'd even come up to the resort and looked it over before making up his mind. She'd liked him better for that. She'd never once regretted her decision to hire him, even when he was annoying as hell because he almost never spoke.

Stella met his dark, compelling eyes. It wasn't easy. Looking into his eyes never was. Sometimes she thought it was like looking into hell.

"I can be gone if you want me that way, Stella."

He said it so quietly at first the words didn't actually penetrate. When they did, her entire body nearly shut down. She had to turn her face away quickly, afraid he'd see the burn of tears. Afraid he'd see the panic she felt.

"Why would you say that to me, Sam?" She could barely speak, barely get the question out. "Because I asked you a question? Why would you say that to me?" She wanted to get up and leave him there, but she was afraid if she did, he would shove all his belongings into his backpack and go and she'd never see him again.

Sam was closed off even more than she was. It was possible he didn't feel anything at all for anyone. Did she mean so little to him? Probably. She'd built up their relationship because she needed someone. He was truly self-sufficient. She thought she was, but in the end, she needed the resort, her friends. *Sam*. She needed Sam. The thought of being without him wrenched at her. Maybe she was just feeling so vulnerable because of the nightmares and uncertainty. Because she was afraid for everyone.

"I know things sometimes if people matter to me. You matter to me, so I know when you feel like shit."

Stella's fingers tightened on her coffee mug. That was the very last admission she expected from Sam. His tone was exactly the same, that low blend of masculine sensuality that sank under her skin and found her somewhere deep. To other people who didn't ever act on little unexplained urges, his explanation might have sounded ludicrous, but to her, it was perfectly reasonable.

It was the first time Sam had ever said anything that might make him vulnerable. He all but implied he had a psychic ability, or at the very least a heavy intuition. She wanted to give him something of herself back. It was only fair. Something real.

"I have nightmares sometimes. Bad ones. Once they start, they come in clusters. I can't get any sleep when it happens. Nothing helps." That was all true. She drank a little more of the coffee and kept her free hand in Bailey's fur.

Sam was silent for a long time. When she dared to look at him, he was looking at the mountains. The sun's rays had scattered color through the trees and ghostly mist. The sight never failed to stir her.

"What kinds of things bring on your nightmares? What are they about?"

Those were good questions. She should have thought he

might ask her questions like those. He was intelligent and he was a fixer.

"Dead bodies floating beneath the surface of the lake." She blurted the truth out. Or half truth. It came out strangled because a part of her felt like it was a lie and he'd given her something of himself. Made himself vulnerable to her after two years of dancing around each other. He'd opened himself up to ridicule and she was still closed off. He was astute. He knew there was something she wasn't telling him, and it had to hurt. She would be hurt.

Stella forced herself to look up at him because he at least deserved that. Those dark eyes of his studied her face. Penetrating. Seeing too much. She knew there were shadows under her eyes. But what could she really tell him? There was no body. Not even an accident yet. She was definitely going to use her day off to drive around the lake and see if she could find the location where the fisherman would be killed if she couldn't prevent it. The worst of it was, there were several lakes in the area popular with fisherman. Still, she was certain the location was her beloved lake.

"Stella, you're the calmest, clearest-thinking woman I've ever come across. I know you're in some kind of trouble." He shrugged. "I'm not going to pry, I don't like anyone asking me questions, so I'm not going to insist you talk to me if you don't want to share. Once you get past being shaken up, you'll do what you always do, think in steps and tackle the problem one step at a time. You'll find the answer. You always do."

There was absolute confidence in Sam's voice and that steadied her. That gave her confidence. He was right. She wasn't a child and the killer was on her home turf. Her beloved Sierras. He had no idea she was already on to him and would be coming after him.

CHRISTINE FEEHAN

"The queen of paranormal romance...
I love everything she does."
—J. R. Ward

PIATKUS